SHE DOESN'T HAVE A CLUE

SHE DOESN'T HAVE A HAVE A CLUE

A NOVEL

Jenny Elder Moke

MINOTAUR
BOOKS
NEW YORK

First published in the United States by Minotaur Books, an imprint of St. Martin's Publishing Group

SHE DOESN'T HAVE A CLUE. Copyright © 2025 by Jenny Elder Moke. All rights reserved. Printed in the United States of America. For information, address St. Martin's Publishing Group, 120 Broadway, New York, NY 10271.

www.minotaurbooks.com

Designed by Omar Chapa

The Library of Congress Cataloging-in-Publication Data
is available upon request.

ISBN 978-1-250-35496-9 (trade paperback)
ISBN 978-1-250-35498-3 (hardcover)
ISBN 978-1-250-35497-6 (ebook)

Our books may be purchased in bulk for promotional, educational, or business use. Please contact your local bookseller or the Macmillan Corporate and Premium Sales Department at 1-800-221-7945, extension 5442, or by email at MacmillanSpecialMarkets@macmillan.com.

First Edition: 2025

10 9 8 7 6 5 4 3 2 1

To Joe,
who doesn't even blink anymore when I say,
"Hey, help me plan a murder."

SHE DOESN'T
HAVE A
CLUE

The mother of the bride was inconsolable.

"My baby," she kept crying, hugging her daughter's body even as the dead woman's head lolled back like an obscene rag doll, mouth hanging open and baring all her teeth. "My sweet baby, no."

"Mia, please," said the groom, gently touching his brand-new mother-in-law's shoulder. Already a widower before the champagne toast. "It was an accident, a terrible accident. But we can't leave her like this. Everyone is watching. Please, for Amelia's sake. There's nothing anyone can do now."

But Loretta suspected someone already had done something. Because as the mother wept into the bride's twenty-thousand-dollar dress, ruining the delicate silk, something in the bride's teeth flashed red. It was nothing more than a glimpse, a tiny detail the rest of the wedding guests and servers easily overlooked in the chaos. But Loretta Starling wasn't one to overlook.

"Mrs. Hallowell, lay your daughter down and step back," Loretta said with authority. It was the same authority she used to cut drunk patrons off at the bar or put her boss/boyfriend in his place when he got ideas about how Loretta should live her life. It brooked no argument, and people's bodies obeyed before their minds could protest.

And Mrs. Hallowell, despite her raging grief, was no different. She laid her daughter down, looking to Loretta with her tearstained face. Loretta had seen enough death to know the damage done to the bodies was nothing compared to the emotional wounds in the loved ones they left behind. But now was no time to lose herself to sentiment for the poor mother of the bride. She had more important details to investigate.

"*Are you a doctor?*" Mrs. Hallowell asked, her voice warbly. "*Can you help her?*"

"*I'm not a doctor, but I can help,*" Loretta said, squatting beside the bride. *She reached into the bride's mouth and fished out a sliver of black and red, holding it up.* "*Rosary pea, a deadly toxin. This was no accident. This was murder, cold and premeditated. There's a killer on this island.*"

EXCERPT FROM *SOMETHING BORROWED, SOMEONE BLUE*

LORETTA STARLING, BOOK 3

BY KATE VALENTINE

Friday

Chapter One

Our story begins, as these stories often do, with an awfully convenient murder.

Not convenient for the murder victim, of course. They probably had plans, hopes and dreams, maybe even a date or a meal left unfinished. No, I guess their murder came as a bit of a shock for them.

It might not even be convenient for the murderer, considering the circumstances. That's the problem with crimes of passion, isn't it? There you are, having a normal day, fed up with your spouse or your cranky neighbor or maybe your boss, and suddenly, BAM! You've got blood on your hands, a blunt object to toss in a river, clothes to burn, and an alibi to line up.

But these murders are admittedly convenient for Loretta Starling, she of the Starling Mysteries, a Florida Keys bartender by night and amateur sleuth by day. This is Loretta's fourth murder in as many books in her sleepy vacation resort town, and, really, it's a wonder no one has gotten suspicious of Loretta herself. I mean, look at Jessica Fletcher. How many people have to kick the bucket around her before you start looking for blood spatter on that typewriter? Murder, She Committed, am I right?

Kate Valentine sighed and deleted the note on her phone, letting her head drop against the back seat of the ride share. She'd thought a change in venue and writing device might have shaken some decent words loose, but so far it was proving as productive as the last six months of trying to force this book out hunched over her laptop in her apartment, surrounded by increasingly distressing mounds of takeout containers.

"You said Pier 66?" said the driver as they traversed the brilliant blue of the Lake Washington Ship Canal, looking her over in the rearview mirror. "That's the clipper terminal, right? You headed to Victoria or the San Juan Islands?"

Kate cut her gaze up sharply. That was the problem with writing murder mysteries; it made a girl far more fine-tuned to the inherent dangers in the minds of men. Any rideshare driver could end up being *The Bone Collector*. Sure, this guy had a picture wedged into his dashboard of what looked like a wife and two kids, but how was Kate to know they were real? The car was some kind of gray SUV that she normally would have clocked the make, model, license, and any visible damage or identifying marks on. This time she'd barely even checked to make sure it was *her* rideshare before chucking her suitcase into the trunk.

"A private island, actually," Kate said, turning her attention out the window. The sky outside was no help for her mood, the glorious golden tones of a Pacific Northwest autumn having given way to the gloomy gray rains of late October. It was the season of SAD lights and short days, a constant drizzle in the air that ruined your hair and turned your socks squishy. How was she meant to imagine the sunny, saturated beach vibes of a Florida Keys summer in this drab gray existence? Normally she loved a rainy day—the perfect excuse to curl up with a hot mug of coffee, a cozy oversize sweater, and the latest Loretta murder. But Loretta was playing as coy with her as the sun behind the clouds, frustratingly out of reach.

"I didn't realize there were private islands out there," the driver continued. "Which one are you headed to?"

"Hempstead Island," said Kate, never one to offend someone who might keep her pinky toe as a memento. That was the problem with being a woman in the real world; not all men were murderers, but you couldn't tell the difference between the ones who were and the ones who weren't just by looking.

Maybe in the new book, Loretta could track down a murderous rideshare driver who asked too many questions and blew through one too many red lights. Kate opened a new note on her phone, typing away furiously.

"Where you headed?" asked the driver, making suggestive eyes at Loretta through the rearview mirror.

"What business is it of yours?" Loretta asked, making hard eyes right back at the nosy driver as she pulled out her lipstick case shaped like a knife and ran the color over her lips for emphasis. Shocking Red, the tube promised, but on Loretta it looked natural.

Of course, there were currently only two rideshare drivers on Big Pine Key, and one of them was Loretta's aunt. The other was the hot British mixologist who worked with Loretta at the Key Lime and had already been accused (and acquitted) of murder in book one. So maybe not a rideshare murderer, then.

"Hempstead?" the man said as Kate deleted the note, his eyebrows rising in surprise. "That got anything to do with the Hempstead building downtown?"

"And Hempstead Park, and the Hempstead Arts Center, and

Hempstead Dormitory at the University of Washington," Kate went on. "Those Hempsteads."

The man let out a low whistle. "That's *old* money. You a Hempstead?"

Kate sighed. "No, I'm just attending a wedding."

"Yeah, I didn't figure you were," the man said, shaking his head. "Money like that, you don't take rideshares. You just buy the car and the damn driver."

When Spencer took Kate to Orca Island for their last anniversary, it was a full-day trek of walking to the bus stop, wedging herself in with a shirtless man in old army fatigues on the last remaining bus seat available, and riding the public ferry with gulls screaming and children wailing, before walking more than three miles from the ferry terminal on Orca to their Airbnb because Spencer didn't want to spend forty dollars for a taxi. And now Kennedy probably helicoptered both of them to Hempstead Island for the weekend without a second thought.

"Pier 66," announced her driver as he parked the car and stepped out. He squinted toward the docks. "That your boat down there? Sheesh, looks expensive."

It did look expensive, the sleek white boat waiting below. Probably a yacht, if Kate knew anything about boats. Which you would think she would, considering she wrote a whole successful series set in the Florida Keys. But her knowledge didn't extend very far beyond "they float in water." She'd gotten dinged in more than a few online reviews on that front. She once put Loretta in the ocean on a pontoon during a storm, which apparently was *not* a seaworthy vessel, according to *DanSeaLife4376*.

"I'll get your suitcase," said her driver as she stepped out. He squinted in the direction of the dock where the possibly-a-yacht waited. "You sure that's your boat? Looks like it's pulling away."

Kate had been too busy rating him five stars—at least one of them out of guilt for briefly assuming he was a murderer—to pay attention to the boat. But now that he'd mentioned it, there was a thin sliver of ocean water between the edge of the boat and the dock. A man stood on the aft deck in a puffy jacket and a thick beanie, watching as another man cast off their dock lines (that, at least, she'd learned from her research).

"I think you're gonna miss it," the driver said.

"Like hell I am," Kate said, hoisting her rolling case under one arm. She took off for the stairs, waving her free arm. "Hold the boat, please!"

Now that she was full-on sprinting across the uneven wooden planks it was plain to see the fat slice of green-black ocean water between the boat and the dock. The man in the puffy jacket stood alone on the aft deck, cupping his hands around his mouth and shouting something. But it was lost in the brisk wind that stirred up the choppy waves. The forecast had been clear all week long, but now the sky looked leaden and threatening for an outdoor wedding. Still, predicting rain in Washington State in October was like predicting bears in the forest or alligators in Florida. An ever-present threat.

As she closed in on the end of the dock there was a gap of about three feet between the boat and solid ground. On impulse, she chucked her luggage across the gap and took four long strides back to give herself a running start. This was obviously an insane idea; she was going to end up splattered against the side of a luxury boat. But her computer was in that suitcase, her life's work stored on its hard drive. She wouldn't jump for anyone except Loretta.

"Look out!" she shouted at the man, who had caught her suitcase in an impressive maneuver, obscuring his face. "Clear the deck!"

She sprinted down the dock and leapt across the gap. Her feet pedaled and her arms windmilled, and she had a split-second realization that she'd been absolutely right; she wasn't going to make it. She was going to hit her head and drown three feet off the docks. At least she'd have a decent excuse for missing the wedding and her deadline. Her own accidental murder.

But then a pair of hands grabbed her and pulled, helping her clear the last foot as she crashed into the man. They both went tumbling back on the sleek deck, her suitcase skittering away. He curled up with a painful grunt, the movement pulling her in tighter against him.

"I'm so sorry," she gasped, struggling to catch her breath after that Olympic-level long jump. "I didn't mean to crash into . . . Jake?"

Her eyes went wide, heart beating in double time as the man beneath her winced out a tight smile and spoke with that gorgeous, buttery Australian accent of his. "Still know how to make an entrance, don't you, Katey cakes?"

Chapter Two

"Jake," she said again, at a loss. Jake Hawkins, former pro surfer turned elite travel guide. Once the most important person in the world to her, not that she had ever told him so. Of all the places she'd imagined seeing him over the last two years—and there had been plenty of imaginings, more fantasy conversations than was probably healthy—the back deck of a boat on its way to Hempstead Island for her ex-fiancé's wedding was *not* one of them.

"I know you'll take this personally, but you're not exactly a sack of feathers," Jake grunted, reminding her that she was still sprawled out on top of him, crushing him with her clumsy weight.

"Oh shit, your back," she said, clambering off and raising a distinct *oof* out of him. "Oh god, Jake, I'm so sorry. Let me help."

"I've got it," Jake said, rolling to one side before going very still. "Actually, no I don't. Give me a minute."

"We should get you inside," Kate said, though she couldn't quite bring herself to reach for him just then. It wasn't like she didn't have plenty of practice helping him in the past, when the injury that brought his pro-surfing career to an abrupt end caused him so much pain he couldn't move. But that had been before *the incident*, before Kate had sworn never to try to touch him again.

He was supposed to be in Borneo this weekend; she'd checked his company's website to make sure. She'd also called her mom and not-so-subtly confirmed it through his aunt. Not to mention she couldn't imagine Spencer actually agreeing to invite Jake to his wedding. So what was Jake doing *here*?

A window slammed open above them and somebody stuck their head out from where Kate presumed all the steering equipment was (hmm, maybe *DanSeaLife4376* had been right to call out her incompetence).

"Everybody all right down there?" the man shouted. "What in hell was that?"

Kate wondered the same thing. "You were leaving me behind."

"They only told me there'd be one last person, so once he was on board I figured we were good. You two better get inside. We've got a real bluster coming up. I'll try to keep it as smooth as possible, but it looks like we're in for a rough ride."

So the ship's captain hadn't been expecting Jake, either. Interesting. Jake had recovered enough to stand, staggering his way toward the sliding doors and the welcoming embrace of what looked like a very luxurious couch beyond. Kate retrieved her suitcase, giving Jake enough time to shuck his jacket and beanie, sink into the couch, and put his feet up on the low coffee table loaded with a charcuterie plate and a bottle of champagne.

He wore jeans torn at one knee and a Henley, the sleeves pushed up at the elbows and exposing the lean lines of his forearms. His skin was deeply tanned, no doubt the result of his latest tropical destination as a tour guide for the extreme adventure company he co-owned with a friend, his hair like spun gold under the soft lights. He looked both exactly as she remembered him from the disastrous last time they'd spoken, and somehow completely different.

Was he still angry with her? It was hard to tell, considering how tight his expression still was as he gingerly leaned forward to pick up a bunch of grapes. Could be her presence he was wincing at, or it could be the twinges of pain that used to render him immobile.

"Do you need your pills?" she asked tentatively.

"Didn't bring them," he said, his tone short. He cocked his head toward her. "Didn't think I'd get cannonballed on the way there."

Two years ago Kate would have known he was joking and would have shot back a quip of her own about how an athlete should stay agile and ready for anything. But right now all she could remember was the last time she'd seen him, his normally open and friendly expression twisted in anger, the accusatory words coming so hot and fast she couldn't keep up with them. He didn't *look* like he was about to unleash another tirade on her, but athletes had to stay agile. Even mental ones.

"So, you're here!" Kate said, trying to sound cool and breezy and landing closer to maniacal. "And not in Borneo. I mean, was it Borneo? Did you say? I thought I heard . . . probably read it . . . somewhere. Or maybe Burma? I get those mixed up, when I think about it. And Burbank, though I think that's a city in California. Was that where they taped *The Tonight Sh—*"

"Kate," Jake said, putting up his hands in exasperation. "Stop. I know what you're doing, and we don't have to do this."

Oh boy, here it comes. He *was* still pissed, and he was gearing up to tell her all the ways she'd failed him as a friend, just like last time. She had enough to worry about this weekend without adding Jake Freaking Hawkins to the mix. She had to get ahead of this.

"You're right," she said, squaring her shoulders. "You are right. We're just gonna . . . face this head-on. No games. No playing around. No saying one thing and meaning—"

"Kate!" Jake said, wincing again. This time she was pretty sure *she* was the pain in his backside, though.

"I know we're not friends anymore!" she blurted out, staring hard at the sweating bottle of champagne and feeling a kinship with its discomfort just then. "Or at all, maybe ever. And that's fine, really.

I'm . . . super cool with that. You have moved on, I have moved on. Time has moved on—"

"*Time* has moved on?" Jake said, somewhat disbelieving.

"You know what I mean," Kate snapped, irritated that she hadn't been allowed to practice this at least a dozen times in the mirror. If she'd known he was coming this weekend, if she'd even so much as suspected he might be in attendance, she would have planned—and packed—*very* differently. She didn't do well under pressure, as evidenced by the last time they'd spoken. Jake opened his mouth as if to speak, but she held up her hands to stop him; she needed to get this out, her way.

"We aren't friends," she said, this time with a gravity to her words that carried all the weight of the past two years without him. "As far as anyone this weekend knows, we are just . . . former work colleagues."

Jake's gaze was nearly intolerable. "Former work colleagues?"

"Yes, who amicably parted before their last project could be completed," Kate finished, feeling pretty good about the story she was concocting in real time. She might not have a grip on Loretta, but maybe she could still salvage this weekend. "So I think we just . . . we call a truce. For the weekend. Pretend . . . pretend we're still . . ."

Still what? Still harboring fantasies about the other person when we're two glasses of wine and half an episode of *The Bachelorette* into the evening? Still have their phone listed in most frequent contacts because we keep typing up long, weepy, apologetic texts and deleting them the next morning? Still can't go to the dim sum shop on the corner without our hearts stopping if someone with tousled blond hair is occupying the back corner booth?

But no, Jake had been off traveling the globe, chauffeuring wealthy adrenaline junkies on extreme adventure tours. Probably leaving a trail of heartbroken women in every far-flung locale he visited. He hadn't given a second thought to Kate in all those years, she was sure of it.

"Pretend we're still what, Kate?" Jake asked, his voice soft and even, an underlying intensity to the words making her skin feel tight and prickly.

"Pretend we still care," Kate said. "About each other."

"Is that what we're doing? Pretending?" His gaze narrowed on her. "That's what you really want?"

Of course it wasn't what she wanted, but Kate had plenty of practice not getting what she wanted. She put out a hand, determined to play the diplomat for the weekend.

"A truce," she said. "And then we can each go our own separate way again. Just like before."

Jake sighed, taking her hand in his warm, calloused fingers and sending a surge of electricity through her that could have powered the whole Pacific Northwest. "If that's how you want to play it. Truce, Katey cakes."

Kate wrinkled her nose. "One time you catch me eating cake and you never let me forget."

"Hang on," Jake said, giving her a grin that turned her bones soft. "You weren't just 'eating cake.' You were hiding in the bushes at my aunt's condo eating a slice of cake the size of your head, and you threatened to fork me in the thigh if I even dared to sniff the frosting. It would have left an impression on anyone."

As if Kate could have forgotten. Her mother had only recently moved into the retirement community and met Jake's aunt through the bridge club. When Mrs. Hawkins threw a welcome party for her nephews, freshly arriving from Australia, Kate's mother guilted Kate into attending. Everyone else was from the retirement community, and his aunt wanted some younger locals to "shift the bell curve of death a little lower." Kate had planned to hide in the bushes with her cake until her mother was ready to leave, but then Jake had come out for some fresh air and caught her lurking.

He'd only been a few months out from the accident that ended his surfing career, still in a back brace and crutches that made getting around hilly Seattle intolerable. Kate's mom had offered Kate as a taxi service, and she'd hardly needed much convincing. Jake was funny, surprisingly self-deprecating, charming, and hot as hell. He had incredible stories of chasing big waves in Morocco, winning tournaments in California, and cave diving with his brother, Charlie, in Australia. He'd toured the world, been to every beach, and had kept a photo journal to prove it. Those aimless drives around the city eventually turned into Kate's first big career break.

A series of part-photography, part-travelogue, all thirst-trap books called *The Wandering Australian*. They featured full-page spreads of pictures from Jake's time chasing big waves around the world—historic architecture, crystalline waters, and waves that looked blown from glass. And in the middle of them all a shirtless, grinning Jake. They'd also featured vignettes of his trips written by Kate, shared over plates of nachos or pho bowls or, one fateful evening, a pitcher of margaritas in her apartment.

"Well, a gentleman wouldn't bring it up again," Kate sniffed, turning her attention toward the distant horizon.

Jake snorted. "A gentleman would have lost his fingers getting between you and that frosting."

They settled into a silence that wasn't quite amicable, but didn't feel so actively hostile, as the waters turned rougher and the sky quickly darkened. Even in the luxurious interior of the boat Kate began to feel queasy, dropping onto the couch opposite Jake and cradling her head in her hands, wishing the hours away until they reached their final destination. When she thought she'd rather go down than suffer another minute of being tossed about, the speaker in the ceiling crackled to life.

"Hempstead Island, coming up."

The private island of the Hempstead family that included Kennedy Hempstead had once been known as Rum Island. Situated to the northwest corner of the San Juan Islands archipelago, it was a prime location for hiding contraband alcohol from police boats during Prohibition. Russell Hempstead took the profits from his timber mill and purchased good Canadian whisky, selling it back to Seattle's elites at triple the cost. He then opened his own bank, solidifying his family's fortune for generations to come.

Kate crawled toward the large windows to watch their approach. At least the waters had calmed in the sheltered cove created by the extended outcroppings surrounding the main island. Still, the sky was a smothering blanket overhead, threatening to open up at any moment.

"I hope they weren't planning on having this shindig outdoors," Jake said from close behind her. He was only a few inches taller than her, five foot eleven to her five foot seven, but in close quarters those four inches might as well have been four feet. Kate turned in surprise, tilting her head back to look up at him, caught again by how different he seemed since the last time she'd seen him. Older, a few more scars, but still Jake.

"Kate," he said, his brows drawing into a frown, but the sliding door banged open just then, startling them apart. An older man in a heavy raincoat with a grizzled white beard glared at them. If he'd had a parrot on his shoulder, you couldn't have convinced Kate he wasn't a pirate. "Come on, then, what are you two lovebirds waiting on?" he groused. "We need to get the boat secured before the storm comes in. Train's a waiting."

"Sorry," Kate said, turning a furious red.

"Train?" Jake said in bemusement.

Sure enough, a small train waited just above the docks, the tracks leading around the lush greenery of the island. It looked more like an old car, like a Model T that someone had outfitted with train wheels, but there was a rack in the back for their trunks and a bench back seat with the door open and waiting. There was even a man in an old-school chauffeur's outfit, complete with a puffy black-and-white-striped hat and dove-gray pants, holding the door.

"Welcome to Hempstead Island," he said in a demure British accent. Of course the Hempsteads would have an imported British butler. Loretta would have a field day with him. The guilty butler was such a trope of the genre, it could almost be a fun twist if the butler actually *did* do it. There were certainly plenty of wealthy, eccentric characters around Big Pine Key who could hire a suspicious butler. Maybe Miss Faraday, the reclusive heiress with dark family secrets and a penchant for Loretta's Gin Rickeys on delivery.

Kate crawled in the back and slipped her phone out of her pocket, the little EMERGENCY CALLS ONLY message at the top giving her heart palpitations. There were no service bars, and she was worried the message about emergency calls was optimistic at best. She hadn't been able to send a text since the Seattle skyline disappeared. They were all alone out here, at the mercy of the comings and goings of a luxury boat currently being battered by the oncoming waves.

She swiped open the Notes app, letting the fun little loop-de-loop of panic in her gut fuel the potential Loretta scene as she typed.

> "Hiya, Jeeves," Loretta quipped, doffing her imaginary cap.
>
> "Good day, madame," said the butler, the pinnacle of propriety.
>
> Loretta snorted. "I've been called a lot of things, but 'madame' might be the worst of them. I'm here for Miss Faraday's weekly delivery. The old gal might be pushing ninety-five, but she drinks harder than most of the twenty-five-year-olds I've seen."
>
> "I am afraid Miss Faraday is . . ." The butler's gaze skittered to the side only a fraction of a second, just long enough for Loretta to know that the next words out of his mouth would be a lie. "Indisposed at the moment. I shall take the delivery for her."
>
> "I don't think so, Jeeves," Loretta said, narrowing her gaze. "I'm going to need to see Miss Faraday myself. In person."

Except now that she thought about it, hadn't Miss Faraday suffered a heart attack and died of natural causes in Loretta book two, *A Dark and Stormy Murder*? Kate would have to consult the series bible, which was currently stored away on her computer safely tucked in her luggage, which Jake had just tied to the trunk. So maybe not Miss Faraday's butler, then.

"All set," Jake said as he slid onto the bench seat beside her, oblivious of Miss Faraday's potential fate. Kate quickly deleted the silly note as the butler climbed into the driver's seat, closing them inside the cabin. It had looked wide and roomy from the outside, but Jake Hawkins had a tendency to take up all the space he occupied. His elbow brushed hers, sending frissons of energy all down her spine. Boy, she really was deprived if all it took was a little elbow friction to get her engine going. Of course, that was when it was Jake's elbow doing the rubbing.

"Brakes released, proceeding ahead," said the driver as the little car sputtered to life and lurched forward on the tracks. It must have been installed around the time Russell Hempstead was bootlegging it up and down the Seattle coastline, because the seats felt hollow and the doors looked too thick, like maybe they had a secret compartment of hooch still in there.

"On your left you will note the hunting lodge, built in 1934 by Franklin Houser, based on an original design by Frank Lloyd Wright," said Jeeves as fat drops of rain adorned the hood and windshield.

"What does an island need a hunting lodge for?" Jake asked.

As if in answer to his question, the train car lurched to a halt, throwing Kate face-first into the hard seat back in front of her. Her forehead connected painfully and she tasted blood as she bit down on her lip, swearing under her breath. That was all she needed going into this weekend, a massive goose egg on her face and a bloodied lip.

"Kate, are you all right?" Jake asked, reaching for her.

"Fine, just . . . surprised," Kate groused as she sat up, more embarrassed than hurt. Well, okay, a *little* hurt. What was that seat back made of, concrete? "We stopped so fast."

"My apologies, ma'am," said the butler, his genteel tone a little distracted and sharp. "There is an . . . impediment on the tracks."

"What kind of impediment?" Jake asked.

"It's best if you and the lady do not look, sir," said the butler, just as Kate crawled forward for a better view.

Though she probably should have heeded his words, considering the gruesome remains of a body strewn across the tracks before them.

Chapter Three

"Oh my god," Kate said, swooning against the back of the seat. She was suddenly glad her grandfather never insisted on taking her on any of his fishing trips. She liked bone and sinew where it belonged, safely on the inside, out of her eyeline.

"'Tis only a deer, ma'am," said the driver, having recovered his sensibilities. "And a stuffed one at that. No harm done."

"No harm done?" Kate said incredulously, cracking one eye open to survey the dead animal on the tracks. The driver was right; that wasn't bone and sinew, as she'd thought, but dense stuffing. Still, it was somehow worse in her mind. How the hell did a stuffed deer end up on the train tracks? Who would do such an insane thing?

Jake was of the same mind. "How did a stuffed deer wander onto the tracks?"

"It must have been from the hunting lodge," the driver said dismissively as they exited the car. "They were probably moving it and it fell off one of the recreational vehicles. Unfortunately, I will need to recover it. Miss Rebecca is very partial to her trophies. You will need to proceed to the Manor on foot at the top of the hill there."

Tall trees surrounded the tracks, the underbrush so thick she could barely see the ground. Kate looked up at the steep climb, wondering how she was going to manage it in ballet flats, when the driver called out sharply. "Sir! Ma'am! I am afraid you will need to take the long way around, on the tracks. You cannot go into the wilds alone."

"Why not?" Kate asked, eyeing the bushes warily.

"It's not safe," intoned the driver, reaching into the car and pulling out a knife the size of Kate's forearm. He held it out to Jake. "You will want to carry this, sir. Just in case."

"In case *what*?" Kate asked, her voice climbing in direct relation to her blood pressure.

"You'll be fine, ma'am," said the driver smoothly, waving her along. "So long as you stick to the tracks and stay in the open."

The sky gave an ominous rumble of thunder, cutting off further protestations from Kate and hurrying the two of them along. She stuck close to Jake on instinct. "You think somebody would have noticed a deer missing from the back of an ATV."

"Kate," Jake said, giving her a funny look. "That deer didn't fall off any ATV."

"What do you mean?"

"Did you get a look at that thing? It wasn't just hit, it was *shredded*. Falling off a vehicle couldn't have done that. Something else tore that deer apart."

"Something else like . . . what?" Kate said, looking toward the trees like that *something* might leap out at any moment. "A person with a grudge? PETA?"

"Or something that thought it was a real deer," Jake said with a shrug, hefting his knapsack and absently swinging the giant knife the driver had given him.

"Wait, you think an *animal* did that?" Kate squeaked, stopping suddenly. "We should go back to the train, wait with Jeeves."

"We'll be fine," Jake said with a wave of the blade. "My buddy Freddy once fended off a Burmese crocodile with a Swiss Army Knife when the thing had my whole arm in its mouth, so this is a real upgrade. Who is Jeeves?"

"Hmmm?" Kate eyed the trees around them warily. "Oh, that's what I named the butler guy in my head. Jeeves."

Jake gave a little half laugh. "Of course you did."

Kate frowned. "Wait, I remember that story. You told me that *Freddy* was the one with his arm stuck in the crocodile's mouth, and *you* were the one who used the Swiss Army knife to rescue him!"

"Did I?" Jake continued on, looking thoughtful. "Well, either way, somebody fended off a crocodile with a knife a tenth the size of this one. That's the important lesson."

"I made you sound like a hero!" Kate said, hurrying after him. "That story was the back cover copy for book two!"

Jake glanced over at her, his gaze considerate as he studied her face, making all the little hairs along her body prickle to attention. "You really did a number on yourself, didn't you? Hang on, I've got something for that."

"Is it that noticeable?" Kate asked miserably as he rummaged around in his knapsack.

"Nah, just looks like you've been in a bar fight. Loretta would be proud. Here." He pulled a dented metal tin from his pack, twisting it open and releasing an unctuous smell. "I know, it smells awful, but it really does the trick. Just be still."

And then Jake Hawkins was touching her lip—not just touching, but tenderly rubbing it, pulling on it to better access the sore spot where she'd bitten into it. The salve gave her a tingly sensation wherever he applied it, or maybe that was the effect of Jake. Touching. Her lips.

"You really got into it this time, didn't you," Blake said, gently tending the wound on her face.

"You should see the other guy," Loretta said dryly.

"I did," Blake replied in the same tone. "He's dead."

"Not through any fault of mine," Loretta said, steeling her resolve as Blake set to work bandaging up the wound. "He was dead before I showed up. It was the other, more alive guy who mistook me for a heavy bag and fancied himself a boxer."

"*You know I worry about you, Lor,*" *said Blake, so close the blues of his eyes were electric, pulling her in. "One of these days, one of these idiots is going to get lucky and catch you out. Won't you come to Thailand with me instead?*"

"*You think I'd be any safer in Thailand?*" *Loretta asked, hardening her heart against the surge of longing and wanderlust that arose at the idea. "Murder has a way of finding me, Blake. I trip and fall no matter where I go.*"

"*Sure, but at least I'd be there to catch you.*"

"Kate?"

Kate blinked back to reality, and it wasn't Blake at the Key Lime anymore, but Jake standing before her on an abandoned stretch of railroad tracks. It was clear he'd been talking to her for some time, and just as clear that she hadn't heard a word of it.

Oops. Sometimes in moments of extreme distress, Loretta had a way of just . . . taking over. Kate spent so much of her time imagining *What Would Loretta Do?* that it was like a second brain nestled inside her own.

"Sorry," she blurted, jerking back. "I was . . . We should get going."

Jake cleared his throat, turning away. "Yeah, of course."

Kate trailed a safe distance after him, not sure what she was more afraid of—whatever had killed that deer, or the way her whole body lit up when Jake touched her. Whichever it was, she wanted to stay clear out in the open so she could see it coming and dodge before it was too late. The wind had picked up considerably, cutting down the open stretch of track viciously and blinding her as they headed in what she hoped was the direction of the house. There was at least some landscaping coming into view, long rows of square hedges abruptly replacing the tall trees. It looked almost like the back of a walled-in garden.

"Do you think that's where we're meant to go in?" Kate called, pitching her voice above the wind. "Doesn't seem quite grand enough for a . . . What did Jeeves call it? A manor house?"

Jake shrugged, changing direction to hike up the hill toward the gate. "Only one way to find out."

Kate hustled after him, her suitcase bopping along on the uneven terrain and flipping over from the force of the wind. By the time she met him at the gate she was more than ready to be out of the oncoming weather, but as Jake rattled the gate it didn't budge.

"It's locked," he said. "We'll have to go around."

"Around where?" Kate asked, looking at the long stretch of building on each side. She wasn't keen to go exploring after the unfortunate shredded deer incident. A flash of movement caught her eye from inside the garden. "I think there's someone over there."

Kate could just see a young woman with blond hair in an ill-fitting blue dress, her face marred by dark drips of mascara down her cheeks. She'd been crying, obviously, but she didn't look like she was crying now. She looked *pissed*.

"Ah, great, we'll just have them let us in," Jake said, raising an arm to catch the woman's attention. But Kate grabbed his arm, pulling him to one side of the gate and shushing him. "What are you doing?"

"She's arguing with someone," Kate said in a low voice, nodding at where the young woman gesticulated with sharp intensity. They couldn't see who she was talking to, but Kate imagined the person was getting an earful. At one point the woman threw her arms wide, like she might consider tackling the other person.

"This feels an awful lot like snooping," Jake said, though he didn't move from where she'd pushed him against the garden wall. In fact, he seemed to lean in closer as the young woman grabbed the other person by the arm, snatching a handful of vibrant floral fabric. "On the other hand, it's rude to interrupt."

"Shh, I can't hear them!" Kate said, crouching and leaning forward for a better angle. The other person—a woman, Kate assumed from the garb—snatched her arm out of the young woman's grip, raising a hand and slapping the blond woman hard.

"Oh!" Kate and Jake exclaimed simultaneously, giving away their position.

The young woman's gaze snapped to the gate. Kate grabbed Jake and darted back, pressing against the garden wall as her heart pounded. She wasn't quite sure what she was so worried about—sure, she'd committed a social faux pas, but it was their fault, really, arguing out in public like that. And she and Jake had a perfectly reasonable excuse to be there. Still, it wasn't the successful start to the weekend she'd envisioned, getting caught snooping like this.

"Do you think they saw us?" Jake asked after a moment.

"I'm going to check." Kate leaned around him, doing her best to ignore the press of his chest against her arm as she surveyed the garden. She half expected the woman to be standing there like a video game jump scare, streaky mascara guaranteed to haunt her dreams. But the gate was clear, the garden empty beyond it.

"They're gone," Kate said, strangely disappointed.

"That was awkward, wasn't it?" Jake said, checking the garden for himself. "What do you suppose they were fighting over? Seating charts? Floral arrangements? Maybe they both brought the same dress for the ceremony?"

"I don't think that had anything to do with the wedding," Kate said with a frown.

"Ah, I see the gears turning," Jake said. "Go on, then, what's your theory?"

This was another bad habit of Kate's. She couldn't help but observe and theorize, like everyone around them was in the middle of their own murder mystery. After spending all day inventing suspicious conversations for Loretta, even the most mundane exchanges took on a tinge of the ominous to Kate.

It used to drive Spencer crazy whenever they went out in public, the way Kate would *accidentally* eavesdrop and *casually* wonder what the people at the next table over were plotting. He said she never really fully returned to reality after spending the day in fantasy Loretta land, and she learned to keep her theories and observations to herself. But now here was Jake, openly asking her what she suspected. Like Blake, who was always game to help Loretta put the pieces of her investigation together. But Jake wasn't Blake, and he would tire of her suspicions as surely as Spencer had.

"My theory is that this is about to open up on us," Kate said, waving at the steely gray sky overhead. "And unless you're scaling this gate, we'd better find another way in."

"Fine," Jake said, heading down the hill. But he couldn't help a final comment, tossed casually over his shoulder. "Coward!"

"I'm not a coward!" Kate said indignantly, slip-sliding down the hill after him. "I'm just not keen on being caught out by the . . . the Deer Shredder!"

Now there was an idea for a Loretta killer. The Deer Shredder. He graduated from torturing animals to torturing humans, and only Loretta could stop him before she became his next victim. Although after what Kate had just seen, she couldn't imagine harming a poor defenseless animal. Even an imaginary one. So back to square one. *Again.*

She could see where the house had been beautiful once, with white plaster walls and red roof tiles and turrets and gables and whatever other architectural flair enormous houses came with. New money spent better than old money, though, and the Hempstead fortune was now several generations old. Which meant the Manor showed it.

Vines overgrew nearly every surface, turning the faded gray plaster into a sentient wall of green and brown. Tiles hung at slanted angles from the roof, one crashing to the ground as Kate and Jake scurried up the front lawn toward the safety of the house. It seemed that efforts had been made in recent years to repair much of the damage, though, as scaffolding covered the back half of the house and piles of fresh siding and paint buckets peeked out from under rain tarps.

The entrance to the house was at least covered, the massive wooden double doors protected by a cupola. Kate crowded close to Jake as they tried to find any small patch of the porch that wasn't getting bombarded by windy rain. Her hand brushed his waist, his nose brushed against her ear, and they were altogether too close for comfort. A girl might try something, and Kate had already learned *that* lesson two years ago.

"I'll knock on the door," she announced, loudly and woodenly like a community theater bit player as Jake set the knife off to the side. She stared up at the elaborately carved door as she banged her fist against it, unwilling to face Jake. Which meant she had to study a panel that she realized depicted a deer with its throat being slashed open.

"What is with the deer?" she muttered, taking a step back as the door creaked open.

"Welcome to Hempstead Manor!" said a little man in a striped suit with an artistic goatee. He spread his arms wide, looking for all the world like Gomez Addams welcoming them to his haunted mansion. "You must be our last guest for the evening, and not a moment too soon. Look at the weather out there! Come in, come in!"

He ushered them into a long, dim hallway with tile floors and darkly paneled wooden walls covered in staid portraits, chandeliers made of antlers hanging low over their heads. The lights flickered, casting long shadows across each portrait until Kate was having flashbacks to university scholarship panels full of judgy white men.

"Pretty ballsy to have a portrait gallery as your entryway," Jake murmured to Kate.

But their greeter moved through it all like it was a luxury resort in the Bahamas. "I'm Abraham from Dreams Come True Event Planning. Our clients value discretion above all else, so while nondisclosure agreements prevent me from naming names, let's just say I've fixed a tear in the bridal gown of a certain American to a certain royal and personally stocked the bar on the private plane of a certain billionaire on the way to his private island wedding."

He continued on like he saw all this luxury and more on a daily basis. Which, considering he was coordinating a Hempstead wedding, might be the case.

"This is the entry hall, and that is Russell Hempstead," he said, waving at an oil painting of a man with impressive muttonchops. "And his children, Ferdinand and Nikola."

"What's with the two empty spaces?" Jake whispered to Kate, nodding at the long stretch of wall after Nikola's painting where two portrait-size gaps stood empty.

"Those are the dissenters," Abraham said in a stage whisper. "The Hempstead family feud? Inspiration for a certain HBO series?"

Kate had read about the feud that had split the Hempstead family apart. Russell willed the bulk of his estate to his eldest son, Ferdinand, with a host of strings attached to how the money could be dispensed. Russell's two youngest children—Georgi and Lydia—were so incensed by the rules (and being cut off from their fun money) that they took Ferdinand to court over the terms of the will. Only Ferdinand's brother, Nikola, sided with him, mainly because he knew where the butter got spread. The younger siblings lost their court case, their inheritance, and, apparently, their portraits in the gallery.

"And this, of course, is our esteemed host for the weekend," Abraham said with a little sigh, stopping in front of a massive portrait of a sharp-looking woman with a severe bob haircut and sparkling blue eyes. "Rebecca Hempstead."

"Her portrait's at least twice the size of the other fellas," Jake observed, looking around the room. "Healthy ego on that one, eh?"

"Probably because that one's net wealth is greater than the GDP of most European countries," Kate said. Was it too much to curtsy to a portrait? Probably, but that didn't stop her from considering it. "Ferdinand might have established the Hempstead family fortune, but it's Rebecca who's put them at the top of the *Forbes* list. They call her the Queen of Wall Street. While our parents were trying to build a decent 401(k), Rebecca was buying up stock in dying legacy companies and turning them into the hottest tickets on the market. She's increased the Hempstead fortune tenfold. I read that the market once dipped a hundred points because she made an offhand comment about the auto industry at a fundraiser in DC."

Jake had slowly turned to her during her observations, his eyebrows raised. "And how do you know so much about Rebecca Hempstead?"

Kate flushed. She could hardly say she'd spent most of the past six months obsessively googling the entire family, learning the ins and outs of their ongoing legal battles over the family trust, scrounging up every interview Rebecca ever did as if she could siphon off some of the woman's success. Rebecca was polished, confident, stylish, and flamboyant—a magnetic magnate. Kate wasn't easily impressed with wealth, especially inherited money, but Rebecca had taken her family's respectable fortune and turned it into a never-ending gold mine by sheer force of personality. She'd also been the center of her fair share of sensational news stories; she'd spent most of her younger life in the press for one reason or another, and had eventually withdrawn entirely from the public eye. But that didn't mean she didn't still control every aspect of the Hempstead family fortune. She was exactly the kind of personality Kate couldn't resist.

And of course, there was the matter of that mysterious letter.

"You forgot her greatest nickname of all," came a loud, expansive voice from down the hall. A man sauntered in, looking very much like the owner of such a voice with his thinning hair aggressively combed into submission, his nose bulbous and pocked from too much alcohol indulgence, and a smirk that rivaled any used car salesman.

"Excuse me, Mr. Sheffield," said Abraham, his tone strained. "I was simply conducting these new arrivals—"

"The Bitch Bull," the man spat, swilling a glass of something dark brown before knocking it back in one massive swallow. "That's what we used to call her. The Bitch Bull of Wall Street. And she earned it, too, oh boy, didn't she? A real bitch she was then, and an even bigger one now. But she'll get what's coming to her, mark my words. This weekend, the Bitch Bull will finally be castrated."

Chapter Four

"Okay!" Abraham said brightly, clapping his hands together. "Moving on. Cocktail hour is at five, though I see you've gotten a head start on that, Mr. Sheffield. Can't be late!"

"Who was that?" Kate whispered as Abraham led them out of the portrait gallery, where the man glared his revenge at Rebecca's portrait.

"Marcus Sheffield," Abraham whispered with dramatic distaste, shaking his head. "He and Ms. Hempstead were once . . . paramours."

"Those two used to root?" Jake said in surprise. "He sounded like he wanted to fuck her *over*."

"Well, I said once upon a time," Abraham said, eyes gleaming at the chance to impart some NDA-free gossip. "According to my sources, they were young and in love, and Mr. Sheffield swore he wanted to marry her. She had a great deal of restrictions on her, being the Hempstead heir and all. Her father didn't approve. Apparently, Mr. Sheffield was quite the drinker and gambler back then."

"Still is, by the look of that nose," Kate murmured.

"Right?" Abraham said gleefully, tapping the side of his own nose for emphasis. "Ms. Rebecca was going to run away with him. But when she got to the airport, he was a no-show. Her father had gotten wind of the scheme and offered him an obscene amount of money to buzz off, and he took it like the fly he is. Broke her heart, and she swore vengeance on him."

"Marcus Sheffield!" Kate gasped, clapping a hand over her mouth. "Now I recognize that name! The Sheffield takeover. Oh my gosh, that's *him*? I didn't even think he was still alive after everything he went through."

It had been one of the more sensational bits in Kate's Google deep dive, which was really saying a lot, considering the Hempstead family history. In the early eighties, before Rebecca had really earned her reputation on the market, she'd staged a hostile takeover of a small family business that had just been listed publicly. But instead of buying up shares at a fair rate, she brutalized them in the marketplace first, fueling rumors of corruption and incompetence, driving the stock price down to almost zero before scooping up the ashes of what remained at a fraction of their value. It had earned her the Bitch Bull reputation and cemented her reign of terror over the market.

"What's he doing here this weekend?" Kate whispered, glancing back toward the man at the far end of the gallery.

"Bad luck for Ms. Rebecca, his son is Kennedy's godfather," Abraham said. "Boarding school buddies. And Ms. Kennedy is very, *very* precious about family, even questionably extended family. So here he is, on her private island, making it his personal mission to drink through the whisky supply before Sunday."

"I'm surprised Rebecca let him set foot on the island," Kate said, shaking her head before cocking it to the side. "Actually, I'm surprised she let *anyone* set foot on the island this weekend. I thought she had a reputation as a recluse."

"Oh, she did *not* want to," Abraham said, pausing just before the exit leading out of the portrait gallery into the main house. "Again, sources I can't divulge, but when Kennedy asked her about hosting the wedding here, Rebecca refused. But Ms. Kennedy has an iron streak up that sweet spine of hers. She went behind Rebecca's back to the board of trustees at the Hempstead Family Trust and requested a vote. She beat Rebecca by one vote. Hers."

"Yikes," Kate murmured. She couldn't imagine sweet, people-pleasing Kennedy Hempstead going up against someone as formidable as Rebecca Hempstead, even if the woman was her aunt. Kate couldn't even stand up to her dry-cleaner lady, who always overcharged her for dresses. Maybe the girl had more to her than Kate realized.

"But you didn't hear it from me!" Abraham said, spinning on his heel and marching them toward a table with a leather bag embossed with Kennedy and Spencer's initials on the front. "And here we have your gift bags for the weekend. Only one left, I'm afraid, so you'll have to share with your plus-one."

"Oh, he's not . . . we're not," Kate started, but she didn't know what to say they *were*.

"I'm a late addition," Jake said, giving Abraham an apologetic smile. "Jake Hawkins?"

Abraham looked down at the list of guests on his clipboard, frowning and clucking his tongue. "Yes, I see you. Kate Valentine and her plus-one, Jake Hawkins. As I said."

"There must be a clerical error or something. We are two separate ones," Kate said, reaching for the clipboard. "I'm a one, and he's a different, completely independent one. No pluses involved. If I could just see that for a minute?"

But Abraham snatched the clipboard to his chest, looking offended. "We do not make clerical errors. He is your plus-one. If he is not your plus-one, then he does not belong here and he'll have to leave the island. Hmmm?"

"I'm sure we can sort this out, mate," Jake said, giving Abraham a shaky smile. "I bet there's a spare cupboard or an empty hallway where I can bunk down, right? I hardly take up any room, and I once survived a week and a half in the jungle on a single protein bar. You'll hardly notice I'm here."

"I thought you said it was two days and there was a shawarma place within walking distance," Kate murmured to him.

"This is not the jungle, and we are not serving protein bars," Abraham said flatly. "The Manor accommodations are full, as is my schedule. So if you are not her plus-one—"

"He is my plus-one," Kate blurted out. "I just remembered."

Abraham looked at her. "You just remembered he is your plus-one?"

"Yes," Kate said, before shaking her head. "I mean, obviously I remembered him. I meant I just remembered that I forgot that I RSVP'd for both of us. But that's him. He's him. The plus."

"Mm-hmm," Abraham said, clearly not convinced but needing to move them along. "The welcome bag has a map of the Manor and the island so you don't get lost. I'm sure you were already warned about sticking to the Manor grounds and not wandering from the designated paths into the wilds?"

"Viscerally," Jake muttered.

"Good. And do please note that Ms. Hempstead has *very* strict rules about the comings and goings in her home. She's graciously opened her doors to us, and we are to treat our access as the precious gift it is. Now! We have cocktails and appetizers in the salon in twenty minutes. Let's get you both to your room."

"Sorry, room?" Kate said, leaning in, sure she had misheard him. "Singular?"

Abraham looked at her with such a professionally blank expression she imagined she wasn't the first unruly guest he'd dealt with. "He is your plus-one, yes? So, you share a room."

"I did . . . say that, didn't I?" Kate said, nodding like the soothing rhythm might save her from the panic of sharing a room with Jake Hawkins. "I definitely . . . did . . . say that."

"Yes, you did," Abraham said, giving her a long-suffering look. "My assistant will show you up. Jean-Pierre! Where is that little Frenchman when you need him?"

Kate was still mildly hyperventilating at the idea of Jake disrobing within ten square feet of her when they passed into the full glory of the house. She stopped under a wide archway, supported by marble columns carved in the expression of satyrs grimacing under the weight, her gaze going up and up as her eyes grew wider and wider.

"What in the ever-loving fuck?" she breathed.

The interior lighting of the Manor looked as if it hadn't been updated since its original construction in the twenties, all yellowed wall sconces and dramatic chandeliers. The walls were paneled in a dark wood, like chocolate bars stacked sideways, with no less than three staircases parading upward from this part of the house. Oil paintings hung on every open surface, all of them looking frightfully authentic. But it wasn't the clearly haunted details of the house that riveted Kate.

It was all the *animals*.

Lions and tigers and an enormous grizzly bear, oh my; but there was also a bobcat, a moose head, several types of deer with varying headgear, an entire family of possums suspended by their tails under one of the staircases, and a large jackrabbit that still had the terrified gaze of its final death throes etched into its furry face.

"I'll find Jean-Pierre," Abraham said, leaving them at the mercy of the taxidermied occupants.

"This is a murder house," Kate said, sightless black eyes following her no matter where she moved. She turned instinctively toward Jake as if his effortless attractiveness could somehow erase this new memory. "I knew Rebecca was into big game hunting, but I didn't know she *kept* them. I figured she just murdered for fun and left them there, like other terrible rich people. So many stuffed animals."

"And yet they couldn't capture the most elusive game of all," Jake murmured. "The dreaded Care Bear."

The comment caught Kate by surprise and she snorted in laughter, smothering her mouth in her sweater sleeve to hide the reaction. But she couldn't hide the way her entire body shook with rebellious laughter, which seemed to please Jake greatly.

"I can't stay here," she said, looking around again in horror. "I can't wake up to a squirrel playing a tiny banjo or a platypus that sings 'Don't Worry, Be Happy.'"

Now it was Jake's turn to snort, though he didn't bother hiding his reaction. The feeling of making Jake laugh shot through her veins like champagne bubbles, rising straight to her head. It was almost enough to make a girl forget her troubles for the weekend.

Almost.

Until a voice echoed through the hall of horrors. "Valentine, you sneaky lying *bitch*."

Chapter Five

Unfortunately for Kate, there were any number of guests that weekend who could have leveled such an accusation her way, and she wasn't keen on confronting any of them. But there was only one person in the world who called her exclusively by her last name, claiming it was far superior to boring old Kate, and Kate's mouth fell open in shock as a compact white woman with dark brown hair dyed a deep red at the ends appeared from a side room.

"Marla!" Kate said. "I didn't know you'd be here. Why didn't you tell me you were coming?"

"Hello to you, too," Marla said wryly. "Nice to see your communication skills haven't improved any since college."

Kate met Marla Lynch her sophomore year at University of Washington, when Kate had been floundering as a business undergrad with secret dreams of being a writer. Marla was the queen bee of the UW literary scene, dubbing their group the Nights of the Round Table after the central fixture in their meeting space, and all Kate had ever wanted was to be in her orbit.

"Sorry," Kate said sheepishly. "I'm just surprised! I mean, I guess you're technically closer to Hempstead Island than I am now, since you moved to the artists' colony on Orca. I just didn't think weddings, or Spencer, or Spencer's weddings were your thing."

"And here I was thinking public appearances were no longer *your* thing," Marla said in her smoky voice.

Kate winced at the implied accusation. After Spencer broke things off with her and her life went to hell, Kate had sort of gone MIA on everyone, Marla included. She'd left Marla in the lurch on more than one occasion and, based on their last text exchange, Kate wasn't sure their friendship was on the most solid ground. "I guess people are still . . . mad that I missed the alumni awards?"

"If by *people* you mean me, who had to drag her happy ass on a three-hour ferry ride back to Seattle to present the distinguished alumni award to you, only to receive a series of increasingly deranged texts from you about having an obviously fake case of mono."

"It was real!" Kate said, far too defensively. "I had a doctor's note and everything."

"Mono is for filthy middle schoolers with loose lips, not hermits whose lips haven't touched more than a takeout order of eggrolls in the last year. But I convinced the dean to pick up the tab for dinner that night, so no lingering bad vibes, babe." Marla's lips quirked into a smile, turning her attention toward Jake. "Besides, I'm just happy to have some stimulating company this weekend. Is this Jake the Hotstralian, finally in the flesh?"

Jake returned her smile, holding out a hand. "And you must be the Marla Lynch I've heard so much about over the years. Seattle's Rising Literary Star, eh?"

Marla was the first among the Nights of the Round Table to get an agent and a book contract, and she was also the reason Kate met Spencer that fateful evening during a Round Table discussion. Marla had just signed with Spencer, and Kate had been so in awe of meeting a real, honest-to-goodness publishing professional, that she'd basically begged Spencer to let her buy him a coffee. That coffee had eventually turned into her first gig as a ghostwriter on a Simon Says project.

Marla made a face. "Don't believe everything you read. It's been a lot less literary output and a lot more boozy input lately. You know us artists. So, you and Kate, huh? After all these years she finally worked up the ovaries to make it happen?"

"That's not . . . we aren't here . . ." Kate paused. Would it cause problems for Jake if she outed him now as not her plus-one? Kate tried to swallow, her throat suddenly sticky and dry. "Did I hear there were cocktails?"

Marla snorted. "Come on, Valentine, let's get you nice and liquored up, let all your little secrets come out like they do after a couple Jolly Rancher martinis."

"Oh god, don't bring those up," Kate groaned as she followed Marla down the side hallway where she'd first appeared. "I still can't smell watermelon candy without dry heaving."

Marla navigated the halls like an expert, already familiar with the layout that still made Kate anxious if she tried to think about how to get back to the main entryway. She'd never imagined a single house could have so many twists and turns, or rooms, or cabinets full of old toddler-size dressing gowns with suspicious stains on them. But when Marla pushed open a door with a flourish and a little "ta-da," Kate had to hand it to her. She'd hit the mother lode.

"Are these wine crates?" Kate asked as Marla pulled a bottle from a crate.

"Don't get too excited," Marla said as she poured. "It tastes awful, but it drinks the same as any alcohol. I was trying to find the good stuff, but apparently they keep it under lock and key somewhere. I'll find a way. I always do. Like the time we drank Professor Gould's Glenlivet." Marla lifted her glass. "To Rebecca Hempstead and her cheap-ass booze."

"Do you know Rebecca Hempstead?" Kate asked, thinking of the letter.

"I know *of* her," Marla said, waving it away like it was no big deal to know one of the richest women in the country. "Everybody in the San Juans does. She donates to the commune, along with a billion other nonprofits. She throws her money around so she can keep everybody in her stranglehold. But I'm not interested in the evils of inherited wealth,

I want to know more about the infamous Jake Hawkins. We used to take bets that you were an AI-generated Ken doll that Kate invented since you never came out when we invited you."

"I didn't realize I was being invited places," Jake said, giving Kate an arch look.

Kate's face warmed. "It was a work thing! I was keeping it professional!"

She hadn't been keeping it professional at all, and she had absolutely kept Jake away on purpose, though she'd rather guzzle all the cheap wine in the room than admit it. Marla had always belonged more to the "free love, nobody belongs to anybody" camp of dating, courtesy of her hippie artist dad. She didn't let things like school policy stop her from sleeping with her professors, and she didn't let a little thing like Kate's long-standing crush on a guy get in the way of hooking up with him after a rowdy session of the Nights of the Round Table. So yeah, maybe she kept Jake to herself a little.

"That's Kate, the pinnacle of professionalism," Jake said. Something about the way he said it made Kate feel like she'd done something wrong.

Marla drained her glass. "But this weekend isn't about boring professionalism or lab room sex or Kate's extremely fake case of mono."

"I had a doctor's note!" Kate protested weakly.

Marla filled their glasses, raising hers. "This weekend is about getting back on track. Eye on the prize. Onward and upward. And the free booze, obviously. To the weekend!"

"To the weekend," Kate echoed, sipping her wine. She could certainly cheers to getting back on track. She'd burned so many bridges the last few months—cancelling book tours at the last minute, asking for deadline extension after deadline extension, ignoring even her own mother's calls. She'd thought she had torpedoed her friendship with Marla along with the rest of her life, but maybe this was a chance to piece together her shattered existence, starting with the two people in this room.

"Here you are!" Abraham said, looking slightly put out as he appeared on the threshold. He glared in disappointment at Marla and the open bottle on the table. "I am afraid those are for the rehearsal dinner, and you are not meant to be in here, Ms. Lynch."

"Just . . . inspecting the goods," Marla said, her lips quirking as she polished off her wine.

"You two, with me!" Abraham announced, turning on his heel and marching out.

"Guess that's our cue," Kate said reluctantly, setting her glass down. "We'll see you at the rehearsal dinner, though, right? We can sit together."

"Mmm, seating for all meals has been carefully arranged by our illustrious hosts, thank you," Abraham said, shooing them along.

"Don't worry, Valentine, you know I always find you," Marla said, giving her a wink as she shamelessly cracked open a new bottle of wine. "Maybe we'll even find the good booze!"

"We will!" Kate promised as Abraham dragged her away, her spirits already buoyed by their conversation.

"This is Jean-Pierre," Abraham said as they reached the main hall and an impeccably dressed young man joined them, his curly hair arranged in an artful bouffant. "Jean-Pierre, this is Ms. Valentine."

He made meaningful eyes at his assistant, whose only response was a thorough, almost insulting perusal of Kate's full figure.

"*Oui?*" he said, drawing it out. "*Comme c'est intéressant.*"

"Indeed," said Abraham, his brows going up and down. "Miss Kennedy selected your room especially for you, aren't you so lucky? See them to her room, please. I need to check with Henri about the hors d'oeuvres."

"Tell him not to touch my bruschetta," Jean-Pierre said. "He knows what I'll do to him. Upstairs, you two. Quickly, if you would."

Jean-Pierre moved awfully fast, and Jake, with his perfectly taut glutes and calves, was right behind him, leaving Kate to bump along with her rolling case in tow. They'd disappeared by the time she reached the second floor, and she stood helplessly on the lush wine-dark carpet looking in either direction for them. Of course, in this house she was more likely to run into the twins from *The Shining* instead.

"Hello?" she called. "Jean-Pierre? Jake?"

Kate wandered down one stretch of hallway, passing a room with a plaque that read *Zebra Suite* and wondering how literally they meant it. Probably very literally. The hallway was deathly quiet, which was why the low hum of conversation from a room several doors down caught her attention and drew her forward. Maybe it was Jean-Pierre and Jake. She moved gratefully toward it.

"She's pushed me to this, Richie," said a tightly controlled voice. "If she torpedoes this deal, I'm fucked. You understand that, don't you? Tell her she needs to listen to me. Otherwise, she won't like what happens next."

Kate halted, body tilted toward the door, ear cocked at a prime listening angle. The voice was definitely not Jake, and lacked Jean-Pierre's accent, which meant this was a private conversation among strangers. A normal person, respectful of boundaries, would quietly move on. But this was another side effect of writing murder mysteries—she assumed all tense, private conversations were meant to be eavesdropped on. Like the bathroom conversation Loretta "overheard" in *A Dark and Stormy Murder*, when Loretta was trapped in the bar during a hurricane with several patrons, one of whom ended up strangled in the supply closet.

"If there's anything she doesn't respond well to, it's threats," said a much younger voice, presumably the Richie in question. "You're pushing her too hard, Steven. Give her time."

"Time is the one thing I haven't got!" said Steven, his tightly controlled voice losing some of its edge. "It has to be this weekend. Rico is on my back. This is my last chance."

"Fine, fine," said Richie, sounding bored. "Can we go to the party now? Gomez Addams down there was real stingy with the pour."

"There's still the rehearsal dinner to get through," said Steven.

"Such a helicopter daddy," Richie said, but his tone was playful. Teasing.

"Don't let your aunt catch you," said Steven.

"My aunt is a prude," said Richie, his tone dancing between bored and playful. "You're not a prude, are you, Stevie?"

"Talk to her, Richie, I mean it," said Steven, his voice stiff. "Before it's too late."

Chapter Six

"There you are!" someone announced so loudly from the other end of the hallway that Kate jumped away from the door like it had spontaneously erupted into flames. Jean-Pierre huffed from his position near the stairs, waving impatiently. "We continue up, yes?"

"Yes, sorry," Kate whispered, hurrying away before Richie or Steven could catch her snooping. She caught the barest glimpse of the men as they moved toward the door, one in a plain navy blazer and the other in a more festive herringbone affair, but she couldn't see their faces. Kate wouldn't be able to identify them unless they kept their jackets on. Not that she planned to do any identifying, but Loretta had taught her that tense conversations about money never ended well. It certainly hadn't for Blake the bartender when the wealthy woman who willed her fortune to him wound up dead.

"What were you doing?" Jean-Pierre asked, his tone professionally accusatory.

"I got lost," Kate huffed, glancing back surreptitiously at the door. The men still hadn't emerged, which was just as well. Even if she wanted one quick peek at their faces.

"Mmm, keep up, please," Jean-Pierre said, turning and hopping up the stairs toward the third floor. Kate started up the stairs that seemed to go on and wrap around with no signs of stopping. How many floors could one manor have?

The answer, in this case anyway, seemed to be four, as Jean-Pierre and Jake were down at the far end of a hall when Kate finally caught up on the fourth floor. She slowed as she approached, looking at the rickety set of stairs leading to a rectangular hole in the ceiling that he had pulled down with a golden cord.

"This . . . can't be right," Kate said, looking up dubiously. "It looks like an attic."

"Because it is an attic," Jean-Pierre said, typing away on a small device in his hands. It must be connected to Bluetooth, Kate figured, because she hadn't been able to get any signal on her cell phone since they left the dock in Seattle. "*Non, non!* Not the heirlooms, the cherry! Why must I be the only competent one? You two go up now. I'm very busy. Abraham is waiting."

Jake looked as dubious as Kate felt, but he nudged her toward the stairs. "Ladies first."

"That's sexist," Kate said, chewing one corner of her lip as she eyed the stairs. "You should go first. As a male feminist."

"Ah, but because I am a male feminist, I can allow a woman to face danger without needing to ride to her rescue as a white knight," Jake countered.

"Okay, but I'm asking you to go first," Kate said through gritted teeth.

Jake was all wide blue eyes and guile. "Because you're scared?"

"You are, too," Kate hissed.

"Yes, but I'm comfortable enough with my masculinity to admit I am."

Jean-Pierre huffed. "My bruschetta will be a nightmare if I leave it to Henri's clutches. Up, up you go."

Kate heaved a sigh, her first step on the rickety staircase warping the whole contraption. The air was positively frigid the higher she climbed, charged with the energy of the storm bearing down outside. She was sure this was just an attic, probably filled with half-gutted animal carcasses missing their eyes or teeth or something else that would haunt her night-mares. Maybe this was a psychological play on Spencer's part, to rattle a plot for book four out of her by sheer terror. Maybe he thought it would inspire her. Hell, maybe *he* was the Deer Shredder.

Her gaze came level with the opening, a yellow glow emanating from above. She paused in surprise with a soft "oh," taking in the attic. The room was absolutely *delightful*. The space looked like a cozy reading nook filled with bookshelves, the light coming from a Tiffany lamp in the corner beside a stuffed leather chair. The whole place was blissfully unadorned with dead animals, although the furry white rug in front of the leather chair was suspect. Still, it didn't have a head, so it would have to do.

"This looks fantastic," Kate said, enthusiastically exploring the space now that the prospect of murder had proven unsubstantiated.

"Not much elbow room, though," Jake said as he scaled the ladder. "You think they expect you to sleep on that stack of books over there?"

"There's a bed back here," Kate said. It looked to be a twin, narrow but comfortable, with fresh white sheets and a soft pink canopy enclos-ing it, the curtains pulled back on either side with a ribbon. Something about the whimsy of it appealed to Kate. Like she could close the cur-tains and shut out the rest of the world for the weekend.

"Well, I won't look if you won't," Jake said, already stripping out of his Henley. Kate caught the barest glimpse of his intercostal mus-cles lengthening and flexing over his rib cage before she whirled around abruptly.

"Yep, nope," she muttered, crawling behind the half wall of books. "No peeking. Nope."

She did her best to wrestle out of her sweater and leggings while also hiding behind the meager privacy screen made of what looked like a bunch of old paperback westerns. She dug out the dress she'd bought a month ago that felt like a good idea then, but now felt too short and tight and way too low cut. There was a brief moment, just after she'd slipped out of her leggings and unhooked her old bra, when she was topless and only a few feet away from Jake. The air was cool, the storm picking up momentum above them, whistling and humming through the eaves, and her skin prickled in response to the electric energy.

"So," she called out, hoping to mask the unevenness in her voice with volume. "Weird that they had you as my plus-one, huh? Must have been some kind of error or something."

"Must have been," Jake said vaguely. She swore she didn't mean to, that it happened by accident, but she caught a glimpse of his backside through a crack in two Louis L'Amour books. Fortunately—or unfortunately—for her, he'd already slipped into his dress pants. "Probably a mix-up because my invite was so last minute. I wasn't even supposed to be here. I only got back from Borneo two days ago. My business partner took ill. We had to medically evacuate him back to the States."

"Oh," Kate said. "I'm surprised you're here, then. With all of that going on."

"Yeah, well." Jake didn't answer right away, which wasn't like him. The only subject she'd ever known him to be cagey about was his dad, who treated him like a failure for chasing surfing and getting himself nearly killed because of it. "I, uh, I went into the Simon Says office. Had some business to clear up. I ran into Kennedy, she invited me, and . . . here I am."

"Here you are." Kate twisted her way into a pair of lacy pantyhose. Another uncomfortable mistake, but she was committed now. Still, she could tell by the tension running through Jake's shoulders that he was lying. She didn't know why he was here this weekend, but it wasn't because of an impromptu invitation from Kennedy Hempstead.

"This wasn't the Spencer wedding I thought I'd be reluctantly invited to," Jake said before Kate could ask any more questions about his reasons for being there that weekend, glancing back at her and catching her eye over the stack of books as she wrangled her boobs into her new strapless bra. He turned his back too quickly for Kate to read his expression. "The two of you got together and engaged so quickly I figured it would be a done deal before I made it back stateside. But I get back from

Borneo and hear from my aunt you two called it off, and he's marrying the peppy marketing girl."

Kate sighed, slipping into her dress and fiddling with the tiny buttons on the sleeve. "Yeah, well, you know the old story. Boy meets girl, boy asks girl to marry him, boy hooks up with cute new marketing hire and ends up leaving girl to marry the marketing girl six months later. Tale as old as time."

"And girl comes to their wedding weekend because she can't resist the temptation of rich people cake?" Jake gently prodded.

Kate sighed. "It's . . . complicated."

Jake snorted. "With you, that's always an understatement."

First there was the invitation with the ostentatious, hand-calligraphed name and address that Kate threw in the trash unopened. Then there was the series of automated text messages reminding her of the deadline to RSVP, which she kept trying to block, but somehow they always popped up again. And then there was the bridal shower invitation, with the personal note from the marketing manager at Simon Says, Juliette Winters, making it clear the invitation was only a courtesy insisted on by Kennedy and threatening bodily harm if Kate dared to actually show up. Not that Kate would dare, especially when she was two missed deadlines deep at that point.

But then there had been the final invitation in an unassuming envelope, her name and address neatly printed as if it had been done up on an old typewriter. And inside, tucked between the luscious cardstock and thin vellum, a personal letter from Rebecca Hempstead herself. *Please do me the favor of attending. I'll make it worth your while.*

How Rebecca Hempstead had heard of her, much less wanted to meet her enough to personally invite her for the weekend, Kate couldn't imagine. Maybe the woman wanted to pull an Evelyn Hugo and publish a tell-all. Or maybe she was a closet Loretta fan; she wouldn't be the first surprise super-reader. Whatever the reason, it was the one mystery Kate couldn't resist. Why did Rebecca Hempstead want her there this weekend?

"Let's just get this over with," Kate said, straightening up and wind-milling her arms to keep steady on her towering heels. "Okay, ready."

"I thought you'd be at least anoth—" Jake began as he looked up from his place in the leather chair. The words died in his throat as his gaze traveled down to her heels and back up, taking in the dress she'd pinned so many of her hopes for the weekend on.

It was nothing like her usual style—in that it *had* a style—a black silk dress with a high waistline and a gathered skirt that fell in soft waves to mid-thigh, the bodice a sweetheart neckline that plunged so low she'd had to buy a new bra just to wear it. It had a floral lace overlay with a high neckline that left her cleavage in deep shadow and ended at her wrists in a small frill. The salesgirl at the boutique told her she wanted to cry when she saw Kate in the dress, and Kate had wanted to cry when the total hit her credit card bill. But the way Jake was looking at her now, like he'd literally forgotten to breathe—she'd pay double, triple, just to have him look at her like that again.

"Too much?" she asked, giving the skirt a little swish.

"No, it's—" His voice was hoarse, and he cleared his throat sharply. He pressed his hands to the arms of the chair like he might try to stand, but he stayed there, fingers digging into the leather. He cleared his throat again, giving his head a little shake. "No, it's . . . You look . . . Kate. It's stunning. *You're* stunning."

Stunning. She'd never been called "stunning" in her life, not even close. Cute, clever, even adorable (until the age of six). But never stunning. And never by Jake Hawkins. Kate could feel that one little word working its magic, making her spine curve and the soft underpart of her feet arch and her hips tilt at an angle. Jake was still staring, his gaze caressing the lines of her calves, the exposed expanse of her thighs, that deep dip of the sweetheart neckline. It had been chilly before, but now the attic was sweltering like they'd turned on dueling heaters.

"Thank you," Kate said, heart hammering. "And you look . . ." What should she say, incredible? Too eager. Stunning? No, he'd already said that. Like a tall glass of icy cold water on a blisteringly hot day that she could slurp down in one thirsty gulp? Highly inappropriate, if accurate. "You look great, too. Should we . . . go?"

Jake cleared his throat for the third time and stood up. "Right. Let's . . . go, then."

The cocktail hour had come and gone by the time they found their way to the ground floor, rain lashing the windows as thunder rattled the panes, and more than once the electric lights dimmed and dropped out before buzzing back to life. Jake seemed to have recovered his sense of self, his smile pleasantly mild and his eyes fixed anywhere but on her. She'd felt so powerful when he'd first looked at her, but now she felt awkward and unbalanced in her heels, a cool breeze gusting up her backside anytime she leaned over. She considered scurrying back upstairs for her flats when Simon Hsu, president and publisher of Simon Says, approached them with a wide smile.

"Jake Hawkins and Kate Valentine!" he said, clapping them on the shoulders. "Two of my most beloved local authors!"

It was Simon's favorite joke, since all of his authors were local. It had been his mission when he'd started Simon Says in 1994, to highlight the talents of writers in the Pacific Northwest.

Simon Says had grown along with their title list, boasting fifteen employees across all departments. Simon liked to think of them as a family, hosting annual summer barbeques and holiday parties, Thanksgiving potlucks at the office and spring break trips up to Vancouver. Kate had tagged along for several of those parties in the beginning, when she'd been a contract ghostwriter for some of their business titles.

"Simon, my man, what's good?" Jake said, grinning and shaking Simon's hand enthusiastically. Kate had never seen Jake so glad-handy with Simon, but she supposed it was the law of bros. Get two men together with potential bro tendencies and watch the "brahs" and "dudes" start flying.

"Life, my brother, life is good! Just riding that wave." Simon put out his hands expansively. "But don't tell me you don't already know. Are we back in business?"

"Ah, yeah, maybe," Jake said, glancing apprehensively at Kate and rubbing the back of his neck. "I stopped in earlier this week but you were out. I figured we could talk."

"Later, later! It's a party tonight, isn't it?" Simon said, pretending to punch Jake in the ribs. "And who better to party with than the party man himself?"

"Ah, yeah," Jake said with a forced laugh. "Maybe over breakfast—"

"And Kate!" said Simon, turning and holding out his arms. "My best-selling-est bestseller! Keeping the lights on for three years running. And you've got another coming this weekend I hear. No getting mono this time around, huh? Though I guess we all know who you got it from now."

Simon looked expectantly between the two of them, grinning, and it took Kate longer than necessary to catch on.

"What?" she said. "No, that's not—"

"Ah, don't play coy with me. The little French guy already spilled the beans that the two of you came together." Simon patted Jake on the shoulders again like he was trying to dislodge a cocktail olive. "Though try keeping this guy pinned down for long, huh?"

"How about some drinks?" Jake asked with a wince. "I'll get us a round."

"Simon, really—"Kate said, desperate to clear up this pesky dating rumor before it got out of hand. Jake was no help, having already booked it for the bar. "I think there's been a misunderstanding—"

"Hey, Gerry, you made it!" said Simon to a passing gentleman, ignoring the increasing strain in her voice. "Kate, great to see you. Gerry, let's talk stocks, my man!"

"Simon, no, wait!" Kate said, stumbling after him as he slipped through the crowd in pursuit of Gerry. But her heel stepped on something uneven, turning her ankle with a sick crunch. She tilted sideways, staggering to the left to try to catch her balance, but instead crashing right into Kennedy Hempstead.

Chapter Seven

"Oh!" exclaimed sweet little Kennedy Hempstead, bride-to-be extraordinaire, as she went flying back into the gift table. All those perfectly wrapped boxes tumbled to the ground and the chatter around them died as Kate looked down at Kennedy, sprawled out among her destroyed wedding gifts. She looked almost ethereal in her flapper-inspired dress studded in crystalline beads that had probably been handsewn by some beleaguered apprentice in Paris.

"Shit," Kate muttered, shaken out of her horrified reverie by the sight of Kennedy crumpled up among the dented boxes and bags. She reached forward, helping the poor girl up, a wave of coconut and lemongrass wafting out of her glossy, perfect beach waves. Except the lacy sleeve of Kate's dress got caught in Kennedy's massive diamond pendant necklace, and when she made to help the girl stand up, she accidentally choked her with her own necklace instead. "Oh, wait, hold still! My sleeve is . . . Hang on. Oh, *shit*."

She struggled with the lace, lamenting the ripping sound as she managed to pull the fabric free. More crunches followed as they struggled upright with a captive audience, Kate teetering dangerously on her heels and Kennedy dazed from the fall. There was a blinding flash and Kate caught sight of the wedding photographer as he flitted through the crowd. Great, now there was photographic evidence. Why would he even take that photo? For blackmail, probably.

"I'm so sorry," Kate said, holding on to Kennedy for balance. "These shoes, they're an absolute menace. I was going to change them—"

"It's okay, Kate," Kennedy said, still a little unsteady. But she gave Kate a brilliant smile that was all perfectly aligned teeth and expertly applied makeup, throwing her arms around Kate's neck in a surprisingly strong hug. "I'm just glad you could make it!"

"Oh," Kate said, put off-balance by her enthusiasm. The surrounding guests were less enthusiastic, watching with judgmental expressions. "Happy wedding weekend?"

Kennedy pulled back. "Spencer thought you might miss the wedding because of Loretta. Didn't you, Spencey?"

"Technically, I said she'd use it as an excuse," came Spencer's baritone from over Kate's shoulder.

Kate tensed, bracing herself to face her fiancé—ex-fiancé, she had to remember the ex—for the first time in six months. At his own wedding. To someone else. Kate pivoted, and damn those stilettos, because her other ankle turned and she lost her balance *again* and face-planted into Spencer's jacket, dragging Kennedy with her. Spencer stiffened as he caught her, Kennedy tumbling to the floor beside them.

"Oh," Kennedy said again in her sweet voice.

"Still a wiz on heels, I see." Spencer grunted. "And that's . . . quite a dress."

"Spencer," she hissed, her gaze darting furtively around the circle of onlookers entranced by this new development in the saga. Kennedy struggled to get up, but Spencer still hadn't let Kate go. "Spencer, your *bride*. Help your bride."

"Right," Spencer said gruffly, abruptly pushing her upright and blinking through his customary tortoiseshell glasses (which she'd learned a full year into their relationship were not actually prescription). He wore a suit just nice enough that she knew Kennedy must have paid for it, and just rumpled enough that she knew he hadn't bothered steaming it before putting it on.

"Sorry, Kennedy," Spencer said, helping his bride up. "All better?"

"Yes, of course, thank you, Spencey," Kennedy said, giving him a smile that he completely missed because he'd already released her, turning back to square off with Kate.

"So, you came," he said, frowning. "I didn't think you would."

"Of course I would," Kate said brightly, as much for the assembled crowd as for him.

"I assumed you would have some other convenient excuse, like the plague or yellow fever," he said. "But since you're here, I expect you have something for me? Some overdue chapters, perhaps?"

"All work and no play," Kate said with a plastered smile, turning to Kennedy. "Kennedy, everything looks beautiful. You must be so happy."

"I'm just so glad you're here," Kennedy said, playing with her diamond pendant. "If it were up to me, we would have invited all of Spencey's authors! So many brilliant minds, it would have been amazing to have you all together this weekend. But he was a stickler about the guest list, even though I told him we have plenty of room here."

"And I told her most editors don't invite their entire author list to their wedding weekend," Spencer said, pulling off his glasses and untucking the edge of his shirt to clean the lenses. It was his poker tell, a nervous habit he'd developed under his mother's increasingly invasive questions about his and Kate's wedding plans. He was hiding something. He put the glasses back on, blinking as if he could suddenly see again despite having LASIK surgery years ago. "But you know Kennedy, we're all one big family at Simon Says."

"Because we are!" Kennedy said. "Simon is walking me down the aisle, Juliette is a bridesmaid, and you're the groom! Of course we're all one big happy family."

"One big happy family," Spencer echoed with far less enthusiasm as Kennedy hugged herself to his side. Spencer went stiff at the contact, which Kate considered odd behavior for a groom. Still, Spencer was as good at public displays of affection as he was at line dancing. Kate

wouldn't be surprised if he insisted on a handshake instead of the customary kiss tomorrow.

"I hope you liked your room okay," Kennedy said to Kate, oblivious
to her future husband's tension. "I picked it out especially for you. I know
it's a bit of a trek to get up there, but it's warm and cozy and filled with
books, and far away from the crowds. It's my favorite room in the house.
I used to stay there when I would visit Grandpa Ferdinand."

"That's . . . so thoughtful," Kate said, and she meant it. "It's perfect,
Kennedy."

And it was perfect, and of course Kennedy had been so thoughtful as
to pick it out for Kate. And that was why, despite everything, Kate couldn't
actually hate Kennedy. Because she was a genuinely, infuriatingly, kind
person.

"I know it's a bit small for two, but I think you'll make it work,"
Kennedy said, giving Kate a wink.

Kate's mouth fell open. "How did you know—"

Kennedy leaned in close, lowering her voice to a conspiratorial whisper. "I knew Spencey would never let me invite him on his own, but if he
came as your plus-one? Well, he couldn't say no then, could he?"

So it hadn't been a clerical error; Kennedy had made Jake her plus-
one. That was . . .

"Surprisingly devious," Kate said out loud.

"I know," Kennedy said with a mischievous smile.

"Kate," Spencer said, in that tone that meant he was about to launch
into a lecture. But then his eyes flickered over her shoulder, his expression turning sour. "Ah, is this the reason why I don't have my Loretta
pages yet?"

"Is what . . . why?" Kate asked, at a loss.

"What did I miss?" Jake asked, handing her a glass. "Got the drinks,
darling."

"Darling?" Kate repeated stupidly, as if she'd never heard the word
in her life. Come to think of it, she'd definitely never heard it directed at
her. And certainly not from Jake Hawkins.

And as if that wasn't enough, he slid his arm around her waist, pulling her in close and nuzzling the soft spot of skin behind her ear with his nose, instantly turning her entire body to jelly. "Play along, Katey cakes. There was some chatter among the guests that's best not repeated, but suffice it to say you could use a lifeline right now."

Kate glanced at the guests trying their best to act like they weren't shamelessly eavesdropping. She should have expected as much, after the stunt with Kennedy and the gift table and Spencer's odd behavior toward his bride. Still, she wasn't going to stay upright on these damn stilettos if Jake nuzzled her one more time.

"So, it's true, then," Spencer said, taking his glasses off to fidget with them so hard he bent one of the arms. "When did this happen?"

"Well, Spence, when was it you and Kennedy got together?" Jake asked, so casually Spencer didn't feel the barb until it was buried in his gut. "Must have been right around then."

For the rest of her life, as long as she lived, Kate would cherish the memory of the look on Spencer's face just then. He looked as if someone had put their fist straight into his gut right as he took a whopping bite of a meatball sub, and the guy to do it had been Cary Grant or Ryan Gosling. His back bowed out, his cheeks sucked in, and his eyes went glassy.

"That long?" Kate managed to get out. "Why, it feels like only . . . today."

"Such is the nature of love, darling," Jake said, tightening his arm around her waist, scattering her last coherent thought. The look he gave her was pure sin, and he leaned in to kiss her on the cheek. But she anticipated it and turned her head so that his lips pressed against hers. His eyes widened in surprise for a moment before he drew her in.

Kate had meant the maneuver as a form of proof to Spencer that she had indeed moved onward and upward. But Jake held her there, so much of him pressed against so much of her, his lips lingering on the fullness of her lower lip. He was holding back, she could swear it, but even at that the contact tingled all the way down to her toes. His lips lingered—regretfully, punishingly—as if to say he knew what she was doing and he didn't approve. Kate was certain of one thing—the full power of his kiss would be absolutely devastating. She wouldn't survive it.

"Thank you," she huffed as he pulled back.

Jake chuckled. "If you're going to thank me for kissing you, Katey cakes, we'll have a long night ahead of us."

Spencer made a choking noise, Kennedy sighed softly, and Kate was positive she'd died and gone to heaven or hell. Or a hot and sweaty combination of both.

"Oh my gosh, I *love* it!" Kennedy practically squealed, drawing both of them into a spontaneous hug. "Love at my wedding! We need to toast this. Oh, I had a champagne glass, didn't I? Where did it go?"

They searched around the wreckage of the guest table, and it was Kate who discovered the cut-crystal glass with the word *Bride* laser engraved on the side. "Here it is! Oh, but it looks like whatever you were drinking might have gotten . . . drunk." More like spilled into a hundred-year-old carpet, but Kate didn't need any more black marks on her record at this point. "How about I get you a refill?"

"Let a server handle it," Spencer said. "You and I still have business to discuss."

"Business?" Kate said, backing away from the conversation and the threat of discussing pages she hadn't written. "At a wedding? Don't be ridiculous. I'll be right back!"

She slipped away before any of them could stop her, setting a determined course toward the bar.

Chapter Eight

Kate reached the bar and held out the glass absently to the bartender, who brought out a hidden bottle of chilled Dom Pérignon when he saw the word *Bride* on the glass. It even had a tiny wedding dress around the neck with a red sash marked "for the Bride" in case the staff got distracted and tried to serve the top shelf to the bottom-feeders. Kate guessed you didn't stay old money by splashing out on expensive champagne for the plebians.

Kate was in no rush to return to Kennedy and Spencer, not to mention Jake's overwhelming presence. What had he been up to with that whole fake dating ploy? It was bound to come back and bite her in the ass, but she was powerless to stop him now. Not when he spread his fingers against the small of her back like that. Asshole.

She lingered by the bar, taking in the lavish decorations. The ball-room was certainly a centerpiece of the Manor, a two-story affair with observation railings above and crystal chandeliers hanging from an ornately carved wooden ceiling. The dinner tables were covered in rose-hued linens and coordinating mauve napkins. Each place setting had at least four forks, which felt like two forks too many to Kate, but what did she know about multicourse meals? She considered eggrolls, fried rice, and a fortune cookie a three-course meal. Glass sculptures filled with vibrant pink tulips adorned each table, which Kate heard had been cultivated for Kennedy by a Dutch tulip master. The bar served a signature cocktail made from small-batch liquors distilled especially for the wedding weekend.

Kate had never gotten very far in her wedding planning with Spencer—truth be told, she'd held three cake-tasting sessions and zero dress fittings—but she knew it would have been a far simpler affair than this. It wasn't that Kennedy flaunted her wealth, but it was obvious in the designer quality of her clothes, the Lexus she drove, the expensive sheen to her hair. Kennedy had never worried about money; she'd never really thought about it. That was the security that inherited wealth afforded her, and try as she might to be egalitarian about it, Kate couldn't help envying such stability.

"It's a fucking disgrace is what it is," someone slurred beside Kate in a husky voice with the faintest hint of a posh accent Kate was never quite sure was authentic. "All this money on a party, and they can't pay authors a living wage. An absolute disgrace."

"Serena," Kate said, turning to the voluptuous older woman draped halfway across the bar beside her. "I didn't know you would be here this weekend."

Serena Archer wore her yellow-blond hair styled in forties' curls and bumper bangs, her generous figure poured into an hourglass dress in a deep green with her boobs propped up like an appetizer course. A fascinator hung precariously from the side of her curls, threatening to tumble into the half-empty martini glass in front of her.

"Oh, they did their best to keep me out, didn't they?" Serena said, recovering some of her posture and her dignity at the prospect of an audience. "That little *chippy* tried to 'friends and family only' me, but I put her in her place. I told her 'Honey, I knew Spencer before you and I'll know him after you're gone. Eleven books we've done together.' I was his first author, you know. First one to believe in him and take a chance on him despite some shaky editorial choices. Do you know he wanted me to rename the Gutter Angels series to something more marketable? I get dozens of emails a week from readers who picked up the books precisely because of the title."

"I'm . . . sure," Kate said. She'd attempted to read one of Serena's books when she'd first sold the Loretta series, but there had been a lot of heaving parts that Kate couldn't keep track of enough to follow the plot.

Serena snorted into her now-empty martini glass. "Don't you tell me about marketing, you little . . . She wouldn't know good marketing if it slapped her in the face, which it will if she doesn't watch herself."

Kate nodded along mutely, knowing from extensive experience at other Simon Says events what a risky combination Serena and alcohol could be. She'd once ended a company Christmas party early by putting on a pair of antlers and offering free reindeer rides to the hired Santa. She seemed in fine form tonight, her cheeks stained a pink that matched the room motif, her upper lip dotted in beads of sweat despite the cool evening air. Lightning flashed through the glass dome overhead, throwing her thick makeup into sharp relief.

"Eleven years, eleven books, and now they want to ghost me?" Serena said, blinking at Kate as if she'd forgotten who she was talking to. "Oh, Kate. When did you get here?"

"Why don't we just . . ." Kate said, reaching for the martini glass to take it away.

"Good idea! Barkeep, another of your finest!" Serena announced, slapping her hand on the bar top. "They think they can let that little fool tank our sales, hold out on our contracts, and refuse our calls? After all we've done for them? Authors like you and me, we made them. They're nothing without our talent and skill. They can't treat us like this!"

"Treat us like . . . what?" Kate asked.

"Oh, please, I know you're Miss Superstar right now, but I was on top once. All it takes is one bad sales cycle, thanks to abysmal marketing by little Miss 'I'm Head of the Department Now,' and suddenly Spencer isn't returning *your* calls, isn't extending *your* options on the next book, and whenever you stop in to speak to Simon, he's conveniently out of the office. And I'm not the only one, not by a long shot. The writing's on the wall, Miss Superstar, and you'd better get your big-girl panties on because shit's about to hit the fan."

"They're delaying contracts?" Kate said in surprise. She hadn't heard anything, but that was probably because she was a good six months past her deadline. "Everyone?"

"Nearly," Serena said with a snort, chewing viciously on the olive from her fresh martini. "To them we're just cogs in a machine, easily replaced. Well, we won't make it so easy for them. We won't go quietly into that good night. Are you in?"

"In for . . . what?" Kate asked, at a complete loss. What if she wasn't just in breach of contract over her missed deadlines? What if she didn't have any more contracts to look forward to? Surely Spencer would have said something to her.

Serena leaned in so close their noses almost touched, her vodka and vermouth breath basting Kate's face. "Midnight," she breathed. "You'll see. Be there. The lion will roar."

"The lion? Midnight? Where?" Kate asked.

Serena winked as she pushed herself off the barstool, sloshing half her martini. "Midnight, Kate. The little chippy will see we mean *business*."

"Serena, I don't think—"

"*Liberté, Egalité, Fraternité!*" Serena announced, tottering off away from the bar.

"That . . . can't be good," Kate said, frowning. Whatever Serena had planned at midnight, Kate was sure she wanted to be as far from it as possible. Still, the news about the contract delays was distressing. Serena's books didn't sell nearly as well as Kate's, but she was right about being a staple of Spencer's list from the beginning. Kate needed to find Marla, ask if she'd heard anything. Marla always had the gossip.

Kate headed toward the bridal dais with Kennedy's glass in hand as the first wave of waiters brought out the soup course, a creamy, buttery smell filling the ballroom and making her stomach rumble. Maybe she'd stop off at her table for a quick bite, a little sustenance before she dropped off Ken's champagne glass. Actually, the Dom smelled pretty good, too.

Kennedy wouldn't notice a sip or two, and Kate could never afford Dom on her own. Just one tiny sip.

"Don't even think about it," Jake murmured, intercepting her as she raised the glass. His hand slid across her lower back, so smooth and intimate, as he guided her toward the front of the room. "You've already launched the bride into her wedding presents like an American football defensive line. What do you think people will say when they see you drinking out of a glass with *Bride* etched into it?"

Kate had only wanted a little taste of the luxurious life, but when he put it like *that*, she sounded unhinged. "Why did you let everyone think we were . . ." Kate trailed off, telling herself to put some physical distance between them even as her spine rounded into his hand.

"Having sex?" Jake asked, infuriatingly chill about the whole thing.

Kate swallowed hard at the blatant description and the way it made her feel like panting. "Dating. I was going to say dating."

"Then you should have said it."

"You're impossible."

"People were talking," Jake said with a shrug. "Besides, Spencer's a twat, and I couldn't pass up the opportunity to let him know it."

The bad blood between Jake and Spencer had started from their first editorial meeting after selling the *Wandering Australian* book. Kate had been working contract ghostwriting jobs for Spencer, but when she'd met Jake she knew his story was too special to pass up. Spencer had been less than enthusiastic, so she'd convinced Simon to take a meeting and let Jake work his magic. He'd done more than that—Simon had badgered Spencer into signing him on the spot. Spencer assumed Jake had put Kate up to it, despite her protests that it had been her idea, and had taken his revenge during that first meeting by eviscerating Jake's ideas. They'd nearly come to blows, and the atmosphere between them hadn't improved much since then.

Jake turned toward her, nuzzling her ear. "He's up there next to his bride now, staring at you, isn't he?"

Kate swallowed hard, momentarily forgetting the English language. "I don't . . . What?"

"Should I give him something to look at?"

And then—*then*—his teeth grazed her earlobe before biting softly and giving it the lightest tug. She let out a sound that was borderline inappropriate for the bedroom, much less a ballroom full of wedding guests. It was craven, lusting, halfway to an orgasm, and Jake's chuckle against her skin nearly pushed her over the edge.

"Please don't . . . don't do that," Kate huffed.

"You don't like it?" Jake asked.

She rather liked it *too* much, which was the problem.

Chapter Nine

"Here we are," Kate announced hastily as she spotted her place card, gold script on thick linen card stock. Unfortunately for her, she apparently had a place of honor at table one, directly across from the bridal dais where Spencer was, indeed, staring daggers at her and Jake. She ducked behind the tower of tulips, obscuring him from view. She still had Kennedy's champagne glass, but she wasn't about to give Spencer the opportunity to pounce and lecture her again, so she quietly set it beside her plate. Maybe they wouldn't notice.

The wedding party had taken their seats as well, including Spencer's awful brother, Eric, and his boring college-roommate-turned-lawyer, Ian. Kate shifted her position before almost making eye contact with Juliette Winters, the ferocious second-in-command of Kennedy's marketing team. The woman was an absolute shark, as formidable in meetings as she was on the dating scene. Kate had no desire to give Juliette any more reasons to hate her tonight after the book tour debacle six months ago.

Next to Juliette, in the maid-of-honor position, was a woman in a dress Kate recognized instantly, thanks to its boxy fit. It was the woman from the garden, only this time Kate was close enough to identify her.

Cassidy Smith, Kennedy's cousin from the banished side of the family. No wonder she couldn't afford a better dress. Kate had met the poor girl a few times over the years at Kennedy's parties, and she'd always seemed on the verge of a nervous breakdown about something. She'd at least cleaned up her eye makeup so it was less raccoon, more Alice Cooper. Who had she been talking to out there, and what had they been discussing that had made the other person mad enough to slap her? Kate could hardly ask Cassidy, even though she was burning up with curiosity.

Jake took the seat beside her, breaking into her suspicious thoughts as he looked over the table decorations. "Kennedy must be a big fan of pink."

"Dreadful, isn't it?" said a young man in a bright red dress shirt, flopping into the seat beside Kate and slinging his jacket over the chair beside him. "It's like being inside of an enormous vagina."

Jake choked on a poorly timed sip of wine, spraying red across the soft pink of the tablecloth in an unfortunate pastiche that seemed to only underscore the point. "I wasn't thinking that," he said. He looked around the table with fresh eyes. "Though, now I can't . . . unthink it."

The new arrival waved an empty wineglass at a passing waiter. "Hello? Refill?"

"I think you've had enough until we get to the main course, Richie, don't you?" said an older Black man in a navy blazer as he took the seat beside Richie. Kate glanced surreptitiously at his place card, where the name *Steven Moyer* was etched in gold. Kate dug her fingers into Jake's arm to keep from gasping out loud. Richie and Steven. As in *she's pushed me to this, Richie.*

"I'm Steven, the family's real estate lawyer," he said, shaking Kate's hand in a formal grasp. "And this is—"

"Richie, the black sheep cousin, and you are Kate and no name, fantastic, we're all friends now," said the younger man, draining half his freshly filled wineglass in one sip and making a face. "God, is this really the best that Auntie R would let them pull from stock? It tastes like cooking sherry mixed with grape juice."

Kate's knowledge of wine ran to the "silver bladder bag in a box" variety, but she thought the wine tasted fine. Then again, that might be *why* she thought the wine tasted fine. She sipped slowly as the waiters brought out the main course. Richie picked at it, complaining about Kennedy's banal choices of chicken or fish, criticizing the plating and the undercooked potatoes as he drained another glass and a half. Kate would have preferred something far less dainty herself, with less fork selection and a paper napkin.

"The, uh, photos are a nice touch," Kate said, her attempt at polite conversation with a man she was rapidly realizing was deeply unpleasant to share a meal with. She waved at the photos embedded in the surface of the tulip vase. "Very . . . retro?"

"They're of Uncle Gordon and Aunt Brielle's wedding," Richie said in a bored tone. "Kennedy's parents, may they rest in peace, blah blah blah. From when they got married here. Ken has dreamed of having her wedding here just like they did ever since she was a little girl. She used to carry their wedding album around and make us re-create scenes from the wedding. I was the only boy, so I always had to play Uncle Gordon. Of course, that was before Auntie R basically banished us from the island under the guise of 'preservation.'"

"If there's one thing your aunt is good at, it's spin doctoring," Steven said with a shrug. "She has the majority of the board in her pocket, too, so she can get away with it."

"Perfect little people-pleaser Ken really got her back, though, didn't she?" Richie snorted into his wineglass. "More cutthroat than the Bitch Bull herself, going behind her back to the board like she did."

"There's no telling what Rebecca will do about it now, though," Steven said. "Hell hath no fury like a Rebecca Hempstead spurned, and she'll bring all hell down on us for it."

Kate thought of Mr. Sheffield from the portrait gallery, whose entire family business Rebecca ruined over a broken engagement.

"You don't seem particularly fond of your aunt," Jake observed.

Richie snorted once again. "Who would be? She thinks because she's made so much money with her little stock market ploys that suddenly she's the only Hempstead worth cashing the family trust checks? It's all

Great-Grandpa Russell's fault, really, willing everything straight to Ferdinand and decreeing some ridiculous inheritance restriction that only the eldest of the eldest can manage the trust. That's some old-fashioned bullshit. But it was Grandpa Ferdinand who really put the ice pick in the family back, cutting out his own siblings because they dared to question the will. And now we all suffer the consequences, bowing and scraping at the divine altar of Rebecca to give us our share."

"You have to ask Rebecca for your inheritance?" Kate asked. She hadn't run across the specifics of their trust during her late-night, ill-advised Google rabbit-holing, but there had been enough litigation among the Hempsteads to power a small village of lawyers.

"It's more complicated than that, actually," said Steven. "According to Russell Hempstead's will, upon his death the entirety of the Hempstead fortune would be placed in a trust, with the eldest child of the eldest child in charge of overseeing and doling out those funds to the family. However, he put an . . . interesting stipulation upon the release of any such funds."

"Interesting," Richie muttered. "More like sadistic and humiliating."

"I believe his intentions were good," Steven said with a frown. "He'd seen many of his peers and their heirs fall to infighting and wasteful living over the fortunes they had amassed in their day. Russell came from farming stock, and he believed in the power of hard work. So he put in a clause—any Hempstead could request their inheritance at any time, up to one million dollars each, but only if they presented their plan to use that money in a significant and impactful way to contribute positively to society."

"Like curing cancer?" Jake asked, bewildered.

"Or starting a business, or a charity foundation," Steven said. "He wanted his children and his grandchildren to work for their money, same as he had."

"Yeah, except he made all his money back in the twenties running rum up the coast of Seattle," Richie said, rolling his eyes. "Significant and impactful, sure, but I doubt anyone would think he was contributing positively to society. Meanwhile, if I want to so much as buy toilet paper,

I've got to run it up the flagpole through the Bitch Bull. She's denied every request I've ever made. Twelve times! Twelve times she's poisoned the board against my perfectly legitimate business plans. I swear, if she tries to intervene next month, I'll—"

"Richie," Steven said sharply, glaring at him. "I think you've had enough, don't you?"

"Of Rebecca, you bet," Richie said venomously. "She can't hold our inheritance hostage forever. Speak of the she-devil now."

Richie turned his sullen attention toward the bridal dais as the chandeliers dimmed and a single spotlight flared to life, illuminating Abraham.

"Everyone, please, can I have your attention?" he called, holding up a hand to block the glare of the spotlight. "Dessert will be served shortly, which means it's time for speeches! And, first up, we have the honor of hearing from a woman who needs no introduction, but who absolutely deserves one. What hasn't she done, folks? Top of the Forbes list, Ernst and Young's Entrepreneur of the Year for six years running, and she even served a stint as a US diplomat in Japan. Please join me in welcoming and extending our sincere gratitude to the woman who made this weekend possible, our esteemed and revered host, Ms. Rebecca Hempstead!"

The room politely cheered as a woman in a bold floral caftan climbed the short steps to the stage. She towered over Abraham, lean and willowy like a former athlete. Kate would have guessed her to be in her forties based on her flawless skin, but the steel gray of her bob haircut and Kate's own googling put her closer to her sixties. Kate had always heard that meeting celebrities in real life was underwhelming, but Rebecca Hempstead managed to be the opposite; sparkling and perfectly put together, tall and imposing while still portraying feminine grace. This was the woman who moved the market before breakfast, who made politicians scramble to get a few minutes with her, who held the Hempstead family reins in an iron fist.

"Good evening," Rebecca said, her voice rich and smooth, as if the generations of fine breeding and top-tier schooling had smoothed any accented edge. "And welcome to Hempstead Manor. I see some very familiar faces in the crowd tonight—John Berry, president of Washington National Bank, the very bank my grandfather started over a hundred years ago. And Prince Abdullah, *As-salaam alaikum*! George and Agatha, so good to see you taking a break from the campaign trail. And what an auspicious gathering to bring such luminous dignitaries like yourselves together! When Kennedy asked for my blessing to hold her wedding here, where her own parents were married so many happy years ago, how could I refuse her?"

Richie made a choking sound, earning himself a glare that would have melted steel.

"After all, it was such a tragedy to lose my brother and his wife in that gondola accident in Switzerland all those years ago, with nothing left of them but this lovely family heirloom necklace that Kennedy wears to this day."

Kate leaned toward Jake. "Actually, I read they found a whole foot in a shoe, too, but I guess that doesn't fit into the wedding speech as nicely."

Rebecca pulled a tissue from her pocket, dabbing at eyes that looked awfully dry from table one's perspective. "I know that for many of you, this weekend is your first time touring the grandeur of our estate. And during the lengthy, numerous, laborious preparations for this weekend, in which I opened my home to strangers, I began to understand what an unrealized gift we have here on our ancestral island. The statuary my grandfather collected from the European art scene; the incredible architectural wonder of Edwin Frothington's neoclassical Romanian castle; the rich history of Hempstead Island as a central point of activity during Prohibition. And, of course, my own humble contributions from a lifetime spent hunting nature's most devious animals and collecting them in my own personal menagerie."

Kate shuddered at the idea of this Chuck E. Cheese funhouse of horrors being billed as a "menagerie."

"And so," Rebecca continued, her smile turning indulgent, "with such a gift in mind, I realized I could no longer keep it from the annals of history. To let time turn its face away from all that the Hempsteads have accomplished would not only be foolish, it would be a true erasure of historical significance."

Richie stiffened in his seat, his posture suddenly as rigid as a Catholic schoolgirl come Sunday morning. "Where is she going with this?"

"I don't know," Steven said, "but I don't like it."

It was true that Rebecca seemed to be picking up steam, barreling toward some destination only she knew, even as she took a dramatic pause to make eye contact with every important person in the room. The room, in turn, held its breath, Kate's lungs burning with the need to breathe even as she couldn't grant them release until she knew what, exactly, Rebecca Hempstead was up to.

"That's why," Rebecca said, eyes gleaming, "in the spirit of great estates like the Rockefeller family's Kykuit before us, I've decided to gift Hempstead Island to the San Juan Islands Historical Trust upon my death. And to support such a generous endowment, I'll also be directing the Hempstead Family Trust to support those preservation efforts in perpetuity."

The collective gasp in the room couldn't have been more dramatic if it had come from a studio audience. But the applause that followed drowned out the thunder raging overhead. Richie sank back into his seat in horror, and Steven had gone preternaturally still, as if Rebecca had dealt him a death blow. Kate couldn't see Kennedy beyond the glare of the spotlight fixed on Rebecca, but she couldn't imagine the woman still sported her bridely glow after her aunt basically stripped her of her entire inheritance right then and there.

"Holy shit," Kate whispered. "Is she saying what I think she's saying? She's turning over the entire Hempstead family fortune to make this place a public park when she dies?"

"Hell of a wedding present," Jake said.

"She can't do that!" Richie whispered harshly. "She can't, can she?"

"If she's announcing it, knowing Rebecca, it's already done," Steven said, looking lost.

"We have to stop her!" Richie hissed. "Call an emergency board

meeting, take her to court, something. Get her checked for incompetence, put her in a loony bin. Something, Steven! We can't just let her do
this. That's my inheritance, too, damnit!"

"I don't think your aunt sees it that way," Steven said, shaking his
head. When he spoke again, his voice was a harsh whisper. "What the
fuck am I going to do now?"

"Thank you, thank you!" Rebecca announced with a polished laugh.
"But this weekend isn't just about me, or about the historic value of
Hempstead Island. This weekend is about the future." Rebecca lifted a
glass, her smile wide and wolfish. "To Kennedy, and the future."

Chapter Ten

"Well, that was certainly . . . something," Abraham said as Rebecca departed the stage on a swell of gossip. "Uh, next up we have . . . the maid of honor, Cassidy Smith!"

Kennedy's cousin took the stage, her voice shaky and her paper crinkling through the mic as she started her speech. Rebecca was a bright spot in the darkness as she moved from table to table, stopping to speak with guests, waving to other members of important families as she approached their table like a tropical hurricane. The closer she got, the more Richie vibrated and Steven turned to stone.

"Richard, Steven, don't you two look cozy and conspiratorial this evening," Rebecca said in a low voice with a sharp smile, leaning down to emphasize her words. A soft cloud of bright citrus and earthy cinnamon notes wafted toward Kate, subtle and rich. "Still plotting to go behind my back to the trust board and convince them to sell Hempstead Island to build your ridiculous luxury resort? You see how well such an endeavor has turned out for Kennedy."

"It's not ridiculous," Steven said in a tone that made it clear how many times he'd tried—and failed—to convince Rebecca otherwise. "It's a sound investment opportunity and my buyer is willing to pay cash up front, sight unseen."

"Yes, your *buyer*," Rebecca said with a sneer. "I know the type of buyer you're talking about, and I'd rather see Hempstead Island sink into the ocean than give a filthy little man like that claim to our historical fame. Does the cash come in sweaty, glitter-stained one-dollar bills?"

"Rico is a reputable businessman—"

"Oh, sure, the illustrious owner of the Diamond Cabaret, wanted at all the most exclusive clubs in the Islands—"

"You can't do this!" Richie burst out, slamming his hands on the table and drawing attention. Even Cassidy paused her speech, looking down at her paper at a loss for words.

"Control yourself, Richard," Rebecca said in a voice dripping with disdain. "You're clearly drunk and you're embarrassing the Hempstead name. It's bad enough Kennedy invited her cousin. Debt up to her eyeballs from a food truck, of all things, and she had the nerve to show up here begging for handouts and making ludicrous accusations. It's no wonder Alexi cut her off finally. The girl can barely hold herself together. Look at her."

Rebecca made a gesture toward Cassidy stammering her way through the speech, and something in the movement triggered a memory for Kate. That same floral pattern, reaching out a perfectly manicured hand to slap Cassidy. She smothered her gasp in her hands. Rebecca had been the one arguing with Cassidy in the garden, and judging by her comment about debt up to her eyeballs, Kate could imagine what Cassidy had been begging for. But what kind of accusations would a woman like Rebecca Hempstead find ludicrous?

"It's not fair, Aunt Rebecca," Richie said, his tone approaching a plaintive whine. "You can't cut the rest of the family out like this. There are rules, requirements for the inheritance."

Rebecca spread her hands wide. "It's already done, Richard. The inspector from the historical society is here this weekend as my personal guest to sign off on all the paperwork, and then it goes to the board for the final vote. I've already got the five-three majority I need. And do you know what that means?"

"That you're a heartless, soul-sucking bitch?" Richie guessed.

The smile she gave him was so cruelly dismissive that Kate felt the whiplash just sitting next to him. Rebecca leaned forward, pressing her hands against the table, her nails digging into the flesh-colored linens. "It means I'll never have to hear another one of your coma-inducing inheritance pitches ever again. I'll never have to field another lawsuit from the loser side of the family, whining that they deserve money for nothing. I'll never have to attend another gala for goddamn feral cats because Kennedy insisted on picking a charitable organization close to her heart. Not a single one of you has worked a decent day in your lives, and you represent everything my grandfather stood against. Maybe now you'll finally get off your ass and do something useful, Richard."

"Holy shit," Kate breathed as Richie deflated in his chair like a balloon with a leak. Was anyone actually happy this wedding weekend was happening? Was this how all wealthy families conducted themselves? Kate was suddenly glad to know she'd never have the wealth to find out.

"Who are you?" Rebecca asked, looking at her in annoyance.

"Oh," Kate said in surprise, trying to stand and rattling the table when her chair got stuck. "Ms. Hempstead, it's such a pleasure. I'm Kate? Kate Valentine?"

"Is that a question? Are you unsure of your own identity?" Rebecca asked.

"No?" Kate said, feeling turned upside down. "I . . . You . . . I'm Kate Valentine. The writer?"

Should she have brought a copy of her book for reference? Maybe strike a pose like her author photo on the back cover? But Rebecca's expression relaxed, as if Kate were no longer a threat. "I see, one of Spencer's people. Welcome."

Was she playing coy? Or did she not want her nephew to know she'd personally invited Kate for the weekend?

"I'm sure we'll get a chance to connect later—" Kate started, but the lawyer had kept his peace too long.

"It'll go to court, Rebecca, you have to know that," Steven burst out. "Richie is right, you can't make these kinds of decisions unilaterally."

"Bring your best, Steven. I'll make mincemeat of you by lunchtime."
Rebecca snapped her fingers at a passing waiter. "Bring me a glass of
champagne. The Dom Pérignon."

"Oh, uh, I'm sorry, miss," said the waiter, juggling a tray of dessert
plates that Kate eyed with interest. "We only have sparkling wine for the
guests this evening. Will that do?"

"No, that will not do," Rebecca said, turning the force of her irrita-
tion on the poor man.

"I'm sorry, it's house orders," he said, shrinking. "The Dom is for the
bride only?"

"Do you know who gave you those orders?" Rebecca asked in a soft
voice that was still razor sharp. When the waiter hesitated, she lifted her
brows slightly in impatience. Whoever did her Botox injections did an
exquisite job of allowing her forehead to move. "I did, because this is *my
house*. I am Rebecca Hempstead. So if I want a glass of Dom, you will
find me a fucking glass of Dom, or the next plate you serve will come
with fries and a super-size drink."

"I'm sorry, Ms. Hempstead," the man stammered, stepping back and
nearly colliding with another passing server. "I'll, uh, I'll ask at the bar."

"Never mind," Rebecca snapped, dismissing him with a curt wave.
"I'll get it myself."

"Oh, Ms. Hempstead!" Kate called, her chair still trapping her. "Ms.
Hempstead, if we could just speak for a moment—"

But Rebecca had disappeared in the direction of the bar as Cassidy
stepped away from the microphone in relief. Everyone clapped as Kennedy took her place, giving a soft smile that sparkled under the harsh
spotlight, and Kate was forced to slump back quietly into her seat. Kennedy's diamond pendant winked along with the crystals on her dress,
making her look like she was made of starlight.

"Friends, family, loved ones," she began, her voice tremulous. "Thank
you so much for joining us on this magical weekend. It means so much to
have everyone we love and admire here to celebrate with us."

She looked down at her speech, hesitating just long enough that the
stretch of silence was punctuated by the clink of forks and a few smoth-

ered coughs. Kennedy blinked, seeming to collect herself, and set the paper down, squinting into the spotlight.

"This place means so much to me. It's the place where I feel closest to my parents. They were married here, as you can see from your table arrangements. And even though they can't be here today physically, being here in this ballroom, full of so many happy childhood memories, makes me feel like they're here now, watching over us."

Kate looked up at the lightning crackling across the dome, wondering how any child could have happy memories of such a place. Maybe there were fewer stuffed gazelles back then.

"It's so important to me that this place—the Manor, the railroad Great-Grandpa Russell built to get around the island, the hunting lodge designed by Frank Lloyd Wright, all of it—is cared for by people who understand its history. Who love what it represents, and will cherish it as much as I have cherished it throughout my life."

It sounded like Richie wasn't the only one upset about Rebecca Hempstead's little coup. Kate wondered how much of a lock on the board of trustees Rebecca really had, if even Kennedy couldn't back her deal to hand over the island and the trust to the historical society. Kennedy had thwarted her once; Kate wouldn't be surprised if she tried to do it again.

"Thank you everyone for making the trip, and here's to a wonderful, magical, life-changing weekend!" Kennedy said, looking down with a frown. "Oh, where did my champagne glass go?"

"Oh *shit*," Kate muttered, the forgotten glass still on the table. "I've got it here!"

Kate held it up and Cassidy hurried down off the dais to retrieve it. She looked startled, and borderline angry with Kate. Or maybe that was just the runny mascara effect. "What are you doing with Ken's glass?"

"Long story," Kate said, waving it off. "Here you go, ready to cheers!"

The woman took the glass and carried it back up to the dais with both hands, like she was afraid she was going to drop it. She handed it up to Kennedy, who smiled as she lifted it.

"Cheers!" she proclaimed, taking a healthy drink that the rest of the room followed.

Kennedy sat down and handed the microphone to Spencer, who adjusted his glasses and tugged at the ends of his jacket as he stood, holding a small stack of note cards. Spencer had always had an intense fear of public speaking, and the few times he'd spoken at her book events he'd had to write out his speeches word for word, including when to pause for breaths.

"Hello, everyone, and welcome," he said in a formal voice. "I just wanted to say a few quick words about my blushing bride here."

"Save it for tomorrow night!" someone hollered from one of the back tables, and Spencer winced. If Kate had to guess, she would assume it was one of his less-savory cousins. "Thanks, Hap, for that. No, I just . . . I wanted to say how lucky I am, to have found someone like Kennedy. Someone who saw more in me than I knew I had. Someone who lifts me up on my down days, and keeps me grounded when my head wants to float off into the clouds."

He kept reading in that slow, mechanical public speaking voice of his, listing all the ways Kennedy was his polar opposite and therefore perfect for him. Except the longer he went on, the more the speech started to feel so . . . familiar to Kate. She wouldn't put it past Spencer to lift his speech from somewhere else. Coming from such a repressed household, he hadn't told Kate that he loved her until eight months into their relationship. The words stirred up a sick feeling in her stomach. She definitely, *definitely* knew the speech he was giving.

"Anyway, I know I'm going on," Spencer said, giving Kennedy a rueful smile. "I guess I just wanted to say, it's you and me, Kennedy. Until the tides carry us back out."

Kate let out a sound that was something like a scream wrapped up in a gasp. It was loud, and stark, and absolutely the only sound in the room. She clapped her hand over her mouth like that might shove the thing back in where no one could hear it, but she could feel it. All the eyes in the room, on her. Watching. Waiting for the inevitable meltdown. And hooo, boy was she about to give it to them, because she finally realized where she knew those words from. Everyone in the room knew those words—at least everyone who worked on the second Loretta book.

It was the big speech Loretta gave her bar owner boyfriend, Geoff, at the end of *A Dark and Stormy Murder* when she tells him she loves him for the first time. It had been one of the hardest scenes Kate had ever written, because Loretta had just shared a steamy kiss with Blake when she thought the hurricane was going to rip the roof off the place. She'd been confused, pulled in two directions, torn between her on-again, off-again boyfriend and this backpacking rebel. Spencer had been furious about the kiss, demanding to know how Kate was going to justify Loretta as a cheater to her loyal readers. The conversation had shaken her up, and so she'd written Loretta's profession of love to Geoff to placate him. But deep down, writing that scene, Kate had known irrefutably that she didn't love Spencer anymore. The words had felt forced, hollow, imposed on her by someone else. More than anything else that happened, it signaled the beginning of the end of her relationship with Spencer.

Why would he read this now? In front of everyone? She could feel the heat of their gazes on her back, as if she had been the one to plant that speech on Spencer. Juliette Winters watched her like a hawk, waiting for her to crack.

"Kate, are you all right?" Jake asked, his touch light on her shoulder.

But it was enough to undo her entirely. She stood up so abruptly her chair tipped over, making the scene she'd been trying so desperately to avoid. Jake reached up to help but she waved him off, needing fresh air or a private corner to quietly curl up and die in. Somewhere that wasn't this ballroom full of prying, accusing gazes. She hurried to the nearest exit, horrified faces passing in a blur as she half collided with a waiter carrying a fresh batch of drinks. She snatched a wine bottle off his tray and bolted, racing through hallway after hallway of rich old white people horrors until she couldn't hear anything but the pounding of the rain.

Chapter Eleven

Why, *why* would Spencer do this to her? Why embarrass her like this, so publicly, at his own wedding? She'd done her best to move on, to stuff the humiliation down deep where it could fester into a tumor. Did he want to punish her? Was this because she hadn't brought the chapters like she'd promised? Hadn't she been through enough already?

Kate got lost in less than two turns of the hallways, finding herself either in a dry sauna or a portal to the hellmouth. She stumbled back out, taking a slug from the bottle of wine with relish and wincing as it hit her tastebuds. Richie and Marla were right, this really was the bargain basement stuff. Still, it drank as good as any other wine, and she took a hearty swallow as she tried to find her way back to more familiar territory.

All she found were the darker, weirder depths of Hempstead Manor. There was the room that looked suspiciously like a medieval torture chamber, complete with a man-size iron coffin and a giant birdcage with spikes on the inside. Then there was the library that looked cozy at first glance, until she realized there was a gargoyle leering at her from his perch over the fireplace, and all the books seemed to be about witch trials and the science of black magic. By the time she made it to the room labeled DOLL SUITE with hundreds of Victorian-era dolls piled on the massive four-poster bed, their heads turned toward the door with unblinking black eyes, she gave up on finding a safe space to polish off her wine in peace.

Figures, she thought as she came upon a set of stained-glass double doors. The wind practically blew them open as she tried the handles, shoving her back as gusts of rain blanketed the carpet and soaked her dress. She'd almost forgotten about the storm outside, considering the one raging within her, and she was more than a little surprised to realize the balcony was all the way up on the third floor. She hadn't even remembered climbing any stairs.

"This fucking house is cursed," she muttered, fighting the wind to close the door. At least she hadn't had to make the crossing in this weather; she couldn't imagine any poor souls stuck out on the Bay now, fighting the elements to get to safe harbor.

She located a set of stairs, tromping down to the second floor for a refill since all the wine in her bottle had mysteriously disappeared. Must have spilled on the balcony. She hummed to herself, no clue of the time or location, the alcohol doing its job to make all her problems seem inconsequential. Somewhere in the distance, much like thunder, a hangover loomed. But that was a problem for later Kate. Now Kate was feeling much, much better.

Until she reached the second-floor landing and was greeted by the rather titillating image of Juliette Winters's rear end pointed at her. Juliette herself hadn't seemed to notice Kate hovering on the bottom step, as she was bent over a door with something in her hand. A key, maybe? Kate pressed her lips closed and worked her way up the stairs until she wasn't in Juliette's direct line of sight, but she could still see what the other woman was doing.

Which looked, the more Kate studied her, an awful lot like she was trying to pick the lock. Which meant, if Kate wasn't too drunk to be mistaken, it wasn't Juliette's room she was trying to access. Curious. Someone came up the stairs from below, the dark brown shaved head of their marketing intern, Veeta, appearing beside Juliette.

"I found it," said Veeta, holding up something that looked like one of those tools dentists use to scrape your teeth. Just the thought of it made Kate shiver. "You think you can get it open?"

"These locks are a hundred years old, most of them go swinging open by themselves," Juliette said, crouching before the door. "Watch the stairs. The last thing I need is to get caught."

"Should we really be doing this now?" Veeta said in a loud whisper, looking anxiously down the stairs to the first floor. It never occurred to them to look up, where Kate watched with wide eyes. "This weekend, of all weekends?"

"It has to be this weekend," Juliette whispered back, annoyed. "I'm running out of time. If I don't give Simon *something*, the whole deal will go bust. I'm not fucking losing out *again*."

Veeta fidgeted with the collar on their pantsuit. "Maybe if you tell Simon—"

"No way," Juliette said, cutting them off. "Nobody can be trusted right now, not even Simon. I'm on the verge of getting everything I've worked so hard for. All that's standing in my way is one little *idiot* who thinks they're clever. And I'm going to take care of them for good this weekend. *Yes*, that's it."

The door clicked open and the two of them slipped inside, leaving the hallway empty. Kate had the overwhelming urge to follow them, to find out what Juliette was on the verge of getting, and who the idiot was, and what she meant by taking care of them for good. She couldn't possibly mean Kate, could she? Kennedy had been named head of marketing less than a month after the book-three-tour-cancellation fiasco, the one Juliette had taken so personally. Juliette had every reason to hate Kate and Kennedy. If Juliette was planning revenge, Kate really didn't want to know what the woman had in store for either one of them.

Plus, Kate realized as soon as she descended the few stairs back down to the second floor, she was *possibly* too drunk to go snooping around without detection. She had a gut-rumbling feeling that *something* was going on this weekend, something bad and possibly dangerous, and potentially involving more than just Juliette and her secret snooping. There was the fight between Cassidy and her aunt in the garden, Serena's cryptic remarks about the lion roaring at midnight, and that tense conversation she casually overheard between Richie and Steven. Her Loretta senses were tingling, telling her that somebody had something more than a wedding planned this weekend, but she couldn't figure out how they were all connected or how far any of it might go any more than she could walk a straight line just then. Her head was beginning to ache, the stairs tilting at precarious angles.

"There you are," came Jake's voice. "I've been looking all over."

Kate made the unfortunate mistake of turning her head too fast in response, the room doing a full 360 even as she was positive her head had stopped moving. She gripped the railing, terrified that Juliette might hear and enact her revenge right there and then.

"Shhhh!" Kate said harshly, far louder than Jake had spoken. She felt her way down the banister toward him, her shoes catching on the deep pile of the carpet. She wrenched them off her feet. "They'll hear you."

"Who will hear me?" Jake asked in confusion.

Kate jerked a thumb over her shoulder. "*Them.*"

"Kate, are you . . . drunk?"

"So drunk," Kate whispered, almost gleeful to admit it. "I don't even know where I am right now. Do you know where I am?"

"Oh boy, you smell like you fell into a wine barrel," Jake said, putting one arm around her waist and wrapping her other arm around his shoulder. "Let's get you to bed."

"Are you trying to seduce me, Jake Hawkins?" Kate laughed, ending in a hiccup.

"Not right now, I'm not," Jake muttered, looking around. "These aren't the same stairs we took earlier. We'll have to go to the ground floor and find our way up from there. This house is too fucking enormous."

"I know, right?!" Kate said, tripping down the stairs beside him. With Jake guiding her, it was suddenly a lot easier to manage walking. She leaned into him, looking up at his profile in a bliss that only her drunken state would allow. "You have such a pretty face, do you know that? Pretty, pretty face. Makes me want to sit on it."

Jake made a strained, choking sound. "Excuse me?"

"You know, I'm not actually sure what that means," Kate said with a frown. "Serena's characters use it a lot. I think it has something to do with oral sex, but the mechanics don't really make sense to me. Anyway, you and me, we should figure it out together."

"Kate," Jake said, his voice wary. "You're very drunk right now."

"No," Kate said, drawing out the vowel. Her limbs had gone soft and pliant from the alcohol and the warmth radiating off Jake. "I'm just the right amount of drunk to hit on you."

"You *only* hit on me when you're drunk," Jake said. "Why is that?"

Kate gave him a blissful smile, her eyes drifting closed. "Because that's when I make all my best bad decisions."

Jake went still beneath her arm, his back muscles rigid where her hand trailed along them. She opened her eyes in confusion, wondering why they had stopped. Jake's expression was as still as the rest of him, though a small muscle in his jaw ticked in time to her heartbeat.

He was so close, if he turned to look at her, she might be tempted to kiss him. And she already knew where that would go. She'd tried it once, drunk on margaritas and panicked at the thought of Jake leaving the country to join this new extreme adventure tourism business his friend had started. He'd rejected her then, as he was probably going to reject her now.

"Why would it be such a bad decision, Kate?" Jake asked, his voice quiet.

"What? You and me?" Kate snorted. "Are you kidding? Kate Valentine and Mr. Jake of All Trades?"

Jake frowned. "Jake of All Trades?"

"That's what the bridge club at the retirement community calls you, you know, but don't tell your aunt. No, I'm breaking the Valentine curse. Or I was, but I guess I didn't, did I? Spencer still left me for a younger, richer thrill."

"What is the Valentine curse?" Jake asked.

"You know how my grandfather died? Treasure diving Florida's Gold Coast. Something went wrong with his regulator, a strong current came up, and *poof*! Never even found his body. He would have liked that, though, belonging to the sea. Grandma always said the sea was his wife, and she was only his mistress. And my dad died in an offshore oil rig explosion, seeking his fortune on a different sea. Same water, though, I guess, so it still counts. We were never good enough to keep them around, the Valentine women. Never enough of a thrill. Spencer was supposed to fix that, but I guess even book editors get antsy."

"Is that what you think?" Jake asked. "That you're not enough of a thrill for me?"

Kate snorted again, a thoroughly undignified sound. "You forget I wrote the book on you. Literally. I've seen the photographic evidence. Running all over the world, seeking your next adventure, leaving a trail of beach bunnies behind? Always chasing something to fill that hole in your chest."

Jake took a deep breath. "All right, I think we'd better get you up to the room now."

Kate reached for him then, putting a hand on his cheek to turn his face toward her, to indulge the fantasy she'd carried for so long. But he took her wrist in his hand and sat her down on the stairs. "I'm not doing this with you when you're drunk."

Kate looked up at him, eyes big and pleading, too drunk to properly mount her defenses. "Please, Jake? Just for tonight? No strings, I promise. It's not like we're working together anymore. We don't have to keep up a professional whatever. We can just . . . get it out of our systems."

Jake looked at her for a long time, his fingers pressing into her wrist, his expression heavy. "Is that what you want, Kate? To get me out of your system? Would it make you feel better about your choices if I proved to be everything you've always told yourself I am?"

Kate didn't care for his accusatory tone, nor for the sharp twist of guilt in her gut at the idea that she might have misjudged anything about Jake. She'd heard his stories, met his disapproving father and his high-achieving brother, knew that Jake often pushed himself to the limit to prove he wasn't afraid. That he was just as worthy. He was always bringing girls around, but never the same ones, and never anyone serious. He was allergic to responsibility, he'd told her once. Made him break out in hives. She knew plenty about Jake Hawkins, thank you, which was why her next words were so defensive.

"Would it make you feel better about *your* choices if you thought you actually were something more?"

Jake's expression froze, but before Kate could rewind time or drop into a hole of self-loathing, a heavy set of boots interrupted them.

"Valentine, you sloppy slut, what the hell was that?" asked Marla, appearing from a nearby hallway with a huff. "I've been looking for you all over. You ran out of the rehearsal dinner like you were about to upchuck a frog or something. Are you okay?"

Oh, Kate was a lot of things, and okay had been torn from the bottom of the list. But she could hardly tell Marla all of that without those feelings—and all that wine—coming back up.

"I'm fine," she gasped, like if she could just get the words out she might believe them herself. "This house is . . . really fucked up."

Marla barked out a laugh. "So creepy, right? I stubbed my toe on a whisky barrel earlier and went face-first into a wild boar. I've never met anyone so obsessed with killing and stuffing things. Though I'd expect nothing less from Attila the Hunter."

"Marla, can you get Kate back to the room?" Jake asked, straightening up. "I have something else I need to do."

"Or someone else," Kate muttered.

"Night, Kate," Jake said curtly before disappearing.

Marla blew out a breath, making a face. "That was awkward. What the hell happened?"

"Nothing," Kate said glumly. "Nothing at all. Same as always."

"I meant what happened at the rehearsal dinner, but I see you've got a few things going on." Marla plopped down on the stair beside her, pencil-thin brows crinkling in concern. "What can I do, babe?"

Kate groaned, dropping her face in her hands before realizing how much worse it made the dizziness. "I screwed everything up like I always do. I drove Jake away, I drove Spencer away, I even drove you away."

"Me?" Marla said. "What do I have to do with any of this? I never boned you."

Kate shook her head morosely. "I haven't been a good friend, I know. Missing awards ceremonies, not answering texts, bailing on our weekends at Dive Bar. I just . . . I lost sight. Of everything. Of myself. Sometimes I wish we could just go back to the beginning, you know? Nights of the Round Table, talking craft, sharing our work. None of this . . . business bullshit."

"Would you really do anything different, though?" Marla said. "You can't tell me it's not nice, the commercial fame and fortune. Shit, your writing pays your mortgage. That's more than most of us can say."

"I just miss it, that's all," Kate said, unable to put the intense feelings of nostalgia and regret into words. "I miss . . . I don't know. I miss hanging out. I miss making fun of Jeremy's terrible haircuts. I miss your dad's weirdo friends bringing in their phallic pottery. I miss you."

Marla twitched her lips in consideration before holding out a hand to Kate resolutely. "I can't watch you mope all night. We need to do something mildly illegal and definitely fun."

"How mildly are we talking?" Kate asked.

"I found out where they keep the Dom," Marla said. "They've got a whole wine cave off the kitchen, used to be for whisky storage. Let's do some casual burgling."

Kate took Marla's hand, leaning heavily into her as the alcohol hit so much harder without Jake to support her. They fumbled their way back to the main hallway, the corridors passing like a haunted nightmare. Kate would have gotten hopelessly lost, a ghost haunting the Manor, if it weren't for Marla's navigation. They reached the kitchen, several servants cleaning up dishes from the rehearsal dinner. They ducked behind a counter to avoid being spotted, and Marla pointed to a stone arch on the far side of the kitchen.

"That's the wine cave," Marla whispered. "I'll grab some glasses and score us some of those crab things they had during the cocktail hour. You find the Dom and I'll meet you down there."

Marla crawled away and Kate headed for the wine cave. A puff of cool, dry air greeted her from the top of the stone steps. It certainly had the feel of a hidden distillery as Kate descended. Earthy and dark, the walls set in close as if they were meant to inspire claustrophobia. Or stop the G-men from gumming up the works while you made a quick escape.

There was something hauntingly familiar about the dark, rocky stairs, even though Kate had certainly never stayed anywhere posh enough to have an entire cave for storing wine. The nubbly feel of the stones beneath her hands, the faint trace of dry dirt in the air, the soft pad of her bare feet against the rough steps, it all felt like something she'd done before. A vivid memory from someone else's life.

The cinematic feel was brought to an abrupt halt when her toes met with a soft, immovable object. She cried out in pain and surprise, falling over just as some demonic motion sensor turned the electric lights on full blast, illuminating Kennedy Hempstead's lifeless face.

"Come on, Lor, be reasonable," said Geoff, leaning over the bar as Loretta wiped it down for the evening. Or the early morning, by the clock, but Loretta didn't keep her hours by the clock. "I know you were fond of the kid, but the police have him dead to rights."

"The police are wrong," Loretta said, snatching up a bin of pint glasses for the washer. "Blake is innocent. And if someone doesn't do something about it, he'll go to jail for a crime he didn't commit. Which means the real murderer will still be out here, roaming free. I can't let that happen."

"What are you going to do?" Geoff snorted, slapping his hand down on her freshly washed bar and leaving behind a smudge. She could hardly tell him to clean it up himself, considering he was both her boss and the owner. She'd had plenty of hound dogs for bosses before, but there was something else to Geoff. Something . . . tender. Protective. It kept her from kicking his ass when she caught him looking at hers.

"I'm going to do what the police can't do. Or won't do. I'm going to find that woman's real killer," Loretta said.

"How do you plan to do that?" Geoff asked, his eyes following her as she replaced bottles on the back bar. "You're not a cop. Hell, you're barely even a bartender. I hired you on as a favor to your pops."

"You hired me on because I bring in the navy boys when they're off duty," Loretta shot back, giving him a long look as he guiltily lifted his eyes away from her ass. "And you've gotten more than your money's worth out of me, Geoff. This is something I have to do."

"I'm just worried about you, is all, Lor," said Geoff, his eyes going soft. "You're in over your head, and a girl like you could get herself in real trouble poking around where she doesn't belong."

"I plan to stir up some trouble," Loretta said, her brows drawing down in a fierce line as she set the last of the tequila bottles to rights. "Whoever thought they could get away with murdering a poor old woman and framing my friend better watch out. Loretta Starling is on their case."

EXCERPT FROM *SHAKEN, STIRRED, AND STABBED*

LORETTA STARLING, BOOK 1

BY KATE VALENTINE

Saturday

Chapter Twelve

Somewhere overhead, a clock clanged midnight, and Kate couldn't stop screaming. She couldn't stop as she dug her heels in and shoved away from Kennedy's body; she couldn't stop as she bumped into a rack of wine bottles and they gave a perilous rattle; she couldn't even stop as voices called down from the kitchen in alarm. She couldn't stop because, despite writing several mysteries with heaps of dead bodies in them, Kate had never personally encountered one.

Until now.

Loretta. Loretta would know what to do. Loretta always knew what to do in situations like these. And Kate needed Loretta now, more than ever.

Loretta stalked the perimeter of the body, her boots clacking heavily against the old stone as she took in the bride's lifeless body. She still wore the lovely crystalline dress from the rehearsal dinner, the hem twisted up around her thighs. Her feet were bare, the heels nowhere to be found, and her glossy curls were spread haphazardly over her neck. Her face was relaxed, as if she'd just laid down for a second in a most inopportune location, but her color was all wrong, her white skin closer to gray.

"Her lipstick is smudged," Loretta said, pointing with the metal swiz-
zle stick she always carried in her back pocket. "See? Just there."

"You think it was the killer?" asked Blake, his eyebrows creeping up.
He was always happy to play second to Loretta's detective, knowing that
she was the only reason he was working the island wedding this weekend
instead of wasting away in jail. "Maybe she was assaulted."

Loretta shook her head, pointing to a twin smudge on the opposite
side of her lip. "I'd guess it's from her glass, the champagne toast. I don't
see the glass anywhere around now. Which can only mean—"

"The Spice Girls preserve us, is that the *bride*?" came a sharp, dramatic
voice that wasn't nearly as seductive or understanding as Blake's. Kate
looked up, startled, at Abraham the wedding coordinator as he stood at
the bottom of the wine cave stairs, mouth dropped open.

"Wha . . . what?" Kate asked, still caught in the fog of Loretta's murder scene investigation. But there was no Loretta, no fictional bride. Kennedy Hempstead was really lying on the floor, and she was really dead,
and Kate had really tripped over her. "Oh, god."

"Help!" cried Abraham, pressing a hand to his chest and swooning
against the wall. He waved that same hand toward the top of the stairs,
as if he could magic someone there. "Please, we need help down here
immediately!"

"What's going on?" called a strident, authoritative voice. Juliette Winters appeared moments later, Veeta trailing behind her, eyes as wide as
saucers and just as unblinking. Kate didn't want to imagine what the company chat would look like come Monday, but she didn't figure she would
feature positively in it.

"Is that Kennedy?" Veeta asked in a hushed tone. "What's wrong
with her?"

"I was told *this one* was spotted trying to steal the good champagne,
and I come down and find . . . this!" Abraham crumpled toward the wall
again as if he were the one who'd face-planted into a dead body.

"What did you do?" Juliette demanded to Kate. "Did you push her?"

"Wait, what?" she said, snapping her head up and making the room spin. Whoops, still drunk. "I didn't . . . What are you saying? I would never . . . I didn't!"

"Oh, so you conveniently found her lying at the bottom of the stairs?" Juliette said, voice dripping with sarcasm as she checked Kennedy over. "Did you even check for a pulse before screaming your head off like an idiot? Or did you already know there wouldn't be one?"

"Oh my god, Ken!" someone screamed from the stairs, and then Cassidy came hurtling across the room and cast herself across Kennedy's body with a sob. "Kennedy! Kennedy, are you okay? Oh my god, say something, Ken, please!!"

"Abraham, we need medical help," Juliette said.

"Jean-Pierre!" Abraham gasped. "He is certified in CPR, among his many other talents. I'll alert him immediately. Oh, it's the Greek heiress's sweet sixteen all over again, isn't it?"

"What did you do to her?" Cassidy sobbed at Kate.

"Why does everyone keep asking me that?" Kate cried.

"Here!" chirped the French assistant a moment later, stopping short with a stage gasp. "The bride? *Non!*"

"Yes," Abraham said with relish, pointing at Kate. "This one found the body. Suspiciously."

"Suspiciously!" Jean-Pierre echoed. "Is she . . ."

Abraham drew a line across his neck, making his eyes wide and dramatic as he mouthed *dead*. If he was aiming for discretion, he shot too wide, because Cassidy gave up a wail the Greek chorus would envy, throwing herself dramatically across Kennedy's body again.

"I can't find a pulse," Juliette said in a low voice to Abraham.

"Murder!" Abraham gasped. "We'll have to inform Rebecca Hempstead right away. Death at a wedding! She'll want this handled quietly. Shall we detain the killer?"

He looked at Kate expectantly, the rest of the room following suit.

"Hang on, wait, that's not . . ." Kate held her head as if that would stop the spinning, and then she held on to her stomach as if that would stop the nausea. "I didn't touch her! I mean, I touched her, when I tripped over her—"

"You tripped over her?" Cassidy said in horror, once again looking like a raccoon. If the woman was going to go around crying all the time, she really ought to invest in a waterproof mascara. "You stepped on Kennedy?"

"No!" Kate said.

"We all saw you shove her into the present table," Juliette said.

"And you made a scene when the groom gave his speech," said Jean-Pierre. "*Such* a scene. So embarrassing."

"No, that didn't . . . You're not . . . You don't understand!" Kate protested, the room spinning faster and her stomach twisting up tighter.

Someone took Kate's arm in a hard grip, making her cry out in pain.

"She killed the bride," Abraham said with a little too much delight. "She's a criminal, we must detain her!"

"Nobody's detaining anybody," came Jake's stern voice. Kate had never heard him speak like that, not even when he was on a tear about his dad. He sounded so protective, so fierce. She wasn't proud of it, but it extremely turned her on. And then he was touching her gently. Kate gave a half sob.

"Kate, are you all right?" Jake asked, just as gentle as his touch.

She wanted to curl up in that voice and block out everything else. The blues of his eyes were stormy but his expression was calm and completely focused on her. Marla hovered just over his shoulder, close enough that it was clear she'd arrived at the same time as Jake. Or had she arrived *with* Jake? Marla had said she'd be down in a minute, but surely she would have come running when she heard Kate screaming? Unless she'd found someone more interesting to entertain her for the evening. Someone like Jake. A spear of territorial jealousy lanced through Kate's insides, stirring up her guts and wrapping her stomach around its handle until it felt like it was a part of her.

Kate gave a little shake, just enough that she could feel her brain hitting the inside of her skull. "I didn't . . . Jake, I didn't."

"I know, Katey cakes," he said, his thumb brushing her cheek. "Sit right here. I'm going to check on Kennedy."

"I'm gonna go find someone actually qualified to deal with this," Marla murmured, backing away.

"Marla, no!" Kate gasped, lurching forward and gripping her hand. "Stay, please. I need you."

"Valentine, chill," Marla said. "I'm just going to get some help."

But Kate couldn't loosen her grip even as Marla tugged on her arm. She needed her friend now more than ever, with everyone watching her so suspiciously, judging her. Jake moved his hands along the slim line of Kennedy's neck. He tilted her head back, checking her airway. He frowned, plucking something from her tongue.

"What is it?" Kate asked, leaning in.

"I don't know, something she ate maybe," Jake said, handing it off. It looked like a sliver of something hard, like a seed. Kate couldn't remember what they'd had at the rehearsal dinner that might have had seeds in it. "Her airway looks clear. I'm starting compressions."

"Give it to Abraham," Marla suggested. "Maybe it will help us know what happened to Kennedy. What if the rest of us ate it?"

But Kate was too distracted to do anything except clutch the sliver in her hand as Jake started his CPR compressions. They were so much harder and more violent than Kate expected, Kennedy's chest whooshing in with each push. These were not theatrical TV imitations; they were the real thing. Kennedy's ribs creaked as Jake finished his first round, leaning over and performing mouth-to-mouth. Kate knew it was hopeless—Juliette said she hadn't found a pulse, after all—but still she hoped. She had complicated feelings about Kennedy, but she certainly didn't want her dead. And she definitely didn't want to be accused of being the one who'd done it.

Jake went through another round of compressions, another round of mouth-to-mouth, the tension in the room tightening until Kate felt like everyone would snap. They were all looking at her, all thinking it, she was sure of it. They'd already made up their minds, and Kate was their patsy. And poor Kennedy was just . . . dead.

"Jake," Kate said, reaching for his arm. She might be doomed, but she could spare Kennedy any more indignities.

But then the strangest thing happened. Kennedy's body convulsed, like she was trying to cough but couldn't get it out. She flung out a hand, nearly smacking Jake in the face, and he quickly rolled her over on her side as she vomited up what looked like the soup course. A sharp, acrid tang filled the air, like vinegar and something rotten. She sucked in a jagged breath before blinking open those luminous brown eyes.

"Mother Mary Tyler Moore," Kate whispered. "She's alive."

Chapter Thirteen

"Holy shit," Marla breathed in true shock, her eyes ready to pop out of her head. Her nails pressed red half-moons into Kate's arm as her grip turned painful.

"Ken!" Cassidy screamed, dropping to her knees and taking Kennedy's head in her lap. "Oh my god, are you okay??"

"What happened?" Kennedy asked, her voice raw and weak.

"This Kate woman 'found' you," Jean-Pierre said, having the audacity to put air quotes around the word. "Lying at the bottom of the stairs here in the wine cave."

"The wine cave? What was I doing in the wine cave?" Kennedy struggled as Cassidy and Juliette helped her to a sitting position, propping her up between the two of them.

"We don't know," Cassidy said, giving Kate a look. There were still a lot of looks being thrown around, Kate thought, considering that Kennedy was not, in fact, dead.

"The last thing I remember is feeling unwell and going to lie down upstairs," Kennedy said, looking around in confusion. "I don't remember coming down here at all."

"I went looking for you," Cassidy said, shaking her head. "Upstairs, when you said you were going to lie down. You weren't there!"

"That's because Kate poisoned her and pushed her down the stairs like the killer in *Something Borrowed, Someone Blue*," Juliette stated so matter-of-factly that Kate almost found herself nodding along with the accusation.

That's what felt so familiar to Kate about the wine cave—so much of the setting reminded her of the groom finding his poor dead bride at the bottom of the grand staircase in book three.

"Kate didn't push anyone," Jake said, standing up and putting himself in front of Kate. "It's clear that Kennedy ate something that didn't agree with her and passed out."

"The oysters!" Kennedy said, recovering more life and tone. "It must have been the oysters in the bridal suite. They must have been spoiled, but I didn't notice because we were so busy getting ready. Cassidy, remember when you had that bad case of food poisoning from the king crab legs on my graduation cruise?"

Cassidy shuddered. "Ugh, yes. I thought I was going to die. I even fainted at one point, trying to go to the bathroom." She clapped a hand over her mouth. "The oysters!"

"The oysters!" Kennedy echoed, nodding.

"Oysters?" Marla murmured. "I've had some cheap-ass oysters, but they never did *this*."

Unfortunately for Kate, everyone else in the room seemed to be of a similar doubtful mind. They shuffled around, casting baleful eyes at her. But they could hardly keep accusing her when Kennedy had made up her mind that it had all been some big misunderstanding.

"We need to get you upstairs and get some electrolytes in you, Kennedy," said Juliette, giving Kate one last warning glare. Between her, Cassidy, and Jean-Pierre, they managed to help Kennedy stand.

"We need to get you to bed, too," Jake said to Kate. He looked her up and down. "You really look a mess, Kate."

Kate looked down at the dress that was supposed to be her triumphant statement to the world that she had moved on and up—torn at the sleeve where she'd choked Kennedy, gashes in the knees of her stockings where she'd fallen when she tripped over the body, the skirt rumpled and stained with cheap red wine. An apt reflection of Kate's emotional state for the weekend.

"Womp womp," Kate muttered forlornly.

"Alright, drunkie, up you go," Jake said, putting her arm over his shoulder and holding her waist. She was too tired, and still a little too drunk, to even appreciate the intimacy.

"I'll help you," Marla said, appearing at Kate's other side and leading her toward the stairs. "Wouldn't want you to have all the fun of putting drunk Valentine to bed by yourself."

"I can manage," Jake grunted, clearly struggling with Kate's lack of balance. "You get some sleep, we'll catch up with you later."

"Don't be stupid," Marla said in that way of hers that always ended any disagreement. "I've cleaned up sick Valentine more than her own mother by this point. Besides, the vibe was getting decidedly finger-pointy down there. What the hell do you think happened? No way was that a bad batch of oysters, huh? Weird that it did seem kind of like Kate's book, too."

"It wasn't anything like her book," Jake said stonily as they climbed the stairs toward the upper floors. "And we're not bringing it up any-more. Kennedy will be fine, though I'm not sure I can say the same for Kate here once she sobers up. How much wine did you drink, exactly? You smell like the inside of a grape press."

"There was at least one bottle involved," Kate said as they reached the fourth floor.

"Here we are," Jake grunted as they arrived at the end of their hall-way. He pulled on the golden cord hanging from the ceiling, the stairs creaking as they settled into place.

It took both Marla and Jake—and the rest of Kate's dignity—to get her up the stairs and into the attic room. There was a distinct breeze in the back as she was half pushed, half shoved upward, and she couldn't imagine what kind of view they were getting below. Not one they wanted; Jake had made that clear enough. But the two of them managed to keep her steady so she could reach the landing, and she army-crawled the rest of the way up.

"... really had to give her a good push," Marla murmured to Jake as she ascended the stairs into the attic room.

"I didn't push her!" Kate cried. "I just found her like that! Which sounds like what someone would say when they *did* push her, but I didn't. I swear it. How could I? Think about the position of her body when I found her. That wasn't the position of someone who'd been pushed down the stairs, it was the position of someone who'd been . . . I don't know, placed there. Yeah, placed there! Which I couldn't have done, could I? Because I was with you the whole time!"

Marla blinked at her as Jake finished climbing the stairs, both of them wide-eyed with surprise.

"I was talking about getting you up the stairs," Marla said slowly, waving to the gap in the floor for emphasis.

"Oh." Kate looked about the room helplessly, as if the answer to what had just happened with Kennedy might be found in this dusty collection of old books.

"Why don't we get you changed," Marla suggested, shooing her toward her suitcase in the far corner.

"I can change myself," Kate muttered, glancing over her shoulder and just catching the look the two of them exchanged. She didn't want to think of it again—Marla and Jake *together*—but her brain was far too full of wine and way too empty on good sense to protect her from the image.

"Last time you insisted you could change yourself, I found you in a bathtub trying to wear my turtleneck as a pair of leggings," Marla said, unzipping Kate's bag and leaning back as it vomited out its contents. "Jesus, Valentine, how much did you pack for this weekend?"

There hadn't been a plan to her packing, so much as a frantic last-minute grab of whatever was at the top of her drawers. Marla dug through layers of ratty sweatshirts and a pile of embarrassingly threadbare underwear and managed to find an old T-shirt and a pair of pajama pants with puppy faces on them that her mother had given her for her birthday ten years ago. They were the pajama pants of a recent college graduate, not an adult woman with multiple bestselling books and a mortgage.

"I really am a mess, aren't I," Kate whispered, mostly to herself. She looked at Marla, so cool and collected, who always seemed to know how to handle herself in a bad situation. She never had to ask *what would Loretta do*, because what would Marla Lynch do was always good enough. Kate raised her voice. "I'm glad you're here this weekend. I know I've been . . . well. I'm just glad you're here. To help."

Marla finished shoving all her clothes back in her suitcase and straightened up. "Sleep on your side and don't puke in the bed, no matter how tired you are. Trust me on that one. Try not to get accused of any other crimes while I'm sleeping."

"You don't have to stay," Kate said to Jake after Marla departed, realizing she'd been holding her hand in a fist the whole time. She opened it up, something black embedded into her skin from the pressure, and brushed it off on the pillow before wriggling into her pajama pants under her dress, losing her balance more than once. "I don't need babysitting."

"Apparently you do, considering what happened the last time I left you alone," Jake said, tossing his jacket over the chair. He paused, glancing at her. "I'll sleep in the chair for tonight. I'm changing now, if you don't mind."

Kate did a little tilting whirl, facing toward the bed resolutely. "It's not like I'm a Peeping Tom or something. I'm not even interested."

"Why's that, because you're sobering up now?" Jake muttered.

"Hey! That's not—" Kate turned, ready to argue, but definitely not ready for Jake stripped down to his boxer briefs and bent over, pulling off his socks.

They were dark gray Calvin Kleins, based on the waistband that she couldn't stop staring at, and they hugged him *everywhere*. Her mouth went dry, all words abandoning her. Jake sensed the shift and straightened, white lines of old scars jagged across his back.

She'd never seen Jake without his shirt in person. She'd seen plenty of pictures while they were making *The Wandering Australian* books, but that had been young Jake. Surfer Jake. Pre-accident Jake. She knew about the wipeout that had fractured his pelvis, broken several vertebrae in his back, and shattered his femur. But she'd never seen the physical evidence, and the feeling it stirred up in her was so immediate and visceral that she lurched forward, hand outstretched.

"Don't," he said, the one word sharp and clear. He took a breath that seemed to involve every muscle in his body, and when he pushed it out his shoulders softened. "Don't, Kate."

"Jake," she said, hand still hovering there. It must have been the alcohol, the late hour, the shock of finding Kennedy, because she couldn't stop the tears that welled up. "Oh, Jake."

"If I wanted pity, I'd have visited my mum," Jake said, snatching a long-sleeved shirt from his bag and quickly pulling it over his head. It fit him like a glove, showing the muscles underneath, but covering the scars.

Kate drew her hand back sharply. It wasn't pity she felt, not at all. It was *hurt*. Hurt for the Jake from those *Wandering Australian* pictures, who'd had the world in front of him. Hurt for the Jake she knew now, living with a shattered body and dream. But Jake didn't want her hurt, any more than he wanted her attention.

"I'm going to sleep now," he said, keeping his eyes resolutely away from her. "You should, too."

"Fine," Kate muttered, crawling over the bedspread toward the pillow. But there was something on the pillow, standing out black against the soft pink comforter, and Kate swept it up with her finger to take a closer look. That shard Jake had fished out of Kennedy's mouth when he was performing CPR. The one that had been stuck against her skin when she changed earlier. Kate brought it close enough to make her cross-eyed, frowning at it. Something about it was so . . . *familiar*.

She'd never seen any oyster shell like this. It was too smooth, too black and shiny, and now, under less stressful circumstances, she realized the tip was bright red. Were there red oysters? Jake was already breathing deep and even, but the sliver tugged at her memory. She should know what it was, she was sure of it.

Kate sucked in a sharp breath, heart pounding. She did know what it was—a rosary pea, a decorative bead used in jewelry and ornamental plants that also happened to be deadly if ingested. And she knew that because it was exactly how the bride had been killed in *Something Borrowed, Someone Blue*, the latest Loretta novel. Juliette had been right about the circumstances, even if she'd been wrong about the culprit.

Kennedy hadn't eaten some bad shellfish. She'd been poisoned.

Chapter Fourteen

Kate was on at least her sixth cup of coffee and her fifteenth sheet of paper borrowed from her Loretta plotting notebook (Loretta would certainly approve) by the time Jake groaned and cracked one eye open, his gaze widening as he took in the state of the attic.

"Kate?" he said, slow and unsure.

"You're awake, *finally*," Kate said, waving a sheet of paper in his face. "Can you tack that up there? Above the creepy portrait of the Victorian child with the blurry face? Actually, go ahead and put it over the picture, she's been staring at me for hours now."

"What's with all the candles?" Jake asked, pushing himself to stand and stretching his arms above his head. The movement exposed a strip of lean stomach muscles that made Kate's already over-caffeinated heart beat even harder.

"Power's out," Kate said, handing him a flashlight. "Storm knocked it out. Abraham says they have a backup generator, but something's wrong with it? I don't really know, he was in high form at four A.M."

"And what is *that*?" Jake asked meaningfully.

Kate looked up at the swath of sheets she had haphazardly taped and tacked to the attic wall. "That? Oh, it's my murder board. Murder wall?

Murder attic? No, that just sounds like an attic where you do all your murders. Murder wall, let's go with murder wall."

"No, I don't mean that." Jake looked at the papers. "Well, I don't *not* mean that. I mean, what are you wearing?"

Kate looked down at herself in horror, suddenly unsure if she'd bothered with a bra at any point in the night. "What do you mean? What's wrong with what I'm wearing?"

"The jumper," Jake said, as if that would explain the whole thing.

"Oh," Kate said, perking up. "It's my sleuthing sweater."

Jake's brows rose. "Sleuthing sweater?"

"Yeah, my mom gave it to me for Christmas after the first Loretta book came out. There's this scene in the book where Loretta's stuck on a clue, so she gets her grandfather's old fishing cardigan out because she's missing him, and the itchiness helps her realize who the real killer is."

"The nephew with eczema, I remember," Jake said, nodding sagely.

"You've read *Shaken, Stirred, and Stabbed*?" Kate asked in surprise.

"'Course I have," Jake said. "And *A Dark and Stormy Murder*. I'm only halfway through the new one, though, so no spoilers. And I only read them for the Blake bits, since he's obviously based on me. That kiss with Loretta when she thought the storm was going to tear the roof off the bar? Wowza."

"He is not based on you," Kate said with an eye roll.

Jake matched her eye roll. "Of *course* he's based on me. He's hot, he's hilarious, he wakeboards, and he's British."

"You're Australian," Kate pointed out.

"Same thing to you Americans," Jake said. "Our names even rhyme. Jake? Blake?"

"That's . . . coincidence," Kate said, turning away to hide her frown. They really did rhyme. How had she missed that? "Anyway, my mom drew an illustration based on the description in the book and had Jan at the retirement community knit it up. You remember Jan? The woman in the corner condo with all the cats?"

"The one with the cataracts and the revoked driver's license because she hit too many parked cars?" Jake said, looking at her sweater again. "That Jan?"

Kate frowned at the repeating motif of sea creatures along the chest of her cardigan. "I'll admit she might have gotten a little . . . creative with the design. In the book I said they were crabs and lobsters, but I think she went more . . . mythological."

"They look like dragons with penises," Jake said matter-of-factly.

"I thought they were jellyfish," Kate said, tugging at the hem. "Or maybe octopi?"

"That one's got horns," Jake said, tilting his head to the side. "Or maybe teeth?"

"I think it was sweet of Jan, and my mom," Kate proclaimed, though now that she could see the teeth, she couldn't unsee the teeth. "Whenever I get stuck on a clue in Loretta, I put it on and the itchiness helps. So."

"And you need the itchiness now because . . ."

"Because someone tried to poison Kennedy last night," Kate said with dramatic flair. She'd never gotten to deliver such a line, just like Loretta, and the dopamine of it lit up her brain like a pinball machine.

"How many of those have you had?" Jake asked, eyeing the cup in her hand.

"Uh, I don't know. I lost track somewhere around four."

Jake raised his brows. "Four cups?"

"No, four in the morning."

"Okay, why don't I just . . . take . . . that," Jake said, forcibly removing the cup from her hands. "And set it waaaaaay over here. And then you're going to tell me why you think Kennedy was poisoned."

Kate was nearly hopping at the chance to explain what she'd figured out hours ago. She'd had to stop herself from waking Jake up several times, reasoning that one of them would need their strength to confront a killer. "Remember that thing you found in Kennedy's mouth last night? When you were giving her CPR?"

"Yeah," Jake said, frowning. "What about it?"

Kate moved to the half wall of books and picked up a piece of paper she'd folded to make a pocket for the sliver. And her mother said her origami obsession at eleven was just a waste of paper. She unfolded it carefully, holding up the sliver to him.

"This is from a rosary pea. It's a decorative plant—"

"I know what rosary peas are, Kate, they're all over the place in Australia," Jake said.

"Then you know that their seeds are highly toxic if ingested," Kate said. "Ground up into a powder, it's called abrin. Even a small amount can cause gastric distress, loss of consciousness, and death."

"But how did that get in Kennedy's mouth? The oysters?"

Kate shook her head. "Abrin is fast acting. She would have started feeling symptoms within thirty minutes of ingestion. She said the oysters were in her room before the rehearsal dinner, so that's out. And all the food courses last night were brought out together, so the poison couldn't have been in her food. No, I thought about it, and I figure the most likely avenue of poisoning was her champagne glass. It would have been an easy target, considering it was the only glass in the room with the word *Bride* etched on it. Plus, Loretta noticed that the champagne glass was missing last night, which means the killer must have taken it with them as evidence when Kennedy passed out! So, we find the glass, we find the killer."

"Did you just say *Loretta* noticed the champagne glass was missing?" Jake asked.

Kate blinked a few times, wishing he hadn't taken her coffee cup. A well-timed sip would have saved her answering his question. She could hardly admit that she'd briefly hallucinated Loretta Starling surveying the crime scene because Kate Valentine couldn't handle what she'd seen. Then she'd have to admit how often she imagined Loretta in times of stress, and why Loretta seemed so much more capable of handling Kate's life than Kate herself did.

"I . . . said . . . you oughta," Kate said. "You oughta . . . have noticed the champagne glass was missing." Kate shook her head, getting herself back on track. She didn't have time to psychoanalyze Loretta when a real attempted murder was staring her right in the face. "The point is, someone poisoned Kennedy last night, and they used the *exact setup from my last Loretta novel*. Loretta gets hired as bar staff at this swanky wedding on a private island in the Keys, right? Except that the night of the ceremony, the groom is discovered with the bride's dead body. And everybody thinks he's pushed her down this grand staircase, right? Except Loretta starts investigating, and she finds a sliver of rosary pea wedged in the bride's teeth. Somebody poisoned her, and wanted it to look like the groom did it! Somebody who read my book used it as inspiration to plan their own attempt at murder!"

Jake crossed his arms. "You don't have to sound so gleeful about it."

"Am I appalled? Of course I am. Am I also a little flattered? Well, I mean, who's to say? The point is, somebody really did try to poison Kennedy, and they used my book to do it!"

Which meant now Kate had the incredible opportunity to play detective in real life, just like Loretta. And maybe prove that Kate Valentine was just as capable as badass Loretta Starling, and she'd be just as fine no matter what chaos life threw her way.

"But Kennedy wasn't actually killed last night," Jake reasoned. "Sure, she said she wasn't feeling well, and she clearly passed out. But she's fine now."

"Exactly!" Kate said, pointing at him with her pen. "Which means whoever started this business isn't done. They'll try it again, and we have to catch them before they finish the job."

"Kate." Jake sighed, and she readied another defense tactic when he held up his hands. "I believe you."

"I know it sounds cra—Wait. You believe me?"

Nobody ever believed her, most especially Kate herself. Even when she was positive she was right about something, there was a nagging voice in the back of her head telling her she was crazy, and everyone would finally see her for the mess she was. But here was Jake being a Blake—a character who had little to no real-life resemblance to him, obviously—supporting her wild theory. It did itchy, tingly things to her skin that had nothing to do with the sleuthing sweater.

"I do believe you," Jake said again with a nod. "Which is why I'm going to find a phone and call the police."

"Oh, you can't," Kate said, turning back to her murder wall. "Phones are all down, too, and there's another storm cell on the way. We're completely stranded."

"Again, so gleeful," Jake said, coming to stand beside her and survey the suspect sheets.

"Because *that* was the exact plot of Loretta Starling book two, *A Dark and Stormy Murder*. Loretta got stranded at the bar during a hurricane and one of the patrons ended up stabbed. She had to figure out who the murderer was before they could escape after the storm."

"Alright, so what are the itchy dragon penises telling you about who poisoned Kennedy?" Jake asked, standing close enough that their shoulders rubbed together. Kate wouldn't think about how firm his muscles felt beneath the soft slide of his sweater, or the thin, nearly transparent weave of the ancient T-shirt she wore beneath her sleuthing sweater. She definitely wouldn't think about how she hadn't bothered to put on a bra since last night. What she *would* do was casually bring her arms around her chest, one hand thoughtfully cupping her chin, so her nipples wouldn't show through the sheer fabric.

"Oh, uh, hmm." Kate cleared her throat, trying to bring her attention back to the more pressing matter at hand. "So, I have a couple of the most likely suspects. Juliette Winters, because she's got a great motive and she's scary. She lost out on a big promotion to Kennedy recently and was pretty upset about it. She and Simon had a big fight in his office after the announcement. And I saw her breaking into someone's room last night, when she said she was close to getting everything she wants as soon as she gets someone out of the way. Plus, she was the first one to notice the setup from my book last night, before I even could. Like she wanted everyone else to notice it, too. So maybe she thought if she killed Kennedy and pinned it on me, she'd get the promotion and I'd be on the hook for Kennedy's murder."

"That's a hell of a way to get a job," Jake murmured, lifting up the sheets to read them more closely. "What about Serena Archer? She certainly seems dramatic enough to pull off something like this, but what's her motive against Kennedy?"

"I talked to her at the bar last night," Kate said, pacing like all good detectives do when working their list of suspects. "Well, *she* talked *at* me. She was really pissed about the marketing job Kennedy did for her last book. Apparently, her sales tanked. And she mentioned that Spencer and Simon have both been dodging her about renewing the option on her contract. She said she thought Kennedy had poisoned them against her. And *then* she made some mysterious comment about something big going down at midnight, and that's exactly when I found Kennedy's body! So maybe she thought Kennedy was responsible for ruining her career, and she wanted to get revenge."

Jake lifted another paper, jerking back in surprise. "Hang on, you've got Rebecca Hempstead here? Why in the world would she want to kill Kennedy?"

"Yeah, she's kind of a long shot. She was obviously furious with Kennedy about this whole wedding business. And last night during her speech, Kennedy made the comment that she wanted to keep the Manor and the island in the hands of those who would love it and care for it. So, maybe Rebecca thought Kennedy might pull another fast one on her, and decided to take her out of the equation instead."

"You're missing something," Jake said, crossing his arms.

"Mug shots, I know! I couldn't find the photographer this morning, though. I thought about doing some illustrations, and then I remembered that my second-grade art teacher called my stick figures 'questionable.' So, we'll just have to use our imaginations."

"You're missing *someone*," Jake said. "Where's Spencer?"

"I don't know. Probably getting ready for the wedding or something."

"I don't mean right now, I mean on your murder wall. Why isn't Spencer a suspect?"

"Oh," Kate said, suddenly uncomfortable. "Well, because . . . Why would he be?"

"Because he's the spouse," Jake said, as if it was the most obvious thing in the world. "It's always the spouse."

"He's not the spouse yet," Kate said, wondering why in hell she was defending Spencer, of all people.

"You have to admit, he was acting all out of sorts last night, even for Spencer. He seemed upset with Kennedy."

Kate didn't have to admit anything, certainly not to Jake, but it was harder to lie to herself when she'd noticed the same thing. Spencer had been cagey, and seemed distant with Kennedy. And he'd obviously been hiding something, but Kate didn't know what. Still, she wasn't going to give Jake any more ammunition in his campaign against Spencer.

"What's his motive? Can't be money, since he won't get any if she dies before they're married. And it's not an affair, because he'd have to be crazy to blow a sweet thing like this." Kate counted off the routine motives on her fingers. "And he's obviously not in the habit of poisoning fiancées because I'm still here. It doesn't fit."

"But he wasn't there last night, was he?" Jake pressed. "When we found Kennedy. He's the groom and yet he was nowhere to be found when his bride nearly died? And he certainly had motive after the way he was looking at you last night."

Kate drew back in surprise. "What is that supposed to mean?"

"It means he didn't look like somebody who had moved on. He looked jealous as hell. It's half the reason I put my arm around you, just to set him off. He's still got feelings for you."

Kate wheezed in surprise, doubling over in laughter. "That's . . . that is . . . I can't breathe. I really can't breathe. That's the most *ridiculous* thing I've ever heard. You're crazy."

"Am I? What about you? What was that little scene, running out of the rehearsal dinner like that? You think I didn't recognize the speech he read? That big, ridiculous monologue Loretta gives in the middle of the hurricane, trying to prove she really loves Geoff when she was obviously still hung up on that kiss with Blake? Don't tell me Spencer didn't pull that stunt on purpose. And in murder mysteries, it's *always* the spouse, isn't it? Even the almost spouse."

"Not in Loretta book three," Kate said defiantly, crossing her arms.

Jake put up a hand. "I told you I'm only halfway through. No spoilers."

"It was the sister," Kate said petulantly.

Jake growled. "Spencer had means, access, and motive. He goes to the top of *my* list."

"Fine," Kate said, throwing her hands out wide. "We'll investigate Spencer first. If only to prove that you're being an asshole and I'm right."

"Fine," Jake shot back at her. "We'll see which one is the asshole and which one is right."

Chapter Fifteen

Kate scrounged up a bra while Jake lowered the ladder and climbed down to the hallway. He looked unfairly refreshed for a man who had slept slouched over in a chair all night. But at least he'd slept; Kate was running on caffeine and adrenaline and, other than her sleuthing sweater, she definitely had not packed for a murder investigation. The only other shoes she had besides her heels were a pair of ballet flats, and the heels had worn a blister on the side of her foot that rubbed against the faux leather of her flats and made her want to weep.

"It's not really possible, is it?" Kate argued as they descended the stairs to the main floor. "I mean, Spencer? *Spencer Lieman?* I used to have to kill the spiders he found in the bathroom because he couldn't handle the squishing sound. And now you think he's graduated all the way to murder?"

"Are you sure you aren't just upset that you dated him all that time and never noticed any of his murderous tendencies?" Jake countered. "Pretty big oversight for a mystery writer."

He had a point, actually. If Spencer really were capable of murder, she should have seen it ages ago, right? Funny taste in her morning coffee, faulty brakes on her car, toaster in the bathtub. He had been acting strangely last night, and Jake had been right that he'd seemed upset with Kennedy. She was positive he was hiding something; but *murder*?

"What would he stand to gain by killing Kennedy now?" Kate persisted, lowering her voice as they reached the main entryway in case any other guests were up and about early. The last thing she needed was panic about the bride being poisoned, much less any more eyebrows raised or fingers pointed her way. "They're not married yet, which means he wouldn't inherit any of her money."

"Unless money wasn't his motivation," Jake said meaningfully.

"You can't still be on this," Kate said, rolling her eyes as the doors to the entry hall were thrown open in a dramatic fashion.

"Everything is fine!" said Abraham from the doorway. "Right on schedule. Going smoother than a certain minor Dutch princess's wedding on a certain lake in Switzerland! I can't say what happened, but let's just say it rhymes with smecret smaffair. A little issue with the generator, but I have my best team members working on it despite none of us knowing how a generator actually works and no maintenance workers on the island!"

"What happened?" Jake asked. "I don't have a lot of experience with electrical work, but I did once make a battery in the jungle with a handful of pennies and a copper wire."

"Oh good, you come with me, then," Abraham said, grabbing Jake's arm.

"Actually, we were just headed somewhere on very important business," Kate said, trailing after them toward the exterior doors.

"More important than fixing the power and rescuing the wedding decorations?" Abraham said, shocked that she'd even suggest such a thing.

"What's wrong with the wedding decorations?"

Abraham pursed his lips. "Nothing is wrong, per se. There's just a *bit* more wind at the moment than forecasted, and we're having trouble keeping the outdoor tent staked down. Rebecca Hempstead must be a late riser because I haven't been able to find her all morning to confirm where we can set up the reception inside the house, much less to tell us how to fix the pesky generator. So fun, planning a wedding in the Pacific Northwest in late October!" He gave a sharp hysterical laugh, dropping his voice into a mutter. "This never would have happened at a certain soccer star's son's wedding, I can tell you that."

A crack of thunder loud enough to rock the island shattered the momentary stillness of the house, a gust of wind making the walls moan and creak. Kate could have sworn she saw them bend to one side and back, even though she knew that was impossible.

"So! We need to fix the generator *and* bring the décor in," Abraham said, a little too cheerily. "Preferably before it floods and ruins a hundred thousand dollars' worth of preparations!"

He hurried out the main doors, a blast of wind tossing them open with a clap. Kate couldn't imagine how much force it took to toss twenty-foot-tall solid wooden doors open like they were lace curtains, but she was sure she didn't want to subject her body to it. The house had a wide patio on either side with thick stone railings and a flight of stairs leading to a perfectly manicured courtyard. Each section had a massive water fountain as its focal piece, one a perfect reproduction of the Trevi Fountain and the other an ocean monster with water pouring out of its fourteen mouths by Kate's count. There were other statues in marble and brass, tinged in a green patina but no less impressive for their detail and size.

"Baby Hemsworth, you come with me," said Abraham, already tugging Jake around the side of the house where the generator was presumably located. He gave a dismissive wave to Kate. "And you go over there, help Jean-Pierre move the decorations."

"Over there" seemed to be a massive white tent that had been erected on the front lawn. She'd missed it yesterday, coming up to the house from the back, but it buzzed with activity now. The tent had indeed sustained damage, one corner completely collapsed and the left wall listing dangerously inward. A line of servers, groomsmen, and younger wedding guests carted out chairs, tables, more glass sculptures, and flower arrangements. Petals scattered into the air and swirled around their heads before being snatched out to sea, and a nearby sound of shattering glass brought out Jean-Pierre's shrill voice from within.

"Support it on all sides!" the young Frenchman shouted. "All sides!"

There were even a few guests holding signs, though Kate couldn't imagine why Kennedy would want crudely drawn handmade signs as part of her wedding décor. They were chanting something as well, crossing through the line of servants carrying chairs and hiking their signs up and down. Serena Archer was at their head, still dressed in her cocktail gown.

"Fairer contracts for all!" they chanted, slightly out of sync. "No more wages from the dark ages! Sign our checks or we'll ring your necks!"

"Serena?" Kate asked in confusion. She recognized a few of the sign holders as other Simon Says authors, though she didn't remember seeing them at the rehearsal dinner. "What are you doing?"

"There you are, Kate, about time!" Serena proclaimed, thrusting a sign toward her as if she'd been waiting for Kate's imminent arrival. "We're protesting the unfair contract negotiation tactics of Simon Says publishing. Simon and Kennedy want to sabotage our careers and ignore our calls? Well, they can't ignore the lion's roar!"

Serena thrust her sign skyward to the scattered cheer of the handful of authors. The moment was rather undercut, however, when three men carrying a glass tower in the shape of a tree bumped her out of the way. Still, Serena was never one to ignore an opportunity.

"Scabs!" she cried, swinging her sign at them. "Crossing a picket line in support of the elite, shame on you! Enjoy your paychecks, lads, because they're signed with our blood!"

"Where did these authors come from?" Kate asked, still confused.

"Snuck them on the island last night," Serena said, obviously proud of herself. "A very clandestine affair, very romantic."

"It was less romantic and more miserable," said a man in his early sixties, looking haggard. "The storm battered us around like a kitten with a yarn ball. We thought we'd capsize."

"Nonsense, Peter," Serena said, waving him back. "Get on the line, don't let up on them, boys!"

"Were you expecting . . . more people?" Kate asked, looking at the meager collection.

"Cowards, the lot of them," Serena said darkly. "A bit of rain and wind and suddenly everybody's got a case of the scaredy cats. We may be small, but our roar is mighty. And they'll hear us, all the way back to Seattle. And you're here now! Simon and Kennedy certainly can't ignore their superstar. With you on the line, we'll have some real firepower."

"Oh, actually," Kate said, shuffling awkwardly sideways toward the entrance, "I promised I would help move some things? It's a time-sensitive matter, you understand."

"Time-sensitive?" Serena said, her eyes bulging in shock. "And our career plight is not? Are you saying you won't join us, Kate?"

"I'm not . . . exactly saying that," Kate said, grimacing.

"You mark my words, Kate Valentine," Serena said, pressing into her personal space and overwhelming her with the smell of flowery perfume and sweat. "You're either one of us or one of them. And if you're one of them, you'll suffer the same fate as them. Mark. My. Words."

Chapter Sixteen

"Scab!" Serena screeched as Kate ducked into the tent. "You all saw her. Kate Valentine crossed the picket line! She's a scab!"

"I'm not a scab!" Kate hissed back through the flap.

"Scab!" Serena shrilled louder. "Kate Valentine doesn't support the working writers!"

Kate ducked farther into the tent to avoid the meager cries of "traitor" by the other authors, turning her attention inward. Even with one corner of the tent down and two dozen men hauling out the decorations, the tent was still magnificent. Like a fairy-tale forest, it had live trees spread throughout as support structures, with blown-glass butterflies suspended among the branches. Each table had a different installation, some with brightly colored mushrooms and flowers, others with lush pads of grass and small fairy houses. There was even a babbling brook that meandered around the dance floor and ended beneath a sheet of heavy-duty glass made to look like a reflecting pond, with fish swimming in an underground tank.

"Gentle with the lights," Jean-Pierre said halfheartedly from the center of the tent, reaching out forlornly to touch a piece of his dismantled creation as one of Spencer's cousins hauled it out. "They are hand-blown! *Faites attention!*"

"It's magnificent," Kate said as she approached, watching one of the supporting trees as six waiters lifted it.

"It was," Jean-Pierre said, his voice hollow. "My crowning glory. We couldn't even get pictures because the photographer was busy at the rehearsal dinner and the tent collapsed overnight."

"Hilarious, isn't it?" snorted a familiar voice behind them, one that made Kate instantly want to take a shower. Jean-Pierre stiffened and did an about-face, striding away.

"Eric," Kate said with distaste, turning to face Spencer's younger brother.

"All this money and they can't keep the walls from collapsing," Eric said, shaking his head and brazenly drinking from a pocket flask. He grinned that shit-eating grin of his, smacking his teeth against a piece of gum that deserved a better fate. "You see those idiots with the signs out there? Hilarious! I asked the little Gomez Addams guy if I could borrow one of Rebecca's hunting rifles, you know? Thin the herd a little. *Pew, pew!*"

He mimed holding up a rifle and shooting, which only made Kate loathe him all the more. Spencer had his inherited flaws, but Eric had perfected them. Spencer had always been strangely defensive of his brother, probably because he secretly knew what an awful human being he was. Spencer had even made Eric his best man, which meant Eric should have the inside line on Spencer's whereabouts.

"Eric, it's never a pleasure," Kate said with a saccharine smile. "You haven't seen your brother around, have you?"

"Why, you looking to make another scene?" Eric said, waggling his brows and braying once again. God, she hated him.

"Sure, I was hoping to throw myself at him in a desperate last-ditch attempt to win him back at his own wedding on his future bride's obscenely wealthy private family island," Kate said flatly. "Have you seen him or not?"

Eric shrugged, his gaze straggling over the tent as if he were already bored with her. "You're the one who ought to know."

"Why would I know?" Kate asked.

"Because he went looking for you after your little shit fit at the rehearsal dinner. We were supposed to bro down, drink some whiskies, smoke some cigars, get a little loose. You know, last night of freedom and all? But he was a no-show. So I had to make my own bro fun, if you know what I mean."

"I'm glad I don't," Kate said. "But Spencer never found me last night. Have you seen him this morning?"

"Nah," Eric said, smacking at his gum. "Missed his tux fitting this morning. That little French guy threw a total tantrum about it. Definitely not bro material."

"Nobody says 'bro' anymore," Kate said, rolling her eyes.

"Yeah, well, you're not gonna be my sister-in-law anymore, so I don't have to pretend to listen to you," Eric said, moving away from her toward a newly arrived cute female server.

"Don't you dare molest that poor girl just trying to do her job!" Kate called after him.

Eric waved Kate off, leaving her to her own thoughts as she moved toward the collapsed corner to gather table linens. Spencer had apparently gone looking for her after she ran out of the rehearsal dinner, but he'd never found her. And he certainly hadn't been there when she'd found Kennedy. So, what had he been doing instead?

Kate was so wrapped up in her own thoughts that she didn't hear the heavier patter of rain on the tent roof overhead, nor did she notice the shout of warning as the collapsed section of roof created a funnel for the water to gather into a downspout. What she *did* register, however, was an unwelcome deluge through the open section of roof, right onto her head.

"Oh!" Kate yelped, the linens in her hands absorbing the majority of the water and dragging her arms down.

"*Non*, oh!" said Jean-Pierre, hurrying toward her.

"I'm all right," Kate said miserably, giving a little shiver.

"The poor table linens! They are ruined now!" Jean-Pierre took the bundle from her, tutting his tongue before realizing that Kate, an actual live human, had also gotten soaked. "Ah, apologies. You should . . . change."

"Thanks," Kate said dryly as Jean-Pierre hauled his precious cargo away.

She wrung out her sleeves as she dodged around two men carrying another tree jangling with fairy lights. She felt no shame, either, in timing her exit with a large table that obscured her from Serena's view. The wind raised goose bumps along her arms as she hurried toward the Manor, the clouds heavy and leaden and far too close for comfort.

At least it was windless inside, if no warmer or more inviting. Somewhere the tantalizing scent of bacon beckoned, nearly derailing her from her course, but she had too much to do. She looked through the doors of the cocktail room wistfully at the towers of pastries and sleek stainless steel coffee urns, promising herself she'd return as soon as she had changed. She headed up the stairs but stopped on the third-floor landing as a thought occurred to her.

She *could* get changed and continue to help bring in the decorations. Or she *could* take this opportunity, while everyone else was occupied, to hunt down Spencer and get the truth. Find out where he was last night and what he'd been hiding. If she wanted to unmask the person who'd poisoned Kennedy and catch them before they tried it again, she'd have to engage in some good old-fashioned snooping, Loretta-style. Snooping was a highly maligned, underrated skill, in Kate's opinion. After all, how else would Loretta have discovered that the groom's sister in book three was the real killer if she hadn't gone snooping in the sister's room and found the family heirloom wedding ring hidden in the lining of her suitcase? It had been Spencer's suggestion, actually.

Was that one of the murder signs Jake had accused her of missing all these years? Spencer really was a quick study at figuring out the most expedient way to get rid of a body in all of her books. Was it from personal experience? A mind that was used to plotting murder? Sure, he hated spider guts, but maybe that's why he chose poison. No bloody mess to clean up.

Kate rubbed her face in frustration. She was losing it. The lack of sleep, the mainlining of caffeine, the wine hangover from last night, it was distorting her sense of reality. Kate didn't have any good answers— only more questions—as she prowled the halls. She'd nearly cleared the third floor with no Spencer Lieman sighting when a door down the hall opened and a different, entirely undesirable Lieman stepped out to stare her down.

"Ohhhhh, there she is," said Spencer's mother, staring knives at Kate. She shined a flashlight directly in Kate's eyes, momentarily blinding her. "The little wedding crasher, come to ruin Spencey's big day once again."

"Excuse me?" Kate said, her gut clenching tight. "What are you talking about?"

"Oh, don't play dumb with me, little missy," said Mrs. Lieman, advancing on Kate. "I know *exactly* what you did, and you won't get away with it."

Chapter Seventeen

Kate's whole existence was just a long list of things that Spencer's mother never approved of, and for the life of her she couldn't figure out which one she was currently on the hook for. And so, as Mrs. Lieman marched down the hall to her, red-faced and huffing, Kate could only stare in bemusement, waiting to find out.

"You thought your little trick would work, didn't you, Katherine? Trying to make him fall back in love with you. You broke his heart, and now here you are trying to sweep up the pieces and tape them back together so you can toss it out later."

In all the time Kate had known Spencer's mother, the woman had never gotten her name right. She'd called her Karen, Katherine, Katelyn, and once, after half a bottle of red wine, Virginia. Kate had never been able to parse that one. She'd also never been able to correct Mrs. Lieman, no matter how many times she or Spencer reminded her that Kate's name was, in fact, just Kate.

"Mrs. Lieman, I'm not sure what you think I did—"

"Oh, we saw that little show you put on with Kennedy last night, didn't we, Frank?" Mrs. Lieman didn't bother looking back at her husband as he stepped out of their room, seeming far more interested in squinting at the wood carving relief of naked forest nymphs along the hallway. "Pushing the poor girl over, ruining her presents, so you could throw yourself at our Spencey. Is that when you did it? Switched them out, thought nobody would notice? Homewrecker!"

"Mrs. Lieman," Kate said, exasperated. "What are you talking about?"

"The speech, you idiot girl, the speech!" A fleck of spit flew from her twisted lips. "You took our poor son's speech and switched it out."

The *speech*. She'd actually forgotten about Spencer's speech, which really said something about what had transpired between the dessert course and now. But Spencer's mother seemed to be under the *very* mistaken impression that Kate had been the one to slip Spencer the speech. Which was absolutely preposterous, and yet the woman was looking at her like she was about to recommend Kate for an eighteenth-century firing squad.

"Mom?" came Spencer's voice from over Kate's shoulder. "Mom, what are you doing? Who are you yelling at?"

Kate whirled around to confront Spencer, who looked—there wasn't a polite way to say it—like an absolute wreck. His hair was pulled in ten different directions and his glasses were smudged, dark circles pressed in under his eyes. He wore his rehearsal dinner suit, the jacket gone, the shirt rumpled and stained under the arms, his belt missing about half the loops on his dress pants. His voice sounded just as bad, hoarse and rough, like he'd been shouting all night.

"Spencer," Kate said, because she didn't really know what else to say.

"Kate," he said, and the look he gave her was so . . . so *hopeful*, it made something sick lurch inside her. "I've been looking all over for you."

"I've been looking all over for *you*," Kate said, remembering what she'd been doing there before Mrs. Lieman's attack. "Where have you been?"

"Don't you dare," Mrs. Lieman said, bustling between them. "Don't you even look at my son, or talk to him, or breathe the same air as him!"

"Mom," Spencer said, fiddling with his glasses. "Please stop. We can hear you all the way downstairs."

"You are making a bit of a scene, Marge," Mr. Lieman said, though he didn't seem to be able to meet the small woman's gaze, either. "Your blood sugar's running low, probably."

"I'll make any kind of scene I want, if it saves my son falling for her mind games again," Mrs. Lieman huffed.

"There's breakfast downstairs," Kate said weakly. "Scones, coffee. And mimosas."

It was the promise of booze that finally kicked Frank Lieman into action. His grip on Mrs. Lieman's arm tightened, the light coming on in his eyes as he dragged her toward the stairs. "Come on, Marge, let's get you some eggs and coffee and leave the kids to work out their business in peace."

"I will not leave him alone with *her*," Mrs. Lieman said, eyes bulging. "You let go of me this instant, Frank!"

"What's he gonna do, Margey? Ask her to marry him? Move in with her? They did all that already. What harm is one little chat gonna do?"

"Your mother is in high form today," Kate muttered while Mrs. Lieman stared bloody murder at the two of them as her husband towed her down the stairs.

Spencer turned to Kate, his eyes dark and serious. "Is that my shirt?"

It was not the first question Kate expected from Spencer, nor was she expecting the intensity of the look he gave her as his eyes swept down the front of her shirt, reminding her how soaked through it still was.

"I need to change," she said abruptly, heading up the stairs toward the fourth floor.

"It *is* my shirt, isn't it?" Spencer said, trailing after her.

"No, it's not," Kate said, tugging on the bottom to look at it. "This is mine. The Turkey Trot run we did our first Thanksgiving together."

"You don't remember?" Spencer said. "You woke up with food poisoning and begged me to run the race so you could get the shirt? Because you'd seen the design and thought a turkey wearing gold hot pants was the funniest thing you'd ever seen?"

"Oh," Kate said, frowning. Now that Spencer mentioned it, that sounded . . . vaguely familiar. "Do you want it back?"

"No, it's fine," Spencer said, in that tone that always meant it *wasn't* fine and she was going to hear about it in little muttered asides until the day she died.

"You can have it back," she said, finding the pull cord with her face. She blinked in surprise and grabbed it. "I need to change into some regular clothes anyway. Or wedding clothes, I guess."

"Yeah, wedding clothes," Spencer said vaguely. But then he grabbed her by the arm, stopping her. "Wait! I mean . . ."

He looked terrified, like she might strip down right there in front of him, glasses flashing as a burst of lightning illuminated the vampire-killer stained-glass window at the end of the hall.

"Spencer, it's fine," she said, turning away so he wouldn't see her rolling her eyes as she pulled the attic stairs down. Without the generator powering the lights, the attic was pitch black, not even a small window to light the interior. She should have grabbed that flashlight from Mrs. Lieman while the woman was waving it in her face. The ladder swayed slightly as she reached the top.

"What are you doing?" she asked Spencer as he mounted the bottom stair.

"I'm . . . going up the ladder?" he said, equally surprised.

"Okay, but . . . why?"

"Well, that's where you're going, isn't it? I'm just following you."

"You can't do that!" she said hastily. The attic was small, and still smelled faintly of Jake. Plus, there was the matter of her murder wall, and Kennedy's poisoning. And Spencer being prime suspect number one, at least in Jake's eyes. "If you come up we'll be bumping into each other. Inappropriately."

"You don't seem to mind bumping into Jake up there," Spencer muttered as Kate felt her way across the room. Though Kate wondered if you could call it a mutter when it was loud enough that anybody on the floor could hear. "So, what's the deal with you two, anyway? Are you . . . dating?"

He said the word like anybody else would say "murdering children."

"Uh, we're . . . seeing each other," Kate said, feeling like that was innocuous enough that she couldn't later be accused of lying. She pulled things out of her suitcase and held them up blindly, trying to figure out what they were by shape. Were these pants or a shirt? Only one way to know. She stripped out of what was apparently Spencer's shirt and pulled it on before wrapping herself in the sleuthing sweater, the wool scrubbing away some of the chill still left on her skin.

"When did that start?" Spencer asked, his voice sounding awfully close. Kate paused and glanced over the stack of books, but she couldn't see a thing. Which meant, hopefully, Spencer couldn't, either. Not that he hadn't seen it all anyway, but still. Things were different.

"It's new," Kate said, still hedging that line of truth.

"Well maybe this *fling* will finally inspire some Loretta chapters out of you," Spencer said. "Considering you've been dying to put Loretta and Blake together since the beginning."

Kate sighed toward the ceiling. "Seriously?"

"At least now you can admit it," Spencer said defensively.

"Blake is *not* based on Jake," Kate said.

"Oh sure, the hot British bartender who was supposed to be the murderer and go to jail in the first Loretta book that you *magically* decided would be a better rival love interest for Loretta is *definitely* not based on Jake."

The sarcasm was thick enough that all Kate needed was a knife to spread it on a piece of toast. Or to stab Spencer with it.

"Their names even rhyme!" Spencer said.

"Why does everyone keep pointing that out?" Kate muttered. She felt around in the suitcase again, trying to locate a pair of pants and maybe some socks. She felt along the inside of the suitcase for the mesh pocket where she kept her bundled socks. Her fingers snagged on a little hole in the lining, the fabric making a small ripping sound. Great, now even her suitcase was falling apart. There was something wedged down in there, hard and small, and it made the sleuthing sweater itch all over.

"I ran into Eric," Kate said casually, digging her fingers into the lining to try to hook whatever was stuck in there. "He said you bailed on him last night. Apparently, you were supposed to have bro time together? What happened?"

"Oh, that," Spencer said, trailing off awkwardly. "Something . . . came up."

"Something like . . . what?"

"It doesn't matter," Spencer said, in a tone that implied it definitely did, and he definitely didn't want to tell her. "Kate, about the speech I gave—"

"Yeah, why does your mother think *I* switched your speech?" Kate demanded.

Spencer grunted, and she didn't need the light to know he was tugging at his hair, another nervous habit from childhood. Kate used to tease him, saying he'd be bald by the time he turned forty if he couldn't break the habit. "I tried to tell her it couldn't have been you, but she's convinced you were trying to . . . I don't know. Sabotage the dinner? Embarrass me? Win me back?"

"Win you back?" Kate said, finally getting ahold of something long and thin and tugging the piece loose from her luggage. The cardigan was so itchy it was like fire ants crawling all over, the delicate chain dangling from her hand with a surprising weight. A keychain, maybe? "Spencer, that's the most—"

Not a keychain. A necklace. Kennedy's diamond pendant necklace.

Kate gasped, standing up so fast she knocked over one of the book stacks and sent them scattering across the attic floor.

"Kate?" Spencer said in alarm, and there he was, taking her by the arms. The necklace swung wildly in her hand, knocking into his wrist. "Are you okay? What happened?"

"Spider," she gasped, the first thing that came to mind. "I thought I felt a spider."

Kennedy's necklace. Hidden in the lining of her suitcase. Just like *Loretta* book three, when Loretta found the family heirloom ring that the groom's sister, Lucretia, had stolen and hidden in the lining of her luggage because she had considered it her inheritance.

"Kate," Spencer said, his grip tightening. Drawing her in closer.

"Spencer," she said, slowly and cautiously. It occurred to her that they were alone, in an attic on the fourth floor, on a remote island several hours off the coast of Seattle with no working phones. Spencer could be anyone in the dark, a complete stranger. A killer who had planted his fiancée's necklace in Kate's luggage to frame her for murder.

"Spencer," she said again, more hastily. "We should go. This isn't . . . We shouldn't be here. You can't . . . We can't be up here. Let's go."

"Kate," Spencer said again, and she knew *that* voice well enough, even though she hadn't heard it in six months. It triggered an automatic, highly inconvenient reaction in her body, which was when Jake fucking Hawkins decided to make an appearance.

"Kate, you up here?" he called, his voice rising up the stairs. "Good news, Abraham said they found a patch for the generator, they're powering it up now."

At which point the lights buzzed to life, illuminating Kate in her sleuthing sweater and no pants, Spencer with his arms halfway around her, and Kennedy's missing necklace dangling from her fist.

Chapter Eighteen

"It's not what it looks like," Kate blurted, which wasn't really true, only because she had no idea what it looked like. She certainly couldn't tell what it looked like based on the blank expression on Jake's face as he took in the scene. Kate jerked back from Spencer's grasp, the necklace chain snagging on his cuff button and ripping out of Kate's hand to drop to the floorboard. The chain slipped through the crack, the pendant snaking through the boards after it and disappearing.

"I see I've interrupted something," Jake said, his tone flat. "I'll leave."

"Jake, wait!" Kate called out, costing herself precious seconds as she scrambled into a pair of leggings. She lurched for the attic opening, practically shoving Spencer out of the way.

"Kate!" Spencer called, following after her. "I think we should talk—"

"No more talking!" Kate said, chasing Jake and his stupid long strides down the hallway. "Talking is overrated! Talking is probably what killed the dinosaurs, all that CO_2 in the air. Jake! Please!"

She caught him at the head of the stairs, snagging his lovely soft sweater. He paused, that expressionless expression so frightening on his normally smiling face. She was going to have to admit that he might be right, that Spencer might really be a murderer. Or at least an attempted one. And that he might have planted Kennedy's necklace in her suitcase to frame her for the job, which was just a real kick in the teeth after everything he'd already put her through.

"What was that about moving on?" Jake asked, his voice low and angry.

"Listen, I think you might have had a potentially valid point. If you'd let me explain—"

"What's there to explain? You're an adult, aren't you? Even if you don't always act like it. And Spencer, well, I don't think any of us should be surprised he's a cheater, right?"

Kate sucked in a breath. "How *dare* you."

Jake rubbed at his face. "You're going to get yourself hurt, Kate."

"I can handle Spencer," Kate said.

"It's not just that." Jake hesitated, glancing behind her, where Spencer was clumsily navigating the rickety stairs out of the attic. Jake lowered his voice. "Someone sabotaged the generator."

"What?" Kate gasped, far too loud.

"Kate?" Spencer called. "Are you all right?"

"Yep! Just give us a minute!" she called back in a falsely cheerful tone. She stepped closer to Jake, trying to ignore how he always smelled faintly of salt and coconut, like he'd just come out of the ocean. "What do you mean, someone sabotaged the generator?"

"I mean, the fuel line was cut. And not very well, either. It was like someone took a handsaw to it."

"Why would someone do that?" Kate wondered.

Jake looked at her pointedly. "Oh, I don't know, because maybe they didn't want the wedding ceremony to happen?"

Kate frowned, chewing at one corner of her lip. She had to admit it looked awfully suspicious. Spencer goes missing overnight, during the same time frame the generator was sabotaged. And he'd been cagey with her earlier when she'd asked where he'd been last night. Still, that didn't mean he was guilty, or that he'd poisoned Kennedy. Loretta would warn her not to jump to conclusions before she had all the facts.

"If someone really did sabotage the generator to stop the wedding ceremony, that means Kennedy is still in danger," Kate reasoned. "Which means I can't stop now."

Jake gave a frustrated sigh. "You need to be more careful, Kate. You go around poking a hornet's nest, you're likely to get stung."

"What would you have me do?" Kate asked hotly. "Sit around and wait for them to come find me? Let them finish the job they started on Kennedy last night? I'm going to find out who's behind this, with or without you."

"Oh sure, what do you need Jake of All Trades for?" Jake said, his tone taking on a bitter edge. He turned away, heading down the stairs. "When you've got Spencer up in your room playing tonsil hockey with you?"

"Excuse me?" Kate gasped, nearly falling down the stairs in her rush to follow him. "I wasn't playing anything. I was trying to find out where he was last night! And *you* made it perfectly clear last night that you want nothing to do with me. Again. So, what do you care what I do with my time or my tongue?"

Jake paused on the stairs, gripping the railing hard before pivoting and surging up to the step just below her. The height difference put them at eye level, which meant she was staring directly into the storm of his gaze when he spoke.

"For the record, the only reason I didn't kiss you last night was because you were clearly drunk, clearly upset, and clearly still hung up on your ex. Who you were just embracing in the dark, I'd like to point out again."

"Well, joke's on you, because you already kissed me," Kate said, crossing her arms. "At the rehearsal dinner."

"I didn't kiss you," Jake said. He'd dropped his voice low, the vibration of it changing her heartbeat. *"You* kissed *me.* And you were doing it for *him.* When I kiss you, it will be for you and me. Nobody else. And you'll be stone-cold sober."

Kate rocked back on her heels, stunned into silence. What did he mean, *when* I kiss you? He'd made it perfectly clear a kiss between them would come the day after a global apocalypse. But Jake was done with the conversation—done with her—and already halfway down the stairs. She wanted to chase after him, to remind him she was in fact stone-cold sober right now. But Spencer was hovering, reminding her she had more pressing concerns than Jake Hawkins at the moment. Even if the rest of her body was in riotous disagreement with her.

"Sorry if I caused any issues with you and Jake," Spencer said. His tone didn't sound very apologetic, though.

"I bet you're heartbroken over it," Kate said. "But that's not what I'm interested in right now. What I want to know is where you went after the rehearsal dinner. I know you weren't with Kennedy, and you might have gone looking for me but we both know you didn't find me. Plus, your brother has already ratted you out about being a no-show for your bro downtime. So where were you?"

Spencer frowned. "Why do you need to know?"

"Why are you acting like you have something to hide?" Kate countered, going on the offensive. "Unless you actually have something to hide?"

Spencer's gaze roved around the hallway. "I . . . was . . . with . . ."

Kate rolled her eyes. "Spencer, I *see* you lying. God, you're bad at this. Where were you?"

Spencer huffed out a petulant sigh. "Fine. It's just, out of context, it's going to sound—"

"Spencer!"

"I was with Ian," he said, glaring. "Until about two in the morning, talking . . . business."

"Ian the estate lawyer?" Kate asked in surprise. "Why?"

Spencer's gaze turned shifty. "Look, I said I know how it's going to sound—"

"I swear to god, Spencer."

"The prenup!" he blurted out. He huffed a sigh, like the effort of releasing that secret had robbed him of air. "Ian helped me with the details and I thought he might know a way I could, uhhh . . . get out of it. You know, legally. Or otherwise."

She could only be grateful that Jake wasn't there to hear Spencer's confession just then, because she was positive the asshole would never let her hear the end of it. He'd visit her on her deathbed only to whisper in her ear *I told you so.*

"Why the hell would you be trying to get out of your prenup?" Kate demanded.

"Not the whole thing," Spencer muttered. "Just . . . certain clauses."

"Which *certain* clauses?" Kate pressed, letting the insult *idiot* infuse her tone.

Spencer sighed, going to town on his glasses again. At this rate, they'd be cleaner than a brand-new pair. "After Kennedy convinced the board of trustees to hold the wedding here, Rebecca forced her to add a damages clause to our prenup. She was afraid that letting this many people on the island might cause historically disastrous destruction. Her words, obviously. I didn't think anything of it at the time, since Ken said of course nobody would go around ripping sconces out of the walls or tearing up hundred-year-old floorboards. But the problem is, the wording is really vague. It said if anything substantially damaging happened this weekend, Ken and I would be on the hook for repairs. The cost of which would be astronomical. You should have seen what the restoration guys charged just to repaint."

"So, what, you were worried about getting a bill from Rebecca for the storm damage?"

"I wasn't worried *just* about the storm," Spencer hedged.

"Then what?" Kate heaved a disgruntled sigh. "For pete's sake, was it me? The rehearsal dinner speech? You didn't really think I would sabotage your wedding over that."

"You were so upset," Spencer said. "And I didn't understand why, at first. You know how I get about public speaking. I was just reading. I wasn't really *reading.* But then you . . . you ran out, and I read over the cards again, and I realized what it was. And, Kate, I swear I don't know how those cards got in my pocket."

Kate crossed her arms defensively. "So, you thought I might go crazy ex-girlfriend and start smashing up the house because of it? And you just wanted to be sure you wouldn't get stuck footing the bill for my emotional trauma–induced property damage?"

"It wasn't like that," Spencer said, propping his glasses on his nose and looking at her earnestly. "Kate, when you ran out, it stirred up a lot of feelings for me, too. I wanted to know my options before it was too late to do anything about them."

Oh, like *hell* she was going to let him do something so stupid as act like he had feelings for her now, of all weekends. She already had one nonexistent relationship causing her heartburn. But at least Spencer had an alibi for the previous evening—he was with Ian when Kate found Kennedy's body. Which meant Kate needed to consider the rest of her suspects.

"Rebecca seemed pissed off about the board of trustees business," Kate said, switching tactics. "And I've heard she can be pretty vindictive when it comes to people crossing her."

"Ah, I see you've made Marcus Sheffield's acquaintance," Spencer said. "I wish I could have seen Rebecca's face when she found out Ken included him on the guest list."

"Do you think she'd try to retaliate against Kennedy like she did against Marcus?"

Spencer tilted his head to the side. "Retaliate? Rebecca can obviously hold a grudge, and she and Ken have had their disagreements. Ken mostly goes along with whatever Rebecca tells her to do as the future heir, though every once in a while Ken takes a stand and they go around about it. But Ken loves her aunt. And she told me they'd already worked it out. Ken apologized for going behind her back, and Rebecca agreed to let us hold the wedding here."

Or maybe Kennedy only thought her aunt had accepted her apology, when really she'd been planning her future demise. Same as she'd done to Marcus Sheffield. After all, Rebecca had been conspicuously absent that morning after so happily playing the doting aunt last night. Maybe now that her schemes were coming to fruition, she wasn't interested in playing the role anymore. Was that why Rebecca had invited Kate? To play the patsy to her scheme to do away with Kennedy?

"Why are you asking me all these questions about Kennedy and Re-becca and the prenup?" Spencer asked. "I thought you wanted to talk to me about the speech."

"Oh, ahhh . . ." Kate could hardly admit to him now that someone had tried to poison his bride, or that he was a suspect. "I saw Serena outside, with some other Simon Says authors. Protesting. I was wondering if that might impact your damage clause."

Spencer groaned. "Oh god, I told Kennedy it was a bad idea to invite her. To invite any of you! No offense."

"Great offense taken."

Spencer gave her an exasperated look. "Ken is always going on about how Simon Says is a family, and Simon's been like a dad to her since her own dad died. I think she gets lonely, despite her family name being on every other building around town. Her aunt is basically a recluse, her cousins are always fighting over the will, and her parents died when she was young. I think to her, Simon Says really *is* like family, and she forgets that everybody else just works there."

"Last night, Serena said you told her that all new contract negotiations are on pause," Kate said. "Is that true?"

"Oh," Spencer said, blinking a few times. His gaze slid to the side. "I'm not really supposed to say."

"So it's true," Kate said, easily connecting the dots. "But why? Is Simon closing the business? Is Simon Says folding?"

"I said I'm not supposed to say," Spencer said.

"Is that why everybody's marketing campaigns have been going so poorly? Because there's no budget to actually promote them?"

"Kate!" Spencer said, exasperated.

"Hey, if I'm out of a job I need to know it!" Kate countered, suddenly worried about her next mortgage payment.

"You know you're not out of a job, not with the way Loretta sells," Spencer said.

"But you *are* hiding something," Kate said. "I could tell last night. You know something, so spill it. What do you want, a pinky promise that I won't tell? Should we spit in our hands and shake on it? Blood pact?"

"Even though I know you wouldn't pass up the opportunity to stab me or spit on me, I'll just take your word." Spencer glanced around the hallway, like there might be a spy lurking in the corridor waiting to catch him in an act of corporate espionage. "There's a rumor—just a rumor, mind you, I don't have real proof yet—that Simon is looking to sell the publishing house."

"What?" Kate whispered, leaning in closer. This was real gossip, indeed. "Why?"

Spencer shrugged. "He hasn't said anything official yet, but there have been . . . signs. He's already made me cut ties with several of my lower-performing authors, and he's holding out on extending anybody else's contracts unless they're high-earners like you. Serena's been down my throat for months now, wanting to move forward on her next title, and I can't. There's another rumor that layoffs are coming in every department."

"Who's on the chopping block?" Kate asked.

"I'd guess the highest earners in every department, like Juliette. She's obviously way more expensive than the interns, and as far as I can tell, most of her job is just telling them what to do. If she gets cut, the department budget basically gets cut in half."

"Does Juliette know?" Kate thought about Juliette sneaking into locked rooms last night. Was that Simon's room she'd been breaking into? Maybe looking for proof that he was going to cut her? Maybe Juliette thought she'd axe Kennedy before Kennedy could drop the axe on her.

"If I've noticed the signs, Juliette certainly has," Spencer said. "There's not much that gets past her at Simon Says."

And if anybody was devious enough to use Kate's book as a blueprint to frame her for Kennedy's poisoning, it would be Juliette Winters. She'd been the first one to connect the dots in the wine cave last night, which made sense if she'd been the one to draw the dots in the first place. Plus, someone had planted Kennedy's necklace in Kate's luggage. A necklace she still needed to find and get rid of before Juliette started a witch hunt to find it.

"I need to go," Kate said, heading back toward her room. "And you need to get to your tux fitting before Jean-Pierre has an aneurysm."

"But we still haven't talked about the speech," Spencer called, sounding disappointed.

"Tux fitting, now!" Kate said, waving him off. She didn't have time for speeches or disappointed ex-fiancés. She had a necklace to find, and a murder to thwart.

Chapter Nineteen

Kate spent a horrifying thirty minutes digging through a room that seemed to consist only of spare doll parts, old linens that smelled of what she swore was brimstone (even though she'd never smelled brimstone), and hulking pieces of furniture. But she emerged victorious and covered in cobwebs, the necklace tucked safely away in her pocket and her feelings pricklier than ever toward Jake and Spencer.

What right did Jake have to be mad at her about Spencer? He was the one who'd rejected her. Twice! And what the hell was Spencer thinking, talking about cancelling prenups and stirring up old feelings? Loretta wouldn't take that kind of guff from Blake or Geoff. She'd have the two of them strung up and put down by chapter three. Besides, Kate had real problems to focus on—like how she was going to get Kennedy's necklace back among her things before the bride noticed her precious family heirloom was missing.

The ship seemed to have sailed on that last one, at least, because Kennedy's distressed voice filtered past the double doors of the bridal suite as Kate reached the second floor. "Have you found it, Cass?"

"Not yet, I'm checking the bed," came Cassidy's voice, muffled under layers of bedding.

Kate pushed the door open cautiously, not yet wanting to knock and announce herself until she knew what she was dealing with. The room was enormous and menacing, the dark wood walls overbearing and the curtains a heavy drape of deep purple that cast the corners in heavy shadows. It must have been the master suite at one point, considering the mural painted on the ceiling made to look like an evil Sistine Chapel, with devils instead of angels and a grinning satyr instead of a god. Kate wondered, not for the first time since arriving on the island, what Russell Hempstead and his Romanian bride got up to on their private island.

The bridesmaids must have camped out in there with Kennedy, at least for the previous evening. There were toiletry bags everywhere, makeup and champagne glasses and hair products on every surface, glittering dresses she recognized from the rehearsal dinner scattered throughout the space. There were several pallets laid out, mattresses that looked like they'd been dragged in from other rooms or sleeping bags and yoga mats piled up to make beds. But everything had been pulled out, turned over, and shaken up in their search for the missing necklace. It looked like someone had set off a bomb in a high-end shopping gallery, with lace bras and sparkling high-heeled shoes strewn everywhere.

"It has to be here!" Kennedy said, her voice pinched tight with worry. She popped up from behind a velvet divan, the light throwing ghoulish shadows under her eyes where Cassidy hadn't yet applied makeup to hide her fatigue. She looked so fragile, with her big hair and her doe eyes and her bare neck, and she blinked in surprise as she spotted Kate in the doorway. "Oh, Kate! I'm sorry, I didn't hear you knock."

"That's okay," Kate said, skipping over the part where she didn't actually knock. "Is everything . . . okay?"

"It's my necklace," Kennedy said, rubbing her hands over her bare chest where the diamond pendant usually hung. "It was my mother's, and I need it for my wedding day."

"Not here, either," Cassidy announced, her hair sticking up from the static discharge of the sheets as they slid off. "I don't understand, you never take that thing off. Where could it be?"

"I thought maybe it had fallen off while I was sleeping, or it got caught when I changed last night. But I can't find it anywhere!"

"You think someone *stole* it?" Cassidy whispered. She looked meaningfully at Kate.

"Have you checked the wine cave?" Kate asked, giving what she hoped looked like a normal smile. The pendant felt like it weighed a thousand pounds, jangling around in her pocket, just waiting to give her away. "Maybe it came off last night."

"Oh, the wine cave, of course!" Kennedy said, smacking the side of her head and grinning at Kate. "Good thing I have Loretta on the case, I'd completely forgotten to check down there. Cass, would you go ask the kitchen staff to give the cave a good once-over? Maybe it got kicked under a wine rack or something."

"Why doesn't she do it?" Cassidy asked, still eyeing Kate suspiciously. "We need to finish your makeup."

"I'll be fine," Kennedy said with a wave, wincing as she stood. "I can do my own foundation, and you can finish my eye makeup when you get back. We have plenty of time!"

Kate knew they did not, in fact, have plenty of time, considering the state of the generator. Not to mention a killer loose on the island. But she kept all that to herself, instead nodding along in agreement as Cassidy moved past her toward the exit. She paused beside Kate, mustering up her best bulldog impression as she stared Kate down.

"Nothing better happen to Ken while I'm gone," she said.

"Well, you'll know who did it if something does," Kate said before realizing how menacing it sounded out loud. "That was a joke! I'm not going to do anything."

"Mm-hmm," Cassidy said, moving to the stairs. "Stay away from stairs, Ken!"

"She's very . . . protective of you, isn't she?" Kate ventured as Kennedy shook her head with a soft smile.

"Cassidy? Oh, she's more bark than bite. We spent all our summers together here on Hempstead Island when Grandpa Ferdinand was still alive. We were inseparable. I guess we were both kind of lonely as only children. We got to pretend we were sisters, and it didn't feel so lonely. I never would have considered anyone else for my maid of honor."

Kennedy turned and hobbled toward the bathroom door, wincing at the movement.

"What's wrong with your legs?" Kate asked, wondering if the poison had any lingering side effects.

"Oh, it's just my feet," Kennedy said with a dismissive wave. "Too many hours in high heels, gave me blisters. That's the last time I wear shoes embellished with Swarovski crystals."

She gave a little laugh, showing off one heel. There were deep scratches running from the back of her ankle to the bottom of her heel, with spots of blue and purple bruising around the edges. Kate could only imagine the other foot looked just as bad. She knew all about blisters, considering the ones her own heels had given her last night, and those weren't blisters caused by any shoes. Loretta would never miss a detail like that, not when the investigation was just heating up.

"Barefoot," Loretta murmured to herself as she examined the bride's body. The groom had said she'd been complaining about her shoes all evening. Had she taken them off? But no, Loretta remembered the way her feet had sparkled as she'd spun around the dance floor. Custom-made in Italy. A bride didn't shell out for footwear like that only to ditch them halfway through dinner. There were scratches, too, along the backs of her heels, as if someone had dragged her bare feet over a rough surface.

"How is that possible?" Loretta asked, pivoting to glance up the stairs. Even if the bride had been poisoned and taken a tumble down the stairs, her feet wouldn't have looked like that. And she'd have more bruising all over. No, the bride didn't fall down those stairs at all, but someone certainly wanted to make it look that way.

"Kennedy, what do you remember about last night?" Kate asked, moving toward the bathroom where the other woman had disappeared to finish her wedding day preparations. She sat at an old-fashioned vanity, complete with a little wooden stool carved to look like a bloom of tulips. "After the rehearsal dinner, and the uh . . . the speeches. Where did you go?"

Kennedy pursed her lips in thought, taking the opportunity to paint a coral pink on them. "Well, I remember taking photos with the wedding party, and I started to feel sort of sick. I came in here to change, but I was so dizzy I could hardly stand. I thought it was the champagne at the time, you know? I don't drink often, so my tolerance isn't very high. I thought I'd lie down for a minute. And the next thing I knew, I was in the wine cave."

"So, you don't remember going down to the wine cave?" Kate asked. "Maybe to get another bottle of Dom?"

Kennedy shook her head slowly, frowning. "No, I don't think so. The last thing I remember is lying down on the bed over there."

Kate examined the room more closely as Kennedy layered on her foundation. There were several garment bags hung up at various points around the room, most likely the bridal party's dresses. If Kate could figure out which one was Kennedy's wedding gown, maybe she could hang the necklace on the hanger without anyone noticing.

"What about your shoes?" she asked, using the excuse to edge closer to the floofiest garment bag. She figured it stood to reason that the bride's dress would have the most floof. The zipper made a loud, horrendous sound as she struggled to open it, and she pitched her voice louder to mask it. "Do you remember taking them off, or what you did with them?"

"You know, that's funny," Kennedy said, coming to the door. Kate snapped her hands to her side, trying to lean casually against the nearby wall before realizing it was a good half a foot farther away than she'd thought. She stumbled, catching herself on the bag and wincing at the flash of diamond clutched in her fist. Kennedy gave her a look of concern. "Are you all right?"

"Yep, just great!" Kate said enthusiastically, recovering her balance and clasping her hand behind her back. The zipper on the dress bag gaped immodestly, and she moved to block it from Kennedy's view. "You were saying, about your shoes?"

"Oh, right. Yes. The funny thing is, I haven't been able to find them either this morning. I don't remember taking them off, but I must have, right? Only they're not anywhere in the room." Kennedy gave a little laugh, touching her forehead. "I swear if my head wasn't attached to my neck, I'd lose that, too!"

Kate gave a weak laugh, figuring that the joke wasn't as far off as Kennedy thought. Kennedy turned back toward the bathroom, and Kate took the momentary advantage to tug at the zipper of the dress bag again. Except Kennedy pivoted just then, and Kate's sleeve got caught in the toothy little bastard, and so she had to twist into a thoughtful position, her fist positioned under her chin while she tried to tug her sleeve loose.

"And now all this business with the generator!" Kennedy exclaimed, politely ignoring Kate's ludicrous impression of Rodin's *The Thinker*. "And, apparently, the water is acting up, too. The toilets won't flush. I know weddings never go as smoothly as you imagine, but I didn't think we'd be fielding this many disasters. And now I've lost my necklace and my shoes!"

Kennedy shook her head and turned back to the vanity, giving Kate the opportunity to finally rip her sleeve loose and stuff the necklace deep in the folds of the dress inside the bag. She tugged the zipper into position before it could give her any more trouble.

"I'm sure they'll turn up somewhere," Kate murmured, though she didn't think Kennedy had misplaced them like she'd thought. Kate figured that Kennedy lost her shoes when her poisoner dragged her down into the wine cave. It was the only way to explain the scratching and bruising. And the only stairs she'd encountered so far that weren't luxuriously carpeted were the rocky stairs leading down into the wine cave. Which meant nobody could have dragged her down from the second floor, across the entryway, into the kitchen, and down into the wine cave without being seen.

"This weekend has me all turned around," Kennedy said ruefully, sweeping a makeup brush across her cheeks. "I even dreamed that someone was trying to choke me. I couldn't breathe. I woke up with my pillow over my face. I was so stressed I tried to smother myself! Can you imagine it?"

Kate could imagine it, but she didn't think Kennedy was responsible for the late-night smothering. She recognized a second attempt on Kennedy's life, even if Kennedy laughed it off. And she knew that whoever was after Kennedy wouldn't stop until they saw the job done.

Chapter Twenty

The kitchen was already bustling with servers prepping the wedding day breakfast. Even in such an expansive working kitchen—an unprecedented seven cooktops—the space was crowded. Kate could barely make it past the entrance, much less across the room to the wine cave stairs. But she wasn't there for the wine cave—at least not yet. There had been several servers in the kitchen last night when she and Marla had snuck in, which meant if someone dragged an unconscious Kennedy Hempstead down the wine cave stairs, someone must have seen something. She just needed to grease the right wheels.

Kate posted herself at the door between the kitchen and the main entryway, where servers carried trays loaded with tantalizing piles of bacon, steaming eggs, and croissants so flaky and buttery they rustled in the faintest breeze. Kate snagged a few strips of bacon for emotional fortification before pouncing on a young man carrying a full tray of mimosas.

"You didn't see anyone come through here with Kennedy Hempstead last night?" Kate asked, crunching down on the delicious strip.

"No ma'am," he said, struggling under the weight and uneven distribution of glasses. "Nobody but staff back here last night. Ms. Hempstead—uh, the boss one, I mean—she's got very strict rules about servers and guests mixing. She says it 'muddies the waters.' She even makes us stay in the old servant quarters, and she put an alarm on the door separating our rooms from the rest of the house so nobody gets tempted."

That tracked with the Rebecca Hempstead she'd met at the rehearsal dinner. Kate didn't mention that she'd been in the kitchen and nobody had spotted her, but she hadn't been dragging an unconscious body. "Were you in here all night?"

"No ma'am, we were in and out of the ballroom, collecting plates and glasses. I'm sorry, I've really got to get this to the breakfast room."

Kate questioned a few more servers as they passed through, but each one of them had the same frustratingly vague answer. Nobody had seen Kennedy, and nobody knew how she'd gotten down to the wine cave last night. She moved into the breakfast room for better access to the pastries, eyeing the guests as she entered.

The breakfast room looked more suited to a jazz club than a mimosa and pastry bar. The walls were the same dark wood that made up the rest of the house with panels of floor-to-ceiling stained-glass installations, the wan morning light casting pearlescent beams of light across the black-and-white-tiled floor.

"It just doesn't make any sense," Kate muttered as she swiped a fresh croissant.

"What doesn't make any sense?" someone asked, startling her into dropping her treat. Marla stood behind her, holding a position Kate knew all too well.

"I take it you kept the party going after you left my room last night?" Kate said.

"Turns out Rebecca Hempstead's wine selection is as cheap as she is, and gives you twice the hangover," Marla said, pressing a hand to her head. "My entire kingdom for a decent cup of coffee and some buttered toast right now."

"I got you," Kate said, slipping away to the coffee stand. The smell alone perked her right up, and she glanced around for any sign of Jake before filling a second mug for herself. Kate was almost positive you couldn't overdose on caffeine, but if anyone was going to find out that weekend it would be her. When she returned, Marla took a long, hot slurp without even wincing.

"Speaking of hangovers," Marla said, eyeing Kate up and down. "What the hell are you wearing, Valentine? They look like erotic krakens."

"I think they're jellyfish," Kate said. "Or a very creative take on mermen?"

"Why are you wearing that monstrosity, whatever the shellfish involved?"

"Oh, it's my sleuthing sweater."

Marla raised her brows. "What are you sleuthing?"

Kate glanced around at the wedding guests crowding into the breakfast room, lured by the heady scent of bacon and eggs. "Can you keep a secret?"

"No," Marla snorted, chugging another swig of coffee. When Kate gave her an exasperated look, she shrugged. "Maybe? I'll give it the old college try."

Kate leaned in, dropping her voice dramatically. "Kennedy was poisoned last night."

Marla choked on her coffee. "After that whole oyster business?"

Kate shook her head. "There was no oyster business. Somebody tried to poison her."

Marla blinked, trying to process Kate's bombshell. "What makes you think that?"

"I know it sounds crazy, but hear me out," Kate said, running through the events of the previous evening, including finding the sliver of rosary pea and Kennedy's missing necklace in the lining of her suitcase.

"Are you shitting me?" Marla asked. "You actually found Kennedy's necklace in your stuff? How the hell could it end up there?"

"The killer must have planted it," Kate said dismissively, as if this sort of thing happened all the time. "Don't worry, I got rid of it."

"Got rid of it?" Marla said. "Isn't that thing worth, like, a small European country's per capita? Please tell me you didn't chuck it down a trash chute."

"Don't worry about the necklace," Kate said. "The important thing is that *someone* on this island is a murderer. Or a would-be murderer. And I'm going to catch them."

"Valentine." Marla sighed, draining her coffee and surveying the grinds along the bottom of the cup critically. "I really need another, and you do, too. Maybe then you'll start making sense."

"I know how it sounds!" Kate whispered as they moved toward the coffeepot.

"It sounds like you've imagined one of your books is real," Marla said dryly, filling her cup. "Are you sure this isn't some kind of, I don't know, weird coping mechanism because of Spencer and Kennedy? I mean, really? Murder at a wedding? Besides, Kennedy is fine, right? If somebody really wanted her dead, they didn't do a great job of it, did they?"

"That's the other part!" Kate exclaimed, drawing the attention of a nearby couple in the pastry line. She gave them a hasty smile, lowering her voice. "Someone tried to kill Kennedy *again* last night. In her room. They tried to smother her with a pillow."

Marla's eyes went wide. "How do you know that?"

"Kennedy told me. She thought it was a bad dream, but I know a murder attempt when I hear one. Whoever is after Kennedy won't stop until they finish the job, unless I catch them first."

"How do you plan to do that?"

"By discovering the evidence they left behind," Kate said firmly. "I'm pretty sure the poison was dumped in Kennedy's champagne glass, which was missing last night. We find the evidence, we find the killer."

Marla nodded along slowly, far less enthusiastic about the prospect of a murder investigation than Jake had been. Kate felt that old, aching longing for Jake. The absence of him loomed large in her life, even when she tried her best to pretend she'd moved on. But she couldn't help Kennedy by mooning over Jake.

"We need to find that evidence," Kate said firmly.

"'We'? As in you and me?"

"I can't interrogate our suspects while also looking for missing shoes," Kate said.

"What about the hotstralian, why isn't he here helping you?"

"He's . . . occupied," Kate said uneasily. "Besides, it could be fun! This house has plenty of inspiration for your feminist fairy-tale reimaginings."

"This house is a nightmare of the patriarchy, but you might have a point." Marla looked at her in consideration. "Sneaking around looking for evidence does sound a hell of a lot more fun than talking to any of these blowhards about stocks or legacy enrollment or whatever it is rich people blather on about. Plus, you're not exactly Brenda Leigh Johnson when it comes to getting info out of people. You'll definitely need my help with these interrogations. Fine, I'm in. How do we find this so-called evidence?"

Finally, the chance to show Marla that her "little detective stories" might actually prove useful in the real world. Sure, Marla wasn't as handsome or effortlessly charming or deliciously distracting as Jake, but that was probably a good thing, right? Now Kate could really focus in on the investigation itself.

Of course, that meant she needed to figure out how to actually find the evidence.

Kate glanced across the breakfast room, spotting the wedding photographer snapping pictures of the pastry tower and getting close-ups of the bubbles popping in the mimosas.

"Oooh, the photographer!" Kate exclaimed, licking the butter and bacon grease off her fingers. She didn't exactly sound—or look—like the expert she was hoping Marla would see her as. She cleared her throat, tempering the excitement in her voice. "I mean, we should talk to the photographer. Maybe he caught something in the background of the rehearsal dinner."

"Lead the way, Loretta," Marla said.

"Hi there," Kate said to the photographer as she approached him.

She gave a friendly, disarming smile. "Are you the wedding photo-grapher?"

The man looked at her and back at his camera. "It would look like I am, wouldn't it?"

"I'm Kate," she said, putting out a hand before realizing both of his still held the camera. She pulled it back, forcing her smile wider. "Kate Valentine. Nice to meet you."

He gave her a bemused nod. "Louis. If you don't mind, I'd like to get a couple more photos of the spread before the guests get to it. We're not called More Than Memories because we skimp on the wedding day captures."

"Great," Kate said, her smile fading. "I was wondering if we could take a look at some of the photos from the rehearsal dinner. Particularly any photos you might have of the bride after the dinner? Anybody who might have been with her maybe?"

Louis paused in front of a silver tower of petit fours. "What?"

Marla gave Kate a frank look, as if to say *see what I mean about Brenda Leigh?* "The bride lost her heirloom necklace last night, and we're trying to help her find it."

"Oh yeah, that's good," Kate muttered. Who looked like the expert now? "I mean, that's true."

The photographer straightened up, holding out his camera. "Fine, but could we make it quick? I've still got the groom's fitting and the bridal room prep to photograph. My partner was supposed to be here this morning but they can't get here with the storm, so I need to be in two places at once."

"We'll be quick," Kate promised, clicking through the gallery. There were the obligatory place-setting photos, a whole series of the bride's and groom's rings in various food dishes, the overloaded gift table. And then there it was, Kate knocking Kennedy into the same table, Kate looking deranged and Kennedy looking like the perfect victim.

"Not a great vibe for you, huh, Valentine?" Marla murmured over her shoulder. She leaned in closer for a better look, her frown deepening as she took in more of the disaster scene. Kate's finger hovered over the delete button, her good sense warring with her sense of self-preservation. Before she could make up her mind one way or the other, Marla snuck a hand in and pressed her finger down, deleting the photo.

"Hey!" Louis exclaimed, jerking the camera away. "What do you think you're doing?"

"Sorry!" Kate said hastily, holding up a hand. "My finger slipped. Bacon grease."

"Happens to the best of us, doesn't it, Louie?" Marla slapped him on the back, the faint whiff of clove cigarettes rising out of her oversize black sweater. She gave Kate a wink, as if to say *you're welcome*. "I'm sure that wasn't one of those precious memories the bride was looking for. What if we skip ahead to the end of the night, huh?"

"Fine," Louis ground out, quickly scrolling through the rest of the rehearsal dinner.

There were photos of Kate running out after the speeches, but she could hardly claim an accident if she tried to delete those now. So, she let the photographer scroll until he reached a series of Kennedy posing with various sets of guests throughout the house. She still wore her necklace in each of the photos, though her face looked increasingly flushed throughout, her smile more strained. Kate clocked the time as it ticked by—11:30, 11:35, 11:42. Several guests flitted in and out of the background of each photo—a bright spot of Rebecca's floral caftan, the back of Richie's herringbone jacket, Serena's fascinator marking the hour of the evening by how low it had slipped over her eye.

The last photo of Kennedy was a candid, in conversation with her bridesmaids as other guests moved past behind them. She looked terrible—sweaty and green, deep circles pressing in under her eyes. But she smiled bravely, where Kate would have already had her head in the toilet praying for the end. She was still wearing the necklace, but that wasn't what snagged Kate's attention in the background of the photo.

It was the cut-crystal champagne glass half hidden by skirts and bodies, held by a hand with bright purple nails that stood out even in the tiny viewfinder. Kate was sure if she looked at the photo on a computer screen she'd see the word *Bride* laser-etched into the side of the glass. And she was also sure that the hand holding the glass belonged to none other than Juliette Winters, smiling like a shark at the camera.

Chapter Twenty-One

"Valentine, wait up!" Marla hissed as Kate dodged through the growing crowd of wedding guests vying for plates of bacon and heaping cups of coffee. "For fuck's sake, you move like a hyperactive toddler on coke. What is it? What did you see?"

"Shhh," Kate said, lurking along the fringes of the crowd and positioning herself in a shadowy corner to do what she did best. "I'm snooping."

Marla gave her sweater a skeptical look. "Hard to be inconspicuous in that thing. Would you just tell me what you saw in the photo that's got you all rattled?"

"The missing champagne glass," Kate whispered. "In that last photo, it looked like Juliette was holding Kennedy's glass."

Marla's brows shot up. "You think she's our killer? I mean, it fits. The bitch is wound tighter than a corkscrew."

"I need to talk to her," Kate said resolutely. "Find out what she was doing last night, and where she was when Kennedy was knocked out. You want to come with me? I can show you the ropes for interrogating what I assume will be a very hostile suspect."

"Sounds thrilling," Marla said, "but wouldn't it be better if I go poking around her stuff while you've got her distracted? Get some of that evidence you've been talking about?"

"Oh, right," Kate said, crestfallen. She'd been enjoying having a sleuthing partner, even if it wasn't Jake. "That's a good idea, actually. But be careful. If Juliette really is our potential killer, she's . . . well, a potential killer. Who knows what she might try."

"I'll be fine," Marla said with a wave. "Besides, Juliette's always trying to rattle everybody else. It'll be good for someone to rattle her cage for once."

Marla slipped off into the crowd and Kate circulated through the room, keeping one eye out for Juliette or any of her other suspects.

"It'll never stand, of course," said an older man in a silk smoking jacket. He'd amassed a small audience of like-dressed people with smooth foreheads and dark blue veins along the backs of their hands. "There's too much precedent against her. Not that I'd want to go up against Rebecca Hempstead, mind you. She eviscerated her cousins over the inheritance rights. Left them poorer than they started."

"It's a bad look, I don't mind saying," sniffed a woman in a diamond-and-emerald necklace. "The press will have a field day with it, of course. It's splashy and tacky, just like her. Always making a fuss, dragging the rest of us into it. They'll be swarming the Dover benefit next month, you know. It's obscene!"

"Can't say I blame her, though," said a man whose cheeks looked permanently red. "The latest batch of Hempsteads is a real mess. Kennedy's an all right egg, but that boy Richard did an internship at Gary's firm a few years ago and was a complete waste of space. Didn't understand the first thing about advertising, much less working in an office. Gary said he'd show up in all sorts of states, drunk, high, who knows what."

"You didn't hear it from me, but how do you think Kennedy got the job at Simon Says in the first place?" said a woman in a raspy voice that Kate realized was Serena Archer. The picket line must have broken up already. "The girl is barely out of short dresses and here she is, running the entire marketing department! More like running it into the ground."

Smoking Jacket Guy gave her a surprised look. "I'd heard from Simon that she was a star, a real up-and-comer."

Serena snorted. "The only reason Simon would say that is because she gave him a healthy infusion of much-needed cash to grease the wheels. Oh, she tried to keep it quiet, but someone spilled the beans about Kennedy being a so-called silent investor in a rather nasty exposé in *Pub Daily*. The publisher's been struggling for years, it's no secret, and hardworking, high-earning writers like us have been carrying it on our backs with barely a thanks. And how does she repay us? By tanking our sales and ruining our careers! Well, it won't stand, I tell you. She'll find she can't ignore us all when we come together in the mighty lion's roar."

"Was that your lion's roar we heard outside?" said the man with red cheeks. He snickered into his glass. "More like a kitten's meow, if you ask me."

Serena sputtered mimosa and outrage in equal measure. "How dare you—Kate, tell him!"

"What?" Kate asked in alarm. She thought she'd been doing a good job of lurking, but as Serena fixed her gaze on her, she realized she was caught out. "I've got . . . things."

"Scab!" Serena cried shrilly in an echo of their previous encounter outside. "You mark my words, scab, you'll be one of us someday soon. Out on the streets with nothing but our author copies to keep us warm! You can't escape us forever. Join the revolution!"

Kate hastily backed away, bumping into a man with a belly like a mall Santa and pirouetting around his wife, who was more perfume than woman. By the time she did a little dance to avoid colliding with a server carrying an urn of piping hot coffee, she was ping-ponging her way through the crowd in an increasingly unbalanced manner. It was around the fourth or fifth muttered "watch it" when she realized this could only end in disaster, which was when she ran chest to chest into someone carrying two full glasses of champagne.

"Oh!" she exclaimed as half the contents of one glass splashed down the front of her shirt, little bubbles rising and popping on the surface. "I'm sorry, it's so crowded, I—Jake?"

"I might have to reconsider nicknaming you Cannonball Kate," he said, though she couldn't tell if his tone was teasing or angry. Her eyes dropped down to the two glasses in his hands, one now half-empty.

"You have . . . two champagne glasses."

His mouth tightened, just the tiniest bit. "I do."

"Oh," she said, hating how small and sad her voice sounded. Not that Jake owed her anything (he didn't), and not that she expected anything (she definitely didn't), but the fact that he seemed to have already found someone else to spend his time with so quickly still hurt.

"Ugh, there you are," said Juliette Winters as she snagged the full glass from Jake's hand and knocked half of it back in one gulp.

Kate's gaze wandered from Juliette back to Jake in shock. "The glass was for Juliette?"

"I sent him to find me one nearly half an hour ago," Juliette said, giving Jake a frank look. "You're lucky you have a beautiful face, because you're a terrible waiter."

Jake rolled his eyes. "A, I told you I wasn't a waiter. B, I know you know who I am. You ran the marketing campaign on the *Wandering Australian* books."

Juliette shook her head, polishing off the rest of her champagne. "That would have been Kennedy, I don't do photography books. No, we've never met, I'm sure of it. I make a personal habit of remembering guys I might have sex with later."

Jake choked on his sip of champagne as Kate blurted out, "He has a brother. Jake does. He's a doctor. The brother, not Jake."

Juliette looked her up and down with a critical eye. "I see what you're trying to do, and you're not subtle about it. But, you're also not wrong. Tell me more about this doctor brother. What's his specialty? If it's feet, I'm out. Or vaginas. I'm competitive, but that's masochism."

"Charlie is a cardiothoracic surgeon," Kate said, hoping Juliette wouldn't ask for details, since she'd thought *cardiothoracic* was a dinosaur era when she'd first met Charlie.

But Juliette scrunched up her nose in distaste. "Charlie? No, that's not happening. That's a terrible name. Imagine calling *that* out in bed."

"Juliette and I were just discussing how things have been going at Simon Says since Kennedy took over the marketing department," Jake said, looking at Kate meaningfully. "Apparently, there have been some hiccups."

"More like fuckups," Juliette snorted.

Jake looked at Kate, tilting his head slightly toward Juliette with an emphatic expression. Which was when Kate realized, with a funny little lurch in her heart, that Jake had been investigating for her. Bringing Juliette a glass of champagne, loosening her up, getting her to talk.

"What kind of fuckups?" Kate asked innocently, giving Jake a wink. Except Juliette chose that moment to look at her, narrowing her eyes.

"What is that? What are you doing? Is this some weird tag team attempt to change my mind about you poisoning Kennedy last night?"

"No, it's not." Kate crossed her arms. "But I'm not the only one with a potential grudge against Kennedy, am I?"

Juliette gave her a desultory once-over. "Are you interrogating me, Nancy Drew?"

"I'm just asking questions," Kate said with a shrug. "Why does that feel like an interrogation to you?"

Juliette's mouth curled up in a slow, predatory smile. "Oh my god, you're trying to pin this on me, aren't you? Your plan must be going ass up if you think anybody would believe I did it. Okay, Veronica Mars, I'll play your little game."

"You sure do know the names of a lot of teen-girl detectives," Kate said.

"Yeah, I was super into them as a kid," Juliette said. "I like Loretta, too. She doesn't think with her dick like all of Serena's characters, and she's not a total bitch like all of Marla's characters. It's one of the few Simon Says titles I actually enjoy reading. So, what's my motive?"

"Knowing you? Revenge. Against Kennedy, and against me."

"Revenge for what?"

"The promotion," Jake said. "You and Kate had a falling-out over the cancelled book tour, and it cost you the promotion that Kennedy got. So, of course you'd want revenge against both of them for the slight."

"Mmm, first of all, we didn't have a 'falling-out' over the book tour," Juliette said, holding up a finger in rebuttal. "I scheduled an extensive book tour involving fourteen bookstores in eleven cities, and Kate pretended to have mono at the last minute because she was going through a breakup. It was unprofessional, expensive, and damaged our relationship with several indie bookstores."

Kate's mouth dropped open, but Juliette wasn't done. She lifted another finger, cataloging her next point.

"Second, it's laughable you think that would cost me the promotion. Yes, I was at one point in consideration for it, but I removed myself from the running. The last thing I wanted was the albatross of all those little ninnies constantly running to me asking what they should do about every single book launch. Your book-three tour disaster taught me that much. My ambitions and my skills are higher than that, which I'll be proving to all of you soon enough. And third, I was with Veeta at the time of Kennedy's staged accident."

"Veeta, right," Kate said. "And what would Veeta say about the two of you breaking into someone else's room last night, hmmm?"

Juliette hesitated the slightest bit, her only tell that Kate had truly surprised her. Her gaze narrowed. "What did that little narc tell you? I knew I couldn't trust them."

"Whose room were you breaking into, and why?" Kate demanded.

"Nobody and none of your business," Juliette snapped back.

"I heard you say you were about to get everything you wanted, and one little idiot stood in your way," Kate pressed.

Juliette crossed her arms, her gaze narrowing. "You were *spying* on me?"

Kate did her best to match Juliette's stance. "What did you mean by 'one little idiot'? Were you talking about getting Kennedy out of the way so you could get the promotion you thought you deserved?"

Juliette glanced around the room before bringing her gaze back to Jake and Kate. "I guess I can trust you two, considering you've been out of the country for six months and you had a very fake case of mono and a very real case of hiding in your apartment like a coward."

"It was real!" Kate protested.

"So you *do* know who I am," Jake said at the same time.

Juliette took both of them by the arm, steering them into a more private corner of the breakfast room. "Simon Says has a mole."

"What, you mean the one above his lip?" Kate asked, confused. "What about it?"

Juliette sighed to the ceiling. "Not Simon Hsu. Simon Says, the company. Someone is leaking confidential information. Details of the sale, investor meetings, potential layoffs. I swear, a week hasn't gone by without a blind item about Simon Says getting reported in the *Pub Daily* emails. Most of them have been unsubstantiated rumors, but a couple of them were about private, privileged information that only a mole could have access to."

Kate had read a few of those emails, including the one Serena mentioned that claimed Kennedy Hempstead had become a private investor in the company. If that one had proved to be true, she could imagine which other ones might have stirred up panic within the publisher.

"Simon tasked me with finding out who it is," Juliette continued. "When I do, he'll make sure I'm compensated. I was checking out Serena's room last night when you were snooping."

"Why Serena?" Jake asked.

"You mean other than the little author riot she's been stirring up out there this morning?" Juliette said dryly. "Well, I found out that Serena Archer isn't her real name."

"A lot of authors use pen names," Kate reasoned.

"Yeah, but it's not just a pen name, it's a fake name. Like, her whole identity is fake. Serena Archer doesn't exist."

That *was* new information. "So, what is her real name?"

"That's what I was trying to find out," Juliette said. "People don't make up false identities unless they're trying to hide something from their past."

Kate thought again of Serena's tirade against Kennedy last night, and her cryptic comment about midnight. What was she hiding from her past, and could it have anything to do with Kennedy's present predicament?

Plus, Kate realized as Juliette counted off all the reasons that she wasn't the one to poison Kennedy that her nails were painted a soft mauve. The nails in the picture were purple, and Kate didn't figure she could have changed her nail colors that quickly. Which meant someone else had been holding the champagne glass last night. Could it have been Serena?

"Where is Serena's room?" Kate asked.

"Why?" Juliette asked suspiciously. "Don't go fucking things up for me, Harriet."

"She was a spy," Kate pointed out.

"And so were you, apparently." Juliette huffed. "Fine, just don't rat me out when you get caught or I'll make sure there's hell to pay. She's on the second floor, east corridor, fourth door down. You don't know me and we didn't have this conversation."

"But you know *me*!" Jake called after her as she wound her way through the crowd. He looked to Kate, frowning in worry. "What are you planning now?"

"Nothing to concern you," Kate said primly. "You wouldn't approve anyway."

"Kate," Jake said, in a warning tone. But she was already slipping out of the breakfast room, headed for the second floor. "Don't do anything stupid . . . er than you already have!"

Chapter Twenty-Two

Kate's steps were muffled by the thick carpet of the grand staircase as she climbed to the second floor, doing her best to follow Juliette's directions. Which wasn't easy in a house like Hempstead Manor, even sober. When she got to the door in question and tugged at the handle, it held firm. It was locked, which she should have expected given Juliette's need to pick the lock last night. Still, she'd done her fair share of research on lockpicking for the Loretta books, and if Juliette could get it open, she should be able to as well.

"What are you doing?" Jake asked directly behind her.

"Jesus Christ at a church bazaar!" Kate said, spinning around and pressing a hand over her heart.

"What are you doing, Kate?" Jake prompted again, his crossed arms making beautifully defined lines along his forearms and biceps that Kate absolutely refused to acknowledge, despite being unable to look anywhere else.

"I told you, nothing to concern you," Kate said, trying her best to look casual.

Jake took another step closer, his gaze narrowing as he closed the space between them until they were standing chest to chest. Kate tilted her head to meet his gaze, taking a deeper breath than her lungs needed so she could catch the faint scent of sea salt that always lingered on him. He'd been so mad at her earlier, and some of that heat still radiated off him, singeing her skin. When he leaned forward, lowering his voice so that it was more vibration than sound, it rumbled through her like a peal of thunder.

"You're going to snoop in Serena's room. Don't try to deny it. You're a terrible liar."

"And what's it to you if I do?" Kate huffed. "You heard Juliette. Serena has a fake identity, she was ranting about Kennedy *poisoning* Spencer and Simon against her, and she made some cryptic comment about something happening at midnight. Which is when I found Kennedy's body! If she's our poisoner, maybe I'll find the missing champagne glass stashed in her room."

He let out a little sigh, his breath bright and citrusy from the mimosa. "You're going to get caught."

"What do you care? I thought I was a complete waste of your time."

Jake gave her a look. "That's not what I said."

"That's what I remember hearing."

Jake grunted in frustration, running a hand through his wavy hair and somehow making it even wavier and sexier than before, which felt like a personal attack to Kate just then. "Then I'm going with you."

"What? Why?"

"Because the last time I left you to your own devices, you got caught with a dead body!"

"In my defense, she's not actually dead," Kate said.

Jake gave a soft groan of annoyance. "That's not the defense you think it is."

Kate crossed her arms, needing Jake to understand without really understanding herself why. "I found Kennedy's necklace stuffed into the lining of my suitcase earlier today, which was exactly how the killer got caught in Loretta book three."

Jake's eyebrows shot up in surprise. "You have Kennedy's necklace?"

"Not anymore," Kate said, shaking her head. "I snuck into her room and put it with her wedding dress. But someone is trying to make it *look* like I tried to kill Kennedy."

Jake ran his hands through his hair again. "Let me help. If nothing else, I can try to keep you from getting us both in more trouble."

"I will let you help me," Kate said imperiously, "if you happen to have a paperclip or a bobby pin on you."

"Why would I have either one of those things?" Jake asked.

"Fine, something small and pointy?"

Jake regarded her for a moment longer, but eventually he relented and pulled a wallet out of his back pocket, flipping it open and pulling a slim object out of the folds.

"I want to be on the record again as saying this is a bad idea," Jake said, holding out the object. "But, this ought to do the trick."

Kate looked at it in confusion. "What is that?"

"A toothpick," Jake said, motioning for her to take it.

But Kate just kept staring. "Why do you have a toothpick?"

"For emergencies, obviously," he said.

"What kind of toothpick-related emergencies are you having?"

"You'd be surprised. Now, do you want to try it or should we just keep discussing it here in the hall until someone comes round to catch us?"

"Fair point," Kate said, taking the toothpick and crouching before the door handle. "But I want to hear more about these toothpick emergencies later."

Kate felt around with the toothpick until she found something she could push in. The lock clicked, the door handle turning freely. It creaked as she pushed it open, and she tried to time it to a low roll of thunder to hide the sound.

"What are we looking for?" Jake asked as she crept in.

"Evidence," Kate said, pressing the door closed.

"Of course," Jake whispered, voice dripping with sarcasm. "Evidence, I should have known."

"Anything suspicious," Kate whispered, throwing him an annoyed look. The room was pretty small, just a bed-and-dresser set with a smaller door on the back wall. "Something linking her to Kennedy's poisoning, preferably."

"A glass bottle with a skull and crossbones. Got it."

"Just look over there, on the opposite side of the room from me," Kate muttered, half because she was annoyed and half because his skin smelled so warm and inviting.

The bed was full size at most, the covers still neatly tucked under the mattress. Wherever Serena had slept last night, it wasn't in here. Still, her suitcase was on a rack in the corner, the contents spilling out like a vintage dress shop gone mad, as well as a glass of water and a prescription bottle on the nightstand that unfortunately seemed to be filled with ordinary sleeping pills. No rosary peas in sight.

Jake seemed to be coming up similarly empty-handed, giving Kate a shrug from the opposite side of the room, when the door handle gave a warning creak. Someone was coming.

"Hide!" Kate hissed, stumbling across the room toward the door on the opposite wall, grabbing Jake by the arm and dragging him along. The room door swung wide open just as they slipped inside what seemed to be a closet.

". . . heartless bastards wouldn't know a decent cause if it slapped them in the face," came Serena's distinctive voice, breathy and self-important. "If only the others had shown up, we'd have given them a real show. Cowards."

"We did nearly capsize twice trying to get out here," came another voice, reedy and pinched. One of Spencer's more literary authors whose name Kate could never remember. But he'd been among the protesting authors.

"You made it here in one piece, didn't you?" Serena said. "Meanwhile, I was the one waiting out in the rain past midnight, miserable and sopping wet, holding out the signal so you knew where to land. I was the real martyr in all of this."

"Still, staging our protest on a private island during a wedding with a press ban probably wasn't our best idea, was it?"

"Don't be shortsighted," Serena snapped. Her voice had drawn closer to their hiding spot, and Kate desperately pushed through what she hoped to all the gods in all the various religions was just a wall of clothes. "This is only phase one. The little chippy needed to know we could get to her anytime, anyplace, no matter how secluded she thinks she is. We won't be ignored! I've already contacted every major news outlet in Seattle, we'll be on the six o'clock news by Monday, mark my words. They'll hear our lion's roar, and they won't be able to deny our contracts then."

Kate pressed on until she hit what felt like the back wall. There were other things in there, things that tugged at her shirt and scratched along her legs, things that made her want to yelp in terror. It was only Jake's solid presence behind her that kept her from screaming out.

A light flicked on from the far side of the closet door, stretching searching fingers toward her as it swung open. Kate bit down on her lip hard enough that the pain cut through the panic, grabbing Jake's hand and pressing into the deepest corner of the closet. There was something heavy and solid on the floor blocking her way, and as she pushed it out of the way, a breath of stale air puffed in her face. The closet door had opened wide enough now, light spilling in at uneven angles, that she could see a small opening had appeared. A secret passage.

"Simon will have no choice but to give in to all our demands," said Serena, whispering her final savage words. "I'll do what I have to to make sure of it."

Kate pressed into the tiny space between the walls, the air so thick with dust it settled in her lungs like a brick. Jake wedged in after her just as the counterweight in the closet tipped back into place, sealing the door shut. The space was so narrow they could both barely fit, and as Kate felt along in either direction it was clear the space didn't go anywhere. Except now, they had no way to get back out with the secret door shut.

Serena's voice was muffled and distant now, drawing away even as Kate felt the walls of their tiny hiding space pressing in, the exposed beams and the smell of rotting wood hanging in the air and smothering her. She did her best to hold all her feelings in her body, but the panic expanded like a balloon, threatening to pop.

Loretta kicked at the wall with her heavy-soled boot, grunting in frustration. "I should have figured a Prohibition house would have hidden compartments."

"We're stuck, Loretta," came Blake's voice, warm and close and the slightest bit panicked. Loretta would have found it cute, the way his accent sharpened with concern, if she weren't too busy trying to find them a way out. "What are we going to do?"

"If there's a way in, there has to be a way out," Loretta murmured, feeling all along the wall. "We just need to find it."

Kate could barely put her arms out with Jake wedged in the space, much less feel her way around for a secret latch or hidden release. Of course Loretta wouldn't panic, but Kate Valentine didn't have the luxury of knowing her author would rescue her from the worst danger. Meanwhile, the panic had spread into her lungs, the pressure building intolerably, and she let out one tiny squeak.

"Kate," Jake whispered, his body wedged against hers.

"Is this a bad time to remember I'm claustrophobic?" Kate huffed. "Because I am. Very claustrophobic. I'm going to scream."

"You can't."

"No, I know. I know I can't. But I'm going to scream a little bit. One tiny scream."

"Kate," Jake said, his voice desperate. Something thumped against the wall on the other side, the sound going off like a shot in their tiny hiding space. The squeak Kate let out was twice as squeaky.

"I can't hold it in!" Kate said. "I'm sorry."

She could feel Jake holding the breath in his chest, mentally weighing something. He shifted against her, reminding her how much physical contact they were in. The space was suddenly overheated and stifling.

"Kate?" Jake said, more breath than word, his body bent over her.

"What?" she replied, the scream lodged in her throat, clawing its way up her body.

"Are you sober?"

"More than I'd like to be right now," she muttered. "That's kind of a rude question, isn't it? What does that have to do with . . . Oh. Ohhhhhhh."

When I kiss you, it will be for you and me. And you'll be stone-cold sober.

His hand brushed her cheek, found its way into her hair. "May I?"

"Oh god yes," she begged.

His lips grazed hers but she was too impatient, pressing into the kiss with her full body, shoving him back against the false wall. It wasn't a particularly smart move, considering how they'd ended up in that hidey-hole in the first place, but she didn't care if they came tumbling out and someone put an axe in her skull at that particular moment. Because she was stone-cold sober and Jake was finally kissing her.

And holy *shit* was he kissing her. He grabbed her thighs and lifted her up, wrapping them around his waist as he gently pushed her back against the opposite wall, bracing her on a cross beam that put her mouth on a level with his. His tongue was rough against hers, his breath hot as he panted against her lips. His stubble had grown in over the last twenty-four hours, rough and scraping against her mouth as he shifted from her upper lip to her lower lip, pulling it between his teeth. He pressed his groin into hers, the friction dragging groans out of both of them. Kate was pure liquid need, pouring into her center, all of it begging for more contact, more tongue, more friction, more Jake. He rubbed against her again and her eyes rolled back, her head dropping against the wall with a thud.

"Jake," she panted as his lips made their way down her throat to her collarbone.

"Mmm?" he said, sliding his hands up under the hem of her shirt and splaying them out along her rib cage.

Only in the dark could she be this bold. "I want you inside me."

Jake shuddered, grinding against her, his teeth tracing lines along her shoulder. "Don't tempt me, Kate."

It was hard enough, putting together words when Jake's lips were working their way lower. But his hands joined the assault, sliding up under the line of her bra, one thumb grazing her nipple. A jolt shot right down to her lower half, making her gasp.

"Jake, *please*. Please, god, please."

"Mmmm, I like when you call me that," Jake said, grinning against the hollow of her neck. He brought his index finger and thumb together, rolling her nipple.

She thrust one hand into his curls as his mouth and his hand met in the middle, the rough slide of his tongue over her breast sending warning prickles down her thighs. With her other hand she reached up blindly to steady herself, her legs already trembling from the effort of staying braced against the wall. She found a wooden beam and grabbed it for dear life. But the beam shifted in her hand, creaking downward, and the next thing she knew there was a cold rush of air and she was tossed out into another room.

She yelped in surprise as she hit the plush carpeted floor, the impact jolting all the sexiness out of her. Jake had fallen to his knees, still inside the hiding space, his pupils contracting quickly. It was the only part of him that was contracting, the line of his erection thick and obvious against the leg of his jeans. He looked at her in surprise, his hair pulled in every direction by her fingers, his chest rising and falling quickly. His gaze darted down, and she realized one breast was still exposed.

"Oh god," she groaned, quickly tucking it back in. It was one thing to give in to every filthy thought she'd had about Jake when they were trapped in the dark; it was another thing entirely to look him in the eye in the broad—albeit wan—light of day. She wasn't even sure what room they were in, if they were alone, or how they were going to get out. She glanced around, looking anywhere but at Jake, trying to get her bearings.

"Where are we?" she panted, still sprawled out on the carpet, not yet trusting her thighs to support her. All she could see from her disadvantage point was about a thousand potted plants throughout the room. "An indoor jungle?"

"Looks like nobody's here," Jake said, standing up and heading toward her with intent. "Which means we won't be disturbed."

"Wait, wait," Kate said, scooting backward into a plant. "We should talk—"

But the weight of the plant was top-heavy, and as she reached up to steady the pot, the tree itself came crashing down on her, raining leaves everywhere. She cried out in surprise, pushing the tree away on instinct, the branches surprisingly soft and heavy. The weight rolled off, a face turning up toward the ceiling, contorted in terror, sightless eyes like glass marbles.

It wasn't a tree. It was a body.

Chapter Twenty-Three

Kate pressed the heel of her hand against her mouth to muffle her scream as she scrambled across the floor, running into Jake as he reached down to help her up. She clung to him, her skin remembering the cold, rubbery feel of the body against hers, shuddering as she pressed her face into his shoulder.

"Holy shit, is that a body?" Jake asked.

"I think it's Rebecca Hempstead," Kate said.

"What, the Bitch Bull of Wall Street?" Jake asked in surprise.

"Okay, I don't love that *that's* the nickname you remember, but yes." She pressed her eyes closed like that might get rid of the memory of Rebecca's lifeless face, but nope—there it was, behind her eyelids in vivid Technicolor. The woman had been so full of vitality, such a presence yesterday, that it felt like a farce to see her reduced to a cold body.

"What happened to her?" Jake asked.

"Well, I'm pretty sure she died," Kate said. "Judging by the way her dead body just fell on me."

"Yeah, sure, but . . . how? She seemed pretty fine last night when she gave that big speech fucking over her entire family."

"She really did, didn't she?" Kate muttered. Jake had a point—Rebecca had been in the prime of life last night, with no hints of health problems or impending mortality. And with Kennedy's poisoning, it was highly unlikely Rebecca would keel over from natural causes in the same night. Which meant Kate was going to have to go poking around a dead body for the second time this weekend.

Okay, sure. She could do this. At least she wasn't drunk and terrified like she'd been last night. And nobody was accusing her of murder—yet. Plus, at least this time she was pretty sure the body would stay dead.

What would Loretta do?

"We need to examine the body for signs of trauma," Loretta said, using her trusty swizzle stick to lift the edge of the woman's dress along her neck to check for strangulation marks. "No obvious signs of a struggle here, but that doesn't mean there wasn't one. The killer could have cleaned up after themselves. The body will tell us—"

"Kate," Jake prompted. "You all right?"

Right, this wasn't a Loretta case. This was a Kate Valentine case, and Kate was going to have to do her sleuthing herself.

The sight of Aunt Rebecca was no less upsetting on second viewing. Her body had landed face up, her mouth contorted to one side and her lipstick faintly smeared along the upper lip. She was wearing a caftan in a bold, geometric print, not the same outfit she'd had on for the rehearsal dinner. So, whatever happened to her, it happened after dinner. Her hair was looser, too, shiny and slightly mussed, like maybe she'd washed it.

"Well, I don't see any bloodstains, no obvious signs of gunshot wounds or stab wounds," Kate said, gingerly picking up one of Rebecca's hands. Her skin was clammy and stiff, the fingers tightly wrinkled and the palms soft. "No obvious bruising, either. She's not warm, so she's probably been here awhile. Her fingers are all wrinkled up, though. That's weird."

"So, what, a heart attack? Brain bleed? Choked on a peanut?" Jake asked.

Kate gently lifted the woman's head, feeling along her scalp for any kind of abrasions or cuts. "She didn't hit her head. But her hair is kind of . . . damp? That's weird, too, isn't it?"

Jake shrugged. "Maybe she was out in the storm last night?"

Kate shook her head. Rebecca didn't strike her as the type to rough it in the middle of bad weather. She seemed far more like the *take a long, hot bath and read a stuffy book while the servants do all the storm prep* kind of woman. Kate leaned in, lifting a lock of hair and sniffing as if she might catch a hint of shampoo. But Rebecca's hair didn't smell like shampoo.

Kate wrinkled her nose. "She smells funny."

"Well, she's dead," Jake reasoned.

Kate shook her head. "Not that. I mean, also that, but she smells like . . . I don't know. Smell her hair."

Jake snorted. "You're not tricking me into smelling a dead body."

"It's not a trick," Kate said. "Her hair smells almost like . . . chlorine?"

"What, really?"

Kate motioned for Jake to smell it for himself, which he did extremely reluctantly. But he frowned as he straightened up.

"Huh, she *does* smell like chlorine. Is that a smell that dead bodies give off?"

"Not unless they've been in a pool recently," Kate murmured. She shifted Rebecca's head to peer at her face, her lips faintly blue beneath her bold lipstick. There was something white crusted around her nostrils, and as Kate tilted her head back farther to look more closely, her jaw fell slack. "Look at this around her nose. And in her mouth! There's foam."

"Foam?" Jake said, frowning. "You think she, what? Drowned? How is that possible? I didn't see a pool on the estate map Abraham gave us. And how the hell did she end up here? Drowned people don't climb a flight of stairs and hide in a plant."

These were great questions. Kate stood, glad to have a task that didn't involve manhandling a dead body, and peeked through the fern where Rebecca had been stuck. "Hang on, there's something back here."

She pushed past the plants, mindful of any other unsavory hidden surprises, to an antique wooden desk. The wood was a deep, rich brown, the drawers set with gold handles that were no doubt real, the top of the hutch open and decorated in a mini-scale replica of the grand staircase down on the first floor. It even had little carved cherubs the size of Kate's thumb. A flat-screen monitor occupied the center of the desk with a mouse beside it, an old-school tower CPU tucked underneath the desk.

"Kate?" Jake asked from the other side of the ferns. "Did you get lost in the jungle?"

"I think this must have been Rebecca's study," Kate said, sitting in the leather seat that didn't even creak when she tilted it back. Probably didn't dare to squeak in the presence of Rebecca Hempstead. "There's a desk back here, and a computer."

She reached for the mouse beside the screen before remembering to preserve potential fingerprints in case the killer had used the mouse. So, she nudged it instead with her elbow, the screen blinking to life as Jake appeared and leaned over her shoulder, distracting her with his warmth.

"What did you find?" he asked, his voice an intimate vibration in her ear.

"Nothing yet," she said. The computer screen was locked. "It says biometric authentication required."

She peered closer at the mouse and realized the left button was transparent, a small red laser shining up from underneath. It must be some kind of fingerprint reader, coded to only unlock for Rebecca. She grabbed Jake's arm in excitement.

"Fingerprints!" she squealed. "I know what happened! Somebody must have killed her, drowned her in some secret pool somewhere. Then they dragged her body up here to use her fingerprint to unlock the computer. Except her fingers were too wrinkled from the pool, so I bet it didn't work. They must have stashed her body in the fern to come back and try again later."

"What do you think is on her computer worth killing for?" Jake asked.

"You said it yourself, she just gave a big speech fucking over her entire family. I bet whoever killed her wanted access to those trust documents. To stop her from signing over the family fortune and cutting them off."

"You mean like our sullen tablemates last night?" Jake said dryly.

"Or the raccoon-eyed cousin," Kate added. "Or, hell, even Kennedy herself."

Jake tilted his head to the side in consideration. "I don't know, she has an awfully compelling alibi. Mainly that she was technically dead herself at the time."

Kate had to concede that point. "True. Oh, of course! Kennedy's poisoning must have been a distraction, and Rebecca was the real target all along! It makes perfect sense."

"But you said Kennedy's poisoning was staged to look like one of your books, to put you on the hook for killing her," Jake reasoned. "So how does Rebecca's death point to you?"

Was this why Rebecca had invited her for the weekend? Because she suspected someone would be making an attempt on her life? Did she suspect they might be using Kate's own stories to plan their attack? Maybe Rebecca had wanted Kate's insights on who would do this and why, but she hadn't had the chance to ask Kate in private. It made more sense now why she hadn't wanted to talk in front of Richie, if she'd (rightly) suspected him of foul play.

How did Rebecca's death point to Kate? Kennedy's poisoning had been so obvious—the sliver of rosary pea, the necklace stashed in her suitcase, the body at the bottom of the stairs. What was obvious about Rebecca's death? She was obviously drowned, just like—

"It's not me!" Kate gasped, turning suddenly to Jake. "It's *you*."

"What's me?" Jake asked.

"Loretta book one, *Shaken, Stirred, and Stabbed*. Remember? The wealthy older woman goes overboard and drowns on the party boat, and everyone thinks she got drunk and fell in. That's how I knew about the foam in the mouth. But Loretta figures out she was pushed, and Blake takes the blame when they find out he was set to inherit the woman's estate. It's not me they're targeting this time, it's you!"

Jake crossed his arms, looking at her narrowly. "So, what you're say-ing is . . . you finally admit Blake is based on me?"

"No," Kate said, going red in the face. That was exactly what she'd just admitted, wasn't it? "But obviously someone thinks he is. And they think you're here with me this weekend, so they're trying to get to me through you. They're setting you up as my accomplice."

"I knew I was going to regret coming to this thing," Jake muttered. "So, what do we do now? Find the authorities? Report Richie and the lawyer and hold them in island jail or something until the police arrive?"

"We can't do that!" Kate said. "The landlines are down, somebody's already sabotaged the generator, and it's not like we're on the ferry route out here. The only way on or off the island is through the private yacht, and Abraham said it was damaged in the storm. We're stuck here until the weather clears up."

Jake put his hands out in exasperation. "We're just going to hang about on an island with a murderer who's trying to frame us?"

"We need to find where she was actually murdered," Kate said. "There may be critical evidence that will lead to our killer."

"Except I don't remember seeing any pool on the estate map in the welcome bag."

"There wasn't a hidden crawl space between two rooms on the map, either," Kate said, looking at the wall they'd just fallen through. "I'd guess Hempstead Manor has any number of secrets it's still keeping."

"So where do you hide a pool on an island estate?" Jake asked.

"The photographer," Kate said suddenly, putting a hand on Jake's arm. "I remember seeing Rebecca in the background of a picture, com-ing out of a red door, holding a *towel*. That must be where the pool is. There was some kind of stuffed . . . dog, I want to say?"

"Hang on, I know where that is," Jake said. "I found it when I was hunting you down last night. I remember because it was a Tasmanian devil, and I had to wrestle one of those bastards once."

"Wrestle?" Kate whispered in horror.

"Hiking trip gone awry," Jake said dismissively. "That red door is on the ground level."

"Which makes sense for a pool," Kate said, nodding enthusiastically. "That's where we go next."

"One small problem," Jake said, staring meaningfully down at Rebecca's body.

"We can't tell anyone about Rebecca," Kate said. "We don't want the murderer to know we're onto them yet. Who knows what they might do if they feel cornered or panicked. We'll just have to . . . keep this to ourselves, for now."

"For how long?" Jake asked, bewildered. "I think people will notice if Rebecca Hempstead goes missing in her own home on her niece's wedding weekend."

"We'll tell everyone," Kate said, gnawing at her bottom lip after she'd said it. She didn't want to imagine how *that* conversation would go. "Eventually. But we can't waste the element of surprise. If we can catch the killer out in a lie, find the evidence we need before they destroy it, it could make all the difference. Plus, I mean, why ruin Kennedy's wedding? Rebecca's already dead, and she's got to get married. What's the harm in waiting?"

"What do we do about the body, then?" Jake asked.

Kate frowned at the woman, but it wasn't like it was her fault she was such an inconvenience. "Right. She's got to go back in the fern."

Chapter Twenty-Four

"I need the world's *longest, hottest* shower," Kate said twenty minutes later as they exited the room and took the stairs down to the main floor. "Scalding. Skin peeling. I want new skin."

"I've crawled through literal shit, and that was still the grossest thing I've ever done," Jake agreed.

Kate paused by the ornately carved cherub decorating the handrail, reminding her of the tiny-scale replica on Rebecca's desk. "Are you talking about the time you and Fluke escaped that illegal house party by climbing through a sewer system? You said it was a water waste disposal. I thought it was, like, nuclear material."

"Technically, what I said was the water was compromised," Jake said, pushing past her and heading down the stairs.

"I made you sound like a Ninja Turtle!" Kate called out.

"And I told you I felt more like a sewer rat. The door is down this way, I think."

They'd just passed a small alcove with several potted plants arranged around a pair of Grecian columns when Kate heard someone clear their throat. She grabbed Jake on impulse and dragged him into the foliage as Steven the real estate lawyer came striding down the hallway from the opposite direction wearing a pair of bright orange swim shorts and carrying a towel over his shoulder. He moved swiftly out of sight, muttering to himself too low for Kate to hear.

"We must be close," she whispered, trying and failing miserably to ignore how close and warm Jake was, and how very alone they were in that alcove. It was like the crawl space all over again, and Kate wasn't yet ready to process all of *that*. Her thighs were still weak from bracing herself against the wall as Jake—

She pushed him hastily out of their hiding space before her thighs got any more ideas.

"It's just down this way," Jake said, thankfully not privy to her filthy thoughts.

She allowed herself the brief pleasure of watching him walk ahead before she trotted after. Sure enough, there was a stuffed animal with a small gold plaque that identified it as a Tasmanian devil, and Kate wondered how anyone could wrestle such a beast, much less walk away from the encounter smiling. Opposite was the red door Kate recognized from the picture, tucked into another alcove and practically unnoticeable in the dim corridor. There was nothing else in the hallway save a large window a few feet down that showcased the rough surf beyond the island's border, fat drops of rain lashing against the window with a rattle.

"This must be it," Jake said. "I don't think a toothpick is going to cut it this time."

Kate's heart sank as she surveyed the door. This was no old-school lock; in fact, the handle didn't have a lock at all. It had a dead bolt installed above it, and a latch for an additional padlock above the dead bolt. The latch was flipped open, but Kate could see the telltale sliver of silver where the dead bolt was set firmly into the door.

"I don't suppose you know how to pick real locks?" Kate asked Jake hopefully.

"Not among my Jake of All Trades skill set," he said dryly.

"I didn't call you that last night, did I?" Kate winced.

"Among other things," Jake muttered.

Kate debated whether or not to apologize or just crash through the window at the end of the hall and keep running until she walked into the sea. But she was once again saved from either unpleasant option by the click and slide of the dead bolt as the door swung open.

"Oh," said Richie Hempstead, pulling up short just inside the door as a wave of warm, humid air and the distinct scent of chlorine wafted out around him. His hair dripped onto the carpet, his body blocking the door too much for Kate to get a good view past him. "What are you two doing here?"

"We're . . ." Kate looked to Jake, suddenly short on excuses. She'd been handing out so many of them lately, she could hardly keep track anymore.

"We're looking for your aunt," Jake said. "The wedding coordinator needs to know where to move all the wedding decorations. The tent outside got knocked over by the high winds and they have to relocate everything inside."

"You haven't seen her, have you?" Kate asked, looking intently at Richie while also trying to sneak a peek past him. It was pitch black in there, as far as she could tell, and far more humid than it should be considering the chill of the rest of the house.

"No," Richie said slowly, stepping deliberately into the hallway and pulling the door closed. He lifted a chain around his neck, a silver key dangling on it, and threw the dead bolt with a resounding click. He then flipped the latch into place and dug around in a canvas knapsack—which also contained a towel, Kate noted, still damp—and pulled out a padlock. He kept one eye on the two of them, like they might try to kick down the door as soon as he turned his back.

"What's in there?" Kate asked, trying to sound casual. Which was obviously not her forte, based on the hooded expression Richie gave her.

"That's off-limits to guests," Richie said archly. "Family only, I'm afraid."

"Oh, is your aunt in there, maybe?" Kate asked hopefully.

"No," Richie said again, clearly annoyed.

"How do you know?" Kate pressed. "Maybe we should go and check. For Abraham. He seemed pretty frantic about it."

"I know she's not in there, because I just was, and she was not," Richie said.

Kate knew she was pushing her luck, but she needed to know what was behind that door. "Can we take a look? Just to confirm?"

"Mmmm, family members only, if you'll recall me saying that about two sentences ago."

"What about last night?" Jake asked. "Was Rebecca here last night?"

Richie sighed to the ceiling. "I don't know what that has to do with anything, but yes, she was. Briefly. She wasn't feeling well, so she left. Last I heard her, she was having some kind of argument with that Sheffield guy out here in the hallway. She's definitely going to tear Ken a new one for inviting him this weekend. Was that what you were looking for? We done here?"

So, Rebecca had argued with Marcus Sheffield. Interesting. Had he dragged her back to the pool and drowned her later, when Richie was gone? Or were Marcus and Richie in on it together? Kate needed to get back to her murder board and reconsider her suspects. She could find a way into the pool room later, when Richie wasn't guarding the door.

"Do you remember what time that was?" Kate asked.

"Oh my god," Richie muttered, taking out his phone and unlocking it to swipe through his photos app. Kate caught only a glimpse of Richie and Steven smiling into the camera before he tilted it away from her suspiciously. When he did, she spotted a fresh blister on the palm of his otherwise unblemished skin. He slid his phone back into the canvas sack. "A little after eleven, I think. Now, goodbye!"

He started to move past them, and Kate signaled to Jake to distract Richie as she slipped behind him, gently sliding her hand into his canvas sack.

"What would it take, mate, to get an invite to that room?" Jake asked, blocking the hallway.

"I don't know, be born with better genes?" Richie said impatiently. But he paused, looking Jake over. "Actually, I bet you look pretty decent in a set of trunks. We might be doing a little private thing tonight after the ceremony, if you ditch the straight here."

Kate had just snagged his phone and dropped it in the pocket of her cardigan when he looked at her over his shoulder. His gaze traveled up and down her simple attire, making his opinion of her fashion choices apparent.

"Will your, uh, friend be there?" Kate asked. "The lawyer, Steven?"

"Okay, you two are asking a lot of weird questions," Richie said. "And unless you're a hot FBI agent or my fashion-challenged parole officer, I don't have to answer them. Now, if you'll excuse me, I need to get ready. This hair doesn't coif itself."

"Oh, well, don't let us keep you," Kate said.

"Yeah, I'm gonna need the two of you to leave this hallway with me," Richie said, shooing them both along. He muttered to himself as they reluctantly followed in his wake. "Auntie R had a point about not letting commoners in the Manor. Atrocious manners."

Chapter Twenty-Five

Richie abandoned them at the bottom of the grand staircase with another muttered complaint about letting "the plebes" into the Manor, but Kate was already taking the stairs toward the fourth floor two at a time before Richie could finish his classist argument. Jake trotted after her, catching up to her at the third-floor landing.

"Kate!" he called, snagging her sleeve and forcing her to slow down. "Where are you headed now?"

"To the murder board!" Kate said, before remembering nobody else in the house knew about the murder or the murder board. She lowered her voice conspiratorially. "To the murder board. We have a whole new set of suspects to investigate, remember?"

"What was that with Richie back there?" Jake asked as they made the climb to the final floor. The lights buzzed and dipped low before struggling back to a soft yellow glow, yet another indicator that time was not on their side. "What was I distracting him for?"

Kate looked both ways down the hall before hurrying toward the golden pull and the attic room beyond, slipping Richie's phone out of her pocket and holding it up triumphantly. "Richie's phone. I swiped it when he wasn't looking."

"Should I even bother to ask why?" Jake pulled the cord and waved for Kate to climb up first.

"Evidence, Jake. *Evidence.* When Richie was checking what time his aunt left the pool room, I saw a bunch of pictures on his phone from last night. It will give us an idea of what he was up to and who he was with when his aunt was killed. Maybe he's a real sicko and documented the whole thing."

"Again, so gleeful," Jake murmured, pulling the stairs up after them.

"Because this is the second body drop!" Kate said, as if that explained everything. When Jake gave her nothing but a blank stare, she sighed impatiently. "Every good mystery has it. You have your first body drop—Kennedy—and it sets our detective off in one direction. But then you get the second body drop, and it changes up the whole investigation! See, that's why our suspect list wasn't working, because we were investigating the *wrong murder.* For all we know, Kennedy's poisoning was a distraction so the killer could deal with the real target—Rebecca Hempstead. We've got a whole new set of suspects to consider, with a whole different set of motives and alibis to line up. This is the break we needed. I can feel it in my sweater."

Kate scratched fiercely at the soft insides of her elbows as if to emphasize the sleuthing sweater in effect. Jake shook his head.

"Are you sure you aren't just itching because that wool is scratchy?" he asked.

"Don't be a Geoff," Kate muttered, turning toward the list of suspects taped up all over the walls.

"Did you just accuse me of being a *Geoff*?" Jake asked, sounding truly offended. "The buzzkill boss who never believes in Loretta but whom she inexplicably keeps dating even though he's a complete twat? When I'm so obviously the Blake in your life? The hot wakeboarding British bartender who would follow Loretta to the ends of the earth if she said there was a murderer to catch there."

"Yeah, well, *be* a Blake, then," Kate said, pulling a Sharpie from her bag and thrusting it at him. "Start listing new suspects."

"I will," Jake said, taking the pen decisively. Here he was again, so willing to play the Blake to her Loretta, encouraging her wild hair to investigate instead of castigating her like Spencer would have done. She hadn't realized how alone she'd felt the last six months, and really the last two years, without him. And now that she'd had him around, even for a weekend, she wasn't sure how to let him go again. The thought of it made her stomach rumble perilously.

"Richie Hempstead obviously goes on the list," Jake said, oblivious to her fraught epiphany as he wrote out Richie's name in big, bold print. "He admitted to being in the pool room with his aunt last night, and apparently, only family members have a key to access the room. And he was pretty upset with Rebecca over the trust announcement. Plus, did you see his hand?"

"The blister!" Kate exclaimed, happy to lose herself in the investigation and ignore those pesky feelings trying to get in the way. "You saw it, too?"

"He's obviously our saboteur," Jake said sagely. "That's the kind of blister you get from working a handsaw without proper gloves. I'd put good money on Richie being the one who cut the generator line."

"If you want to put good money on someone, put his lover on there, too," Kate said, stepping up beside Jake and writing /Steven Moyers beside Richie's name. "He was there last night, too. Plus, he was trying to convince Rebecca to make some shady real estate deal. They're obviously in on it together. If Rebecca's dead, there's no one to complete the petition process for historical designation. The island is open for business again."

"You think he killed her over a real estate deal?" Jake asked.

"People have been killed over a lot less," Kate reasoned. "And we're talking about a multimillion-dollar deal, which means Steven's cut, if he manages the sale, would be astronomical. For all I know, the guy could have a gambling problem. Maybe he likes the ponies but the ponies don't like him."

"That guy didn't look like he had a problem with the ponies," Jake said. "He looked like his wallet has a padlock on it. Though it would make sense if both of them tried to kill Rebecca and Kennedy, since that would put Richie next in line to inherit, right?"

"Good point!" Kate said, waving at the sheet. "Add it to the motive. Whoever killed Rebecca could easily have targeted Kennedy as well, and Richie is a prime suspect in that regard."

"But we still don't know how Steven would have gotten into the bridal suite or gotten Kennedy down to the wine cave without being spotted."

"Which leads me to my next suspect," Kate said, wielding her pen dramatically. "Kennedy Hempstead. She's the heir, she just had a big falling out with her aunt over holding the wedding here, and she also seemed upset that her aunt was giving away the family farm. She said she wanted to be sure the island stayed with people who would properly care for it."

"But we already established she was poisoned at the time."

"Which is exactly the kind of thing a diabolical mastermind would do to escape suspicion," Kate countered. "Consider this—it's pretty amazing she had enough poison in her system to knock her out, but not kill her. That takes some precise measuring. Now, do I think Kennedy Hempstead is a diabolical mastermind? Behind that sweet, people-pleasing demeanor?"

Could she imagine it? Of course she could, she was a writer; she could imagine anything. It would certainly fit right into a Loretta novel. In fact, she would log that idea away for a potential book four storyline. But did she really think Kennedy Hempstead was a true psychopath, playing a role her entire life, biding her time to strike? She was the exact kind of nice that could mean she was hiding something. Kate couldn't quite rule it out, even though it made her feel strange to put Kennedy's name up on a fresh sheet of paper.

Jake narrowed his gaze on her. "Would that make you feel better about everything, if Kennedy did kill her aunt?"

"What?" Kate asked. "What is that supposed to mean?"

But Jake shook his head, clearly already regretting having said anything. "Never mind. Kennedy goes on the board. Who else?"

Kate frowned at him, but he refused to look at her, so she grabbed another sheet of paper. "Cassidy, the cousin. Remember, we saw her arguing with Rebecca in the garden when we first arrived. My guess is she was begging Rebecca to put her back in the will and Rebecca refused. Apparently, she's got some huge debts from a busted food truck business. Her life is in financial ruin, her aunt has ample means to save her, and yet she won't over some old family squabble. Whatever she said to Rebecca was enough to make her aunt slap her. Maybe she thought if she got Rebecca out of the way, Kennedy might be more forgiving as the new heir. They're basically like sisters, according to Kennedy."

"Speaking of old petty squabbles," Jake said, "what about the guy in the portrait hall? Didn't Richie say he heard his aunt arguing with him when she left the pool room?"

"And he said the Bitch Bull was finally going to be castrated," Kate agreed, nodding. "Marcus Sheffield. Maybe he saw his chance this weekend to exact revenge against Rebecca ruining his company and his life all those years ago."

"Doesn't really explain why he'd poison Kennedy, though," Jake said. Still, he wrote Sheffield's name beneath Cassidy's.

"Good point," Kate conceded. "But maybe it was the distraction he needed, like I said. And it would explain why she was poisoned enough to knock her out, but not enough to kill her. Because she wasn't his real target all along."

Jake gave a low whistle. "Now *that's* a diabolical mastermind. Poisoning his son's goddaughter so he could kill a woman he thought about marrying decades ago."

"I know, right?" Kate said, nodding enthusiastically.

"Why set you up to take the fall for it all, though?" Jake asked. "You've never even met Marcus, have you?"

"No," Kate conceded. "But even I have to admit I make a pretty good patsy. I mean, someone's got to take the fall for a murder, and after the whole rehearsal dinner thing last night, everybody was real quick to believe I'd poisoned Kennedy. Why not her aunt, too? And this weekend is tailor-made to fit my last book. It writes itself. It's like I wrote it as a practice run or something. Someone's obviously setting me up to look unhinged. But they don't know just how unhinged I can be. In a good, catch-a-killer kind of way, I mean."

Jake gave a funny little laugh. "You really are a special breed, aren't you, Kate?"

Kate tilted her head to the side. "I'm not sure if that's a compliment or an insult."

"You know, I'm not really sure, either. What I am sure of, though, is that it's never boring with you around."

Kate grinned, pointing at him. "Now, see, that one *almost* sounded like a compliment."

Jake smiled. "You know, I almost meant it as one."

They stood like that, smiling like idiots at each other, and for a moment Kate could convince herself that everything was fine between them. That nothing happened two years ago, that they were still friends who hadn't just made out in a crawl space while tracking down a murderer. That her feelings for Jake weren't a mishmash of hope and fear and a longing so deep it scared her. But apparently she wasn't doing any better of a job at keeping those thoughts off her face than she was at keeping them out of her head, because Jake's expression shifted the longer he looked at her.

"Kate," he began, and she knew she didn't want to hear whatever words were on the other side of her name.

"We should go interrogate!" she said loudly, waving at the suspect list. "Before we, you know, run out of generator power. Or the storm destroys the house. Or the murderer figures out we're onto them and we're next."

Jake took a breath, forcing it out in a sigh as he reached for her shoulders and turned her to face him. "Kate, I'm going to say something."

"I don't think you need to do that."

"I do. And these things historically go tits up between us, so I'm going to try to be as clear as possible so you don't misunderstand me. I want to have sex with you."

She blinked several times, waiting for her brain to catch up and tell her she'd misheard, or misunderstood, or mis . . . something. But Jake was still there, his hands still on her arms, his gorgeously gorgeous face still looking intently at hers.

"What?"

"Normally I would think I'd made that plenty obvious, but communication with you on this topic has always been a bit dicey. So I thought, better to just come out and say it. I'd really like to have sex with you. Very badly. Right now, preferably."

Whatever her brain was doing, her body got the message loud and clear, her heart thumping hard and her belly warming and buzzing in anticipation. But her mouth was too connected to her brain, and all that came out was "Why?"

His brows arched up. "Why do I want to have sex with you?"

Kate shook her head. "No, I mean . . . why now? You rejected me last night!"

"Last night when you were drunk off your ass and said we were making a huge mistake?" Jake asked. "*That* last night?"

"Okay, fine, but what about two years ago?" Kate demanded. She lowered her voice, as if anyone might overhear them alone in the attic. "What about *the incident*?"

Jake leaned in, his expression intent. "What *incident*?"

Great. Fucking great. The biggest regret of her life and he didn't even remember it. Of course he didn't, he was Jake Freaking Hawkins. He probably had to fend off girls throwing themselves at him all the time. They probably blurred together.

Kate gave a huff of impending embarrassment. She was really going to have to recount the whole sordid thing for him. "The *incident* where I tried to kiss you in my apartment and you totally turned me down. That incident?"

Jake's lips screwed up in a contemplative frown. "Are you talking about the night you made those awful watery margaritas?"

"It was the blender's fault!" Kate protested. "And, yes, I'm talking about *that night.*"

Jake crossed his arms, studying her for a long moment. "What exactly do you remember about that night?"

Oh good, they weren't done reliving her humiliation. "I remember you coming over to pitch ideas for a third *Wandering Australian* book, and I remember talking about the novel I'd sold to Spencer."

Jake nodded. "The first Loretta book, I remember. Go on, what then?"

"Are you really going to make me do this?" Kate whispered.

"Oh, I definitely am. What happened next?"

Kate sighed to the ceiling, digging back into that awful memory she'd buried for two years. "I remember you talking about a new business venture, too. That you were going to join up with your friend . . . I want to say his name was Trout? But that's not a human name."

"Trent. Go on."

"Trent! Yes, Trent. So, Trent was starting this new extreme adventure tourism company, and he wanted you to join as a partner and lead the expeditions. Which meant you'd be gone six months at a time."

Jake's gaze was steady, unrelenting. "And then what happened?"

"I . . . remember I accidentally emptied the whole bottle of tequila into the next batch of margaritas because I thought it would somehow make it less watery? Which, in hindsight, is ludicrous, but I'd already had three of them by that point. And I remember you saying you'd have to call an ambulance instead of a rideshare if you drank any more of them, so I said I would finish off the batch because it was good tequila and I couldn't let it go to waste."

Jake tilted his head to the side in question. "You see where this is going?"

Kate huffed out a sigh. "So, I got a . . . little drunk."

"A little?" Jake gave a disbelieving laugh. "Kate, you tried to prank call the *police*. Lucky for both of us you dialed 822 instead and got some weird answering machine. On which you left, if I recall, a *very* racy voicemail."

Kate winced. She didn't remember leaving a voicemail, but she did have a sudden memory of advertising mustache rides for a dollar.

"And then you swore you could climb the fire escape to the roof to look at the stars, despite it being rainy that night and your building not even having a fire escape. And, if all that wasn't bad enough, you tried to kiss me while promising it was just for the night and nobody would find out. Like I was some kind of . . . shameful secret. You were a complete mess, Kate. I told you last night I wouldn't take advantage of you like that, and I wouldn't have done it two years ago, either. We were friends, Kate. I cared about you. And, yeah, maybe it could have been something more, but you were always going on about maintaining a professional relationship, not crossing professional boundaries. I figured it was your way of telling me you weren't interested. And after I left and I heard you and Spencer started dating, I knew that was it."

"Jake, are you *crazy*?" Kate could have laughed, if it weren't all driving her crazy, too. "I only said all that stuff to remind *myself* not to make a move on you, which obviously didn't work when it came down to it. You had all these stories of your wild adventures and the girls you'd been with. I knew if I let you, you would . . ."

Well, she couldn't come out and say he'd break her heart and ruin her for any other man, could she?

"Meanwhile," Jake continued, "I get a call from Spencer two days later saying they were putting another cowriter on the *Wandering Australian* book because you were too busy with Loretta edits to write a third book. And it pissed me off, sure, but I wanted you to succeed. I thought Loretta sounded brilliant, and I knew you'd do a cracking job with it. And you did. But you dodged my calls and texts, you iced me out when I came to your apartment to talk to you, and it was like I just . . . it was like you couldn't give a fuck about me. Like you'd had your success out of me, and now you were on to bigger and shinier things. It fucking *hurt*."

Kate's eyes went wide. "You think that was over Loretta? *You* were the one who asked to stop working with *me*."

"What?" Jake said, incredulous. "I never said that. Why would you think that?"

"Spencer called me the day after *the incident* and said you'd called him up and said that I had crossed a professional line and you weren't comfortable working with me anymore." Kate buried her head in her hands, her face glowing hot. "And you were right. I definitely crossed a line and you had every right to not want to work with me anymore. But then you were just so . . . so mad that night outside my apartment. I know I fucked up, but I don't do spontaneous confrontation, okay? I need prep time. I need flowcharts and alternate scenarios and maybe some light dialogue prep. And then you said you were gonna leave the fucking *country* and I don't know. I guess it . . . I don't know. It . . . broke me."

"Kate," Jake said, stunned. He didn't try to touch her, which she didn't think she could handle just then.

"I thought we were friends," she said, and oh god, here they came. The snotterworks. Why couldn't she be a dainty crier, like Natalie Portman or something? Maybe they got surgery, actresses. Tear-duct reductions or something, so only one solitary tear could trail down their perfectly sculpted cheeks. "But I guess I messed that up, didn't I? I shouldn't have tried to kiss you, I know. I was drunk, which is obviously no excuse. And I was scared, also not an excuse. You were talking about Trout and the adventure business, and how you'd be gone for months at a time. I always knew you would leave someday. I knew you couldn't stay in one place for very long, but I guess I thought . . . I don't know, some dumb part of me thought maybe you would stay instead. Just for funsies. It wasn't fair, and I had no right. And I know these all sound like excuses and I swear they're not. Or maybe they are?"

"Kate," Jake said, and now he did touch her, his hand sliding up along the side of her face to thumb away her tears. And it was just as unbearable as she'd thought it would be, even as she hiccupped a little and leaned into it. "Kate, I never called Spencer."

"I said sorry! Wait. What did you say?" She looked up at him with big eyes; his gaze so serious. Boring into her, seeing right through all the artifices she'd worked so hard to put in place this weekend, all of them stripped away one disaster at a time.

"I said, I never called Spencer. I never would have called Spencer, because I was never upset with you for trying to kiss me. I wanted you to kiss me. I wanted to kiss you. I want to kiss you right now. But not as some drunken mistake you could laugh off later. I was only pissed because I thought you were trying to get rid of me. Like you didn't care. If I had known what you were actually feeling, I might have given you more time and space to cool off. I had no idea about Spencer calling you. I don't even know how he would have found out. I certainly never told him."

"I definitely never did," Kate said, shaking her head. "Or maybe I did? I don't know, I was kind of a mess that night. I could ask Spencer."

"Oh, don't worry, I've got some questions for him," Jake said darkly, heading for the attic trap door. "Questions that might involve my fist and his face."

Kate grabbed his hand. "Jake, wait."

"I know it's his wedding, Kate, but the twat deserves it."

"I know he does," Kate said. She barely had the courage to look at him, much less ask what she really wanted to know. "But . . . what . . . what would you have done? If I'd been sober, if Spencer hadn't interfered. What would you have done?"

Jake's gaze shifted, the pupils expanding. "You want to know what I would have done?"

Kate nodded, swallowing loudly. "I think . . . Yes. I want to know."

He stepped close enough that she took an instinctive step back, her calves bumping into the overstuffed chair. Jake closed the space, his thighs brushing hers, his hand feathering along her jaw and down her neck. He gave her the faintest smile, his fingers digging into her scalp, pulling her mouth toward his. "What if I show you instead?"

Chapter Twenty-Six

It was one thing, kissing Jake Hawkins in the dark, and another to kiss him now, face-to-face, with the soft lamplight dusting his lashes and burnishing his hair like a sunset. She could tell now that kissing him in that crawl space had been like a fantasy, all touch and taste and physical reaction. But the little glimpses of Jake she took between breaths, the deep blue rim of his half-closed eyes, the soft line where his neck sloped into his collar bone, the tickle of a wayward curl against her forehead, all of it was so very deeply *Jake*.

Jake, who always smelled of the ocean; Jake, who patiently recounted his travel stories while she scribbled down her notes; Jake, who made sure he brought fresh flowers every time he saw his aunt because that's what her late husband would do; Jake, with his sexy accent and easy smile and super-human patience. This was something more than want, something more than lust, and something that completely terrified Kate. But she couldn't stop herself from giving into it just then, even if she wanted to. Which she absolutely did not.

Jake took his time with her, his hands staying firmly above her neck, his tongue running along the soft skin of her upper lip, his teeth tugging at her lower lip. She groaned and leaned into him, chasing that tongue, too hungry for decorum. But he only leaned her gently away from him, his thighs pressing against hers, his lips trailing across her cheek to her ear.

"I've waited years for this," he said, his breath warming the inner shell of her ear. "And I'm going to take my time. Every last minute of it, Kate. Until neither of us can stand up again."

Kate gasped as his teeth sunk into her earlobe, his tongue flicking against the soft tissue there, turning the lower half of her liquid. He slid his hands down to her waist and held her tight against him, kissing her as he slowly turned her and walked her back toward the bed. They had far too many clothes on for Kate's taste, and she tugged impatiently at the hem of his sweater. He gladly drew it up over his head and tossed it to the side, returning the favor and tossing her sleuthing sweater and her shirt in the overstuffed chair. She was down to her bra and leggings, and suddenly self-conscious about which underwear she'd chosen that morning. When she'd packed for this weekend, sex with Jake Hawkins had genuinely been the furthest thing from her mind.

Not that she was complaining.

"God, you're so soft." Jake groaned, burying his mouth where her neck and collarbone met. He ran his tongue along the bone there, swirling it in the hollow at the base. "And you taste so good. Like a ripe, luscious fruit."

"That might be actual fruit. I dropped a cantaloupe on myself at the breakfast bar." Kate sighed, pushing him back a little. "No fair. You shouldn't get to do all the tasting."

Jake's gaze was practically feral, but he bowed his head with a small grin. "By all means, ladies first."

Where to start with Jake Hawkins? How many parts of him had she imagined tasting? All of them. All of the parts. And now here he was, and she didn't even know where to start. She reached out hesitantly, putting a hand on his stomach, feeling the bands of muscle there. His breath caught as she slid her fingers up, brushing his nipple. She leaned forward and gently ran her tongue around the edge, scraping her teeth gently over the tip.

"Kate," Jake said, his voice choked.

"You don't like it?" she said, burying a smile.

"Now I know you're teasing," Jake said, his words thick.

"Maybe," she said, letting her hands slide down his belly toward the button on his jeans.

"Oh, I don't think so," he said, catching her hand. "My turn now."

"I don't know what you—" she started to say, but her bra was unhooked and on the floor before she could finish the sentence, and the rest of the thought evaporated as Jake lowered his head, fixing his mouth on her nipple. "Oh my *god*."

"That's more like it," Jake said, his lips stretching in a smile against her skin.

Kate could only put her hands on his shoulders and hold on as he ran his tongue from one tip to the other, bringing up one hand to cup the weight of one breast as he sucked on the other. It was a shock, the erotic intimacy, as he rolled her nipple between his fingers.

"I knew you'd have the most incredible breasts," he said, running his nose against the sensitive flesh there. "You're always wearing cardigans and sweaters, but I knew. I could tell they'd have weight."

Kate sighed, cradling his head and tipping her own back. Her leggings were already feeling too restrictive, too abrasive, chafing against sensitive thighs as he eased her back on the narrow mattress. He hovered over her, arms braced on either side.

"Kate, love, you deserve a four-poster king. Soft pillows and cool silk sheets. You're absolutely incredible. Smart, funny, sexy as hell."

She reached up for his shoulders, her voice surprisingly thick. "I'd rather be on a twin bed in a haunted attic with you than on a four-poster bed with anyone else."

Jake's only response was a groan as he lowered his head to kiss her, no longer slow and gentle but rough and urgent, the pressure of his body over hers pushing her down into the mattress. Kate gasped as his chest pressed against her, the skin-to-skin contact so intimate she nearly came right then and there. His tongue swept against hers as she ran her hands up his back, teasing every bunch and stretch of his muscles there, her nails scratching over the lines of scars. Jake hissed in a breath and she stopped, frowning.

"Does it hurt?" she asked, curling her fingers into fists to keep from the temptation of touching him again.

"The opposite," he said, kissing the corner of her mouth and down her jaw. "I'm just not used to it."

Kate wanted to ask if anyone else had touched them, if other women—of course there had been other women, this was *Jake Hawkins*, after all—if other women had run their fingernails over them. If they'd held a small piece of their heart for Jake and the pain of his past like she did. No matter how hard she'd tried to cut that piece of her heart out.

"I don't have to touch them, if it bothers you," she said, sighing as his lips found her nipple again. Her back arched of its volition, pressing her breast into his mouth. "I know you don't like talking about it."

He raised his head slightly before running his tongue along the soft flesh under her breast. "If you're able to talk, I'm not doing my job well enough."

"Oh, I think you're doing . . . you're doing . . . swell," she said, sighing again as he moved down her stomach. "This is just . . . what my brain does."

"Swell," Jake said, chuckling against her stomach, planting a kiss just above her belly button. "You really are a treasure."

"Do you ever miss it?" Kate asked, tangling her fingers into his hair.

"Surfing?" He paused over her hips, running his fingers up her sides and back down, making her shiver. "Sometimes, but not often. I'll always love the ocean, but she's not the kind and gentle mistress people think she is when they're watching from the beach."

"That I believe," Kate said, remembering the swell and crash of the waves when they arrived. She closed her eyes and tilted her neck back as Jake's fingers swept just under the waistband of her leggings, raising goose bumps all along her legs. "Still, I always imagined you might take me out one day and show me how. To surf."

Jake's hands paused on her hips, just over the stretchy fabric of her leggings, and after a moment she opened her eyes to look at him. Oh great, she'd fucked it up again, talking about a commitment beyond here and now. Jake didn't do commitments.

"For the books, I mean," she said hastily. "You know how I like to do my research before I write. Not today, though. Today is for . . . other things."

"Right," Jake said, his gaze shuttering as it moved down her body, growing hot again. "Other things like these leggings being somewhere else."

"Oh," she said, words rapidly failing her at the look in his eyes.

"Lift your hips," Jake said, his voice suddenly gruff.

She pressed up obediently as he hooked his fingers in the waistband, sliding her leggings and her underwear down her thighs, slow and sensual. It had been a good while since she'd made any attempts at personal grooming, but luckily she'd made a trip to her aesthetician before the weekend. That painful waxing was paying off as Jake freed her feet and tossed the leggings aside, swallowing loudly as he gently opened her legs.

"Oh, that's not . . . You don't . . ."

Jake met her gaze, holding her knees in place, his touch still gentle. "I won't do anything you don't want me to, Kate. But I'd like to taste you."

Oh god, how could she refuse *that*? She nodded wordlessly, letting her head fall back. Her legs shook, her breath came in short pants, and her heart hammered away in her chest. No one had been between her legs in years—not even Spencer, not that she could conjure up his particular name at the moment. But she'd never really enjoyed oral sex, had only come twice when Spencer had tried it, and had eventually asked him not to do it. She had assumed it just wasn't for her, that she worked differently.

But the first lazy, mischievous swipe of Jake's tongue nearly sent her off the mattress. He flicked the tip of his tongue against her clit and it shot straight up her spinal cord and lit up all the pleasure centers of her brain, making her gasp. He kissed her softly, sucking slightly, and her fingers buried themselves in his curls.

"Did you like that?" he asked, the smile in his tone.

"Like is . . . an understatement," Kate panted.

"Good." Jake laughed, sliding a finger inside her.

His tongue and fingers worked in tandem, her muscles tightening with each assault until she was crying out his name, edging on the precipice of glory. But every time it felt like she might tip over the edge, he slowed his pace, his tongue roving, his free hand caressing the curve of her calf. And when Kate's heart would slow, the thudding in her flesh subsiding, he slid a second finger in, stretching her, working her until she was nearly screaming.

"That's . . . not . . . fair," Kate finally managed, when he'd brought her up and let her sink back down a third time.

"Was there something you wanted?" Jake said, his voice so buttery and teasing. "All you have to do is ask. Nicely."

"Jake, please," she said, as he curled his fingers and made every muscle in her body clench.

"Please what?" he asked, his tongue swirling just around her clit without touching it.

"Please, Jake—Oh *god*, please. Please make me come."

"Only because you asked so kindly," Jake said, giving her a wicked smile from between her thighs before dipping his head again.

And now she knew he'd only been playing with her this whole time. His tongue pressed against her, rough and hard and quick, and her climax came so fast she swore she could see into another dimension. It rode through her like the coming of the end-times, bowing her back and stealing her breath, her entire body shuddering. Fireworks of every color exploded behind her lids. It was almost a relief when Jake slid his fingers out and sat back on his heels, watching her like he could devour her whole. Which he sort of had done.

"That was . . ." She lay back, staring up at the ceiling, the lights flickering around her. "I don't . . . They haven't invented a word yet for what that was."

"Good?" Jake said, holding back a laugh.

"How dare you," Kate said accusingly. " 'Good' is an insult. A slap in the face."

Jake's body shook with the effort to keep from laughing. "So, great, then?"

Kate smacked him with her knee. "Such impudence."

The lights flickered, dropping out for a moment before buzzing back to life at a dimmer level, and Kate realized it wasn't just the aftereffects of her orgasm.

"What's going on with the—" Kate began to say, but a sharp, abrupt sound sent her upright in a panic. She couldn't quite make it out, and there was a brief, heavy lull as the sound dissipated. Maybe she'd imagined—

But no, there it was again, somehow louder and more insistent. A blaring, harsh alarm clanging through the house as the lights buzzed dangerously low again.

Chapter Twenty-Seven

Kate barely had time to slip her clothes back on, her hair in disarray and her shirt inside out. Jake had to support her down the rickety stairs so she didn't lose her balance on shaky thighs, as other concerned wedding guests popped their heads out of their rooms. The alarm blared on, jangling her nerves.

"I didn't even realize this place had an alarm!" Kate cried over the sound. At first it had seemed to be coming from everywhere, but now she realized that was because it was coming from the head of the stairs, down on the first floor. It was simply echoing up, spreading through the house like a virus and drawing out the various weekend guests.

"The question is, what's it for?" Jake called out as they pushed their way through the crowd down to the third floor and headed for the second. "It sounds like a Klaxon from a sci-fi movie in the seventies. Which fits this place, I guess, only I haven't seen any—"

Jake stopped abruptly as they reached the second-floor landing. The first floor was too crowded to go any farther. They could see over the railing to the main entryway and the source of the alarm. Abraham stood on the black-and-white tiles, phone in his hand, the alarm blaring from the tinny speakers. Kate was shocked it had reached the fourth floor, until

Abraham lifted what looked like some kind of megaphone and played the alarm through the mouthpiece. The sound amplified tenfold, slightly screechy, and she winced and covered her ears.

"Aw, what the hell?" griped Spencer's brother, Eric, in half a tux and basketball shorts. "I was mid-poop!"

Abraham gave a professional, apologetic grimace as he turned off the alarm on his phone and lifted the megaphone to his mouth. "Apologies for the alarming measures, but we have a few small problems. Well, not so small. Our fuel supply on the generator is running just a smidge lower than we anticipated. The new storm cell has apparently decided to change course and come directly over the island within the next hour, and we'll most likely lose power again. For good this time. And the place might flood. Historic houses, folks, am I right? So! The wedding ceremony originally planned for two o'clock is being moved up to now. As in, right now. As in, you all have twenty minutes to get dressed and make it down to the sunroom, which you'll find marked on your estate maps. So . . . hurry!"

His voice cracked on the last word, and the megaphone caught the beginnings of a lengthy and imaginative curse before he shut the power off, shooing guests back to their rooms to prepare for the ceremony. Several of the guests were loudly protesting a variety of issues—including Eric's aforementioned bathroom woes—but Kate spotted one guest in particular who was putting up such a fuss that Abraham and two of the burlier men on the waitstaff had corralled him off to a corner. Kate headed down the stairs for a closer look.

"You can't keep us here like this!" bellowed Marcus Sheffield, eyes bloodshot and cheeks puffed out and red. He was putting on a good show of it, shoving against the waitstaff, calling out for civil rights attorneys, swearing vengeance on anyone and everyone who came near him.

"Sir, please," Abraham said, his professional veneer as thin as black ice as Kate and Jake approached. "For your own safety—"

"I'm not staying one more minute in this hell house!" Marcus shouted, the wave of whisky breath rolling out of him so potent that

Kate was impressed the man still stood. "You've got no right to hold me here, and I want off this damn island!"

"What's the problem?" Kate whispered to Jean-Pierre.

"A shorter list would be to ask what isn't the problem," the Frenchman said in a clipped tone. He glanced at her, doing a hasty double take. "The ceremony is in eighteen minutes."

"I meant with him," Kate asked, pointing at Marcus as he threatened to wrestle the two servers. "What's got him so rattled?"

"He claims to be the victim of some sort of conspiracy, and he's already threatened to sue both Ms. Hempsteads, Abraham, and the American Civil Liberties Union. I'm not sure what the last one is or how it factors in, but this is why I always advocate no alcohol before the ceremony. There's always a drunk uncle."

"Why is he threatening to sue Rebecca and Kennedy?" Kate asked. "What kind of conspiracy is he talking about?"

Jean-Pierre gave her the longest of long-suffering looks. "We have no water, no power, the catering company could not deliver the wedding day dinner so we are scraping together meals from what exists in the kitchen now, my décor is ruined, and there is no DJ or officiant. Please. I beg of you. Plague me no more."

"Right, yep," Kate said, nodding in sympathy. She glanced again at Marcus Sheffield. "You know what? Why don't we help you guys out and take him off your hands?"

Jean-Pierre eyed Kate's frame. "And how could you possibly do that?"

Kate smiled broadly. "By giving him what he wants. Mr. Sheffield? Mr. Sheffield!"

"What? Who's that? Whaddya want?" Sheffield turned his bleary gaze toward Kate, huffing like a dragon that had run out of fire.

"Mr. Sheffield, why don't you come with me and we can let these guys get back to the ceremony?" Kate offered. She stepped past the burly waitstaff, leaning in conspiratorially. "I know where Rebecca keeps the good whisky."

"That right?" Marcus said, straightening up and suddenly playing the good citizen. "Sorry I had to get up on my hind legs with you boys, but a man can only take so much."

"We'll be going now," Kate said, leading him past Abraham and Jean-Pierre with a wink. She gestured to Jake to follow after her, leading Marcus toward the storage room Marla had shown her the night before, when everything had felt like it might actually proceed reasonably. "You know, Mr. Sheffield, I know how you feel about this place. The whole island must be cursed. I mean, think of it. No power, no water, a storm that wants to wipe us off the map. It's like something is drawing the bad energy here. Or some*one*, if you know what I mean. We need to get the hell out of here before it takes us down with her."

"Damn right," Marcus barked, punching a fist in the air for emphasis. "The Bitch Bull is going to get what she deserves, one way or another."

Kate gave Jake a meaningful look as they slipped into the storage room. The place looked like it had been raided once already, but she found a bottle of the awful wine and unscrewed the cap, handing it over to Marcus. She figured he wasn't in a state to complain about the palate.

"Rebecca Hempstead, huh?" Jake said, leaning casually against a crate. "She's a real piece of work. That speech she gave last night—yikes."

Marcus snorted, a fleck of red wine speckling his shirt. "That's nothing compared to what she did to me twenty years ago. Destroyed my family's legacy, put good people out of work, and all over some big stupid misunderstanding from when we were kids."

"You were going to get married, right?" Kate said as he took another swig. "Really dodged that bullet, didn't you?"

"You don't know the half of it! She thinks I took some kind of lousy payout from her dad, the devil take his soul. But I didn't even want the money! Not back then. I loved her, if you can believe it. When we met, Rebecca was like . . . well, she was like a wild filly. Always thumbing her nose at the old man, staging protests at his manufacturing mill over environmental concerns. You know she had a motorcycle? Yeah, rode around town on a Kawasaki. She had long hair, all the way down to that peach of an ass. Man, could she ride."

He sighed into the wine, making a low, forlorn whistling sound down in the bottle.

"What happened to her?" Kate asked, genuinely curious. That description wasn't remotely like the woman she met yesterday, and certainly not the Bitch Bull's reputation.

"What always happens? Money." Marcus scoffed. "Money changes people, you mark my words. Takes a hot piece of ass like Rebecca and turns her into the bitter old crone she is now. She went from caring about things that mattered to caring about the share price on a stock. IPOs and mergers and whatever other crap gets her off now. That's why I broke off the engagement. The sad truth of it was, I just didn't like her no more. Didn't recognize her. It'll happen to little Kennedy, too, you quote me on that. There's no saving somebody from the poison of inheriting a pile like that. She's already turning into a crone, just like her aunt."

"What did Kennedy do?" Jake asked.

"She tricked me into coming here!" Marcus burst out, throwing his arms wide and splashing wine on the floor. "That's what. Told me it would mean the world to her if I was here. She promised to talk her aunt into giving my company back. Letting me buy it over time, soon as I could get the works up and running. You know that bitch gutted all our holdings as soon as she took over? She's not even running the damn company, but she won't release the name. That's my family's name, and she'd rather keep it to spit on than let me have it back and build it into something worthwhile again."

"Is that why you were arguing with her last night?" Kate gently asked. "Her nephew, Richie Hempstead, heard you fighting about something outside the pool room last night."

"She just wouldn't see reason!" Marcus said. "And Kennedy, that little two-faced bitch. I get here and find out she hadn't even spoken to Rebecca! I fly all the way to Seattle, take that crummy skiff out here, and spend the weekend simping around Rebecca's hell house, for what? For Kennedy to tell me 'now is not a good time, Uncle Marcus. The situation has changed, and I need to focus on my family.' Like, what the hell does that even mean? So, I figured I'd handle things with Rebecca myself last night. For all the damn good it did me."

Kate frowned, speaking more to Jake than Marcus. "What situation could have changed? Do you suppose she meant Rebecca's announcement about donating the island and the trust to the historical society?"

"Who gives a shit?" Marcus hiccupped, swigging more wine. "I tried to find her after the rehearsal dinner, maybe join forces against her aunt. But she was nowhere to be found when I needed her last night. Well, she can bet I'll be nowhere to be found when she needs *me*."

Kate didn't figure it was worth mentioning she had been poisoned at the time. "That must have been so . . . enraging. Rebecca still punishing you after forty years. I don't know what I'd do if somebody treated me like that. I'd just want to, I don't know. Throttle them. Hold them under water until they drowned."

Jake gave her a look, as if she were being a bit too on the nose, but considering the state of Marcus Sheffield's nose, she figured subtlety wouldn't get her very far.

"Exactly!" Marcus exclaimed, before shaking his head. "Damn, I wish somebody would. Put the rest of us out of our misery. But you can't drown a vampire. Gotta stake 'em through the heart. Expose her to sunlight."

It wasn't the slam-dunk confession Kate was hoping for, but it wasn't an alibi, either. Marcus Sheffield seemed exactly like the type of person to drown somebody in a rage, but he also didn't seem like the kind of careful planner who would carry Rebecca's body upstairs to use her fingerprint to access her computer. Whoever did that needed knowledge of Rebecca's office, and her computer system. Which pointed once again in the heir's direction. Still, Marcus could have killed Rebecca, left her in the pool room, and someone else could have taken advantage of the opportunity for their own gain.

"Where did you go last night, after you fought with Rebecca?" Kate asked. "You must have been pretty steamed. I know I would have been."

"Oh, you believe your ass I was," Marcus said. "I was ready to punch some walls, throw some priceless family heirlooms. But a good steam was exactly what I needed, I guess, since that's what I did."

"What do you mean?" Kate asked.

Marcus shrugged. "That kid, what did you say his name was? Ronald? Ricardo?"

"Richie," Jake supplied.

"Yeah, the surly one. He let me in the pool room, said any enemy of his aunt was a friend of his. They got a real swank sauna down there. I nearly fell asleep in that steam room. They were doing some kind of crazy party, but I'm too old for that crap. All I need these days is a good glass of whisky and a nice schvitz and I'm in heaven."

If Marcus had been in the pool room during the party last night, there was a good chance Richie had caught him in the background of his photos. Kate could confirm the time and location on his phone. Plus, she didn't figure Marcus Sheffield could have rage-drowned someone like Rebecca without a whole pool room full of witnesses. Not unless Richie and Steven were covering for him. But he'd said something that had triggered Kate's interest, and if she'd had time to put her sleuthing sweater on, she was sure it would be itching right now. In fact, her arms were still red from scratching. Maybe Jake had a point about the wool.

"Marcus, it's been a real . . . well, it's been real," Kate said, tugging Jake's arm. "But we've got to get ready for the ceremony."

"Ceremony, ha," Marcus snorted, blinking at her blearily. "Good luck to that poor bastard. That's one bullet you can't dodge. Shoulda taken the old man's payout, then at least I'd have had the money to pick myself up after the Bitch Bull wrecked my life. This fucking family."

The Bitch Bull had certainly paid with her own life, Kate thought. And it was looking more and more like it had been at the hands of this fucking family of hers.

Chapter Twenty-Eight

"Since I know you can't possibly be this eager about the wedding ceremony, I assume we're going back to the murder attic?" Jake asked as Kate practically sprinted up the stairs toward the fourth floor again. She was really getting her cardio for the weekend.

"I need to check the photos on Richie's phone to confirm Marcus's claim that he was in the spa after he argued with Rebecca," Kate said as they climbed the ladder into the attic, picking up Richie's phone where she left it on the armchair and scrolling through his camera roll as Jake changed into his wedding outfit. "Well, Marcus was right about one thing, at least. Seems like Richie and Steven hosted some kind of after-party down in the pool room. Ah, there's Marcus in the background. He looks super pissed, so this must be after he talked to Rebecca. He is in a towel, though. And it looks like he's going into some kind of side room and—Oh! Okay, well *that* is a penis."

The pictures got decidedly more R-rated from there, bare chests and other parts, groups of wedding guests swimming in what looked like an underground pool. Kate checked the metadata on the pictures, disappointed to find that they spanned far beyond the time frame of the poisoning window last night. Richie and Steven were in most of the photos, as was Marcus a good hour after he entered the steam room, looking like a cooked potato. But Rebecca was conspicuously absent. Which tracked with Richie's timeline that she left the pool room after arguing with Marcus. But how did she end up drowned, and who did the deed?

"Unless you're planning on showing up to the ceremony in your sleuthing sweater, you should get changed now," Jake prompted, gently taking the phone from her.

"Wedding, right," Kate said, frowning over her suspects list as she dug through her suitcase for her dress for the wedding. "The photos from the party seem to prove Marcus was in the steam room when Rebecca was killed."

"Doesn't that alibi out Richie and Steven as well, then?" Jake wondered.

"I guess it does." Kate grunted, wrestling herself into the strapless bra from the previous evening. "And to your point, Kennedy has a rock-solid alibi for the time her aunt was killed."

"Being poisoned and unconscious, you mean," Jake supplied.

"Yes," Kate said. "Except that Marcus said something interesting about Kennedy. He said that she lured him here to the island by promising to talk to Rebecca about giving his family's business back. But when he got here, suddenly she's talking about it being a bad time because the situation changed."

"Which makes sense, if Rebecca blindsided her about the historical society," Jake said.

"It would make sense, *if* she'd been blindsided," Kate said, shimmying into her dress. She wouldn't have time to fix her hair or even contemplate makeup, but it hardly mattered, considering they'd be doing the ceremony in the dark at this point. "But what if Kennedy somehow found out about her aunt's plans before this weekend?"

"You mean somebody on the board snitched to her?"

"Think about it. Rosary peas aren't naturally occurring here, and I certainly haven't seen any in the house or on the grounds. Which means whoever brought the poison was prepared. So maybe Rebecca thinks she's hoodwinking her family, making the big announcement last night.

But what if one of them already knew? Like, say, a real estate lawyer? Or her heir? Or a disgraced cousin desperately seeking a cash infusion to stave off her food truck debts?"

Jake turned around in surprise. "You think all three of them were in on it?"

"They all stood to gain from Rebecca's death, didn't they?" Kate reasoned, wincing as she worked her feet back into her high heels. "Kennedy would lose access to the family fund and the island where all the precious memories of her parents are, Richie would lose his inheritance, and Cassidy would never get the opportunity to inherit at all. But with Rebecca out of the way, Kennedy takes over and stops the deal with the historical trust. And, as head of the board, she can approve Richie's request *and* have Cassidy reinstated in the will."

Jake gave a low whistle, his gaze traveling up the length of her bare legs and back down. He blinked, clearing his throat. "That's a helluva motive for all three."

"I need to talk to Kennedy," Kate said. "If I can get her to admit she knew about the deal before Rebecca's speech, that proves she had motive. And if the three of them were in it together—Kennedy providing the distraction, Richie and Steven sabotaging the house, and Cassidy doing the deed—then all we need to figure out is where they actually drowned Rebecca. There's got to be some kind of physical evidence there."

"I've got your evidence right here," Jake said, holding up Richie's phone. When Kate looked at him in surprise, he gave a shrug. "What? You told me to be a Blake, I'm being a Blake. I went through his text history, and listen to this one from Steven: 'You know what Rico will do to me if this deal doesn't go through. We need to take care of your aunt this weekend, or else.' And this one, from Cassidy, sent yesterday morning: 'R can't stand in my way any longer, I've made sure of it.' Sounds like the hatching of a plot to me."

"See, now you're getting into the spirit." Kate grinned. "Let's go talk to the bride."

Kate and Jake hurried down to the main floor, suddenly aware of how much time had passed since Abraham's announcement. But it hardly seemed to matter if they were late or not, because it felt like the house was under assault from the storm outside, the wind finding its way into all the cracks and weak points a hundred-year-old house halfway through renovations will have. The lights flickered more noticeably now, like a heart monitor tracking the last pumps of a dying muscle.

"Seems kind of ludicrous to be trying to hold the ceremony now," Kate said, unconsciously pushing in closer to Jake as the long shadows of the house took on a more sinister feel. "Shouldn't we, I don't know, be seeking emergency shelter somewhere instead?"

"On an island like this? The whole thing could go underwater. The only safe place is somewhere else entirely." He glanced at her as her fingers dug into his arm, her eyes gone wide. "I mean, we'll be fine. This house has seen its share of storms, I'm sure. Nothing stands for a hundred years without taking a few beatings."

"Okay, well you clearly have not read 'The Fall of the House of Usher,' then," Kate muttered.

"Whatever happens, there's a fully stocked wine cellar, right?" Jake said with a shrug. "There are worse ways to go out."

"How do you do that?" Kate asked.

"Do what?"

"Stay so calm, when everything is complete chaos? How are you not freaking out?"

"I've been all over the world, yeah?" Jake said. "Ferrying Wall Street types on their version of an Eat, Pray, Love tour. Rich boys with high adrenaline thresholds looking for an extreme experience they can brag about to their dates back home. And I've got to make them feel like they're always facing danger without actually ever letting them be in danger, which is easy when you're designing a roller coaster. But, in my experience, things rarely go how I think they will. That's the nature of Mother Nature. I nearly lost my pinkie toe to frostbite in Nepal, had a shark try to bite my arm off in Tahiti, and was sicker than I've ever been in my life in Borneo. If I tried to control everything, I'd be a mess. So, I've learned to embrace the chaos."

"But I don't want to embrace the chaos," Kate said, shaking her head. "I want to . . . to organize the chaos."

Jake chuckled. "It's chaos, Kate. By its very definition, it can't be organized."

"Only because no one's tried hard enough yet," Kate said with grim determination.

Jake let out a full-bellied laugh. "That's what I love most about you, Katey cakes. Your unshakeable belief in your organizational skills."

Kate had a *lot* of questions about that off-the-cuff statement, but they had found their way to the sunroom and the guests were already packed in the crowded arrangement of chairs. It was sweltering, even from the hall, so many warm bodies putting off heat in such a small space. Sweat tickled Kate's underarm, blooming into the silk backing beneath the sequins. She'd probably have to toss the dress by the end of the weekend; there was no saving silk from sweat.

Abraham and Jean-Pierre had made a valiant attempt to re-create the fairy forest magic from the tent outside, but due to the small size of the room and the large number of people trying to fit into it, the efforts felt more constricting than transportive. Glass butterflies knocked people in the forehead, several guests had to use the roots of the trees as seats, and the glass pond was propped up in one corner, tilting perilously as each person squeezed past it. Kate could only imagine how the exotic fish were faring in their underground tank outside.

"I'll find us some seats," Jake said, moving into the thick of the crowd.

"Hey," Marla said, appearing beside Kate during a rolling peal of thunder. Kate jumped, startling Marla right back.

"Marla!" Kate exclaimed, the shortness of breath making her sound huffy. "Where have you been?"

"Where the hell have *you* been?" Marla shot back. "I've been all over this nightmare house looking for this evidence you swore would just be lying around somewhere, but I haven't found shit. I got trapped in a weird cabinet that I'm ninety-nine percent sure was a medieval torture chamber at one point, and I startled an entire family of *living* possums in a bedroom that was full of vases and vases of dead flowers. Meanwhile, you're nowhere to be found, and apparently the whole house is about to lose power during a massive storm, so yeah. It's been a less than ideal day for me."

"Oh, Marla, shit, I'm sorry," Kate said. "I was . . . I was investigating, too. I guess our paths just . . . never crossed."

Except that wasn't exactly true, was it? Kate had done plenty more than just *investigate*, and she'd been so busy with Jake and interrogating new suspects and Rebecca's untimely body drop that she'd once again forgotten all about her friend. This was supposed to be their weekend to reconnect, to find the magic of the Nights of the Round Table again. And instead, Kate had done what she'd always done, focused only on herself.

"Marla, I really am sorry," she reiterated when Marla didn't answer. Marla stared hard at the crowd of gathering wedding guests, but Kate knew where her anger was really directed. "I swear I won't forget you this time. I promise. I'm so close, I know it."

Marla looked to her in surprise. "Did you find something? The champagne glass? A new clue?"

Kate shook her head. She could hardly get into Rebecca's murder here in the open. "Not exactly, but mark my words. I'm going to find the killer before this day is out."

"Ahem!" said Abraham, drawing everyone's attention to the back of the room. Or maybe it was the big crash of thunder that rattled the windows in their frames, or the fantastic flash of lightning just before that silhouetted him like the big reveal in a murder mystery. Whichever event it was, all eyes turned to the back as he held up what looked for all the world like an old iPod. "Would everyone stand, please?"

He tapped the screen and a tinny, plodding version of the wedding march fought a losing battle for attention against the furor of the storm outside. He stepped to the side, frantically pressing the volume button as if it wasn't already at top level, as Juliette appeared on the arm of the first groomsman.

"Is that an iPod?" Jake whispered.

"Should have used that megaphone," Kate murmured, preoccupied with the bridesmaids coming down the aisle. Each one gave her a warning look like she was going to jump up and declare her love for Spencer any second now. Cassidy was the worst of them, outright glaring at Kate as she paced down the aisle on Eric's arm.

The crowd turned to the windows at the back with hushed breaths. Even Kate couldn't help tipping up on her heels to catch a glimpse of Kennedy as she stepped into the sunroom. There was something so magical about the moment the bride appeared. And Kennedy was no different—pale, but radiating joy, her dress a gorgeous satin with a draping skirt that made her look as if she'd stepped straight out of an old Hollywood film. She smiled, eyes fixed at the front of the room, holding on to Simon Hsu's arm.

They were really going to do it, Kate thought. They were really going to make it through this damn ceremony.

Which was when the lights dropped out, everybody screamed, and a sharp crack shattered the floor-to-ceiling window directly behind Kennedy.

Chapter Twenty-Nine

In hindsight, Kate would understand she had brought this on herself. You never jinx a perfect game, her father always said, and she should have known the same would be true for disastrous wedding weekends among a maybe cursed family.

All that insight would come later, because now the room descended into absolute chaos. There was screaming, shoving, and Kate even swore she heard squawking. Heaven help them all if a bird got into the room. The lights flickered on and dropped out again, the generator on its last dying gasps, as someone screamed for order.

"Kennedy!" someone called. "Are you okay?"

"I'm okay!" came Kennedy's voice, warbly and off-kilter. "I can't see anything, though. There's glass everywhere."

"Get her up here!" said the bridesmaids as a chorus.

"Please, we need to cover the window!" came Abraham's voice, shrill and frantic. "Quickly, before it floods!"

And in the darkness and confusion, Kate saw a chance to do exactly as Jake had said and embrace the chaos. She could just make out Kennedy's silhouette against the flashing lightning, Simon trying to find his way through the crowd toward the front where Kennedy belonged.

"Jake, I need you to distract Simon," Kate said, already heading for the aisle.

"How do you expect me to do that?" Jake asked, exasperated. But he followed after her like a good Blake.

"Make him help you fortify the window," Kate said. "I need to talk to Kennedy."

While Jake called loudly for help securing the window, Kate pitched her voice high and said she was bringing Kennedy somewhere safe, hoping nobody would recognize her voice. She took Kennedy by the elbow, the other woman giving a little squeak of surprise as Kate pulled her free of Simon's grasp.

"Don't worry, it's just me, Kate," Kate said, thinking that maybe her presence might not be as reassuring as she expected. "Let's get you somewhere dry while they repair the window."

"Okay, sure," Kennedy said breathlessly, letting Kate lead her into the hallway. Kate grabbed randomly at passing door handles until she found one that was unlocked, practically shoving Kennedy in just as the lights staggered back to life. "Oh, it was so stuffy in there! I was feeling swoony all over again. Thank you."

Kennedy was shaken and pale as she plopped into an upholstered chair, looking every inch the worn-out bride ready to be done with her wedding festivities. The room was crowded with old furniture in dusty coverings, and Kate managed to lean against something she hoped hadn't been alive at one point. The lights in the room were older and dimmer, the glass smudged and the bulbs such a deep yellow they bordered on orange. It lent the room a spooky glow, especially when the lights sparked bright and dropped low again.

"I should just give it up, shouldn't I?" Kennedy said, sounding as miserable as Kate had ever heard her. "This whole weekend has been a sham."

"It must be quite a topsy-turvy weekend," Kate ventured. "Your aunt's big announcement last night was pretty upsetting. Donating the island and the family trust to the historical society? That must have been a real kick in the teeth when you found out. Last night."

"What?" Kennedy blinked in surprise before shaking her head. "Oh, I knew about the donation ages ago."

Wow, was Kennedy going to make it this easy for her? "You knew she was going to donate the island? Did you try to stop her?"

"Just the opposite, actually. I was helping her with the historical society."

"Really?" Kate said, disappointed. The confession wasn't going as swimmingly as she'd imagined.

"I mean, I was surprised she announced it this weekend, and I didn't know anything about her inviting an inspector to finalize the deal, but this has been in the works for months. She'd gotten pretty secretive about the final details once she started working with whoever this inspector is from the society, but that's how Auntie R always is. She doesn't like to jinx things."

"But in your speech you said you wanted the island cared for by people who understood its history, who loved what it represented."

"Oh, I do," Kennedy said, nodding enthusiastically. "That's why I thought the historical society was such a great idea. Who better to care for an old place like this than a bunch of history buffs? I knew the rest of the family wouldn't feel the same, though. I was hoping maybe my speech would inspire them to see this for the opportunity it was, to let the real experts keep our family legacy alive. I love my cousins, but they're not exactly fiscally responsible. And no one really understands how much upkeep the Manor requires. It's constantly flooding, the wood warps, none of the doors close right, and it's impossible to get reputable contractors out here to the islands. Auntie R has kept up with the place because she considers it our legacy, but the rest of us prefer, you know, civilization."

Well, that certainly shot Kate's theory in the foot about Kennedy being angry at Rebecca for giving away the island and the trust. Still, maybe there was a different angle to work here.

"What about your inheritance money? I heard she could—er, can be a bit of a stickler about letting people have their money."

"Oh, I took my inheritance a few years ago," Kennedy said.

Yet another new piece of the puzzle to consider. "What for?"

"Simon Says needed a cash infusion to stay alive, so I became a silent partner in the business," Kennedy said. "I used to visit his offices, you know, with my dad when I was little. It felt like a second home away from home. When I knew Simon needed help running things, I couldn't turn my back on him. I never really planned on claiming my inheritance, but it was worth it to keep Simon Says going. Even Auntie R could hardly deny the importance of the arts to the local culture."

"Your aunt seems in the habit of denying most things," Kate murmured, thinking of her heated exchange with Kennedy's cousin. "What about Cassidy? It must be so hard for her, being cut out of the will entirely."

"Oh, Cass." Kennedy sighed, shaking her head. "I love her so much, really I do, but sometimes I wish she'd just . . . pull herself together. I know her dad basically cut her off, but she really did rack up an impressive amount of debt in a shocking amount of time. I tried to talk her out of it, you know. The food truck. I told her start smaller, work in a kitchen, get your feet under you before branching out on your own. But I think she was just so fixated on the Hempstead idea of making your own way in the world. It's kind of been hammered into us since childhood. I'm worried she thinks she can talk Auntie R into letting her into the will, that she's banking on getting her inheritance back to pay off the loans to keep her business afloat." Kennedy shook her head sadly. "But Auntie R has taken such a hard line with the inheritance fund. And once the historical society deal goes through, well . . . I suppose that's it for the Hempstead family fortune. I'll be fine, I never really wanted to play the pampered heir and I've got savings from my mom. But Richie and Cassidy . . . I worry about them."

Which brought Kate's suspicions back around to Richie, Steven, and Cassidy. The three people who stood to lose the most if Rebecca gave away the family trust.

"Kennedy—" Kate started, pausing with a frown. "Do you smell that?"

"Smell what?" Kennedy asked, scrunching up her nose. "Wait, is that . . ."

"Smoke!" Kate said, peering into the depths of the crowded room.

The furniture was so musty and the lights so dim she'd hardly noticed it at first, but now there were greasy black plumes obscuring the lamps and choking the air in the crowded space. The lamps popped and buzzed, unused to the surges of electricity pulsing through them, and Kate wondered if they'd even been used in the last century.

"We need to get out of here!" Kate cried, as Kennedy inexplicably moved toward the source of the smoke. "Kennedy, what are you doing?"

"The entire estate is made of hundred-year-old timber," Kennedy said, pulling a blanket off a nearby armoire with a flair. Kate had the inexplicable thought that Kennedy would make an excellent magician's assistant. "The lights must have short-circuited, and this room is full of dry old fabric. If we don't stop the fire, the house will burn."

Kate looked longingly toward the door, so close and yet so far. Kennedy was right; this whole place would go up like a box of loose matches if they didn't stop the fire. Not that she wouldn't mind shutting down this Haunted Mansion ride, but if it were going to burn she'd prefer it wait until she was well off the island.

"Kennedy, wait," Kate said, struggling with a heavy tarp. She didn't have nearly the same grace as Kennedy, but what she lacked in finesse she made up for in strength. She gathered it in her arms, hauling it toward the far end of the room where Kennedy was already beating at the smoky flames eating through what was probably a priceless antique.

Together they managed to smother the flames before they spread to the rest of the room, but they couldn't stop the noxious smoke that gusted out each time they flapped their blankets, smothering the air and settling heavily in their lungs. Kate remembered reading about how most victims don't die by fire, but rather through smoke inhalation, the hot ash irreparably damaging their esophagus. She coughed, her throat feeling ragged.

"We have to get out of here," Kate rasped, sure that she could already feel her throat muscles disintegrating. She tugged at Kennedy's arm as the smoke billowed out, burning her eyes and filling the room with black soot. Kennedy's dress was ruined, not that that would matter if they suffocated. "Kennedy, the fire is out, but the smoke will kill us!"

"Okay," Kennedy said, giving the smoldering ruin of a stuffed armchair one last vigorous smothering. Smoke burst upward and Kate cowered back, but the smoke didn't come for her. Instead, it seemed to get sucked away, toward the wall. Kate's eyes were streaming and she could barely see, but she could swear there was a crack in the wall. Another secret opening.

"Hey!" someone shouted from the far side of the room, and Juliette Winters stood on the threshold, waving away the smoke. "What the hell is going on?"

"There was a fire," Kate said, and even she knew how stupid it sounded.

"A *fire*," Juliette repeated as Kate led Kennedy through the mess of furniture and ducked out into the hall, both of them coughing. "So now you're resorting to arson?"

"No!" Kate yelped, which sounded way guiltier than she wanted it to. "I was just getting Kennedy somewhere safe and dry while they fixed the window."

"They covered the window several minutes ago," Juliette said, still glaring at her. "Which you would know, if you hadn't kidnapped Kennedy and held her hostage in here. What did she try to do to you, Ken?"

"Oh, Juliette, don't be silly," Kennedy said, before dissolving into another fit of coughing. "Kate and I were just talking and one of the lamps shorted out from the power surge. It's a good thing we were in there, to be honest. If we hadn't been, we might not have caught the fire in time. We should send someone to check the rest of the house. We didn't include the lights and wiring in the latest round of restorations."

The lights buzzed low and sputtered back at half their power, as if to prove Kennedy's point. Kennedy sighed as she looked up at them, her hair in disarray and her dress streaked in gray and black. Still, even with the damage, she looked like a movie version of someone in a disaster, a single smudge on her face only highlighting the curve of her cheekbone. Kate didn't imagine she looked so glamorously disheveled.

"We'll have to delay the ceremony," Kennedy said, her voice small and sad. "Spencer will be crushed."

"We're not delaying anything," Juliette said, giving Kate a hard look. "You're getting married today, and *no one* is stopping it. Come on, I can fix you up in two minutes."

"Really, Juliette," Kennedy started, but Juliette took her hand possessively and mouthed something threating that Kate didn't quite catch. Which was probably just as well.

"No arguments," Juliette said, leading Kennedy back toward the ceremony room. "You're getting married right now."

"Okay, let's get married!" Kennedy cheered. But even she couldn't maintain her usual cheer in the face of such a tumultuous weekend. Kate could only hope they could get her to the altar unscathed. Because she was almost positive it hadn't been the lights that started the fire, even though someone wanted it to look that way. Someone had used a secret passage to finish the job they'd started last night and kill Kennedy.

Chapter Thirty

Jake and the other volunteers had managed to secure the window by the time Kate returned, trailing a good distance behind Kennedy and Juliette. They'd forgone the walk down the aisle in favor of expediency, which was just as well considering the wind howling through the heavy curtains they'd hung to block the broken window. Kennedy hurried to stand beside Spencer, and Kate slipped into her place beside Jake. Spencer gave his bride's appearance a startled look, and ripples of gossip undulated through the crowd, but Kennedy only smiled bravely and signaled for the ceremony to proceed.

"Well, better get this over with before the whole place comes crashing down," Spencer's cousin and current officiant shouted over the wind. The joke cracked the tension in the room, drawing surprised laughs out of everyone. "Dearly beloved, we are gathered here today to see this man and this woman engaged in holy matrimony. The sooner the better, am I right?"

"Are you okay?" Jake whispered to Kate, taking her hand. "What the hell happened?"

"Another attempt on Kennedy's life, I think," Kate said grimly. "And this time I had a front-row seat. Did you notice anybody leaving after the window broke?"

"I wouldn't know. We were too busy trying to block the window with some old drapes. It was all I could do to get them up, with the wind gusting like it is." He shook his head, frowning as he looked back over his shoulder.

"What?" Kate asked, sensing his discomfort. "What is it?"

Jake leaned in closer, his voice a ghost in her ear. "Somebody buggered with the wooden frame on the window. On all of them. I checked. The boards were pried apart, the glass hanging loose. That's why it crashed so easily. Somebody sabotaged the frame."

Kate's brows shot up in surprise. "Richie and Steven?"

"They look awfully pleased with themselves up there, don't they?"

Kate had to agree, the black sheep of the Hempstead family looked very conspiratorial with his partner in crime, smirking around the room at the other guests as Spencer's cousin droned on. First the generator, then the water line, now the windows in the ceremony room. Not to mention the fire. Had they sabotaged the wiring down here? As a member of the Hempstead clan, Richie would certainly know about the secret passages.

"The, uh, the rings?" Spencer's cousin/officiant asked loudly, nudging Cassidy. "Anybody got the rings?"

"Oh!" Cassidy said in surprise with a nervous little giggle. "Sorry. I have them right here."

Cassidy fished around in the pocket of her bridesmaid dress—so convenient, Kate thought, putting pockets on everything these days—and pulled out a small wooden box. Something clinked to the ground as she withdrew her hand, flashing in the glare of a lightning strike, and everyone in the bridal party leaned down to look.

"Cassidy," Kennedy said, her voice full of confusion. "Is that . . . my *necklace*?"

"Oopsies," Kate sang sotto voce. When she'd assumed that Kennedy's dress was the poofiest garment bag, she hadn't factored in Kennedy's old Hollywood style. Her dress was smooth satin, nowhere near as decked out in crystal and tulle as Cassidy's maid-of-honor dress.

Cassidy gasped. "I don't know where that came from."

"It came from your pocket," Juliette said, loud and clear from the other end of the line.

Cassidy shook her head, looking around like she was just catching on to what this might mean for her. "Wait, that's not . . . I didn't take your necklace, Ken, I swear it! I have no idea what that was doing in my pocket. Someone must have planted it there!"

"I thought you said you put it back in Kennedy's wedding dress," Jake whispered in Kate's ear.

"I thought I did," Kate said out of the side of her mouth, unable to tear her gaze from the drama unfolding at the front of the room. "There were multiple bags. I picked the poofiest one and assumed it was the wedding dress."

But in Kate's defense . . . well, she didn't really have a defense, did she? The necklace was definitely planted, and she was definitely the one who'd done it.

"Oh my god, I know what this is!" one of Kennedy's bridesmaids, a friend from college, cried. "*You* are the one who's been trying to mess up Ken's big day all along! What did you do, put something in the oysters? Make her sick on purpose so you could steal the necklace and hock it to pay off your food truck loans?"

"No, of course not!" Cassidy cried, focusing on Kennedy. "Ken, I would never—*never*—do anything to hurt you. You're my . . . You're like a sister to me. Really, you don't even know. Please, this is some huge misunderstanding!"

"Kate, you have to say something," Jake murmured.

"I know," Kate said, gnawing at her bottom lip. But did she, really? The only defense she had was the truth, which was the exact same thing Cassidy was claiming right now. And Kate could see how well that was going. If she stood up and said it was her, that she'd planted the necklace, then she'd be the one everybody was yelling at now. And she'd had quite enough of that this weekend, thank you very much.

And there was still the business of Rebecca's body in the fern upstairs. Someone had killed her, and Kate had seen Cassidy arguing with her aunt the day before. She might not have taken the necklace, but Kate was sure she wasn't innocent here, either. Really, Kate couldn't even be sure Cassidy wasn't the one who'd taken the necklace in the first place. Someone had taken it and planted it among Kate's things; who was to say it wasn't Cassidy?

Still, it was hard to watch the woman get raked over the coals about it now.

"Kennedy, please," Cassidy sobbed. "Just let me explain."

"I bet this is about the money, isn't it?" said another of the bridesmaids. "You blame Ken for not backing you up to get access to the inheritance fund!"

Kate winced, and Jake gave her a hard stare. "Kate."

"Shhh, I can't hear," she said, putting a hand over his mouth.

"It's not a soap opera, Kate!" he said, his voice muted beneath her fingers. His lips did feel nice, though.

"I know," she hissed. "But this whole scene could force a confession out of Cassidy, and wouldn't that be in everyone's best interest? I don't want to derail them now."

"If anybody was going to hurt Ken for the money, it wouldn't be me!" Cassidy said, her voice pitching above the growing noise in the room. "It would be Richie. He's the one who needs more cash to pay for his addictions!"

The room swiveled as one to where Richie sat, looking like he *was* watching a soap opera. He was caught mid-grin, which Kate figured wasn't about to go well for him.

"Uh, excuse me, I don't have anything to do with any of this," Richie said, putting up his hands with an affable expression. "I don't know anything about any oysters or a necklace. I just came for a show, wedding or otherwise."

"Except that's not all you're here for, is it?" Cassidy said. "You and your lawyer boyfriend have been trying to strong-arm Aunt Rebecca into selling Hempstead Island for the past year for some kind of dumb luxury development."

"My suggestion to Rebecca about selling the island was in her best interest," Steven said, putting on his best lawyer voice. "Just look at the safety issues we've had this weekend alone. Kennedy could have been seriously injured. This house should never have been put up for an inspection, and I can't imagine it will pass now that—"

"We know about the gambling debts, Steven!" Cassidy said, practically hysterical by now. "Everybody knows, okay? Richie told us about how you got in over your head with your bookie and now he's forcing you to make Auntie R sell him the island to pay off your debts."

Kate turned in triumph to Jake and mouthed *ponies*.

"It was a lucky guess and you know it," Jake whispered.

"Any *alleged* debts would not be anybody's business but mine," Steven said stiffly, but there was noticeably less wind in his sails. "The real estate proposal is a sound investment, and the house is in a hazardous state."

"Why don't we all just calm down," Simon said, his voice projecting cool control through the space. "I'm sure if we all discuss this like reasonable adults—"

"What would you know about reasonable, Simon?" came Serena's voice from the doors, where she'd appeared in a dramatic clap of thunder. Kate imagined she must have been waiting for such a cue to announce herself. She puffed up like a songbird preparing to give the greatest aria of its little life span. "You thought you could silence the lion's roar, but we're too mighty. We know you're selling off Simon Says and sending us all down the river in the meantime! Some family business you turned out to be. You're as ruthless as the big boys in New York!"

"What?" Simon said in shock. "What gave you the idea—"

"Who's our new overlord?" Serena demanded. "Is it Kennedy? Is that why you're here this weekend, schmoozing? So you can convince Kennedy to buy you out?"

Simon put his hands up defensively. "Now, if we can just take a beat, this really isn't the right place to discuss—"

"Where is the right place, huh? Because you've been avoiding us for months! The joke's on you, bub, because we're unionizing and we're not going to allow you to sell! And certainly not to Kennedy Hempstead. She's already hosed our books with her crappy marketing."

"Serena, please," Kennedy said, her voice soothing. "I know you're upset about the delay in contract negotiations, but as we told you last month, marketing a series is a very different beast from a brand-new book. Series fatigue is real, and your readers—"

"Don't you dare try to lecture me about my readers! My readers are loyal and reliable, which is more than I can say for you, little chippy. If Simon thinks he can put you in charge of the whole shebang, all you can guarantee is that we'll be bankrupt by Christmas!"

The small cadre of Spencer's authors behind her dissolved into boisterous outrage. The lights took the advantage and dropped out again, and Kate felt like a flower pressed between two steaming hot rocks.

"We need to get out of here," Kate muttered as the atmosphere in the room ratcheted up to unbearable heat levels. She pushed into the aisle, intent on making a discreet and graceful exit, but unfortunately it only put her in Juliette's crosshairs as the lights pulsed back on.

"There's your real culprit," Juliette said, pointing a finger square at Kate.

"Me?" Kate squeaked.

"Look at her, she's even trying to flee," Juliette pressed. "I mean, come on, Kate is the most obvious culprit here. This whole weekend is literally the plot of her book. She's the one who conveniently 'found' Kennedy passed out. And I just caught her holding Kennedy hostage in a room where a fire conveniently started. Plus, she's Spencer's ex-fiancé. He dumped her for Kennedy and she's looking for revenge. She's clearly still in love with Spencer."

"I *knew* it," Spencer said, so fucking smug Kate could punch him. "You do still have feelings for me, don't you? That's why you asked me up to the attic."

"No, that's not . . . I didn't . . ." Kate put up her hands. She needed to organize the chaos. "I just . . . I just wanted to get through this weekend without . . ."

Without what? Making an absolute fool of herself? Becoming the object of everyone's pity? Losing her cool in front of an audience? Loretta would *never*.

"Everyone sit down and shut it," Loretta snapped, glaring down the assembled crowd. A more diminutive, soft-spoken woman might have had to stand on the bar or wave her arms around, but Loretta had plenty of height and volume to command the attention of the room. "What we're not going to do is lose our cool right now."

"Let's not . . . lose our cool?" Kate said, but the ending sounded an awful lot like a question.

"Oh, Katelin," Spencer's mother scoffed, and something in Kate snapped. Clean in two. Forget Loretta, forget her dignity, forget saving face for the weekend. Kate had absolutely had enough.

"My name is not Katelin!" she shouted. "It has never been Katelin! I have tried to correct you so many times, until I was sure you were doing it on purpose. But you're not going to be my mother-in-law, so I don't have to be nice to you anymore! You were never kind, never welcoming, and frankly it always felt a little icky how much you fawned over Spencer. He's an ordinary man! He can't drive a stick shift, he doesn't know how to tie his own tie without watching a YouTube video, he overpronounces every Italian word he speaks because he spent one summer there in college, and he was only mediocre at oral sex!"

None of that was meant to come out, but that last little detail was definitely one she had strictly instructed her tongue to keep inside her head. It was Jake, standing there, being sexy as hell and just casually mind-blowingly good at oral sex, that must have rattled that fact loose. Still, she clamped her hand over her mouth as soon as she'd said it. Spencer's brother, Eric, gave a braying laugh and slapped his brother on the back, still smacking that obnoxious gum.

That was nothing compared to Spencer's mother, though. She had long since passed red and dipped into disturbingly purple. "How *dare* you, you awful woman."

"That's not true," Spencer declared, glancing at Kennedy. "Right, Ken?"

"Oh, Spencey," Kennedy said, patting his arm like she was consoling a grieving relative at a funeral. "We'll talk later, honey."

"Oh," Spencer muttered, looking deflated as he glanced sullenly at Kate. "You never complained."

"I never knew better," Kate said, her gaze automatically flicking to Jake, who couldn't have looked more pleased with the whole outing.

"Oh, for fuck's sake," Spencer said. "At my wedding?"

"Yes, Spencer," Kate said heatedly. "At *your* wedding. To *someone else*! You don't get to be self-righteous about this!"

"She admits it," Juliette said, crossing her arms. "She's jealous about the wedding and only came this weekend to get rid of Kennedy."

"Juliette, we've been over this," Kennedy said, giving a hasty smile. "That was all a big misunderstanding. Kate would never hurt me."

"Exactly!" Kate said with a nervous little laugh. "I'm not jealous, and I definitely wasn't the one who poisoned Kennedy!"

"So you admit Kennedy was poisoned?" Juliette pressed.

"You're twisting my words—"

"Your exact words were 'I'm not the one who poisoned Kennedy,' how am I twisting that?"

She needed Loretta, her strength and confidence. What would Loretta say?

"You're acting awfully guilty for someone so loudly proclaiming their innocence," Loretta said. "Pointing fingers at everybody so nobody points one back at you, huh?"

Right, Juliette was still a suspect here.

"I saw you, sneaking around with Veeta last night—"

"Now you admit you were spying on people, too?" Juliette charged. "Is that what you're here to do this weekend? Stick your nose where it doesn't belong?"

"What? No! I wasn't spying—"

"She's a scab, too!" Serena declared. "Kate doesn't support the working author!"

Kate rolled her eyes, exasperated. "Serena, that's not—"

"I caught her creeping around the family pool room, too," Richie said, looking far too gleeful about his part in the accusation makings.

This was *rapidly* getting out of hand. What would Loretta do? Grab Abraham's alarm app and force everyone into silence? Make a Molotov cocktail out of a vodka bottle and escape in the disarray? Kate's Loretta connection was short-circuiting, visions of her heroine jumping out of burning buildings and fighting wedding guests flicking through her head like broken film. And interspersed between it all was a very real vision of Rebecca Hempstead, her skin so cold and rubbery, her expression frozen in grim surprise. Kate pressed her hands to the sides of her head, wishing for one moment of silence.

"Admit it!" someone shouted—probably Juliette. "Admit you tried to kill her!"

"I didn't kill her!" Kate exclaimed, exasperated. "I didn't kill Rebecca Hempstead!"

Chapter Thirty-One

If Kate had considered Cassidy finding the necklace to be a harbinger of chaos, her own accidental declaration was the eye of the storm. The whole room dropped into a dead silence, severely undercut by the howling of the wind outside the broken window and the dull, wet flapping of the makeshift curtains against the wooden frame. All eyes turned on her, bright and accusing. "What did you say?" Kennedy asked in confusion, the first to break the spell.

"Did you say Auntie R is dead?" Cassidy asked.

"Did *you* kill her?" Richie asked, looking almost impressed with her.

"I just said I didn't! I only found her body!"

"Wait, she really *is* dead?" Kennedy said, before bursting into tears. The sound of her sobbing broke the spell in the room, and suddenly the accusations were flying. Someone called Kate a murderer, someone else accused her of stealing their diamond tennis bracelet at the rehearsal dinner, and a deep voice in the back called for a pitchfork, of all things. This was rapidly getting out of hand.

"Did you poison her, too?" Juliette demanded.

"I didn't do anything!" Kate cried, sounding way too frantic to be innocent. "She was already dead when I found her. I only put her back in the plant for safekeeping."

"You stuffed her in a *plant*?" Cassidy cried.

"This isn't going great," Jake said, surveying the room.

"I know this isn't going great," Kate hissed. "Help me get it back on track!"

"Hang on, everybody, it's not what it sounds like," Jake said, holding up his hands and trying to calm the crowd with his trademark smile. "We were very careful with her—"

"You were there, too?" asked Abraham, looking shocked and disappointed. "You are her accomplice? Such physique, such a waste."

"No, no, no accomplices!" Kate looked to Jake helplessly. "It wasn't like that!"

"Oh my god!" Cassidy gasped, as a brutal gust of wind blew out another window, dousing the back half of the room in rain.

"We need to get out!" someone screamed. "Before we all drown!"

"But the ceremony isn't done!" a bridesmaid cried.

"Oh, believe me, honey, it's done," said Serena loudly, holding up a protest sign and waving it as if she were directing air traffic. "Let's go!"

"Wait, what about Aunt Rebecca?" Kennedy cried, shoving against the rising tide of fleeing guests to reach Kate. "Where is she? Did you mean it, what you said? Is she . . ."

Kennedy gulped, the sound lost in the crush of departing guests, but Kate could see her throat bobbing hard. Richie and Steven came to stand behind her, as well as Cassidy and Spencer and his parents, all of them forming a wall around Kate. Trapping her.

"It's not what you think," Kate said.

"Is she dead or not?" Mrs. Lieman demanded.

Kate swallowed hard. "Yes, Rebecca is dead. But I didn't kill her!"

Kennedy burst into tears once again. Cassidy could only stare, presumably in shock, while Richie looked far more discerning in light of this disastrous family news.

"I don't even know your name, but I know enough to know you've been the center of every controversy this weekend," Richie said, crossing his arms. "You put on that little show during the rehearsal dinner. And then you *conveniently* find Kennedy down in the wine cave, but oh it was just some bad oysters, right? So, what did you do to Auntie R, drop a toaster in her bathwater? Tranquilizer dart to the neck? Stab her with a decorative letter opener?"

"Those are *so specific*," Kate said. "But I didn't do anything to her. I never even met her before this weekend!"

"Maybe she caught you with the poison," Juliette said, taking a defensive stance beside Kennedy. "And you needed to keep her quiet."

"I didn't poison Kennedy!" Kate said, throwing up her hands in exasperation.

"If Ms. Hempstead truly is . . . deceased," Steven said in his most lawyerly tone, "I'll need to confirm it."

Yeah, Kate bet he would need to *confirm* it. She looked hard at him, then at Richie, then back at him, waiting for one of them to twitch or sneeze or cough, some kind of tell that they were guilty. But they looked stern and bored, respectively, no sign of guilt that she could tell. She'd have to press them harder, as soon as she wasn't everyone else's prime suspect.

"Where is she?" Cassidy asked. "Take us to her."

"Of course," Kate said, reaching for Jake's hand for stability as she led their small group out of the sunroom. Juliette and Cassidy closed ranks behind Kate, prodding her forward. They closed off the door to the room and sealed the gaps around it as best they could with layers of sheets and heavy furniture to keep the door braced against the howling wind.

They followed Kate and Jake up the stairs to the second floor and the office where she had discovered Rebecca's body what felt like a lifetime ago. Her steps slowed as they reached the landing, her toes practically dragging through the heavy carpet as Cassidy charged forward and swung the office door open. The interior was relatively serene, the raging of the storm outside muffled to a dull roar, but Kate would have preferred braving the hurricane-force winds to the storm Cassidy looked like she was about to unleash on them. Kate hung back by the door, which got her a sharp prod from Juliette.

"I was all state in track, don't bother running," Juliette muttered.

"Innocent people don't run," Kate said absently.

"Where is she?" Cassidy demanded. Gone was the sobbing girl from the rehearsal dinner, and in her place was a no-nonsense, vengeance-seeking woman. Briefly Kate wondered which version of Cassidy was the act and which one was the real deal, before Juliette nudged her again.

"Quit stalling," Juliette murmured.

Kate sighed, moving toward a thick fringe of fern leaves and closing her eyes against the sight of poor dead Aunt Rebecca. "This is where we found her."

There was a solitary gasp, then a long, surprising silence. Kate cracked an eye to catch the rest of the bridal party looking at her expectantly. Kate thought it was rather underwhelming, all things considered.

"There's nothing there," Cassidy said finally.

Kate frowned, realizing she hadn't bothered to actually check for the body before revealing the body, and turned to the frond. Sure enough, there was nothing there, just a pot of soil and a few wilted leaves.

"Somebody moved her!" Kate said, and that got her a few gasps of shock, which was, frankly, more like it.

"Kate," Jake said from across the room, drawing all eyes to him. He looked almost pained to say it, but continued, "she's over here."

"Oh," Kate said, deflating. She'd picked the wrong fern.

Jake swept back the fronds of a tree closer to the false wall—which was obviously the right spot, now that she was actually paying attention to the room—and there was poor Aunt Rebecca. She looked a little grayer, a little stiffer, and a whole lot deader.

"Oh, Aunt Rebecca!" Kennedy cried, turning to Spencer and burying her face in his shoulder as sobs hiccupped out of her.

"This will require a great deal of paperwork," Steven said with a sigh.

"Why didn't you tell anyone?" Cassidy demanded, looking just as upset. But Kate wondered if she was upset for a different reason. After all, she'd only recently been accused of potentially poisoning Kennedy. "You just left her there to rot in the fern. Who does that?"

SHE DOESN'T HAVE A CLUE

"Some of us could have been planning new inheritance requests now that the witch is dead," Richie said.

"Richard," Cassidy said, so severely he immediately clammed up.

"You don't have to call me Richard," he muttered sullenly, turning away. "You sound just like her."

"I wasn't leaving her there to rot!" Kate protested. "I—we—left her there because . . ." Oh boy, here it came. The really big reveal. "Because someone murdered her."

Kennedy buried her face deeper in Spencer's shoulder as Richie sidled up and placed a hand on her shoulder. "Hey, cuz, it'll be okay," he said, patting her awkwardly. "What you should really focus on right now is getting all the paperwork squared away so we can talk numbers and timelines for the November inheritance request meeting."

"There's a great deal of work to be done before then," Steven said, giving Richie a reproachful look. "Like talking about allocation of assets, for one. Including Hempstead Manor and the surrounding lands."

"Oh my god, not the resort business already," Richie said, rolling his eyes. "She's barely cold, Steve."

"And these matters need attendance," Steven said, his brows falling into a severe line.

"Both of you should be ashamed," Cassidy said, crossing her arms and staring them down. "Poor Ken has just had her wedding ruined and lost our aunt, and all you can talk about is money."

"Oh, like you wouldn't take a piece of the pie if you could," Richie said, rolling his eyes. "Don't act like you didn't come here to beg Aunt Rebecca to let you back in the will so you could make your inheritance claim. We all know about your massive business loans. Honestly, a food truck that only serves hush puppies? What the hell were you thinking?"

"They were sweet and savory," Cassidy said hotly. "They covered the full umami spectrum! And that's not why I'm here this weekend. I came because I love Kennedy, and I wanted to be here for her."

Except Kate knew that wasn't true, because she'd seen Cassidy arguing with Rebecca. She'd seen Rebecca slap Cassidy, and now more than ever, Kate wondered what it was Cassidy had said to elicit such a reaction from her aunt. And how she might have retaliated.

"Awfully convenient for you now, isn't it?" Richie muttered. "With the she-beast out of the way and the family fund still in the family. Kennedy will definitely let you back in the will."

"I don't need to be let back in the will," Cassidy ground out.

Why didn't she need to be let back in the will? Kate wondered. Unless her debts magically disappeared, which Kate knew from her own college experience was not possible. Most people she knew would be paying off student loans until they croaked. Kate had paid her loans down to a manageable lump, thanks to Loretta's royalties, but she couldn't imagine what kinds of debt Cassidy had, going to a private culinary academy. Even Marla sometimes complained about the cost of her master's degree, and what it had really done for her in comparison.

Richie and Steven might have been her best suspects for Aunt Rebecca's death, but Cassidy had just jumped up to the top of her list. She had means, motive, opportunity, and she seemed awfully confident about not needing to be let back in the will. What did she know about the Hempstead inheritance and her place in it, now that Rebecca was out of the picture?

"Oh please, we all know Uncle Alexi cut you off when your mom died," Richie said, waving a hand. "You made a big enough show about it when you got here."

"That's not what I was doing," Cassidy said, her voice getting thick. "And he didn't cut me off. He told me . . ."

Richie couldn't stop prodding. "Told you what? To pay your own debts for once?"

"You're one to talk," Cassidy said, pointing at him viciously with her freshly manicured nails. Kate wondered where she'd gotten the money to have them done, considering her financial troubles. Maybe Kennedy had paid to have them done, to match her mauve bridesmaid dress. Although Cassidy's nails were more purple than anything—

Kate smothered a gasp of recognition. The hand in the photo holding the champagne glass had purple nails, the exact same shade as Cassidy's manicure. It hadn't been Juliette; it had been Cassidy, standing right beside her in the picture, smiling to the point of pain. Kennedy stepped up between her cousins, pushing them apart.

"Both of you, please, just stop!" Kennedy said. "Please, for me. For Aunt Rebecca. She wouldn't want you fighting like this."

"Are you kidding me?" Richie said. "She'd *love* it."

"Yeah, she really would," Cassidy said, looking down at Rebecca's body mournfully.

"Can we please just . . . find a better resting place for her?" Kennedy sniffed. "I can't bear to think of her in those potted plants again."

While the family members made arrangements for how to respectfully handle Rebecca's body, Kate slipped out the door leading into the hallway and hurried to the bridal suite.

It had been filled with an ocean of satin and organza since the last time Kate was there, making it hard to wade through the seaweed of discarded bras and the undertow of a pair of very stretchy leggings. These girls made her apartment look like Martha Stewart's jail cell. Of course, they were probably used to someone cleaning up all their messes.

She didn't have much time, and she wasn't sure which suitcase might belong to Cassidy, so she started unzipping bags and rifling through each one with impunity. It wasn't until the third suitcase that she spotted the woman's ill-fitting rehearsal dress, price tag still attached. Her hand hit a hard yet delicate object, wrapped in an old T-shirt and stuffed in a plastic bag for some reason. Kate pulled it out, sucking in a breath at the sight of cut crystal.

"Gotcha," Kate declared quietly, holding up the missing champagne glass. *Find the glass, find the killer.*

"What are you doing?"

Kate whirled around to face Cassidy glaring at her from the door to the bridal suite, blocking her only exit.

Chapter Thirty-Two

"Cassidy!" Kate declared, sweeping the champagne glass behind her back. "I thought you were moving Aunt Rebecca."

"We are," Cassidy said flatly. "What are *you* doing?"

"I . . . am . . ." Kate had told Jake that she wasn't good at spur-of-the-moment confrontations, and she'd meant it. She looked around the room desperately, hoping something would jump out as a reasonable excuse for why she was lurking around the bridal suite, pawing through other people's things. But unless her excuse was that she was a perv for expensive fabrics and other people's underwear, she had nothing. So, she decided to turn the tables, holding up the champagne glass in the thick plastic bag.

"What are *you* doing with *this*?" she demanded, matching Cassidy's stance.

Cassidy gasped. "That's not yours! Give it back."

She hurried into the room and Kate moved to the far side where the bathroom door stood open, a narrow band of light barely illuminating the room. There was something in the bag with the champagne glass rattling against it, distracting Kate's attention. She frowned, raising the bag closer so she could see it. It was some kind of long tube—maybe the poison? But no, there was something in it. It looked like a cotton swab, the long, skinny kind they kept in a doctor's office. And there was a sticker on the side of the tube with a logo.

"Family Ties?" she read aloud. "Isn't that one of those find-your-ancestors kind of deals? Like you're twenty-three percent Scottish or whatever? Why do you have one of these?"

"That's none of your business," Cassidy growled, lurching for Kate and missing the bag. "Give it back!"

Kate tracked around the room, keeping her eye on the exit door, trying to keep a piece of furniture between her and Cassidy at all times. She had to hop over several suitcases and piles of clothes in the way, making her balance less steady. "Wait, are you . . . Were you doing a DNA test for . . . for Kennedy? Do you think Kennedy isn't a Hempstead?"

Maybe that was why Rebecca had slapped her, for suggesting that the heir apparent wasn't so apparent anymore. But Cassidy pulled up short, looking confused.

"That's stupid. Of course Kennedy is a Hempstead. Just look at her jawline."

"Then why . . ." Kate looked down at the bag, trying to fit the pieces together. If Cassidy knew Kennedy was a Hempstead, why would she secretly test Kennedy's DNA?

Kate gasped, clasping the test to her chest as Cassidy once again made a move toward her. "It's you, isn't it? You're not trying to prove Kennedy *isn't* a Hempstead, you're trying to prove you *are*."

"Of course I am," Cassidy said, scowling at her. "Everybody already knows that."

But Kate shook her head, the pieces finally coming together. "But you're the wrong kind of Hempstead. You're on the broken branch of the family tree, the relatives that got cut out of the inheritance after the family split. Unless . . . unless you're not?"

Cassidy went so still Kate could barely see her in the dimness. She was still between Kate and the exit, and Kate wasn't feeling very confident about her ability to sprint in heels, so she kept talking, kept distracting Cassidy as she tried to edge closer to the door.

"That's why you need the DNA test, not to prove Kennedy is a Hempstead, but to prove you're related. Except you're already related, so how? Unless you're trying to prove you're *differently* related. Closer than cousins. That's what you said to her, at the ceremony. You started to say 'you *are* my sister' but you stopped yourself. But that's what you are, isn't it? And that's the bomb your father dropped. Not that he was cutting you off, but that *he wasn't your father*. Her father is your father, too, isn't he? Except he died when Kennedy was young, so you couldn't get a paternity test. The closest match you could make would be a sibling."

"I just had to be sure," Cassidy said, sounding desperate. She dodged to the right as Kate tried to make a break for the door. "I know how it looks, but it's not what you think!"

"Why now?" Kate asked, trying to scout out an alternate escape. She could try to shout for help, but she was so close to the truth. She just needed Cassidy to say it. "Why did your dad tell you now? After all this time?"

"Because my mom died earlier this year," Cassidy said, sounding utterly distraught. "He'd been keeping the secret for her, all my life. My dad couldn't have children. Biologically, I mean. And my mom had wanted them so badly, so they'd . . . they'd made an arrangement with Uncle . . . with Gordon. For him to donate his . . . you know. He'd gone to school with my mother, at Princeton, so it wasn't as weird as you would think. They'd even dated a bit, I think. But then he met Ken's mom, and it was over between them. But my mother never got over it. She'd wanted to be a Hempstead so badly, on the right side of the family. So, when she had the chance to do the same for her daughter, I guess . . . I guess she took it. They never spoke of it. Not even to tell me. Until now."

"But that makes you . . . next in line after Kennedy," Kate said, frowning. "Now that Rebecca is gone, if something happened to Kennedy—"

"No!" Cassidy said, practically shouting as she lurched for Kate. This time, though, she didn't aim for the test. She grabbed Kate by the arms, her grip tight as her eyes loomed close in the darkness. "That's not it."

"And all that debt?" Kate pressed, her gaze flickering toward the door. "What happens to you if you default?"

"I'm working on it," Cassidy said, not convincing either one of them. "I meant what I said. I came here to support Kennedy. My . . . my sister."

She sounded so sad and small as she said it, and in those two words Kate could imagine a very lonely childhood. She'd been an only child, too, but she'd had her mother, and her grandparents, and an active extracurricular life. She'd never been alone, but she'd often been lonely. It was hard when your dreams were so odd, and so specific, like being a published author. She imagined Cassidy might have felt the same way about her culinary dreams.

"You can't say anything," Cassidy said, giving Kate a little shake. "Not to Ken, not to anybody else."

"Cassidy, your aunt was *murdered*. And Kennedy almost died."

"And I told you that wasn't me!" Cassidy said, shaking harder.

"I didn't say it was!" Kate cried. "But someone also tried to smother Kennedy with a pillow in her sleep."

"What?" Cassidy cried, looking truly surprised. "When? How?"

"In her room, after we found her in the wine cave. She thought it was a dream."

"Oh my god," Cassidy said, rubbing one hand across her mouth and smearing her lipstick like the Joker on a bender. "That explains it!"

"Explains what?"

"I heard her thrashing around last night, and I thought maybe she was going to be sick. We all slept in here, you know, to keep an eye on her after. And when I went in, she was sitting straight up in bed, squeezing all the feathers out of her pillow. She said she'd had a nightmare. I didn't think anything of it after what she'd been through. But how could someone get in her room without me seeing them leave?"

They wouldn't, Kate thought, if they *were* Cassidy, but she did seem genuine in her shock. Still, Kate couldn't ignore the facts. If Cassidy was right, and Kennedy's father really was her father, then she stood to inherit everything if Rebecca and Kennedy were out of the way. She'd also had plenty of access to Kennedy's food and drink, since she'd sat right beside her through the entire rehearsal dinner. And she was about to default on a massive amount of debt.

"What were you arguing with Rebecca about in the garden?" Kate pressed. "I saw her slap you."

"That was you?" Cassidy said, once again surprised. "I tried to reason with Auntie R, tell her the truth, make her understand. But she said my father was only doing it to weasel his way into the will, and she wouldn't allow it. I told her I would get a DNA test, and she slapped me and said that proved more than anything I wasn't a real Hempstead, not from the worthy branches of the family. I wouldn't disgrace our name by putting us in some national database. She threatened to get a court order to stop me, to have me expelled entirely. That's why I had to do the test in secret, so she couldn't stop me."

"Kennedy deserves to know the truth."

"Not yet," Cassidy said, frantic. Her grip was so hard on Kate's arms that Kate was positive they would leave bruises. "You're going to ruin everything. I can't let you do that."

Okay, here was definitely where Kate should scream, confession be damned. She opened her mouth and sucked in a breath, but Cassidy slammed her into the wall again, knocking the breath out of her. She bent forward, wheezing, as Cassidy reached over her head and pulled something down. Probably an old rusty sword, or maybe a heavy stuffed badger, something she could bludgeon Kate to death with. Kate was prepared to fight any manner of weaponry to protect herself, but instead she felt the wall dropping away behind her, tumbling her into an empty space.

"What?" was all she could manage, staring up at Cassidy as the wall that had opened behind her started to close up again, like two massive jaws coming together. "No, Cassidy, no!"

"I'm sorry, Kate, but you gave me no choice!" Cassidy whispered as the wall clicked shut. Cassidy said something from the other side of the wall, but it was so muffled Kate couldn't make out the words.

"Cassidy!" she screamed, lurching to her knees, the rough grain of the wood floor tearing up her skin. She banged her fist against the wall, panic gripping her chest. "Cassidy, don't leave me in here!"

Cassidy's voice was nothing more than a faint murmur from the other side, and while Kate couldn't make out any words, she imagined one of them took the shape of the word *sorry*.

Chapter Thirty-Three

Well, *fuck.*

Kate wore out her voice and her fists banging on the wall and screaming for help. She tried fitting her hands into the crack where the walls joined, but they were made of metal and completely immovable. She also tried feeling around the space, but quickly abandoned that as it seemed to be cluttered with years of junk and spiderwebs. She scrubbed her hands against the sequins of her dress, trying to dislodge some of the stickier webs.

Loretta ran her hands over the wall, curling her lip at the spiderwebs. "Spiders. Why did it have to be spiders?"

Nope, that was Indiana Jones, not Loretta Starling.

Loretta zipped off her leather boot, wielding it menacingly at the wall. "Just try to get me, you damn dirty spiders!"

And that was from *Planet of the Apes*, definitely not Loretta. What was wrong with Kate? The harder she asked herself *What Would Loretta Do?*

the murkier the answers became. And *what would Kate Valentine do?* certainly hadn't done her any favors. She couldn't even summon Loretta right now, in her literal darkest hour of need. Why had Loretta forsaken her?

Because Loretta never would have been so easily fooled. She would have solved this thing come morning and celebrated by making everyone Tequila Sunrises to go with their wedding day breakfast. But Kate knew she was nothing like Loretta. Loretta had always been a fantasy for Kate; sure where Kate was doubtful, confident where Kate fretted, sexy where Kate was awkward and insecure. Everything about Loretta's life had been an escape, from the carefree bartending nights to the super sleuth investigations of the daytime. Kate's life was nothing but a computer screen, death investigator websites, and takeout dinners. She'd been lying to herself and everyone else, pretending she could ever be normal this weekend.

She sank into a ball in the pitch black and let herself be miserable, just for the moment. She hadn't ever grieved, not properly, and felt like now was as good a time as any. Because the truth was, she did grieve her relationship with Spencer. Not because of Spencer, but because of her future. She'd had everything planned out, and even if her life had sometimes made her hyperventilate, at least she'd known what was to come. There had been comfort in that, an organization to the chaos. And when he'd broken up with her, he'd broken up her plans for the future and left her unmoored in the chaos.

She might be unmoored, but she was still alive. Though she wouldn't be for long if she didn't find a way out. She stood up and turned back to the door, running her hands over the wall on each side, looking for a release that might open the doors. The space itself was relatively narrow—she could touch the wall on both sides by stretching out her arms—and her hands brushed something rough and woven. A rope, running up the side of one wall. She gave it a tug, thinking it might lead up to another floor or a light.

What she didn't expect was the entire floor of the storage area to lurch and drop several inches. She stumbled back as something overhead groaned and screeched like the metal teeth of a disgruntled dragon. The floor kept dropping, the wall slipping away from her as the small space filled with a series of thuds and screeches.

"No, no, no, no!" she huffed as she scrabbled for something to hold on to, each "no" climbing the octave until they came out as a succession of squeaks instead of words. The opening Cassidy had pushed her through had just enough of a lip that she could hook her fingers onto it, but the floor was descending at a much faster rate. She stretched onto her tiptoes and out of her shoes, trying to keep hold of the ledge. The floor was completely gone, but the screeches and groans kept going for several moments more, until the space filled with a resounding thud and everything went silent.

"Help!" Kate gasped against the brick wall. Her bare feet scrabbled for purchase, little bits of brick dust crumbling away beneath her toes as the sequins on her dress caught against the rough surface and ripped off. After a few tries, she was able to notch her toes into an opening so she wasn't hanging by her fingers alone. She took in a jagged, shallow breath, the expansion of her rib cage pushing her precariously away from the wall.

She screamed for help, as much as her position would allow, and got a puff of stale breath back in her face for the effort. Somewhere in her mind Kate wondered if this, actually, was her lowest point. But no, her lowest point waited wherever the rest of the room had gone, possibly hundreds of feet below in the pitch black.

Panic set in, making her arms tremble and her heart pump so hard she was afraid it was going to push her right off the wall. She couldn't even suck in enough breath for a second scream, and what good would it do her, anyway? Nobody could hear her.

Something creaked overhead and suddenly Kate could see the brown brick in front of her face. She looked up through a haze of cobwebs and swirls of dust, and twenty feet above was a head of glorious golden curls looking down at her through a shaft of pale light.

"Kate?" Jake called.

"Jake!" she cried, nearly losing her toe grip in the process. "Jake, help!"

"What are you doing down there?" Jake asked, completely bewildered.

"Can I explain when I'm not hanging by my fingers and toes?" Kate asked, trying (and failing) to keep the hysteria out of her voice.

"It looks like there's some kind of pulley system up here," Jake said. "Kate, I think this might be an old manual lift."

Well, that would explain the floor suddenly dropping out from underneath her feet. "Can you pull the rope? I'm a bit indisposed at the moment."

"Hang on, let me give it a go," Jake said, and then the narrow shaft was filled with creaking and groaning and shrieking again. Only this time she knew it wasn't a dragon, but the pulley system of the elevator that probably hadn't been oiled in several decades. Her fingers ached and she was pretty sure she felt something crawling over the top of her foot, and she squeezed her eyes shut and willed her hands to hang on for just a few minutes longer. But she wasn't a rock climber, and soon her fingers were slipping and uncurling no matter what she threatened to do to them if they let go.

"Jake, I'm slipping!" she cried.

"This rope is full of splinters," Jake grunted. "It's hell on my hands."

"My hands are doing just great!" Kate said sarcastically.

"I think I see the lift coming up!" Jake said. "Just a second longer!"

But Kate had used up all her seconds, and her trembling hands lost their grip entirely. She screamed as she plummeted down into the pitch-black abyss below.

Or would have plummeted down, except Jake was right about the lift coming up. Instead of crashing several stories below and breaking all her bones, she landed on her backside with a muttered "shit" and only a slight bit of bruising to her tailbone.

"Are you okay?" Jake called.

"I'm okay now," she said, grimacing at the network of spiderwebs between her and the top of the elevator shaft. Maybe she would have been better off plummeting to her death. "How did you find me?"

"Well," Jake grunted, hauling her through the sea of webs, "the Hempsteads were all arguing about who wanted to kill their aunt more, and next thing I knew I turned around and you were gone. I thought you might have gone to the room for your suspects list, but you weren't in the attic. Then I heard this awful screeching sound, which I thought might be you screaming, but turns out it was just these unoiled pulley gears. And then you really did scream, and I found this cabinet door here in a bedroom, and when I opened it up there's a lift door behind it. And here we are."

The elevator platform had reached the top of the shaft, and Kate was now covered in cobwebs and face-to-face with Jake, who had the nerve to grin at her.

"Don't you dare," she said, holding up a wispy finger.

"Caught you in my web," Jake said, his eyes gleaming.

"I hate you," Kate said miserably.

Chapter Thirty-Four

"How did you end up in a freight lift?" Jake asked as she crawled her way out of the elevator, her legs shaking as she stood.

"Cassidy," she said grimly, reaching for an antique armoire for support. She pulled at the sticky clumps of spiderwebs draped over her arms and shoulders, shuddering as she tried to rub them off her hands onto a velvet upholstered stool beside the armoire. "She locked me in there. I'm not sure she realized it was an elevator. I can't imagine that thing's been used since Russell Hempstead's time. She probably thought it was just another secret passage."

"Why in the world would Cassidy lock you up?" Jake asked, bewildered.

Kate sighed. "Because she's Kennedy's sister."

"Ahhhh," Jake said, nodding, before pausing and shaking his head. "Nope, I'm going to need more than that."

"Cassidy's dad is not her dad," Kate said, flicking away more webs. "Her dad couldn't have kids, and her mom really wanted them, so they made some kind of deal with Gordon Hempstead, Kennedy's father, to get Cassidy's mom pregnant. Apparently, Cassidy didn't know until recently. But it means if Rebecca and Kennedy are both dead, she becomes—"

"The next heir to the Hempstead fortune," Jake said, realization dawning. "Which means she could use her access to the family funds to pay off all those debts she's about to default on."

"But she needed proof of paternity, and since Gordon Hempstead has been dead for almost two decades, Kennedy was the next closest thing. I caught Cassidy with a DNA test. If she can prove they're a sibling match, she jumps the inheritance line, right to the top."

"So, she's our murderer?" Jake said.

Kate frowned at the mass of webs that only stretched and stuck the more she tried to extricate them from her hair. "She's definitely a primary suspect, since she's obviously willing to do whatever it takes to protect her secret."

"Let me help," Jake said, moving behind her and gently extracting the webs. "You know, this isn't as bad as the time Charlie and I went spelunking in Chillagoe Caves in Australia. Spiders the size of your face. I found a sac of them in my bag when we got home. My mum nearly burned the house down."

"Not helping," Kate said miserably. "I think I ruined my dress in the elevator shaft, too, when I was holding on to the wall. It was so cute, too, and so expensive."

She ran her hands over the frayed strings and broken sequins where the wall had scraped away the delicate design, looking down just in time to spot a large brown spider crawling down the front of her dress and disappearing into the shadows of her cleavage. She let out a sound somewhere between a screech and a dog whistle, tumbling back into Jake and wriggling in panic.

"Kate, what is it?" Jake asked. "What's wrong?"

"Spider," she wheezed. "Spider. Spider! Get it . . . get it off. Off!"

"What? Where?" Jake asked.

"Get it off!" Kate huffed, twisting her arms around to try to reach the flimsy little zipper along the back. She imagined she could feel the spider in there, rooting around, making a little web home, laying its little spider babies. She needed out of the dress, and possibly a cleansing fire, before she would ever feel safe again. But her fingers only caught at sequins. Why did they make fancy dress zippers so tiny and ineffectual? It was like they wanted you to have to get cut out of their expensive dresses and buy a new one every time.

"Jake, get it off!" she cried, her voice still reedy and panicked. "Get it off!"

"I can't get it off if I can't see it," Jake said, trying to hold her still.

"Not the spider, the dress," Kate snapped. "Get the dress off!"

"Hang on," Jake muttered, tugging at the zipper. "This zipper is garbage."

"I know," Kate said. For all she knew, the baby spiders had already hatched and were running a little spider empire in her bra.

Jake worked some kind of magic and suddenly the dress dropped to the floor in a sequined heap. The spider crawled out from the folds, scurrying off indignantly.

But Kate could still feel it crawling on her skin, despite the fact that she could now see most of her skin with the dress gone. She wore a strapless bra and a pair of highly impractical lace panties, neither of which was substantial enough to hide a small spider army. But still she couldn't stop the feeling of something tickling across her chest, and she wriggled back against Jake on instinct, as if the friction created between them might burn away the sensation. At least until he sucked in a breath through his teeth, his hands dropping to her hips in a tight grip.

"Kate," he choked out. "Stop that."

"Why?" she asked, shivering. He groaned, his fingers digging into her hip bones, hard and unyielding. And it was only as that thought occurred to her that she noticed something else hard and unyielding, pressing against the lace outline of her panties. She'd forgotten she even packed them until she was getting dressed for the ceremony. But they made her ass look great, a fact she was rapidly becoming aware of as Jake's erection pressed harder into her back.

"Kate," Jake said, his tone impossible to read. His fingers still gripped her hips, either stopping or holding her there, she couldn't tell. He didn't move, just held her still, his body radiating heat into her skin.

She gathered all the courage it had taken to hang on in that elevator shaft and arched her back, purposefully grinding her hips against his. His reaction was immediate and swift, a groan rumbling through their connected skin as he held her hips down and still, his forehead dropping against the slope of her shoulder. His breath burned her skin where it touched her, hot and fast, like he was having his own version of a panic attack.

There was a murderer loose on the island, Kate had nearly been pancaked by a hidden elevator, and Kennedy was still in danger. But all her worry, all her puzzle-solving, dissipated under the heat of Jake's caress. She could barely remember to breathe, much less think straight, with his body pressed against hers. Besides, Rebecca wasn't getting any deader.

"Jake?" she ventured.

"What?" he panted, turning his face so his nose dragged across the curve of her shoulder, like the smell of her was a drug he needed in his system.

"I'm very, very sober," she whispered.

He gave an unsteady laugh, his mouth against her throat, and she wasn't shivering from the cold alone anymore. "Are you sure?"

She knew he didn't only mean her state of inebriation, though she certainly felt drunk on the sensation of Jake's fingers, Jake's chest, Jake's heat. Drunk on Jake. It was an addiction she'd quit cold turkey two years ago, had thought herself long over it, but now, with him pressed up against her, it seemed almost laughable that she would have ever gotten over this. She let her head drop back against him, sighing in anticipation.

"I'm absolutely sure," she said, raising a hand to his head as he pressed his lips against her throat, using his hands on her hip bones to pull her in closer, both of them panting at the friction it created. "Jake?"

He paused, the tension in his body like a coiled serpent. "What?"

"You have too many clothes on."

He grazed his teeth over her skin in answer. "Let me fix that."

"Let me," she said, already turning in his arms, tugging at buttons and fabric until she finally, blissfully, had his scorching skin against hers.

His lips found hers as her hands tangled in his hair, rising up on her tiptoes to press her entire body against his. It was astonishing how quickly she was getting used to kissing Jake Hawkins, even as it felt like something brand new and incredible every time. It was a feeling she was afraid to get used to, a craving she would carry the rest of her days that she already knew no one else could satisfy. His tongue flicked against hers, a rough slide that turned soft and playful as he traced along her upper lip, his teeth catching the curve of her lower lip and tugging on it.

"God, you taste delicious," he said, fingers sliding into her hair and pulling her head toward him. "Like a dessert wine, or a plum cake. I want to eat you whole."

Kate went liquid at the pure lust in his tone, the possessive way his other hand kept hold of her hip as he guided her back toward a bed in the far corner of the room that was blessedly free of stuffed creatures of any kind, her thighs bumping against the soft edge. It was easy to convince herself she was dreaming, that this was all a fantasy, or that she'd really lost her grip and plummeted to the bottom of the elevator shaft and this was heaven. But the feelings were too pointed, too sensory. The soft scratch of his golden chest hair rubbing against her breastbone; the faint trace of orange juice still on his tongue; the way her toes cracked from the cold as she curled them into the lush carpeting.

"You're cold," Jake said, his arms sweeping up the flat plane of her back.

"I'm not," Kate whispered, digging her fingers into the waistband of his dress pants and tugging him closer.

He growled against her mouth as she kissed him again, Kate working the button and zipper on his pants as he flicked her strapless bra open in one deft maneuver. She knew it was probably from plenty of practice, but she didn't even have the headspace to be jealous just then. Only to be grateful to all those other women for molding this version of Jake, who knew exactly where to touch her to fill up the rest of her headspace.

"You are cold," he said, shaking his head as he tossed her bra on top of her discarded dress. "Your skin is covered in goose bumps."

"That's not why," Kate said, her nipples tightening into sensitive peaks as they rubbed against his chest.

She finished fumbling with his zipper—with far less finesse—and stripped him down to his underwear, a black pair of boxer briefs that looked like they were painted on. Her mouth watered so hard it hurt. She brushed the back of her hand against him, soft and playful, and he groaned against her lips.

He reached behind her and pulled the fluffy bed coverings free. "In."

"Fine, but only because I want to, not because you told me," Kate said, turning around and climbing up on the bed. But Jake's hands were on her hips, stopping her before she could crawl under the covers, spreading out to span the roundness of her ass. One finger slid under the edge of the lace, running the length of it.

"These are a sin," he said, his voice hoarse as he leaned down and kissed the edge of the panties along her lower back. His thumbs swept up and pressed into her lower back on either side of her spine. "Why did you even bring these this weekend? What were you planning to do with them?"

"I don't know," Kate said honestly. "I thought they would make me feel sexy enough to be confident."

"And do you?" Jake asked. "Do you feel sexy enough to be confident right now?"

"I . . ." Kate faltered. Did she feel sexy enough? It had never really been a consideration for Kate, certainly not around someone as effortlessly sexy as Jake. But how did she feel now, knowing he wanted her, knowing she wanted the same? Could she measure up to her own expectations, much less his?

"Should I tell you?" Jake whispered, leaning forward, his breath warming the length of her spine. He gently guided her up on the bed, laying her down on her belly and pulling the covers up over her legs. The rest of her he warmed with his own body, lowering himself to one side of her. "Should I tell you how badly I want to fuck you right now? Should I tell you how incredible your ass looks in these, and how I want to take them off you and keep them for myself so you never wear them for anyone else? How it made my heart stop when I opened that lift door and saw you hanging there, thinking what would have happened if I'd been just a minute later?"

Kate turned her head, his face so close she couldn't ignore the earnest roughness in his expression. "I was figuring it out."

He grunted his doubt against the curve of her neck. "This whole weekend you've been testing the limits of my patience, and I think it's only fair that I test yours."

And he did, running his tongue from the nape of her neck down her spine to the top of her panties, his hands gravitating toward the curves of her ass like they couldn't help themselves. She sighed into the pillows as his hands moved everywhere, sliding up the sides of her hips and into the dip of her waist, tickling the sensitive skin under her arms before cupping her breasts and rolling her nipples.

"Your tits are amazing," he breathed against her neck. "A perfect handful."

"Jake, I want to touch you," Kate whispered, squirming back against the weight of him pressed to one side of her.

"Who am I to deny a lady?" he said, smiling as he let her turn in his arms.

Her hands went to the waistband of his underwear, her fingers sweeping just below the elastic in the same teasing motion he'd used on her only moments ago. He sucked in a breath and let it out in a sigh, kissing her as either a reward or a distraction.

Kate let herself touch Jake everywhere she'd always imagined touching him, along the tight ridges of his abdomen, down the rock-hard length of his thighs, and gently over the scars from his accident. He explored her as she explored him, touching and tasting and teasing until Kate was moaning and begging, driven to the edge of her patience as he promised.

"If you want something, Kate, all you have to do is ask," he teased against her mouth as he slid the lace of her panties lower, exposing more of her skin to his fingers.

"I want you," Kate said, repaying the favor and sliding his boxer briefs down. "Oh, you're so . . ."

"So what?" Jake asked, grinning as he kissed down her neck toward her breasts.

"So . . . thick," Kate said, biting her lip as she wrapped her hand around him. "Ohhhh."

"Keep doing that," Jake said roughly, putting his hand over hers and moving her up and down. He was hot and smooth in her hand, growing longer and thicker as she worked him up and down.

"Do you have anything?" Kate whispered, afraid to break the spell.

"Ah," Jake said, leaning over the edge of the bed and rustling around until he came up with a black foil wrapper. "For emergencies."

Kate frowned at it. "Where did you get that?"

"My wallet," Jake said, tearing open the top.

"Not next to the emergency toothpick, I hope," Kate said.

Jake grinned. "No."

And then she didn't really care if it was next to the emergency toothpick or not, because Jake was laying her back and hooking his hand under one knee to make room for his body between her legs. And then he was easing into her in little rocking motions, his solid thickness stretching her with each motion, the movements making slick noises until he slid all the way in and they both groaned as their groins connected. He stopped there, giving them a moment to adjust, and all Kate could do was look up at him.

She'd never been this close to Jake, not in all their years of friendship and all her years of not-so-quiet pining. She'd thought she knew every aspect of him, but up close he was more flawed, which somehow made him more perfect. He had a small scar above his left eyebrow, and his ears stuck out more than she realized, the effect minimized by the length of his hair. It made her want to tug on one playfully.

There were so many things to discover, but this was still Jake. Jake, who had been her first and most enthusiastic fan when he'd encouraged her to finish the original Loretta novel; who'd made a game of trying new restaurants each time they met to discuss the *Wandering Australian* series; who always brought her takeout when they were on deadline; who had so gamely played the role of partner in crime-solving all weekend despite its many dangerous twists and turns; the true inspiration for Blake (though she'd die before she admitted it to him or Spencer at this point). The man who had introduced her to so many new places and people and experiences, who had truly opened up Seattle in a way she'd never managed to crack before meeting him. The man who had finally made a place she'd once thought of as just a city she lived in truly feel like home. The man she'd built so many fantasies on, and now he was inside her.

"Kate," he said, brushing his lips against her temple. "Is this okay?"

He wasn't experiencing the same rising tide of emotions that she was; he couldn't be. Because it had robbed her of the power of speech, had taken up all the extra room in her throat until she felt she might choke on the emotion. This was her Jake, but he wasn't her Jake. He never would be. She'd go back to her one-bedroom apartment and he'd pack another bag for some new exotic destination and it would be months, maybe years, before she saw him again. When she hadn't been this close to him, she'd convinced herself she could handle it. But now, he was too close, her heart too unguarded, and even as she tried to steady her breathing and keep her chest from bursting open and offering her heart up on a platter to him, tears welled in the corners of her eyes and spilled down her temples, pooling into her ears.

"Kate," Jake said, pulling back to look down at her. His expression so full of concern. "We can stop. It's all right."

"No," Kate said, shaking her head. "I don't want to stop. I just . . ."

How could she tell him? How could she express the feelings she'd buried so deep she'd been afraid to admit them to herself? She was too overwhelmed, too stripped bare physically and emotionally to lie to herself now. It was Jake. It had always been Jake. It always would be Jake, even when she knew it never could be Jake.

But she couldn't say any of that out loud, not now, not ever. All she could do was reach up and cup his face with her hands to pull him down into a kiss, pouring all of the things she couldn't say into the gesture. It was the closest she could ever get to telling Jake how she really felt about him, and she made it count, canting her hips up so that he sunk another inch deeper into her. He groaned against her mouth, drawing back and sliding in, setting an intense rhythm that quickly had both of them panting against each other.

"God, you're so wet," Jake said. "You feel . . . Kate, you feel so fucking amazing. You're so fucking amazing. I've never . . . I can't . . ."

His breathing turned ragged and harsh, his thrusts bordering on frenetic, his muscles slicked in sweat. Kate ran her hands up his back, so gentle over his scars, until she reached his shoulders. She dug her nails in hard, reaching up to whisper in his ear.

"Come for me," she said, before biting into his earlobe.

He shuddered and groaned, thrusting in hard and making a sound Kate could only describe as helpless. He thrust a few more times, long and deep, burying his face in her neck as he came hard and fast, panting her name over and over as her own orgasm hit and she clenched around him, making him shudder again.

"God, Kate," he said, collapsing against her, heavy and boneless. "God."

She smiled up at the ceiling as she raked her nails softly down his back, her tears nearly dry. She swore to keep it that way. "I like it when you call me that."

Chapter Thirty-Five

Several minutes passed—or hours, possibly days; time was a very loose construct after all that exertion—before Kate regained the capacity for speech. Even when rational thought returned, the words uncurled out of her like a soft, slurring purr. She had tucked herself into Jake's side, one leg hitched high over his hip, her head on his chest and her arm wrapped around him and tucked under his ribs. They'd burrowed under the covers on the bed, which were surprisingly soft and normal, all things considered.

"You're so warm," Kate said, snuggling into all of his soft corners. "I want to cut you open like a tauntaun and crawl inside you like Han Solo."

To his credit, Jake only tucked her in closer.

"Something is still bothering me." Kate sighed, fighting against the heaviness of her body and the gritty feeling every time she blinked.

"Then I haven't done my job properly," Jake said with a grin.

"About the murder," Kate said, pushing at his shoulder playfully. "And Cassidy. If she'd wanted a DNA test on Kennedy, why take the poisoned champagne glass? I mean, she could have just swabbed Kennedy as soon as she passed out. Why take the one piece of evidence that connects her to the crime? Unless she didn't *know* the glass was poisoned."

Jake propped himself up on one elbow to face her. "So now you're thinking Cassidy wasn't the murderer?"

"I mean, if she'd taken the glass as evidence—to hide it, or get rid of it—I'd be sure it was her. But she took it to swab it for Kennedy's DNA. Which implies she didn't realize that was how Kennedy had been poisoned."

"So, what then? We're back to Richie and Steven as our murderers?"

"They both certainly have motive," Kate reasoned. "And I'm positive they're the ones who have been sabotaging the house. Probably to tank Rebecca's chances with the historical inspector. But their efforts have been rushed and poorly thought out. I mean, cutting the generator fuel line? They were just as likely to blow themselves up as anything else. And whoever planned Kennedy's and Rebecca's deaths really planned things out. I mean, they used my books as a blueprint, for pete's sake. That kind of planning and foresight doesn't exactly seem like Richie Hempstead's forte."

"That certainly knocks out Marcus Sheffield, then," Jake said, rolling on his back and propping up his head with both hands. "Which puts us back at square one, doesn't it?"

Kate huffed out a breath in annoyance. "After all these years of dreaming up Loretta, I thought I'd be better at solving a real-life murder mystery. It's not nearly as fun as I imagined."

"And yet it's just as disastrous as I imagined, having read Loretta all these years. I was genuinely angry with you when the fourth book was delayed, although I obviously didn't know why when I saw your Instagram update from Borneo."

Kate didn't want to think about Borneo right now, not when she finally had a naked Jake Hawkins wrapped between her thighs. She didn't want to think of the heartbreak that would ensue when he inevitably left again.

"I need proper clothes," she said, suddenly feeling shy. "You'll have to get them for me, since I'm still a wanted woman. And because I'd rather parade around this house naked than ever put that dress back on."

"Mmmm, I might make you get them yourself just to see that," Jake said, grinning as he dipped his head toward the soft curve of her neck.

"There's something I'm still missing," Kate said, sighing and stretching her neck to afford him better access. "I can feel it. I just don't know what. So, I'm going to need my suspect lists, too. Please."

"Are you sure you wouldn't rather stay here and convince me *you* aren't the murderer?" Jake said, shifting and pressing against her and making it clear how much he didn't think she was a murderer.

"After," Kate gasped, giving into his kiss. "Catch a killer, get off this absolutely cursed island, then this all over again. Several times, preferably."

Jake sighed, pushing up off the bed. "I was out of condoms, anyway. Which is an oversight I'll never make again."

"Hurry back," Kate said as he slipped out the door, attempting a sultry smile that was undercut by the yawn that erupted from her. She really ought to go over the evidence again, or find her way back to Kennedy and warn her that she was still in danger, or do something. But instead she relinquished herself to the blissful sleep that only a fantastic sexual encounter could bring, a sleep so deep it felt like only seconds later when the handle of the door rattled, dragging her back to the surface.

"That was fast." She sat up, the covers slipping away as the door swung open, revealing not Jake, but—"Spencer?"

Spencer looked up from the door handle with a frown. "Kate? Why are you naked?"

"That is . . . a long story," Kate said, pulling up the covers for some modesty. "What are you doing up here on the fourth floor?"

Spencer looked around in confusion. "Is this the fourth floor? What am I doing on the fourth floor?"

Kate leaned in closer, peering at his bloodshot eyes. "Spencer, are you *high*?"

"Shhhh!" Spencer said, looking around the hall again.

"Oh my god, your mom is going to kill you," Kate said in a jubilant whisper.

"I know that," Spencer said, exaggerated. "That's why I'm hiding in here. Do you have anything to eat? I could murder a charcuterie board right now."

"How high are you?" Kate asked on a half laugh.

"In case you hadn't noticed, it's been a stressful couple of days for me," Spencer muttered. "I took some gummies from Richie. I thought it would help me relax, but I can't feel my face and I have no idea how to get around this fucking house. And now Rebecca's dead, and Ken and her cousins are fighting, and Ken ate some bad shellfish last night, apparently? I didn't even know because I was too busy being a selfish asshole asking Ian how to get out of my prenup. Ken deserves better than this. Better than me."

He groaned and slumped down onto a nearby ottoman, burying his face in his hands. Kate had to wrestle the giant comforter loose from the bed and wrap it around her nakedness as she dragged it across the room and sank down to the floor at his feet, patting his knee.

"There are some . . . issues to sort out, sure."

"Issues." Spencer snorted. "That's the understatement of the year. She works so hard, and she cares so much, and she just . . . she deserves the best. Better than any of us are giving her."

Kate had been so focused on Rebecca's murder, so sure that Kennedy's poisoning had been a distraction, but what if she was wrong? Loretta would tell her not to go jumping to conclusions and assume Kennedy wasn't the target all along. If someone had a grudge against Kennedy, Spencer might know something about it. "Spencer, do you know if anybody has been . . . I don't know, upset lately? With Kennedy, I mean. I know about the fight with Rebecca over the wedding, but what about anyone else in her family? Or the board of trustees? Or at work?" A thought occurred to Kate. "Maybe even someone who might be upset with me, too?"

Someone who might want to frame Kate for their crimes.

Spencer gave her a look. "You mean besides Serena Archer and her mighty lion's roar picket line out there?"

"Why *is* Serena so upset with Kennedy?" Kate asked. "At the rehearsal dinner, she was going on about Kennedy poisoning you and Simon against her, and people having their contracts withheld. And I know you said Simon might be looking to sell the company, but that doesn't explain why he'd hold back on all contracts. And what does any of that have to do with Kennedy? She's head of marketing, sure, but she doesn't run the place."

Spencer side-eyed her. "Unofficially and off the record?"

Kate rolled her eyes. "Seriously? At this point?"

"Kennedy isn't quite the silent partner I said she was," Spencer said. "I think she meant to start out that way, but once she was involved with the finances, she realized how much better Simon is at reading books than he was at keeping them, if you know what I mean."

"Simon Says wasn't profitable," Kate guessed.

"It wasn't just not profitable. It was hemorrhaging money. Simon was paying out these big advances for local authors who would sell maybe a thousand copies, if we were lucky. I mean, he shelled out a hundred grand for Marla's first book. And, yeah, it got some decent coverage, won a few local awards, got reviewed in *The New York Times*. But a hundred grand for an esoteric feminist fairy-tale retelling?" Spencer shook his head. "And she wasn't the only one. Serena hasn't earned out on her last seven books, but Simon kept buying them for the same money. Renewing her contract even as her sales dropped. Simon kept saying we needed to invest in local talent, but those investments weren't paying us back. We're a small publisher, we don't have the protection of big-name bestsellers to make up for our losses. The Loretta books have been the only thing keeping us afloat the past three years, basically."

"Oh," Kate said. She knew they were profitable, considering her royalty checks, but she hadn't considered how much they might mean to everyone else working at Simon Says. "So, what did Kennedy do after she gave Simon Says her cash infusion?"

"Look, Kennedy might seem like the cheerleader sorority type, but she's not the future Hempstead heir for nothing." Spencer made a ghastly face. "I guess she's the actual Hempstead heir now. God. Am I going to have to live here?"

"Spencer?" Kate prompted. "The money?"

Spencer shook his head. "Right. Ken knows her way around a checkbook, and a family like the Hempsteads doesn't stay as wealthy as they are without learning how to balance the budget. Once she saw the trajectory Simon Says was on, she knew she had to right the ship. So she started holding budget meetings with Simon, looking at where they could cut expenses to keep the doors open. And one of the first places, the most obvious, was book advances."

"So Kennedy was the one who decided to cut contracts?" That was a prime motive for Serena to want revenge on Kennedy, indeed.

Spencer shrugged uncomfortably. "Sort of? I mean, yes, technically. But it's not like anyone else knew. Or they shouldn't have, if it weren't for . . ."

"For what?" Kate asked. She held up a finger. "Don't tell me you're not supposed to say, Spencer, I will end you."

"Somebody's been . . . leaking privileged information," Spencer said begrudgingly.

"The mole!" Kate gasped, remembering her conversation with Juliette.

"That sounds like an Ian Fleming novel, but yes, sure. The mole. That's how Serena and the others found out about Kennedy becoming a partner in the business, and how they found out that she was the reason their advances were so much smaller, or why their options weren't picked up on their newest books. It's been a huge mess, and we haven't been able to figure out who's been doing it. For all I know, it's Serena herself."

Juliette certainly seemed to think so, considering the fact that she was snooping in Serena's room last night. Still, it didn't explain who killed Rebecca Hempstead, or why.

Spencer sighed, rubbing at his already bloodshot eyes. "I can't even get married without everything blowing up in my face."

"Hey, hey, it's gonna be okay," Kate said again, patting his knee awkwardly.

"Is it?" Spencer groaned, looking at her through his fingers. "Because it feels like a pretty disastrous start right now."

"It's . . . not the most auspicious of beginnings," Kate admitted. "But, hey. Nowhere to go but up from here, right?"

"Don't do that," Spencer said, closing his fingers up again.

"Don't do what? Try to make you feel better?"

"Dismiss my feelings," Spencer said. "You always made me feel like shit."

"That's not what I was trying to do," Kate said in surprise. But Spencer was still going.

"'Why are you sad about not getting the executive editor position when you said you didn't want the responsibility anyway?'" Spencer pitched his voice up in what she guessed was supposed to be an imitation of her own. "'Hey, I know your dad ignores your existence, but at least yours is still alive!' Or, my personal favorite, 'of course I love you, Spencer, why would you even question that? I'm just emotionally unavailable, daydreaming about Jake as Blake the bartender. But you're the one I'm sitting on the couch with, so it's all fine, isn't it?'"

"That's . . ." Kate frowned to herself. "Possibly a valid point. But you're not innocent here! You cheated on me with Kennedy!"

Spencer sighed, pulling at his hair. "I kissed her once, Kate. And I came home and confessed right away. I thought it would finally be a wake-up call to stop dragging your feet on the wedding. But you acted like it meant the end. Like you couldn't wait to get out. I ended things because you made it so obvious it was what you wanted."

"What I wanted?" Kate said, sitting up in shock before remembering the comforter. Spencer's eyes followed the fluffy white material as it dropped dangerously low, before she snatched it back up. "You are not making this my fault. You fell in love with someone else!"

Spencer looked so ragged it squeezed her heart. "Just because I fell in love with her didn't mean I fell out of love with you. The only difference was she loved me back."

"I loved you," Kate said, quiet, hurt.

"Maybe at one point." Spencer sighed. "But not in the end. Not for a long time. I was just a security blanket for you, and you were the kid who couldn't grow up and learn to sleep alone."

It was a hurtful accusation, if possibly a true one. Still, there was something that needed resolving in this weekend of mysteries. "Spencer, when Jake and I had our falling-out . . . how did you know I tried to kiss him?"

"Oh." Spencer's expression turned sheepish. "I was kind of hoping that would never come up."

Kate narrowed her gaze. "What did you do?"

"For the record, I just want to say it happened years ago, and I've grown since then—"

"Spencer!" Kate said, prodding him hard in the leg. "What did you do?"

"Ow," he said, rubbing at the spot. "Fine. You called me."

"I did not!" Kate said. "You called me, and said that Jake had called you!"

"No, no, I mean, you called me that night. After he'd left. I think you thought I was Marla. I guess our names must be in your phone right next to each other."

Lieman. Lynch. It never occurred to Kate that they were. That explained why Marla had never called her back that night.

"Anyway, you left me a voicemail, and you were pretty hysterical. Saying you'd screwed things up with Jake. So, I called Jake the next day, and I swear I only intended to fix things. To figure out what exactly happened, and make sure Jake didn't file an HR complaint or something. But once I started talking to him, it just kind of . . . spiraled."

"Spiraled?" Kate echoed, deadpan.

"I'm sorry," Spencer said. "It was wrong, and deceitful, and definitely unprofessional. It's just . . . I liked you so much. I'd been trying to work up the courage to ask you out for so long, but I didn't want to compromise our working relationship. And then you met Jake, and it was like the sun came out for you. I figured he would pass out of your life eventually, but you started working on the *Wandering Australian* books. When you called me and said you tried to kiss him, I just felt like I needed to do something. I never thought it would go as far as it did."

"You mean destroying our entire friendship and ending the book contracts early and then dating me without telling me the truth?"

"I know, I know!" Spencer moaned into his hands. "I'm such a fuckup. Honestly, when I proposed, I figured you would say no. You were always half out the door, anyway. I was just as shocked as you were when you said yes."

She had been shocked—not that he'd asked, but that she'd said yes. And she *had* been half out the door their entire relationship, even when she'd told herself she was over Jake and ready to build a life with Spencer. It was all so clear now, from the other side. But they'd had to wade through all that shit to get here.

"Aren't we a pair." Kate sighed, laying her head against Spencer's leg. "I'm sorry, Spencer. For everything."

He ran his hand over her hair. "I'm sorry, too, Kate. For everything."

They sat like that for a while, ruminating on what could have been, what never would have been, and what must be now. At least, that was what Kate was doing. She assumed Spencer was doing the same thing, until he spoke again.

"Do you ever think about how squirrels have all the data they need to overrun the human race?" he asked. "Ferrets, too. They're like long squirrels."

"Come on, Cheech, up you go," Kate said, struggling to straighten up with the comforter still wrapped around her as she offered him a hand.

"What if I'm not good enough?" Spencer asked, staggering to his feet.

"Good enough to fight off the squirrels? I'm sure you'll manage."

"For Ken," Spencer said, looking like a lost puppy. "I was never good enough for you."

Kate sighed. "You weren't not good enough for me, Spencer. You just weren't right for me. And I wasn't right for you. I think that's why I got so obsessed with Loretta. She was an escape from a life I didn't want."

"I suppose that makes sense," Spencer said glumly. He frowned. "Did you mean what you said, about the . . . the oral thing?"

Kate grimaced. "Ahhhh. . . ."

She was saved the embarrassment of answering by the man responsible for the statement in the first place as Jake slipped in the room. "Found your clothes and a couple of torches to—Ah. Spencer's here."

"He was just leaving," Kate said, giving him a friendly push toward the door.

"Right," Spencer said, slapping his hands against his thighs. He took a deep breath and closed his eyes, stepping up to Jake. "I'm ready."

"Ready for what?" Jake asked.

"For you to punch me in the face."

Jake looked bewildered. "Why would I punch you in the face?"

"No, it's okay," Spencer said. "I insist. I tried to take your woman, it's your right."

Jake looked to Kate, incredulous, but she only shook her head and mouthed *he really didn't*, trying her best not to break out laughing.

"Spencer, mate, look at me," Jake said.

"I am looking at you."

Jake sighed. "No, you're not. Your eyes are closed."

"Oh." Spencer blinked his eyes open, looking around. "Oh, that's why it got so dark all of a sudden. I thought the power went out again."

Jake took Spencer by the shoulders and looked at him earnestly. "I'm not gonna punch you right now, all right? Consider it my wedding gift to you."

"That's really good to hear, honestly," Spencer said, his shoulders slumping forward. "I really didn't want to get punched in the face. You're a good, handsome man, Jake."

"Same to you, mate," Jake said, ushering Spencer out with a shake of his head.

Chapter Thirty-Six

Jake waited until the door was properly locked before turning to Kate. "What the hell happened in here?"

"You wouldn't believe me if I told you," she said, finally letting loose the laugh she'd been holding in. "Did you happen to scrounge up any snacks while you were out? I think I got a contact high just sitting next to him."

"He *was* high, wasn't he?" Jake looked back at the door in bemusement. "What was he doing in here?"

Kate shrugged as she pulled on the clothes Jake had brought. "He said he got lost."

"And you believed him?" Jake said incredulously. He turned away from her, his voice dropping to a mutter, but it didn't keep her from hearing him. "Of course you did."

"Why wouldn't I believe him?" Kate asked. "Jake, he was high as a kite. He's like a Sims right now, I'm positive he'd get stuck in a corner if there wasn't someone there to turn him around. And believe me, he was just as surprised as I was that I was naked."

"You let him in here while you were naked?" Jake asked.

Kate pointed at her recently acquired clothes. "I didn't have much of a choice. And technically he let himself in, so."

"Because you were supposed to lock the door behind me," Jake said, annoyed. "And you really think, of all the dozens of rooms in this haunted hell house, he just happened to find yours? What if Spencer is the murderer and I hadn't come back when I did?"

Kate snorted, collecting the suspect sheets Jake had brought with him and shuffling Spencer's to the bottom of the stack. "Spencer can be a lot of things, but he's not a murderer. We have plenty of other suspects with much better motives to focus on right now. Besides, he's got an alibi for the window of the poisoning."

Jake crossed his arms. "And what is this alibi?"

"That's . . . not important," Kate said. His alibi didn't exactly exonerate him, and the last thing she needed was to give Jake more ammunition against Spencer.

"I don't understand your obsessive need to defend him," Jake said, and Kate could practically hear his teeth grinding together. "The guy is a complete twat. He cheated on you, left you to marry the other woman, and yet he keeps finding all kinds of ways to be around you this weekend. He's clearly still hung up on you."

"That's not what's happening here," Kate said, her own jaw clenching. "I wouldn't expect you to understand."

"Understand what?" Jake asked, crossing his arms and staring her down.

"My relationship with Spencer is . . . complicated. Our lives are entwined. He's my editor, for pete's sake! I can't just . . . abandon him."

"Oh, you mean like I abandoned you? That's what you're saying, isn't it?"

"Maybe it is, yeah," Kate said. "I mean, come on, you're not exactly Mr. Stick Around Guy. You're only here this weekend because your business partner got sick, and I'm sure you'll be jetting off somewhere else as soon as the boat reaches the docks in Seattle."

"Except I won't!" Jake said, throwing his arms wide. "I'm trying to sell my share in the business. I'm sick of living out of a suitcase, catering to Wall Street bros and their egos. I'm sick of literally being sick, getting twenty different shots and vaccines just to catch some new strain of what's going around. That's partly why I even came to this fucking wedding. I needed to talk to Simon about a new book. Something that would make me enough that I could afford to quit."

"You mean another *Wandering Australian* book?" Kate said, stung. "Without me?"

"It's not like you were willing to write it with me, now, is it?" Jake's tone was bitter.

"It wasn't like that," Kate protested. "I told you. I mean, I was busy with Loretta, and you were talking about gallivanting off on some trip, and I didn't even know what the future was for the *Wandering* books! You didn't want to work with me anymore, and Spencer said that Loretta could really be something, and I—"

"And that's why you chose Spencer, isn't it? That's why he was worth breaking all your dumb little rules about maintaining professionalism and I wasn't, isn't that the truth? Because he was reliable, nothing like Jake of All Trades."

"He *is* reliable," Kate said quietly. "And, yeah, that does matter to me. I know what it's like to be alone, abandoned. That's nothing to sneer at."

"Except he wasn't reliable, when it came down to it. He proved to be just as much of a fuckup as you seem to think I am."

"I never said that," Kate said in surprise. "I've never thought you were a fuckup."

"Oh sure, I'm just the bad decision, right? The one-night stand you get out of your system. No strings attached, you said that last night. And two years ago. I can never win with you, Kate. I've always been Jake the Wandering Australian to you, some . . . fantasy idea you built up in your head, based on stories I told you about my life a decade ago! You were always trying to make me sound like something more myth than man. Making me look like Tarzan, or a fucking Ninja Turtle. It doesn't matter how much I've tried to grow, or change, or prove I'm not that idiot anymore. Everyone's gonna see me that way. You, Charlie, my dad, even Simon treats me like a party boy. That's all I've ever been, my whole life.

Jake of All Trades, Master of None. The Wandering Australian, never good enough for a home. The second son."

"Jake," Kate said, heavy and heartbroken. She'd never seen him like this, laid so bare, and it wrenched her apart to know she'd caused it. "None of that is true, you have to know that."

"Then why does everyone keep saying it?" Jake snapped. But under the anger, she recognized the root emotion: self-loathing. She raised a hand, hoping to bridge the divide that had opened up between them two years ago—that had always been between them, maybe—but Jake wasn't finished.

"That's the only reason you hit on me that night two years ago, wasn't it? Because I was the bad decision before you settled down. I knew Spencer was into you, I knew it from the very first meeting we had with him about the *Wandering Australian* books. He was so obvious, and you were typical Kate, completely oblivious. But I knew. I was the kind of guy you hooked up with when you were drunk, and Spencer was the kind of guy you married. But you managed to fuck that up, too, didn't you?"

Kate shrank back as much from his bitter tone as from his accusatory words. "You have no idea what happens in a long-term relationship. All the ways it can go wrong."

"Maybe not, but I know you," Jake said. "You've always lived in your own head. You'd rather fantasize about Geoff and Blake and Loretta than live your own damn life. Because then you can control all the variables and tell everybody how to feel without their pesky emotions getting in the way. You think I'm the one who runs away? I'm the thrill seeker? Why don't you admit the truth—you've never fully committed to a person in your life. It was always no strings attached with me, and you always had one foot out the door with Spencer. Neither of us could ever live up, no matter how hard we tried."

The accusation hit a little too close to home, considering the conversation she'd just had with Spencer. Maybe if she'd had more time to think, to process, to eat at least a portion of her feelings in ice cream form, she might have come up with a more adult response. But Kate was never good at dealing with big emotions in the moment, and this emotion was so big she couldn't even feel the edges of it.

"I want you to leave," she said, wishing she wasn't trembling, wishing it wasn't so obvious in her voice. "Now."

"I thought that was my big flaw, leaving," Jake said, staring her down. "Which is it? Should I stay or should I go? I'm fucked either way, aren't I?"

"Get out," Kate said, vibrating now. With anger, and that big emotion. What a fool she'd been, considering this some new incarnation of herself. It had been the adrenaline and shock talking; she was still plain old Kate Valentine, and she always would be.

Jake gave a growl and stalked toward the door. He paused with his hand on the handle, and Kate's traitorous heart leapt like it always did with him; like maybe things could end differently this time. But when he turned to her, his face was like stone.

"Good luck catching your murderer, Loretta," he said, before jerking the door open and disappearing.

Chapter Thirty-Seven

Well, wasn't this a fan-fucking-tastic mess she'd made of things now. She could only stare at the door Jake had disappeared through, waiting for her brain to tell her what to do next. Waiting for Loretta to give her a single fucking clue about what to do now.

"It can't go on like this, Loretta," said Blake, running his hands through his wavy hair in frustration. "I can't go on like this. You have to choose. Me or him. Us or not. You can't keep leading me on, jerking me around, making me feel things for you and then punishing me when I do. You have to choose."

"I choose myself, Blake, every time," Loretta said, putting on a precise layer of alarming red in the dingy bathroom mirror at the Key Lime. "That's what you and Geoff don't get. I. Choose. Myself."

"Then let us go, Lor," Blake said. "If you want to be free, fine. But let us be free, too."

She wouldn't let the pain in his voice or the anguish so clearly etched on his face get to her; she couldn't. Too many people were depending on her to save them. He thought she was free? Ha. She was just as trapped as the rest of them.

"You know where the door is and how to use it," was her only reply.

And use it he had. But this time it hadn't been Blake, and she hadn't imagined it. She'd had Jake, and she'd let him walk away. And not even Loretta could save her now. Oh god, was she going to have to admit that Jake might be right? That she might be doing exactly what he'd accused her of—hiding in her fantasies, unable to face reality, more comfortable manipulating the fake lives of her characters and their emotions to suit herself. But now she couldn't even manage that. Jake had ruined Loretta as thoroughly as he'd ruined her.

So what if she asked herself *what Loretta would do* far more than she asked what Kate Valentine would do? That "fantasy" had been paying her mortgage for the past two years. Of course, that "fantasy" had also landed her at her ex-fiancé's wedding in an isolated manor during a storm with at least one murderer and several sociopaths. So maybe the argument could go both ways.

Her stack of suspects now felt childish and stupid as she stared at them in her neat, organized handwriting. Like they were in a Loretta story, with tidy backstories and clear motives that made them obvious suspects in a web of suspects that eventually led to a clear murderer. But that's not how motives worked in real life; in real life, they were messy and overlapping and chunks of time went unaccounted for and everybody had a reason to kill everybody else but nobody cracked and fessed up. She ought to just hole up until the storm passed, catch the first floating craft out of there, and let the police sort it all out.

But Kate was tired of doing what she ought to do. Doing what she ought to do had kept her safe, but it had never made her happy. She'd rather walk into the storm-tossed sea than admit it, but Jake had a point. She couldn't keep turning to Loretta to solve her problems. And it wasn't like anybody else was going to find Rebecca's killer or save Kennedy from another poisoning attempt. The closest thing Kennedy had to Loretta was Kate, so Kate would have to do.

Her gut was telling her she was still missing something. A suspect she'd overlooked, or a motive she hadn't discovered yet. Everyone she'd investigated so far had good reason to kill Rebecca, or Kennedy, or

Rebecca *and* Kennedy. She'd even found the missing champagne glass, but she wasn't convinced it had led her to the murderer like she thought it would. Cassidy had plenty of motive, but Kate believed her affection for Kennedy was real. She didn't think Cassidy would try to poison her cousin, much less her half sister. Richie and Steven certainly had plenty to gain from getting Rebecca out of the way, but their attempts at sabotage had been clumsy and obvious. No way had Richie Hempstead had the foresight to bring a specialty poison for the weekend. And everybody else—Marcus, Juliette, Spencer, even Serena—all had alibis for the time of Kennedy's poisoning. Plus, there was the matter of staging Kennedy's poisoning to look like one of Kate's books, which could mean that whoever wanted Kennedy dead *also* wanted Kate to pay for it.

"I need to go back to the scene of the crime," Kate said out loud, testing the sound of it. It sounded . . . good? She needed to understand the evidence. She'd also done enough research for Loretta to know that often it was the hundredth time an investigator walked the scene that put all the pieces together for them.

Someone had obviously made a run on the wine cave since the last time she'd been down there; several of the racks were empty, and there were foil wrappings littered all over the place. Kate hadn't registered much about the place the night before—Kennedy's dead-at-the-time body and all—but now she realized how extensive it was. It must have spanned half the length of the house, the deeply polished wooden racks going back forty to fifty feet. It was also obvious it wasn't originally built to house wines. Large wooden shelves stacked all the way up to the ceiling must have been used to store contraband barrels of whisky and rum.

She pressed into the depths of the cave, toward a line of refrigerated units in the far reaches, their motors quiet, their doors heavily padlocked. She spotted the coveted Dom Pérignon behind one of the glass doors, and absently reached for the padlock to give it a tug, just to check. She'd never had Dom, and she'd always wondered if it really did taste ten times better than her ten-dollar sparkling wine.

But when she tugged on the padlock, the unit moved slightly. She frowned, tugging a little harder, and it rolled forward a full inch. She bent down, looking for wheels, but the unit seemed solidly set on the floor. She shined her light on the floor, pulling once more, and realized it was because the unit itself wasn't moving—the floor was. The entire unit was set on a rotating disc, opening to reveal a secret passage behind it.

"How many hidden passages does one manor house need?" Kate wondered. But her voice wasn't the only sound filling the space— somewhere deep in the darkness of the secret passage was a thumping sound, with occasional high-pitched whining sounds. Like someone . . . crying out for help? Or in pleasure? It was hard to tell.

She shined her flashlight into the space to get a better feel for it, and realized it was also more extensive than she'd first realized. It followed the wall behind the refrigerated units in both directions, dusty and narrow with exposed wooden beams and stone floors and not much else. And there again was the thumping sound, the whining coming through more clearly as a melody. Music. There was a wooden lever at about head height on the opposite wall, and Kate had firsthand experience with how it must work. She pulled it down, and the section of wall slid silently open. At least she wasn't braced against it half-naked this time.

A wave of warm, humid air hit her as she stepped through the hidden door into a tropical paradise. The space must have been at least as large as the wine cave, cavernous with massive stone pillars holding up the edges. The walls were a kaleidoscope of aquatic colors—deep turquoise and brilliant blue and seafoam green with gold and red accents. Every square inch of the place was decorated in tile motifs, with sea nymphs frolicking in the waves and gods with their tridents commanding schools of fish and pods of dolphins.

An Olympic-size pool took up the majority of the space, with private alcoves for changing and showering, as well as a hot tub big enough to hold thirty people, with a gold statue of Poseidon as its crowning glory. Even down here, in a complete absence of sunlight, there were Rebecca's fronds and potted plants, making the whole place feel worlds away from the dreary weather outside. Kate could have been in Tahiti or Jamaica down here.

The pool room. She'd found the site of Rebecca's murder.

And floating in the middle of the murder scene—which boasted a tile floor in a repeating floral motif—were Richie and Steven on matching slices of inflatable pizza. They both wore sunglasses despite the fact that there was very little light from the few large flashlights they'd set at the edge of the water, and they spun in lazy circles around each other.

"Hello," she said.

"Jesus!" Richie exclaimed, upending himself off his pizza slice and dropping into the water with an unceremonious splash. Steven's only reaction was a single harrumph as Richie resurfaced. "How the hell did you get in here?"

"What are you doing down here?" Kate countered.

"We're celebrating," Richie said, wading to the edge and lowering the volume on a Bluetooth speaker. He tossed his glasses and held out a hand expectantly to Kate. When she didn't move, he huffed impatiently. "Towel?"

She turned to a lounger behind her where there were, sure enough, a stack of fluffy white towels. She took one and handed it to Richie.

"What are you celebrating?" Kate asked. "Rebecca's untimely demise?"

"Don't be macabre," Richie said, wiping his face. "I mean, yes, but it's tacky to say it like that. With Rebecca out of the way, the family trust stays where it belongs: in the family. Cassidy and I managed to convince Ken to delay the whole homestead donation business a few years, so she can have more time and money to dedicate to all her little charity causes."

"And so you can get your inheritance?" Kate said dryly.

"Yes. Ken has graciously promised to intercede with the board on my next inheritance request," Richie said primly, "and I promised Steven I'd cover his debts with Rico so he doesn't get his legs broken. With interest, of course. I'm not the fucking charity lover in the family."

"A prince among paupers," Steven said to the ceiling.

"Hand me the bottle, will you?" Richie said, snapping his fingers. "And the glasses?"

Kate turned to the lounger and the table beside it, where a bottle of red wine and two glasses waited. She started to hand them to Richie, who put his hands out to take them. But when he held his hands up, there were red blisters along the pad of his thumb on both hands. Kate snatched the bottle back and set the glasses down with a clink, snagging Richie's hands.

"Hey!" Richie protested. "What the hell?"

"You *were* the one sabotaging the house all weekend," Kate said, letting him go. He splashed back into the water, coming up spluttering. "You cut the generator fuel line and sabotaged the windows in the ceremony room!"

Richie sniffed. "You can't prove anything."

"It was my idea," Steven said placidly, running his hands through the water and spinning in circles. "I also shut off the main water line down here earlier. The inspector won't be so willing to approve the historical designation after they've spent all weekend not showering or pooping, whoever they are."

"But this one made me do all the dirty work because he's got delicate wrists," Richie said, rolling his eyes.

"I have carpal tunnel from all the contracts I've written up for your aunt over the years," Steven said primly. "She insisted on handwritten first drafts, said she didn't trust email for contracts. I don't even think she owned a computer."

Kate knew for a fact she did, and someone had used her drowned body to access the family fortune on it. But if Steven was lying, he was either doing a really good job at it, or a really bad one. He spun around in lazy circles as Richie paddled their drinks back out to him, his wine sloshing into the pool water and swirling like drops of blood. Which reminded Kate that she was standing in the real scene of the crime. And Richie had lied to her about Rebecca leaving on her own.

"You said Rebecca was here last night," Kate said.

"So what if I did?" Richie asked, struggling to remount his pizza slice. He finally managed it, ungracefully, before swirling dramatically and eyeing her. "Oh, you're doing, like, a detective thing, aren't you? That

Juliette woman warned me about you snooping around like you're a real whatever her name is. Nancy Grace."

"Nancy Drew," Kate said flatly. "And I happen to know Rebecca didn't leave here alive, because she drowned. Which means somebody dragged her body upstairs while somebody else was dragging Kennedy's unconscious body to the wine cave."

Richie snorted. "Several eyewitnesses will tell you Steven and I were down here when Ken had her little spill. They would have noticed Aunt Rebecca floating like a turd in the middle of the pool. If Auntie R drowned down here, she did a good job of pretending she was fine when she left. Well, except for puking in the changing room. Woman can't hold her champagne."

Kate frowned. "What champagne?"

Richie waved at an alcove on the opposite side of the pool. "Take a towel with you and mop it up, will you? It still smells like ass in there."

Kate skirted the pool, the water and the lamps throwing disorienting fractures of light in her path. Twice she almost stepped into the pool because she couldn't see where she was going, and she had to turn on her own flashlight to find her way to the alcove that she realized was a separate room with teak cabinets and stacks of fresh towels. The floor looked like it had been cleaned recently, but Richie was right about the distinct tinge of vomit in the air. It was sharp and acrid, same as Kennedy's the night before.

Kate poked through the cabinets filled with swimsuits, cover-ups, and leather sandals. But the last cabinet had a carefully folded garment in a bold floral print—Rebecca's rehearsal dinner dress. And tucked behind the dress was a champagne bottle, the label gold with black writing. A doll-size wedding dress hugged the neck of the bottle wearing a red sash, the words *For the Bride* printed in a florid white script.

Kennedy's personal bottle of Dom Pérignon.

Rebecca had gone to the bar to get her own bottle of Dom at the rehearsal dinner, but apparently she'd swiped Kennedy's instead. She hadn't been feeling well, same as Kennedy. And she'd thrown up, same as Kennedy. And Kate knew from her research for Loretta book three that abrin poisoning could also cause foaming in the respiratory tract if a lethal dose was ingested. Rebecca had obviously been in the pool last night, but what if Richie had been telling the truth? What if Rebecca really had left the pool room after not feeling well last night?

Kate dashed out of the locker room to the edge of the pool where Richie and Steven had consolidated to one slice of pizza, their limbs entangled. Kate imagined it was only a matter of time before their party got R-rated again. "Hey!" she said, loud enough to snag their attention. "I need a glass."

"So go to the kitchen and get yourself one," Richie said.

Kate looked around until she spotted a long-handled pool net mounted on the wall. She took the net and wielded it in Richie's direction, knocking his wineglass out of his hand and scooping it up with the net despite his protests. She rinsed it out and brought it to the locker room, shaking the water out and setting it in front of her flashlight. She poured the remaining contents of the champagne bottle into the glass, a thick trail of white powder lumping around the opening of the bottle. And there, in the glass, a single shard of black and red.

"The champagne glass was a red herring," Kate whispered, disappointed in herself for falling for the oldest trick in the book. It wasn't the glass with *Bride* etched on it that had done Kennedy in; it was the whole damn bottle. And now Kate knew how Kennedy had been poisoned, and she finally had the answer to the question *who killed Rebecca?*

"Rebecca killed herself," Kate whispered.

Rebecca had swiped the bottle of champagne earmarked for Kennedy, which had been poisoned with the rosary peas, and brought it with her to her evening swim. When she'd started to feel bad, she must have suspected sabotage after her big announcement. She'd rushed to her office to finalize the paperwork, but the poison would have fully hit her system by then. She'd tried to go for help and gotten tangled up in the potted plants. Kate had been so focused on all the reasons why someone would want to murder Rebecca—to be fair, there were a lot of reasons—that it never even occurred to her Rebecca had been the collateral damage, not Kennedy.

"Richie!" she shouted as she entered the pool room once again.

"*How* are you still here?" Richie complained.

"The secret passages," Kate said. "What do you know about them? Where do they go?"

"Who knows?" Richie said, sweeping his arms out and turning their slice in a lazy circle. "All over the house, I think. Apparently Great-Grandpa Russell built them to hide his imported Canadian whisky. He was super paranoid about the G-men even up to his death, so he never told anyone where the secret passages were or how to open them. Aunt Rebecca spent years trying to clear them out and catalog them after she inherited. Found four skeletons. *Four.* Two were animals, but one was a child-size human and the other was clearly a man in a suit. We have no idea who they were, how they got in there, anything. I *never* set foot in those passages."

"You said Rebecca cataloged all the passages she found," Kate said. "Do you know where she kept the documentation?"

"No idea," Richie said, starting to sound irritated. "More importantly, I don't care."

"The trust," Steven said, giving a little laugh. "Rebecca would have had to submit original blueprints to the San Juan Islands Historical Trust with construction dates and architect names. She probably would have marked the passages on those documents."

The historical society. The secret inspector. What if . . .

Kate needed to find Kennedy as soon as possible.

Chapter Thirty-Eight

Kate took her best guess of the layout of the house and turned left inside the passage, accidentally ramming her toe into a whisky barrel tucked just around the corner and cursing the throb of pain that shot up her leg. She imagined the place even smelled like old whisky, a heady combination of wood and jet fuel. She did her best *not* to imagine those four skeletons Rebecca had supposedly found in the wall, or how they got there, or why no one had cared to find them until they were nothing but bones.

Left had at least worked out for her, directionally, as the passage reached a set of stairs. Kate shone her flashlight on the edges of the stairs where the wood was the roughest, little splinters sticking out. The ends looked discolored, and as Kate scraped her finger against them, red dust caked up under her fingernail.

"Dried blood," Kate whispered, shining her flashlight up the stairs.

This was it. This was how someone had gotten Kennedy from the bridal suite down to the wine cave without anyone seeing. She found Kennedy's missing shoes from the previous evening strewn along the steps farther up, all the proof she needed that this was how the bride had been moved. Her shoes came off during the transport, and that's how she got those odd scrapes and bruises on her heels. Kate reached the top of the stairs and found the door-release lever.

It swung open into the master bedroom. Of course Russell Hempstead would want a passage from his bedroom to his illicit goods storage room. Kate stepped into what looked like an impromptu sleepover, with Kennedy and her bridesmaids in matching pajamas. There were a few other guests—Veeta the marketing intern, Abraham and Jean-Pierre, and Louis the photographer capturing the cozy moment. They looked up at her in surprise, huddled around a computer screen that looked like it was showing—

"*Mamma Mia*?" Kate blurted out in surprise. "You're watching *Mamma Mia*? You know they don't end up getting married, right?"

"That's why we're watching it," Kennedy said with a little smile, her eyes sad. "Felt appropriate for the weekend we're having. Plus, Aunt Rebecca loved ABBA."

"That is . . . surprising information," Kate said.

"Where did you come from?" Juliette asked.

"Secret passage." Kate pointed over her shoulder as Cassidy not-so-subtly crawled for the exit. "Relax, Cassidy. I'm not here for revenge. At least, not yet."

"I was just . . . looking . . . for my contact," Cassidy said, sweeping her hands over the floor with wide strokes.

"So you snuck in here through a secret passage just to stand around frowning?" Juliette asked. "Seems like you could have done that on your own somewhere else."

"No," Kate said, shaking her head. "I've gathered you all here today—"

"You didn't gather us here," Veeta said in confusion. "We were already here. You're the one who just showed up."

"Okay, well . . . be that as it may," Kate said, determined to soldier on, "I've *metaphorically* gathered you all here today to reveal, once and for all, the true murderer."

Juliette rolled her eyes. "Kate, you're not a real detective."

"Well, I'm not a real killer, either," Kate snapped. "Didn't stop you accusing me."

Juliette only shrugged. "I'm still not convinced you're not the murderer."

"Just let me do my fake job," Kate said, exasperated.

"Fine, Nancy Drew, what's your evidence trail? Who are your suspects?" Juliette clapped her hands together. "Let's knock this out."

"Well, it's not that simple," Kate mumbled.

A heavy, expectant silence hung over the room, all eyes on Kate. She hesitated just long enough that Juliette gave up a groan. "Oh my god, you don't know, do you?"

The rest of the room burst out in similar groans as Kate leaned into Juliette. "You know, you could do a little less heckling and a lot more helping."

"And miss this crash and burn?" Juliette countered. "Never. You really don't know?"

"I have . . . hunches," Kate ground out.

"Hunches?" Juliette said derisively. "Hunches are worse than gut instincts. Hunches are the tinfoil hats of investigative work. You should be confirming alibis, revisiting the evidence, leaning on people. God, don't you read your own books?"

"I was just about to do all of that before you started heckling me!" Kate burst out, rubbing her face. "Kennedy, what do you know about your aunt's historical designation process? Did you ever see any of the documents she had to submit?"

"Oh, sure," Kennedy said, nodding. "I had to sign off on all of them as a witness. She said she didn't trust anybody else in the family, not until the deal was done. It was such a mess. I think Auntie R thought if she donated a huge amount of money, the trust would let her do what she wanted. But they were stubborn about following protocol. They had to see all the original architectural documents, and they insisted on an in-person inspection to confirm the state of the Manor. She was so angry she threatened to fire all of them, but then she found out they're mostly volunteers."

"This really would be so amazing as a historical site," said Jean-Pierre wistfully.

"I'm surprised she found someone willing to do the in-person inspection," Kennedy continued. "Most of them hated her so much by the end they refused to speak with her. They even staged a walkout at some point. That's why she had to get me involved. They all called her Attila the Hunter behind her back, because of the taxidermy. And because she was so ruthless."

Atilla the Hunter. It wasn't the first time this weekend Kate had heard that name. But it had to be a coincidence, right? Marla couldn't possibly . . . *possibly* . . .

"Kennedy, did you invite Marla this weekend?" Kate asked, needing the answer to be rational. Logical. Of course Kennedy invited Marla for the weekend, and Marla probably just overhead that nickname at her artists' commune here on the islands. Marla couldn't have done all this, it would be . . .

Well, it would be psychotic, wouldn't it?

Kennedy frowned. "Marla Lynch? No. I mean, I wanted to. I wanted to invite all of Spencer's local authors. But he told me not to, because of the contracts stuff. I guess he changed his mind, though."

But Kate didn't think he had. And if Marla wasn't there by Spencer or Kennedy's invitation, it meant someone else had invited her. The only other person on the island with the authority to do so. Rebecca was the only one who could confirm her suspicion, and she wouldn't be divulging her secrets anytime soon. Still, Kate was sure she had it. She knew who had poisoned Kennedy, who had dragged her down the secret passage stairs and stubbed their toe against a barrel they couldn't have possibly known was there, because they'd only ever seen the passage on blueprints and not in person.

"I need to sit down," Kate said, dropping to the carpet beside Cassidy before the other woman could properly make room for her.

"Hey!" Cassidy said, tugging her leg out from under Kate's butt. But she made a face as she considered Kate. "You don't look so good."

"I don't feel so good," Kate muttered, staring at the Greek chorus of

Mamma Mia narrating her fate. She and Marla might not be the good friends they'd been back in college, and they might have drifted apart, but Marla couldn't have done *this*, could she? Poisoning Kennedy? Framing Kate? Why would she do such a thing? And why offer to help with the investigation?

Unless she was only offering to help so she had an inside line into what Kate was investigating. Kate had thought they were reconnecting and bonding, but now that she really thought about it, Marla had been too keen to find that evidence Kate swore was lying around. She'd probably planned to take the champagne glass and use it to implicate Kate even more, but she hadn't expected Cassidy to steal it for the DNA test. And Kate would bet she hadn't expected Rebecca to take the poisoned bottle and stash it in the pool room, either. Still, none of that evidence conclusively pointed to Marla, not without the rosary peas. Kate could barely stomach the idea of one of her oldest friends doing something so diabolical; she certainly couldn't go around accusing her of it without more solid proof.

Louis maneuvered in beside her, snapping a picture of her mid-solve. She had the urge to demand he delete that photo, and hadn't he taken enough unflattering photos of her for the weekend? But then she remembered the photo that Marla had "accidentally" made her delete, and turned to him with a sudden flash of inspiration.

"Louis, can I—"

"No way," the photographer said before she could complete her request. "I just got the bacon grease off the buttons."

"And I apologized for that," Kate said patiently. "But the last time I looked at your photos, my . . . friend deleted one. Can you recover it? In high resolution, preferably."

Louis straightened and sighed. "Maybe, but I would need my computer for that, and I don't have it with me right now. Obviously."

Kate turned to Kennedy. "Can we borrow your laptop?"

Louis took the SD card from his camera and plugged it into Kennedy's reader, the raw photos coming up in a file. He worked some technical magic Kate didn't understand, and the deleted photo popped up.

"Boy, she really tackled Ken, didn't she?" mused Cassidy as the full-size image loaded.

"It's not the most . . . flattering of captures," Kate murmured, but she wasn't focused on the scene she and Kennedy were causing in the foreground. She scanned the background, trying to find what it was Marla hadn't wanted anyone else to see. And there, small but distinct in the far left corner, was the evidence she needed.

"Is that . . . Marla?" Juliette asked, leaning in close. "What is she doing?"

"I believe she's poisoning the bride's bottle of Dom Pérignon," Kate said, a heavy weight settling in the pit of her stomach. Marla's distinct red-tipped hair and lace-up boots identified her more than her face, and while Kate couldn't see specifically what was in her hand, she was positive it was a small bag or vial of crushed rosary peas. Kate could at least make out the bright red *For the Bride* sash the bartender had put around the neck of the bottle in her other hand. The same bottle Kate had found in Rebecca's locker in the pool room. The bottle only Kennedy was supposed to drink out of for the weekend, before Kate had knocked her glass out of her hand and then distracted Kennedy with the scene she had caused during Spencer's speech.

"You know, in a way, I think I actually saved your life," Kate said, bemused. She shook her head, knowing she had the evidence she needed, but missing the most critical piece—*why*.

"You think Marla did all this?" Juliette asked.

"We need to find her and talk to her," Kate said, her voice sounding funny even to herself. She couldn't begin to imagine how or why Marla had done what she'd done. She'd found Kate after the speeches and lured her down to the wine cave, conveniently abandoning her in the kitchen under the guise of looking for glasses. She'd been in Kate's room helping her change, digging through her suitcase. She could easily have planted the necklace then.

But why? Why poison Kennedy at all? Why frame Kate for it? She couldn't possibly have done this, could she?

Juliette took a long, slow breath, letting it out in a huff. "I'd believe worse of her with less evidence. Her books always had too much body horror for feminist retellings. Where's your low-rent Hemsworth stand-in? Why isn't he here to back you up?"

Kate looked away. "We had a . . . misunderstanding."

Juliette snorted. "See, this is why I only fuck guys I don't like. Then when I have to cut them off, I never feel bad about it. You need backup?"

Kate looked at her in surprise. "Are you offering it?"

"I'll search Marla's room," Juliette said. "Since you are clearly no Loretta when it comes to real-life investigations. This doesn't make us friends."

"And here I was, ready to give you half a heart necklace that says *Be Fri*," Kate said dryly. "If you find her, don't do anything until I can talk to her."

"You know I won't promise that," Juliette said grimly.

Chapter Thirty-Nine

They gathered all the wedding guests they could muster—at least, the soberest ones they could find—and combed the house from top to bottom with no luck finding Marla. The worst of the storm seemed to be passing, the rain little more than a misting as they directed their search to the grounds surrounding the Manor. Kate still hadn't seen Jake, and she tried not to worry about where he might be and whether or not he might be safe. He was the freaking Wandering Australian; he'd weathered far worse than a tropical storm in a decrepit manor house, right? Of course, that meant he was just avoiding her, which didn't feel much better.

Kate was so caught up with trying to decide whether or not she was mad or worried or mad *and* worried that she missed the first crash down at the boathouse. But she didn't miss the sharp curse that followed, turning her attention to the washed-out remnants of the trail leading to the dock. Debris littered the hill, driftwood shoved into the mud and the occasional dead fish that Kate avoided looking at too closely. She never imagined the water had made it that high; how close they had been to disaster.

The door to the boathouse was slightly open as Kate approached, something heavy bumping around followed by a more emphatic curse. Kate stepped inside the dim and moldy building, scrunching up her nose as she looked for the source of the sound. A particularly inventive curse came from her left, and she turned half-blindly toward it.

"Marla?" she said into the dimness.

The vague shape of a woman straightened with a start, eyes gleaming like a raccoon. "Satan's ass cheeks, Valentine, don't sneak up on a person like that!"

"What are you doing here?" Kate asked. She could just make out the racks of boats, and a long object Marla was currently wrestling with that looked an awful lot like a canoe.

"I am . . ." Marla looked around, as if just realizing where she was. "Getting a boat."

"Why?" Kate asked, bewildered.

"Because the yacht is damaged, and there's no other way off this godforsaken island, apparently. So I'm gonna row to shore!"

"It's eighty miles to the mainland," Kate reasoned. "You can't canoe across eighty miles."

"Well, I'm sure as fuck gonna try!" Marla said with a hysterical bark of laugh. "I saw that bitch Winters breaking into my room just now, and I sure as hell am not sticking around for whatever witch hunt you and Loretta have planned."

"Marla," Kate said, uneasy with the tension vibrating off her friend. "What did you do?"

"Is this where I make my big villain reveal speech like the destitute cousin in your first book, huh? I mean, never mind that all of Loretta's evidence was circumstantial and she wasn't an actual cop and couldn't do anything to him, he just gave up the ghost as soon as she put the screws to him! Like he was impressed that she'd figured out his plan when he was the actual mastermind who came up with it! Is that what I should do, Valentine? Spill my guts to you because I'm so impressed that you figured it out?"

"Okay, well," Kate muttered, "kind of feels like that's not what you want to do—"

"No, that's not what I want to do!" Marla snapped, shoving her hands into her hair. "I just need to think."

"Marla," Kate said, hesitant. "Juliette is going to find the documents from the historical society that prove you were the inspector Rebecca invited for the weekend."

"That doesn't prove anything," Marla said, waving dismissively. "It's circumstantial."

"Louis recovered the photo you deleted," Kate pressed, needing to get the truth out even if she had to be the one to say it. "The one that shows you putting the poison in Kennedy's champagne bottle. You called Rebecca 'Atilla the Hunter.' You stubbed your toe on the barrel in the hidden passageway. You were the one who led me down to the wine cave."

Marla paused, back hunched as she struggled to lift the canoe again, every line tense and waiting. And then she let it drop with a clang, making Kate jump.

"Why don't you ask what you really want to ask," Marla said, her voice wound tight. "I mean, unless you're down here for some recreational rowing yourself."

"Marla, did you . . ." The words came slow and reluctant, as if she didn't want to let them out. "Did you poison Kennedy?"

Marla gave a little laugh, shaking her head. "Did I poison Kennedy? No. No! No. *You* poisoned Kennedy. *You* did. Of course you did! Isn't it obvious? You're the crazy ex-girlfriend. You're the one with the overdue book and the broken engagement. You're the one who made a scene over that simpering Loretta speech that Spencer read at the rehearsal dinner. You're the one who was found with Kennedy's body. You were supposed to be the one who stole her necklace and hid it in your suitcase just like the idiotic sister in your dumb book. You were blinded by a jealous rage. You couldn't let her have him, of course not. And you knew how you were going to get your revenge, because you'd written the damn book on it. Poison in the champagne glass, just like Lucretia."

"You *were* poisoning the champagne in that photo," Kate said. "That's why you deleted it. You couldn't let anyone see."

"Well aren't you the clever little fucking detective," Marla said with a sneer. "Did you have to hallucinate Loretta to figure that out, or did you come up with it all on your own? I tried to do it in the storage room when

I first got here. I didn't know they kept the good stuff under lock and key. Like they thought us regular folks would go hog wild or something if they left it out. Pompous assholes. God, I hated Rebecca. She was the worst one of all. So demanding, like her shit was made of gold."

Kate shook her head at the cold bitterness in her friend's tone. Marla had always been above it, or removed from it, but Kate had never heard her like this. So small and mean. "Marla . . . *why*?"

Marla kicked the canoe out of her path with a vicious thud, reaching for a nearby oar in a rack and flipping it toward Kate. "Why? You want to know *why*? You know, when I met you, you were a fucking *business* major whose greatest ambition in life was maybe owning a bookshop someday. You'd never written a thing in your life! I let you into Nights of the Round Table because I felt *sorry* for you. You were clearly out of your depth at UW, with no friends, and I thought maybe some of my shine would rub off on you. *I* was the one who started the writing salon everyone wanted to get into. *I* was the one who got her first book deal before graduation. *I* was the one who got written up in *The New York Times*. *I* was the one *The Seattle Times* called "Seattle's Rising Literary Star." Me!"

Kate had backed up as far as she could go, bumping into the doorframe as Marla swiped the flat of the oar menacingly.

"And then Spencer hires you for some random, stupid ghostwriting project, and he's only doing it because he wants to bone you so bad. And I figure, fine. It's sellout work, it's someone else's story, it's like writing cereal box copy. It's not the real deal. It's not *art*. And you write a couple more, fine. Good for you. Even those stupid books you wrote with Jake were just masturbation material for housewives and frat bros. You weren't writing anything worth being proud of. But then you finally manage to crap out that detective story you'd always mooned over, and Spencer only bought it because he was so in love with you and hoping you'd finally notice him. It was never supposed to go anywhere! But suddenly, you're on the bestseller list, you've got a movie deal in the works, you're getting invited to all the alumni events, you're winning the fucking awards. You got every good thing, and you deserved *none of it*!"

"But . . . you were winning awards, too," Kate said. "And Spencer was buying your books, too."

"Except he *wasn't*," Marla hissed, close enough that Kate could smell the wine on her breath. "Spencer called me into the Simon Says offices eight months ago to tell me that not only were they not going to buy my next book but they were pulling everything else out of print. They were going to remainder my books. Do you know what happens to a remaindered book? They fucking *shred it*. Pulp it. Send it back to the earth, like it never was. Like you never even wrote anything at all."

"Marla, I'm so sorry." Kate took a deep breath. "I didn't know. If I'd known—"

"You would have what?" Marla challenged. "Promised to do something and then completely bailed, leaving me holding the bag like you did for the alumni award ceremony?"

"So the lingering vibes *are* bad," Kate said, remembering their conversation in the wine room.

"Of course they're bad!" Marla shouted.

"But I don't understand, you moved out here to the creative commune. You're living the dream!"

"It's not a dream," Marla griped. "It's a fucking *nightmare*. Half the time there's no running water, nobody knows how to cook a decent burger because they're all pretend vegans, and every morning Derrick plays his awful ukulele music at sunrise. I only moved out here because I couldn't afford the rent on my apartment anymore. Nobody lives on communes because they *like* it, they're just on too many drugs to care! I only started going to the historical society because the museum served free hot dogs with admission on Wednesdays. I found out about Rebecca's big plan for the island, and how nobody at the society wanted to touch her with a ten-foot pole. So, I volunteered, logging the blueprints, learning the layout of the house. And when it came time for the in-person inspection, Rebecca insisted it happen this weekend so she could tell her family to fuck off to their faces. Everybody at the society was only too happy to let me be the one to do it. I could finally get my revenge."

Kate hugged her chest defensively. "Why poison Kennedy?"

"Because that bitch is the reason they scrapped all my work! I saw the blind item in the *Pub Daily* email. Kennedy threw her family money around and thought she could call the shots at Simon Says. Like that walking ad for *Legally Blonde* would know a *thing* about real art. She was the one who made the decision to remainder my books, to shred my life's work, because it was cheaper than paying to store them. She destroyed my fucking career. I couldn't let her get away with it. And who better to kill her than the jealous ex? I just had to send you the invitation Rebecca sent me, make you think she was personally inviting you."

"That was *you*?" Kate said in shock. But it finally explained why Rebecca hadn't seemed to recognize her at the rehearsal dinner; because she hadn't been the one to invite Kate.

"Well, I knew you sure as hell wouldn't show up without a cause that actually served *you*," Marla said. "It wouldn't be enough to show up for anybody else. I learned that lesson at the awards dinner. But if a reclusive rich lady invited you under mysterious circumstances? I knew you'd eat that shit up."

It was a classic case of right motive, wrong suspect. Kate had suspected Serena for the same reasons, but she'd missed the suspect right under her nose. She should have known it at the rehearsal dinner, but she'd been so distracted by everything else she'd made the wrong assumptions.

"So, you were going to kill Kennedy and frame me," Kate said. "But you accidentally poisoned Rebecca Hempstead instead, when she stole Kennedy's champagne."

"That wasn't my fault!" Marla said, hysterical. "It was her own fault, really. Basically suicide. They can't blame me for that!"

Now that Kate really thought about it, it was clear she'd imagined most of the parallels. Rebecca hadn't drowned after all, nobody was trying to frame Jake, and there wasn't a party boat in sight. She'd been a victim of her own theory, making the most basic of investigator mistakes—jumping to conclusions without all of the evidence.

"That's why you were genuinely surprised when Kennedy woke up," Kate said, working through the evidence now that she had most of the pieces. "You thought you'd given her enough to kill her, but she never finished the bottle. So you tried to smother her instead."

Marla gave her a wary sidelong look. "How do you know about that?"

"You came in through the secret entrance, but her cousin interrupted you," Kate said, the pieces finally all fitting together. "So you tried again, during the ceremony. You started that fire in the storage room, not faulty wiring."

"You were getting too close to the truth!" Marla snapped. "I tried to find the champagne bottle and the glass and get rid of them. I combed that whole haunted house from top to bottom."

Kate knew where they were, and why Marla hadn't been able to find them, but that hardly mattered now. "So, the fire, it wasn't for Kennedy. It was for . . . me."

"Two birds, one match," Marla said darkly. Her gaze had gone practically feral as she surveyed Kate, a sudden gleam in her eye that Kate didn't care for in the least bit. "If at first you don't succeed."

"*No*," Kate said in horror. "This can't be what you want!"

"Why not? I already killed once this weekend, what's another body on the pyre? Maybe I'll finally get Kennedy before Juliette catches me, huh?"

Kate took a step forward, hands out in supplication. "Marla—"

"Get back!" Marla shouted, swiping the oar at her. "I'm getting off this island, and you are getting back there."

"What do you want me to do back there?"

"Burn," Marla said, her voice guttural.

"*Please*," Kate said, but another swipe of the oar drove her farther into the dank recesses of the boathouse.

"Don't try to stop me, Valentine!" Marla said, backing toward the door. "I'll make it quick. Maybe the smoke will get you before the fire does."

Kate winced at the hard tone in her friend's voice. "You should know—"

"I don't need advice from you on anything, ever," Marla said, edging toward the exit.

"Marla!" Kate said as Marla stepped out. Marla slammed the door shut and dropped something heavy across it. When Kate tried the door, it didn't move. "Marla, wait!"

It took several attempts to break the door open with her shoulder before she realized bones were more breakable than wood. She found an old axe in a tool chest and gathered all her pent-up anxiety from the weekend, going to town on the door. Once she'd made an opening large enough to crawl through, she squirmed out and headed up the muddy hill. Marla stood at the top, oar clutched in her hands. Kate made sure to stop at least an oar's length behind her.

"What are they doing?" Marla breathed in a panicked whisper.

The crowd around the Manor had more than doubled, the wedding party lookie-loos gossiping among themselves as they caught sight of Marla and Kate. Marla went even more pale and white than usual.

"Looking for you," Kate huffed, suddenly exhausted. It was one thing to write a murder mystery wedding with made-up strangers. It was another thing entirely to find out your friend was a murderer who tried to frame you out of envy. "It's over."

"I'm not going to jail," Marla said, taking off at a dead run toward the end of the island where the land sloped up into a thick line of rugged trees.

"Marla, wait!" Kate sighed loudly, shaking her head. "Why do they always run?"

She trudged toward the house in the opposite direction, the crowd spilling out off the front porch as she approached.

"Is that the one who killed Aunt Rebecca?" Cassidy called out as Kate approached.

Kate nodded. "Unfortunately, I think so."

Cassidy shook her head. "Well, she belongs to Fluffy now."

Kate raised her brows in question. "Fluffy? Is that, like, a bunny or something? Cute little squirrel, maybe?"

Cassidy watched the line of trees in the distance where Marla's black-clad figure disappeared through the underbrush. "Fluffy is a cougar."

"Cougar!" Kate choked out. "There's a loose *cougar* on this island?"

"Technically, I did warn everyone to stay on the designated paths when you arrived," Abraham said, raising a finger from the side of the crowd.

"That's why there are the paths," Cassidy said. "Out in the open with a clear line to the house. Everything else is Fluffy's domain."

"Why in the hell is there a cougar on the island?" Kate asked.

"Aunt Rebecca was a big game hunter when she was younger," Cassidy explained. "Used to take a safari trip every year. PETA protested year-round. Eventually she got tired of the long flights with poor legroom so she had the game shipped to her. Fluffy was the last animal she brought to Hempstead Island, but he was a clever one. She tracked him for months, but Fluffy was always one step ahead. He got into the house once and tore up an entire salon of her animals. He's the one that got away. Now he's going to eat your friend."

Kate gasped as another missing puzzle piece locked into place. "Fluffy is the Deer Shredder!"

Cassidy gave her a wild look. "What?"

"How is that the weirdest thing I've said this weekend?" Kate whispered to herself. But she shook off the realization in favor of more pressing issues. "We can't leave her out there. Abraham, can we organize a search party of anyone with, I don't know, wilderness experience? Surely Rebecca knew some big-cat wranglers in her time?"

"Oh no," Abraham said, shaking his head and cutting his hands through the air viciously. "This is far worse than the weekend I spent on a certain tech billionaire's private island in a certain tropical archipelago when the groom wanted to walk down the aisle to a dubstep song and the bride was so high she couldn't pronounce her own name during the vows. I am *done* trying to salvage this weekend. I draw the line at pursuing a murderer through a mountain lion's hunting territory."

"But she won't make it through the next hour, much less through the night," Kate said. "She might be a murderer, and she's definitely a bad friend, but she doesn't even know there's a cougar out there. We at least need to warn her, give her a chance to return to the house and face her fate here."

Abraham crossed his arms, looking her down resolutely. "Then you do it. She's your friend, after all, and technically not an invited guest for the weekend anymore. So, she's out of my purview."

"Cassidy?" Kate said, turning to the young woman in desperation. "You know this island, don't you?"

"She murdered my aunt and poisoned my sister," Cassidy said flatly.

"Fair point, fair point," Kate said. She looked around the gathered guests, who suddenly found the wooden paneling on the massive front doors fascinating. Nobody would make eye contact, much less jump at the chance to go track Marla down. It was up to Kate to save her.

"I wish I knew where Jake was," Kate muttered. "He'd know what to do."

"I know where Jake is," Spencer said, raising a hand. "I ran into him when we were searching the house."

"You did?" Kate said, wheeling on him in surprise. "Where?"

"Eh, he asked me not to tell you," Spencer said, giving her an apologetic shrug.

"And you listened to him? Why?"

"Because we're mates now," he said, like it was the most obvious thing in the world.

Kate sighed. "Do you think you can go ask your mate to help, then? Apparently, I'm going after Marla, and he's the only person I know who might actually be able to save us if the cougar finds us."

"I'll ask, but I won't push," Spencer said with a sniff. "I think you really hurt his feelings. He seemed pretty broken up."

"Great." Kate sighed, turning back toward the tree line. "If I get mauled by a cougar, I'll consider it my due justice."

Chapter Forty

Kate made it no farther than five feet into the underbrush before she realized what a terrible idea it had been to go after Marla. She had no way to defend herself, no flashlight to cut through the rapidly descending darkness; she didn't even have a pair of sturdy boots or jeans to protect her from the scrubby brush. Jake would know what to do, what tools to bring, probably which plants were safe to eat, where to step and what to avoid.

If she survived this cougar encounter—which was, let's admit it, extremely doubtful at this point—she swore she would tell him the truth. About her feelings, what she wanted, what she hoped for. She couldn't expect him to meet her there, but she could trust herself enough to say them. To want for things, even if they felt dangerous and scary.

"Speaking of dangerous and scary," she muttered, squinting to see through the heavy tree cover. The light had grown distressingly thin, nearly nonexistent, and she could see only the tree trunks closest to her. She wasn't sure of the exact protocols when there was a cougar on the loose, but she figured shouting Marla's name and drawing attention to herself wasn't it.

So, Kate pushed on. The less light she had to work with, the slower her progress. The rain had mostly abated by then, but the trees were still heavy with rainfall that chose the creepiest moments to crash over Kate's head. Several times she yelped, swiping at pine needles and twigs that sluiced down her neck.

"Okay, I change my mind," she said after what felt like hours, her hair an absolute wreck and her teeth chattering. "Marla, if you're out here, I'm leaving you to the wilderness. You like to write about haunted forests and stuff, you'll fit right in."

Kate paused, looking around, trying to tell one tree from another, or remember which direction she came from. She was quickly devolving into a panic over how to get back to the house when a twig snapped to her left, followed by the rustle of leaves. Kate made a strangled sound, going rigid, hoping the fear sweat prickling her underarms made her smell less appealing to any predators that might be nearby.

"Marla?" she called out, her voice tight and high. Her only answer was another twig snapping, and something in her snapped in response. "Fluffy?"

"Shut up!" came a hissing voice, before Marla stumbled out of the brush, her dress tattered along the hem, her boots caked in mud. "There's a motherfucking *cougar* out here!"

"I know," Kate hissed back. "That's why I'm here, to rescue you."

"With what?" Marla looked at her with wild eyes, red scratches across her cheeks from what Kate hoped were the tree branches. "Do you have a gun?"

"I thought you were against animal cruelty," Kate said.

"Not when I'm on the dinner menu," Marla snapped. "So, what's the plan here, I just need to run faster than you?"

Kate was about to protest that she didn't intend to be anyone's bait when she looked up and caught the gleam of a pair of greenish-yellow eyes in a tree overhead, too far apart to be an owl, too steady to be fireflies. She swallowed a scream, her heart squeezing so hard in her chest she could barely breathe.

"It's in the tree," she said through the coffee straw–size opening in her throat.

"Oh god, this is how I die," Marla moaned. "Mauled by a cougar with *you*."

"You don't have to say it that way," Kate said. The eyes were still there, yellow and gleaming, and Kate could just spot the flash of long white teeth as she took a tentative step backward. "Oooooh my god, it's so big. Are they always that big?"

"Why do you think they're called big cats?" Marla snapped.

"I guess I thought they were, like, I don't know, fat house cats," Kate said, nearly shrieking as she bumped into a tree. The eyes drew closer as the cougar followed their movements, climbing down a large branch of the tree. "It's following us!"

"No shit it's following us," Marla hissed, shoving past Kate. "It's a fucking predator."

"You know what, if I'm going to die by big cat, I will at least die with my last words being you're a terrible friend, a terrible person, and frankly, an *awful* writer," Kate said.

"Excuse me?" Marla said in a loud voice, whipping her head toward Kate. "I wouldn't expect a schlocky writer like you to understand what I was doing with my books."

"First of all, I knew exactly what you were doing," Kate said, doing her best not to stumble over tree roots as she blindly walked backward. "Your themes were as subtle as a high school sophomore discovering gothic poetry for the first time. Second of all, I'm not a schlocky writer. I'm a damn good writer. Mysteries are incredibly hard to craft, which you wouldn't know, because your books have never seen a plot to save their lives."

"How fucking *dare* you," Marla said.

"How fucking dare *you*," Kate snapped back. "How fucking dare you pretend to be my friend while manipulating me. I've spent so long feeling bad about losing touch with you, but now I realize I was actually protecting myself. You were always so envious and bitter about my success, and I convinced myself that it was somehow my fault. That I was the bad friend and the sellout. But if I'm going down by cougar, you're going down with me, and you'll deserve it."

"Like hell I am," Marla said, as a steady rumble rolled down from the trees.

At first Kate thought it was the distant warnings of thunder, another band of the storm that had upended the last twenty-four hours of their lives, but then it hit a high note and Kate realized it was coming from the cougar. She grabbed Marla on instinct.

"Let me go," Marla said, scratching at Kate's exposed wrist.

"Hey!" Kate said, letting go in surprise. Marla took the advantage and booked it for the trees in the opposite direction.

The cougar leapt from the tree branch and landed directly in front of her, and Kate realized she'd somehow still underestimated its size. Its head was as big as hers, the body at least four or five feet long, the tail swinging along behind it. Its paws were huge, claws gleaming as it flicked them out and retracted them. It lowered its head to the ground, hind quarters swinging high, muscles bunching as it prepared to leap.

Chapter Forty-One

"Jake!" Kate screamed, because it seemed the thing to say when one was about to get shredded like a smoked pork butt at a family barbeque.

"Kate!" someone yelled back, and for a moment she thought she might have imagined it. But then Jake was there, crashing through the trees, shouting at the cougar and holding up a canister that released a pepper-scented mist. The cougar let loose a roar so close to Kate that its hot breath blasted in her face. It twisted away from them, landing in the underbrush and curling around with its paws swiping at its face.

"Kate, come on!" Jake yelled as he grabbed her and dragged her in the same direction where Marla had disappeared.

"You came for me!" Kate called out like an idiot, as the cat roared again with a grating howl that sounded straight out of a movie soundtrack.

"Of course I came for you," Jake said, looking at her like she was crazy. "Spencer told me you went after Marla into a cougar's hunting territory. Why wouldn't I come for you?"

"I just thought . . ." Kate's throat was thick, possibly with emotion, possibly an aftereffect of whatever Jake had sprayed at the cougar. Her eyes prickled and teared, her skin tingling with an odd sensation. "What was that?"

"Bear spray," Jake said. "Next time you go into the wilderness after a murderer, at least change your shoes, would you?"

"I'm not planning on making this a next-time type of thing," Kate said, blinking back tears. "Jake, I'm so sorry. I was an idiot. A jerk. Whatever other insults you want to call me. I was scared that you would leave again, and I would be left behind."

Here it was, her chance to be brave. She took a deep breath, ready to spill all her various feelings, when Jake nearly tripped over Marla, whose boot had gotten so firmly wedged under an uprooted tree root that she couldn't pull it loose. The cougar roared behind them.

"It's coming after us!" Kate said, her heartrate spiking. "Marla, leave the boot!"

"I'm trying!" Marla squealed, jerking at the laces that knotted the boot. "It's too wet, I can't get the laces undone!"

Jake reached into his back pocket and pulled out a small knife, slicing through the laces in one quick jerk. If they hadn't been on the precipice of disaster, it would have been the hottest thing Kate had ever seen. Even on the precipice of disaster, Kate allowed herself to admire the way the muscles in his shoulders tightened as he hauled Marla up, her foot coming loose with a wet, sucking sound. The delay was just enough that the cougar had caught up with them.

"Oh god," Marla moaned, clinging to Jake, trying to claw her way around him to put him between her and the cougar. "What a miserable end to a fucking miserable week."

"Does feel like poetic justice for Rebecca and Fluffy, though," Kate said.

"Cover your ears," Jake muttered to Kate.

"What?" she asked, looking at him wildly. The cougar lowered itself into a leaping position, and her heart threatened to do the cat's work for him and explode out of her chest.

"Just do it!" Jake said, raising his arm with something clutched in his hand. He pressed his other hand to his ear, and Kate just had time to press both hands to her ears before he pushed the button of an air horn. It blasted through the trees, startling a flight of birds overhead, and sending the cougar howling in the opposite direction.

Marla, who'd had no such warning, fell to the ground clutching the sides of her head with a scream. "What the *fuck* was that? My ears!"

"Serves you right," Jake muttered, dragging her up.

They broke the tree line a few minutes later, booking it across the open lawn toward the Manor where the remaining wedding guests had gathered beneath the overhang. Money changed hands among the guests as they approached, and Richie scowled at them.

"You couldn't have gotten one good swipe to the face, huh?" he said, reluctantly handing over a one-hundred-dollar bill to Spencer's brother.

"You were taking bets?" Jake said.

"Not on you, Kangaroo Jake," said Richie. "On the Evanescence stan over here. I thought for sure Fluffy would get her."

"What?" Marla shouted, shaking her head. "I can't hear a fucking thing. This asshole blasted that air horn like two inches from my ear. I think he blew out my eardrum."

Jake shrugged, handing Marla over to some of the wedding guests to detain her until they could contact the authorities on the mainland. "There wasn't time to warn her."

"And what about you?" Juliette asked, looking at Kate.

Kate smiled ruefully. "Apparently there was enough time to warn me."

Juliette cracked a wicked smile. "She got what she deserved, after all. Though I agree with Richie, one swipe to the face would have been pretty satisfying."

The guests retreated into the safety and warmth of the house, but as Jake made to follow them Kate tugged on his sleeve, drawing him off to one side where a small courtyard had been overrun by vines.

"You know there's a recently pissed-off cougar still roaming the island, right?" Jake said.

"Right, thank you for the rescue," Kate said.

"Oh, I intend to be well rewarded for it, too," Jake said. He cocked his head to the side. "So, what's so important we're risking the rise of Fluffy out here?"

It was a lot easier to be brave when she thought she was moments away from getting mauled by a big cat. That had felt like the proper time to blurt out feelings in the drama of the moment. Whatever she said now—whatever she admitted—couldn't be blamed on alcohol, or life-threatening circumstances. But she owed Jake better than hiding behind excuses. She owed both of them a chance, regardless of the outcome.

"Jake, I . . . Well, I already said I was sorry, but I still am. For how I treated you, for not considering your feelings, for . . . for making you feel cheap. You're not a one-night stand. You're the furthest thing from it. You're . . . Okay, here goes. I can do this. You're the most important person to me. In the world. Except maybe my mom. And the Golden Palace delivery kid, Tan. But that's negotiable, depending on your willingness to pick up lo mein. That was a joke, in case that's not clear. It sounded funny in my head, but you're not laughing, so maybe it wasn't as funny as I—"

She might have gone on like that for several more excruciating minutes if Jake hadn't gently and firmly taken her face in his hands and kissed her. And now she could tell he was smiling, his lips stretching against hers. He tasted so lovely, his tongue so warm and just the right amount of rough as it slid against hers, his chest so solid. She sighed, giving in to the sensation, her arms sliding around his neck of their own volition.

"I interrupted you," Jake murmured against her lips. "Did you want to keep going?"

"Not even a little bit," Kate said, kissing him again.

Jake pressed his forehead against hers. "Kate, I wasn't completely honest with you earlier. I didn't just come this weekend to talk to Simon about a new book deal. I came because I knew you'd be here."

"You came back for me?" Kate said in surprise. "But on the way here, I thought—"

"I know what you thought, and I was too much of a coward to just come out and say it. You wanted a truce, so I pretended I did, too. But that's not what I want at all, Katey cakes. After two years of slumming through jungles and huffing up mountains and sleeping in flea-infested hostels, all I wanted was to come home. But home wasn't my apartment with Charlie, or my aunt's house, or even the entire continent of Australia. It was a feeling, something I wanted to come back to at the end of every day. And you're it for me, Kate. *You* are home. And I thought if I could just see you one more time, if I had another chance . . . I swore I wouldn't let either of us fuck it up again."

"Oh," Kate said, her voice thick, her chest filled with too much emotion to contain. But she promised herself she would be brave. She would embrace the chaos. "Well, you can't possibly leave the country now, not after that. Probably not ever, if I'm being honest. Unless you're taking me with you."

Jake lifted his head, his stormy ocean eyes fixing on hers. "Are you sure?"

Kate reached out, pulling him down for a kiss. And underneath everything—the easy smile, the tousled hair, the surfer-boy cool, Kate could taste the hesitancy. The insecurity. She'd never imagined Jake Hawkins worrying about a single thing, but now it was so obvious he was worried about *her*. About her feelings for him, her interest in him. It was so preposterous it made her laugh, and he pulled back with a frown.

"It's never a good thing when a girl laughs while kissing you."

"I'm not laughing at you, I'm laughing at . . . I don't know. The situation. Jake, I've been . . . well, obsessed feels like a creepy word, so not obsessed. But I've wanted you for as long as I've known you."

"And now that you've had me?" Jake said, raising his brows.

Kate shook her head. "No, not like that. Well, I mean, not *just* that. That's obviously . . . that part is, well . . . that part is working *great*. No, I mean *you*. Jake Hawkins, former pro surfer, globetrotting adventurer, secret cat lover. Absolute weirdo about Alfredo sauce."

"Because it's disgusting," he reasoned.

"Because your taste buds are broken," Kate said, smiling.

"And if I'm not that globetrotting adventurer anymore?" Jake asked.

"Good," Kate said, smiling blissfully. "More time for me to make it my personal mission to make you enjoy Alfredo sauce. I will cook *so much* pasta, you'll be forty pounds heavier and absolutely miserable."

"You know, on second thought, the tech bros don't sound so bad," Jake said, stone-faced, and Kate laughed and punched him lightly in the ribs.

"I like you, Jake Hawkins," she said. "I like you so, so much. A lot. All of the time."

"I like you, too, Katey cakes," Jake said, smiling. "So, so much. A lot. All of the time."

And because she couldn't think of anything else to do, she kissed him again, until they both lost the power of speech for several more minutes. Or hours.

Our story begins, as these stories often do, with someone else's end.

Loretta Starling, bartender by night and amateur sleuth by day, had seen her share of other people's ends. She'd caught a murderer in the middle of a hurricane, solved a bride's poisoning during a luxurious weekend wedding getaway, and found justice for a wealthy woman pushed overboard on a party boat. She had foiled all manner of murderers: clever schemers, desperate deceivers, and one particularly obnoxious overachiever. She'd gotten good at uncovering clues, sussing out secrets, breaking alibis, and eliciting confessions. She'd foiled as many murder attempts as the deaths she had solved, and rescued more than one falsely accused friend from a bad murder rap.

But Loretta would soon face an end that even she couldn't see coming; a murder so cleverly plotted and so deviously deployed that it would strike closer to home than ever before. She wouldn't know who to trust or which havens were safe. She would need all of her hard-earned investigation skills, her brilliant insights, and her street smarts to foil a murderer dead set on destruction.

Loretta Starling would have to solve the most important murder she'd ever faced: her own.

EXCERPT FROM *AN OLD-FASHIONED MURDER: TO THE
ANGOSTURA BITTERS END*
LORETTA STARLING, BOOK 4 (COMING SOON)
(FOR REAL THIS TIME)
BY KATE VALENTINE

Sunday

Chapter Forty-Two

By the time dawn broke Sunday morning, Kate had finally managed a solid eight hours of sleep, unlike the rest of the wedding guests. They'd worked in shifts through most of the night, cleaning out the ballroom where they'd held the rehearsal dinner and salvaging what furniture they could from the sunroom to erect a makeshift altar and seating arrangements. There was at least a quiet sense of peace as Kate slipped downstairs to hunt down the last container of coffee. She boiled the coffee on the stove, stealthy as a CIA operative, and made two mugs before sneaking upstairs on her final mission before the ceremony.

"Is that coffee?" Spencer asked as she slipped into his room, his hair an absolute mess and his eyes so red they looked like a cartoon drawing. He sat in a wingback chair beside a crackling fireplace, providing some much-needed heat to the room. He looked at the mugs in her hand with big puppy-dog eyes. "I will never bother you about another Loretta novel again if you give me one of those right now."

Kate smiled, holding out one of the mugs. "I have good news on the Loretta front. I mapped out the whole book this morning and knocked out the first five chapters. And I brought you your T-shirt. I figured the bride shouldn't be the only one who gets something old and something new."

Spencer took a grateful sip, not even bothering to scrunch up his nose at the terrible powdered creamer Kate had found in the pantry. "You finally did it, huh? After all these months, Loretta is back. Simon will be happy to have the series on track again."

"About that," Kate said, sinking down in the chair opposite him.

Spencer frowned as he flipped through the opening chapters, looking slightly less corpse-ish as he sipped his coffee. " You're not killing off Loretta, are you?"

"Not exactly," Kate said, tapping the outline. "Read the rest."

Spencer scanned the outline, his frown deepening. "Loretta becomes the target of a mob hit after her best friend—who is apparently an FBI informant—lies to the mob and claims that Loretta is the actual informant? A little bit of art imitating life, huh?"

"You *could* read the mob as an allegory for a wild cougar, sure."

"Have you been to see her this morning?" Spencer asked.

"I tried," Kate said. "But in an ironic turn, *she* is refusing to see *me*. Which is just as well, all things considered. There's nothing I have to say to her that can't be said through three inches of Plexiglas and an unflattering orange jumpsuit."

"Hang on," Spencer said, flipping to the last page of her handwritten outline. "Loretta has to go into the witness protection program at the end of the book to survive? I don't understand. Where do you see Loretta going from here? This sounds an awful lot like the end."

"That's because it *is* the end," Kate said tentatively. It was the first time she'd said it out loud since the idea occurred to her, and the rushing sense of relief and grief that followed the words nearly overwhelmed her.

Spencer blinked slowly, his gaze steady on her. "What's that now?"

Kate took a deep breath, struggling to put into words the revelation that had been haunting her since she'd mapped out Loretta's last book that morning. "All this time, I've been using Loretta as an escape hatch from dealing with my own life. She got to be all the things I never thought I could be. But in creating her, I ended up holding myself back. I could make Loretta fix all the things I thought I got wrong, but I never learned how to fix them myself. I think Loretta was a crutch, and I want to learn to walk on my own again. I don't want to ask what Loretta would do, I want to know what Kate would do."

"But . . ." Spencer looked about the room, lost. "What will you do without Loretta? What will *I* do without Loretta? I can't imagine my life without . . . her."

He looked at Kate then, so much meaning in his eyes. She smiled softly, reaching across to pat his hand. "Me either. But it's time, isn't it? For both of us."

"I'm going to fuck it up," Spencer said, shaking his head.

"Oh, you definitely are," Kate agreed, laughing at the look he gave her. "Don't worry, I fully intend to as well. I've already left Jake alone with Serena, which feels like leaving a beautiful gazelle to roam with a cougar lurking about."

"What was that like?" Spencer asked. "I really do think Jake blew out Marla's eardrums with that horn."

"Let's just say it's cured me of the desire to ever go hiking," Kate said.

Spencer let out a breath, toying with the shirt in his lap, his glasses slipping down his nose. He pushed them up, fidgeting with the arms to get them to stay. "So, you and Jake, huh?"

"I don't know what will happen with Jake," Kate said, smiling. "But I want to find out."

"I think he's good for you." Spencer looked up at her, blinking. "I knew he liked you. I'd seen it whenever the three of us got together to work on the *Wandering Australian* books. I just . . . I liked you, too."

"It all worked out the way it was supposed to," Kate said, standing as someone knocked softly on the door. "Speaking of which—"

She swung the door open and Jake stood there holding up a garment bag, looking fresh as a daisy despite helping with the arrangements through the night. Spencer frowned, hugging his coffee mug closer to his chest.

"What is that?" he asked.

Jake grinned. "The only clean suit left on the island. Apparently, it belonged to the late, great Russell Hempstead."

Kate tugged the zipper open to peer inside. "Oh, good news. We found your something borrowed *and* something blue."

The ceremony was small, quiet, and quick, as if everyone had agreed to get it over with as quickly as possible. But the power stayed on, the storm finally past, and Kennedy and Spencer were married as warm yellow rays of sunlight streamed through the glass dome of the ballroom. Kennedy was radiant in a makeshift gown someone had pinned together from leftover tablecloths, draped over her like an elegant toga. Kate figured she could get married in a literal potato sack and still be the loveliest person in the room. Spencer managed his best in his borrowed powder blue tuxedo, his glasses smudged and his hair in disarray. But his smile was genuine. Tears prickled the corners of Kate's eyes as Spencer's cousin declared them man and wife and Kennedy threw her arms around his neck to kiss him enthusiastically.

"You all right?" Jake asked, putting his own arm around her and pulling her in close.

"I think I'm as all right as I've ever been," she said, smiling up at him.

"Wait until you've seen the wedding reception fare," Jake said. "Abraham had to make do with island rations. I've never seen so much Spam. I don't know what Aunt Rebecca was preparing for, but from the looks of it, a nuclear apocalypse was only the start."

"Poor Rebecca Hempstead." Kate sighed. "Such an inglorious end for the Queen of Wall Street. Though, I suppose it's better than getting shredded by her archnemesis."

"Speaking of Fluffy," Jake said, turning to her as the other guests filed out after the bride and groom. He put his hands on her hips, pulling her in with a sly smile. "I never got my reward for rescuing you from the cougar."

"Reward?" Kate said, tilting her head and frowning. "I don't remember there being discussion of any kind of reward. Can you remind me, maybe? Of the terms?"

"Oh, I'd be happy to," Jake said, dipping his mouth toward hers.

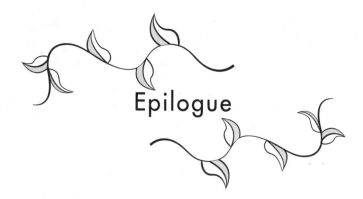

Epilogue

Kate dared a peek out from the makeshift curtain the bookstore had put up over the storage room they'd converted to a green room. The shop was small, but it was absolutely packed, with a line of people waiting outside and still twenty minutes before the launch started. Kate dropped the curtain back in place, doing a nervous little dance.

"You're fretting," Jake said, lounging in an old tweed chair tucked in one corner beside a stack of boxes filled with copies of her book. Copies she hoped to sell out of by the end of the day. He flipped through one he'd pulled from the top box, even though he'd read the manuscript at least half a dozen times to give Kate notes on her scene with the cougar attack.

"Of course I'm fretting, there're, like, a hundred people out there," Kate said, pacing back and forth. "What if they hate it? What if they're mad at me for ending the series? What if they blame you because we're finishing the third *Wandering Australian* book instead? What if they don't like where I've left Loretta? What if they never buy another book from me again? What if I'm run out of town on a rail?"

"I've never understood that phrase," Jake said, setting the book down and crossing the tiny room to take her by the arms and still her pacing.

"It comes from colonial times," Kate said, still jittery. "If someone was suspected of being a British loyalist, they were tarred and feathered and tied to a wooden fence rail and carried out of town."

"Sounds very unpleasant," Jake said with a half smile.

"I imagine it was uncomfortable, yes," Kate said.

"Kate," Jake murmured, lowering his head.

"Yes?"

"If you wanted me to tie you to something, all you had to do was ask."

He captured her gasp with a kiss so slow, thorough, and consuming that by the time he let her catch her breath she'd entirely forgotten what they'd been talking about. Or what she was worried about. Or, possibly, what they were even doing there.

"Mmm, more," she said, pushing up on her toes and dragging him down.

The curtain took that unfortunate moment to twitch open, admitting Spencer, Kennedy, and Juliette. Jake pulled back, his gaze promising all that and more later, before smiling pleasantly at the newest arrivals.

"You smudged her lipstick," Juliette said, clearly annoyed as she pulled a tube and a tissue from her pocket. "You couldn't have waited until after we took the publicity photos?"

"Good afternoon to you, Juliette," Jake said. He turned his attention to Spencer and Kennedy. "And how was Bali?"

"Amazing," Kennedy said, swooning into Spencer. "Your recommendations were spot on. We couldn't have had a better time. Except poor Spencer stepped on a stingray the second day we were there and spent the rest of the trip in a cast."

Jake grimaced. "Bad luck, mate. Those things pack a punch."

"Yes, they do," Spencer said, noticeably limping. "But it gave me plenty of time to read your latest proposal and sample pages, Kate, and I think you've really got something."

"Really?" Kate asked, feeling her face go warm. She had three—and, hopefully, four—bestsellers under her belt, but somehow that didn't stop her nerves from jangling at the idea of sharing something new with someone else. Jake had already read her latest manuscript half a dozen times and told her how much he loved it, but Spencer was a much more difficult judge of her work. "Do you think Loretta fans will go for such a . . ."

"A bumbling idiot?" Spencer asked in that no-nonsense tone that she knew wasn't meant to be insulting, but she still took as an insult.

"I was going to say a work in progress," Kate replied flatly. The idea had come to her on the yacht ride back from Hempstead Island after her own less-than-Loretta attempts at solving a murder. A sleuth who was a true everywoman, who got by not on badass one-liners and hard-soled boots, but on persistence and sheer dumb luck. A heroine Kate could truly relate to.

"I think she's brilliant," Jake said, putting his arm around her shoulders and giving a squeeze. "She just needs a book or two to see it for herself."

"I loved it," Kennedy gushed. "I can't wait for it to be our flagship title next season."

"Will there be a next season?" Kate murmured to Juliette. The rumors of financial struggles and layoffs hadn't died down since the wedding.

"Of course there will," Juliette said, finishing her final touches on Kate's lipstick. The glint in her eye was unmistakable as she lowered her voice so only Kate could hear. "It's a new era, and I'll be the one to usher it in."

"I pity anyone who tries to stand in your way," Kate said.

There was a knock on the wood and the curtain lifted briefly, admitting a taller, leaner version of Jake with darker hair that still curled despite the product he'd clearly applied liberally.

"Charlie the doctor!" Kate exclaimed, smudging Juliette's efforts to fix her makeup.

"Kate the author," Dr. Charlie Hawkins said. He wore a pair of black-rimmed glasses that lent him an air of gravitas, making it clear he was the elder brother.

"You made it, mate," Jake said, slapping him on the back.

"You said it was an emergency," Charlie said, frowning. He held up a prescription bag. "I have the Xanax, but she looks fine to me."

"That's because I applied my own special brand of medicine," Jake said with a wink.

"Did you say Xanax?" Juliette asked, striding over. She snatched the bag, tearing it open and pulling the bottle out. "Perfect."

"I wouldn't recommend she take one if she's got a public presentation to make," Charlie said, holding out a hand to stop her.

But she twisted out of his reach, popping open the bottle. "Please, it's not for her." She dumped a pill out and knocked it back, no water, making direct eye contact with Charlie as she swallowed. "So, you're Charlie the doctor, huh? Interesting."

"You are . . . not who those were prescribed for," he said.

"Report me to the board," she replied, dropping the bottle in the bag and shoving it back in his hand. "If you two didn't look exactly alike, I wouldn't believe you were brothers."

Jake and Charlie sighed in unison. "We get that a lot."

Kate looked between Juliette and Charlie, a small smile growing as she glanced at Jake. "Charlie, you should join us for drinks after the book launch. Everyone's going."

"Who is everyone?" Charlie asked, watching Juliette in bemusement as she stalked back over to Kate to finish her ministrations.

Jake dropped an arm over his brother's shoulder. "You're in for it now, brother."

"In for what?" Charlie asked, utterly confused. "What's happening?"

Jake shook his head, smiling at Kate as she cut her eyes to the side and smiled back. "Just embrace the chaos, brother. Embrace the chaos."

Acknowledgments

Only true book lovers and weirdos read the acknowledgments, and as one of those book loving weirdos I say: welcome and thank you. I wrote this on two cups of coffee and less than seven hours of recommended sleep, so buckle up.

To my agent, Elizabeth Bewley, for reading more than your fair share of duds before saying this was the one. I always value your instinct, your insight, and most important, your tenacious negotiating skills. I'm lucky to know you.

To Lisa Bonvissuto, a million thank-yous for taking a chance on me and my murder-rom-com-franken-book. Your vision and enthusiasm made this a reality, and for that I'm forever in your debt. You have my sword, which is just a really stabby pen.

And to Lily Cronig, thank you for so seamlessly and graciously taking up the baton and carrying this one over the finish line. I can't wait to see what magic we work together on the next one.

And to the whole team at Minotaur—editorial, design, marketing, publicity, the whole shebang—thank you for the joyful covers and elegant interior design, as well as the love and support. Books take a whole team to make it out into the world, and I'm grateful for everyone on mine.

To my family—I love you, you're so supportive, for the love of pete, please don't read this one. And if you do read it, let's never, ever discuss it. I love you.

To Max and Lily—you're monsters and I wouldn't have you any other way. And you are a hundred percent not allowed to read this ever, not even after I'm dead.

To Joe—geez, you've already got the whole book dedicated to you, what more do you want? So demanding.

And to my readers, both old and new alike, thank you thank you THANK YOU for your continued support and dedication. I don't take such a privilege lightly, and I am grateful for every reader who picks up one of my books. And if you love it enough to pick up another one? I love you exponentially more. No pressure, though. Well, some pressure.

About the Author

Brenna Hodge

JENNY ELDER MOKE is the author of award-winning children's and adult literature. She enjoys fast-paced adventures with plenty of mysteries, surprising turns, and laughs along the way. When she's not writing, you can find her knitting, puzzling, or fighting imaginary crime as a tae kwon do black belt. *She Doesn't Have a Clue* is her adult debut. Jenny lives in Denver, Colorado.